# the lessons

# of a

# student

# midwife

## je rowney

Novels by this author

Charcoal
The Derelict Life of Evangeline Dawson
Ghosted
I Can't Sleep

THE LESSONS OF A STUDENT MIDWIFE
SERIES:

Life Lessons
Love Lessons
Lessons Learned

Copyright © 2020 JE Rowney

This is a work of fiction. Names, characters, businesses, places, events, locales, and incidents are either the products of the author's imagination or used in a fictitious manner. Any resemblance to actual persons, living or dead, or actual events is purely coincidental.

# life

# lessons

## je rowney

## the lessons of a student midwife

BOOK ONE

# Chapter One

Tangiers Court is unexceptional, but I can hardly contain myself when we reach the front door. Number twenty-one. Our new home.

"So, this is it."

I look at Zoe, and she looks back at me. I'm trying to keep a straight face, and contain my excitement, but my best friend has already completely lost it.

"This is definitely it." Zoe pushes her key into the lock and pauses for dramatic suspense, looking at me with a huge grin on her face. "Ready?"

I nod, no longer even trying to hide my emotions. I can't. We have both waited far too long for this. She reaches her other hand down to take hold of mine while turns the key.

"Well…" she says.

She's in front of me; I can't see into the house, into our house.

"Is it okay? Let me see!" I nudge her slightly and she moves over.

It's a very average, ordinary hallway. The walls are magnolia, the carpet is beige and all-in-all it is unremarkable.

"I love it!" We shriek at each other and if

1

there was enough room in this narrow space to jump around, we would definitely be doing that.

Close enough to be able to visit our parents if we want to, but far enough away to feel free. Zoe and I have arrived at our lodgings for the next year. We have finally made it to university

"Choose rooms first or get our stuff?"

I nod towards the staircase. Zoe runs without a second thought and I'm not far behind.

We are the first to arrive at the student house, so we get the pick of the rooms. The accommodation spreads over three floors, with two bedrooms on the first floor, and two more up top. The upper rooms are converted attic areas, with slanted ceilings and not nearly as much space as the ones below.

Zoe takes one look into the higher bedrooms and screws up her nose. I smile, and we race back down to the rooms that we are about to claim as our own. The other students will have to take what's left.

The rooms are more-or-less the same size, Zoe heads into the room on the left of the landing, and I go right. It's an arbitrary decision; it's not like we would ever argue about something like this. We've been friends for far too long to fall out over anything.

Hauling our belongings out of Zoe's Corsa, along the road and up the stairs in our student house, today feels like the beginning of an epic adventure.

There was never any doubt that we would choose to go to the same university, the only doubts I had were whether I would get the grades I needed to get here. It's been a tough few years, but here I am. Wessex University. I made it. A week from now I will be embarking upon the start of my student midwife training. In three years' time I'll be a qualified midwife.

At least if I make it through the course I will.

"Are you off in your little dream world again?" Zoe says.

I've stopped because the two bags of clothes and accessories that I'm carrying are a lot heavier than I expected, but, yes, I'm also miles away, or rather years away.

"Just taking it all in," I smile. I hoist one of the bags onto my hip and start moving again.

"It's going to be so much fun living together. All the booze, boys and –"

"Books. We won't have any time for the other stuff," I say, and I almost believe myself.

"You think it's going to be back-to-back lectures and hitting the library every night?" she laughs. "You do that if you like, but my first job, as soon as we've got the rest of this," she nods at the box in her hands, "in there", she bobs her head towards the house, "is to go and find the student union bar and get absolutely…"

"Wasted," I smile.

We push back in through the front door and head up the stairs. Zoe is still laughing along with me and manages to catch the corner of the box she is carrying against the bannister. The cardboard container and its contents spill down the stairs like a landslide. I hop to the side, and barely miss being swept away by 'Wuthering Heights', 'Pride and Prejudice' and the slightly less classical, but classic all the same, 'Bridget Jones's Diary'.

"Oh pants!"

"Luckily not pants, just books." I plop my bags down on the hallway floor and start to gather up the texts for her. She teeters down to help.

"I brought way too much. You're probably right though: I don't think we will have much time to socialise. Teaching and midwifery aren't the same types of courses as say…" She pauses while she tries to think of a standard uni course. "Sociology, or, English or something. They are like five hours a week of classes. We are going to be in all day every day."

"And then some. I start my first placement next month."

"It's going to be tough, even if I don't start mine until the new year," she says.

I put the last couple of Zoe's books on top of one of my bags and carry them the rest of them for her.

"It's going to be great. Trust me. The two of us, here together. How could it not be?"

Zoe grins, then turns and makes a second attempt at carrying her stuff upstairs. This is our third trip from the car to our rooms, and we each still have a couple of suitcases to drag up. Zoe's parents offered to come and help, but saying goodbye at home felt so much easier.

My mum doesn't drive; she could have come with Zoe's folks, but I tried not to make too big a deal about me leaving. I'd rather that she thinks I am only a short distance away, and that I haven't really left her. Zoe's parents have each other, my mum and I have only had each other for the past year. At least, my dad left *physically* last year, but emotionally, he's been absent for as long as I can remember.

"You worrying about your mum again?"

Zoe stands in the doorway of my room, and looks in on me. I've put my cargo down and sat on the edge of my new, single bed in my new single room, and my thoughts are obviously wandering back to home. She'd know what I was thinking about even if it wasn't obvious. She's been my best friend for fifteen years, she knows everything about me, and I know everything about her.

I nod and try to cover up some of the sadness in my expression, but she can see through me. She knows. She always knows.

"It's okay," she says. She sits down on the bed next to me and puts her arm around me. "Oh, your bed is way more comfortable than mine. Feel that bounce!" She lifts her bum off the duvet and drops it back down. "Mine's like a rock."

"We can swap. I really don't mind."

"No way! You know I have a better view."

As better views go, it isn't much. I can see the street from my room, and Zoe gets to look out over the small patch of grass that the landlord called a 'communal garden' in the advert.

"Far better. *Way* better. I don't know what I was thinking." This is what she does, she picks me up and lifts my mood from brooding to laughing, just like that.

We have a bathroom on our floor, and there's another toilet upstairs. Whoever designed this place was definitely into their plumbing. I'm not complaining. I am a huge fan of long soaks in the bath, and I am not going to feel half as guilty about indulging knowing that anyone desperate to clean themselves or, well, whatever, can use one of the other facilities.

Downstairs there's a shower room slash toilet combo, shared galley kitchen, and a living room that could either be described as cosy or compact, depending on how much you wanted to dress it up. It seems spacious now, but once there are two more people living here, I can imagine that it might start to feel cramped.

Zoe doesn't let me wallow in my thoughts for long.

"Shall we finish off getting the stuff?" she says, "I've left the car open." As an afterthought, she adds, "And it's on the double yellows."

I nod. "Let's do it. But Zo..."

"Yeah?" She's stood up and she's reaching her hand to pull me to my feet.

"Even if we are going to spend the rest of our student lives with our heads in books, living the life of sad spinsters –"

"Less of the sad!"

"Okay, *happy* spinsters. Let's go out tonight. Let's celebrate being here."

She reaches her second hand out too and pulls me up and towards her into a hug.

"Absolutely. We've earned this. Let's make the most of our week before classes."

"I'll definitely drink to that!"


It takes us the best part of an hour to finish unloading and unpack our belongings into our rooms. The process is punctuated by the pair of us popping across the landing to visit each other's rooms, sharing our excitement. There's not much in my bedroom; a bed, a desk, a wardrobe. Luckily, I don't have much to fill the space with. Clothes, books, make-up, some scented candles. Despite the fact that my best friend will be living across the hall from me, I have a photo of the two of us printed out and framed that I put at the back of my desk, next to my ceramic pen pot.

Her deep red hair almost tangled in my boring brunette, her bright green eyes glowing in contrast to my muddy brown. Both of us laughing. I don't even remember the moment this photograph was taken. I can't recall what it was that was so funny, because it could have been anything. I have so many photos of the two of us like this on my phone.

She has been there for me through everything. Happy times like the ones in all those photographs, and the less happy times that I would rather forget. Before I head back into Zoe's room to help her finish up, I sit on the edge of my bed and take a moment alone. I send Mum a text to let her know that I am here, and that I am safe.

I never thought I was good enough to get to university. I struggle with exams; I struggle with self-confidence. I did it though, I made it. I always knew that I wanted to be a midwife. Not a nurse. I never wanted to be a nurse. I mean, there are a lot of similarities, but the things that are different are the things that appeal to me the most. Being with a woman during such an important, emotional experience as pregnancy, labour and the postpartum period is such an amazing privilege and honour. I never thought I would make it here though.

I'm lost in my thoughts when Zoe pops her head around the door.

"You okay?" she says.

"Yeah."

"Having a moment?"

I smile.

"I had one too." She walks in and sits on the bed next to me.

I made it this far, and with Zoe by my side I'm almost certain that I will succeed.

True to our words, when we have finished unpacking, we get ready for our first night out as university students. The main campus is a ten-minute walk from Tangiers Court, or at least it should be according to Google maps. It's starting to get dark, and there's a park to cut through, so before seven o'clock we are on our way out.

Zoe pulls open the front door and thuds directly into a tall, dark, and rather scruffy male.

"I'm sorry -"

He smiles, and she stops talking. She's standing with her mouth open, and I give her a subtle prod and shake my head.

"Zoe, be cool," I whisper into her ear.

She clears her throat.

"Can I help you?" she says in the most put-on accent I have ever heard her use. This is the face-to-face equivalent of her telephone voice.

The man tilts his head, looks at her, and then at me. I notice that he looks at her for longer, even if it is only a matter of seconds. Zoe's earlier comment about not having time for relationships pops into my head. I shake the idea away.

"I'm Luke," he says. He holds out his hand to her, and she looks at it.

"Zoe," she replies. "Can I help you?" She tentatively reaches to shake hands.

"No, it's fine, thanks. I couldn't find anywhere to park, so I wanted to check that I could get in first."

"Get in?"

A look of realisation passes over his face.

"I live here," he says. "Or at least, I am just about to."

Zoe mimes a little facepalm expression. I'm standing behind her, trying to fade into the background. She waves her hand to me and says, "This is Violet. We live here too."

11

"Lovely," he says.

There's an awkward pause, Luke on the outside of the doorway and Zoe firmly in the entrance. She's still staring at him. I nudge her again and she turns to me. I nod my head to the side of the door a couple of times, hoping she will catch on, and she does.

"Sorry, sorry," she says again, and steps out of Luke's way. "I'm an idiot. At least we have got that out of the way."

He actually laughs, and I see Zoe's face turn a fiery shade of red. It suits her; it blends well with her hair.

"Not at all." He steps into the hallway and shakes my hand too.

"Nice to meet you." I give him a mock-apologetic smile, and Zoe digs me in the ribs playfully. "We were about to head out to the union bar." I say it as in invitation, but Luke doesn't bite.

"I need to bring my things in, maybe unpack a little, and…" He sniffs his armpit melodramatically. "I probably need a shower."

"There's one on this floor. And a bath on the first. Your room will be one of the ones on the top floor I'm afraid," Zoe says. She's still curt and business-like.

"So, I do need a shower?" he smiles.

"I didn't…I mean…"

"I think he's messing with you," I say, and Zoe facepalms again. I love this girl so much.

"Top floor is fine for me. You two bagged first floor then?"

We both nod.

"I need the exercise anyway," he says and gently pats his stomach, which appears to be completely flat despite his intimation.

"No, you…" Zoe starts to speak and then stops herself.

"We should probably be going then," I say, linking arms with my best friend. I need to get her out of here before she says something she might regret.

"If I finish sorting everything out, I will come and find you." Luke gives us a nerdy salute, I nod, and Zoe tries to replicate his gesture.

"Later," I say, pulling Zoe out of the door.

"Yeah, see you later!" Zoe echoes.

I close the door behind us and pull Zoe into a hug.

"You're so funny," I say, my face pressed into her.

"He seems very, er, nice," she replies.

"Just remember that his room is on the top

floor, and yours is on the middle. No getting lost in the night."

She laughs again, and we stand there on the doorstep of our new home, collapsing in hysterics.

This is the beginning of something special, I just know it.

# Chapter Two

Four hours later, Zoe fumbles her key in the lock, and we tumble back into the house. We have learned three things tonight. Number one: gin is a pound a shot in the student union bar. Number two: it takes approximately four and a half measures of gin each to get giggly drunk. Number three: seven gins are around two too many.

"I don't feel so good," I drawl.

"I don't feel anything. Let's not do that again."

"Not tonight anyway." I wobble along the corridor and flop into the living room without turning the light on.

Zoe keeps walking, her arms outstretched to either side of her, hands on the wall, supporting her and guiding her, and maybe keeping her upright.

I sit in the darkness, trying to focus on stopping the room from spinning.

From the kitchen I hear the sound of Zoe turning on the tap and making a pained groaning noise. Despite the fact that the room feels like a roundabout that I can't keep my balance on, I get back up to my feet and stagger

15

down the hall after her.

She's standing over the sink in what I can only describe as the 'about to chunder' position.

"Oh Zo! Hey. It's okay." I reach over her and scoop her hair back into a ponytail, holding it up, behind her, just in case. "I'm here. You're going to be alright." I'm not even sure if *I* am going to be alright, but I can't bear to see Zoe suffering. For the past fifteen years, it's just been the two of us. She and I have looked out for each other and have been there for each other for as long as I can remember.

Instead of heaving, she sways a little and starts to fall in my direction. I plunge my hands down to catch her, and stumble backwards a half step, knowing I am about to fall, her on top of me, me crushed and just as bleary drunk below.

But that's not what happens.

I lean back into a tall, man-shape. Zoe collapses onto me, and at my rear, our new housemate, Luke, catches us both.

"Good night was it?" He is squashed against the fridge, and although he's trying to hide his discomfort, I can tell he is straining to keep us semi-vertical. The space between the sink and the fridge isn't exactly huge, and it is definitely too small for two sprawling drunken teenage girls and one well-meaning rescuer,

"Something like that," I say, and gradually move so that Zoe slides gently to the floor. That leaves Luke and I standing, his arms looped beneath my armpits.

"Er, thanks," I mumble, and step over Zoe, out of his grasp. "Sorry."

"Kind of wish I had come out with you now. Housemate number four doesn't seem to have moved in yet though, so I don't know who would have stepped in to catch me." He has a friendly smile, and despite my deep embarrassment to have made such a bad early impression, he still manages, somehow, to make me smile back.

"We would have behaved better if we had a good influence with us."

"Yes, so I hate to imagine what would have happened if a bad influence like me had been there." He winks, but more in a joking way than flirtatious. At least, that's how I interpret it. "Have you had some water?" He steps over to the sink and pours out two tall glasses from the tap.

Zoe seems to have settled into a rather uncomfortable sleeping position on the floor.

She looks like a cross between a discarded ragdoll and a starfish. I pull off my sweatshirt and tuck it under her head.

"You're okay," I whisper. "You're okay here." I think she is. She's better off horizontal here than vertical anywhere else right now. Luke and I can step over her. It's fine. I'm sure it's fine.

"She'll be fine," Luke echoes my thoughts. "Maybe get her duvet? Don't think we should move her."

"She would be mortified if she knew you had seen her like this," I say, and then I cover my hand with my mouth. I have said too much.

"I'm sure that living together this year we are all going to see a lot of things. What happens in Tangiers Court stays in Tangiers Court."

He hands me the water and we clink glasses.

We don't repeat the excesses of that first night during the rest of Freshers' Week. I'd like to claim that we got it out of our system, but to be honest, Zoe couldn't face another morning of waking up on the kitchen floor wondering where she was and how she got there.

During that week we found out where the nearest supermarket is (five minutes in the car, no problem), joined up to several university societies that we will probably never attend (Zoe went for yoga, and I was taken in by an allotment-tending club, don't ask me why). We have also worked out where the lecture blocks for our first week's classes are. It's not a large campus, so even though Zoe and I are in separate faculties and different buildings, we won't be far apart.

Sunday night, the evening before week one of classes, I have planned to check my timetable on the online app, make sure my bag is packed with everything I will need, and pick out a cute outfit for tomorrow. I know that my cohort will be mainly female, it's a profession that is dominated by women, even though there are, of course, male midwives, I'm not trying to impress anyone. That's not my style anyway; I've only ever cared about what I like, never about what anyone else thinks. That was my plan anyway. Instead of getting ready I have been sitting on my bed for the past half an hour, my head spinning and my stomach feeling as though I have swallowed a block of ice. I can't do anything. I can't concentrate. All I can do is sit and hope that this feeling passes.

Ten more minutes pass, maybe fifteen, and I

hear the thud of footsteps on the stairs. A flash of red hair whips around the doorframe and Zoe pops her head in.

"I thought you were taking a long time. You okay?"

I shake my head. I can't even speak. Not even to Zoe.

She takes a seat next to me and puts her arm around me.

"Hey. It's alright," she says.

She's seen me like this before. So many times over the years.

My anxiety started in my first year at secondary school. I was eleven years old; there was a lot going on in my life, and I guess I couldn't deal with it all. It was probably a culmination of all the stressful factors, or at least that's what my GP told my parents. School work, family life, growing up, all those things. Up until the end of primary school I was the brightest in class, and I loved it. Once I started at Kingsbury Grammar, I was back at the bottom of the pile, a newbie struggling to find my feet. My mum and dad were teetering on the brink of the divorce that would take six more years to finally happen. Add those together, sprinkle them with a dash of onset of puberty, and apparently that's the recipe for crippling anxiety. Through it all, I have had Zoe. Always.

I mutter a few words and Zoe scrunches up her face in concentration trying to decipher them.

My hands are clammy and cold, but my head feels hot and heavy.

"I can't do it," I say. Each word is painful to produce. There's a tight ball in my chest where my heart should be. I'm breathing too shallowly, too quickly. Zoe puts one hand on the centre of my back.

"Ssh. Slow it down. Slow. It's okay. You're okay."

"I'm not."

She moves her hand in a circle, stroking gently, trying to bring me down. It's like she's trying to get me on track, to realign me. It usually works, eventually.

"You will be. Hush. It's okay, Vi." She kicks out at the door, which I had left open and she in turn hadn't closed when she came in. Now it's she and I, and the rest of the world doesn't matter. I breathe in, and then exhale a shaky sigh.

"I can't do it. I really want to, and I thought I could, but I can't."

She keeps moving her hand, and she shakes her head. "It's not you saying this, it's your anxiety. You know that you can do this. You wouldn't be here, about to start university if you couldn't do this. They don't let just anyone in, you know. You passed your A-Levels, you got through the interview, and you made it." She's looking straight at me, her entire focus upon my face, watching my reactions, and trying to find the right words.

I don't have a counterargument.

"You've wanted this for as long as I have wanted to be a teacher. This has always been our dream. The two of us, here at uni together, working towards our ideal careers. We have done it. Don't pussy out on me now, Vi." She gives me a huge smile and pats my back gently. "You're going to be fine."

All I can think about is walking into that classroom tomorrow with all the other students, who are all going to be better than I am, in every way. I'm not clever enough, not good enough. I feel like a fraud. Yes, I passed my exams, but it must have been a fluke. There must have been some kind of mistake. I don't deserve to be here.

My breathing rate has increased again, and

Zoe frowns at me.

"Really. Come on. Don't let your brain do this to you. Don't let your anxiety spoil this moment for you." I close my eyes and concentrate on regulating my inhalations, slowing down, exhaling deeply. "That's it," she says.

When my parents were fighting, when they divorced, when I had a hopeless crush on the boy I sat next to in maths class, just so I could let him copy off me, when I thought I would never pass my GCSEs, when I thought I shouldn't have gotten into college, when I split up with Jared, my first boyfriend, my first love, when I was certain that A Level biology was going to destroy me…all of those times and so many more, Zoe was there for me.

I suck breath in so sharply that I feel the kick in the back of my throat.

"That's it." She pulls me in towards her and wraps both arms around me in that familiar comforting hug.

"I'm sorry," I say. "I'm such an idiot."

"No, no, no," she says, stroking my hair. "Your brain is an idiot sometimes, that's all. You'll show it though. You can do this, and you will do this."

I wish it was as easy as believing her and believing in myself. It isn't. The feelings that have been brewing within me will continue to bubble, but I can't let them take over. Not now.

We sit for a while in a silent embrace. I listen to her heartbeat thud against my ear and feel her warmth. The only sound is our breathing, we don't need anything else.

# Chapter Three

Monday morning, the first day of term; my stomach is churning. I barely slept last night, and when I did, I had dreams that I had missed my alarm bleeper. My mind is buzzing, so I get up at seven, rather than trying to get back to sleep and I sit at my desk, reading through the course pages on my laptop.

There are six weeks of lectures before we get let loose in the community. By let loose, I mean that we are each assigned to an experienced community midwife, who will guide us gently into the first stages of our 'hands-on' training. The community teams provide antenatal care in clinics, sometimes in the hospital, and sometimes in women's homes. They do postnatal visits, and sometimes intrapartum care and delivery. It's possible to experience nearly every facet of maternity care during the community placement, so it's a great place to start. Like I said, that's six weeks away, and that six weeks feels like forever.

My timetable shows an induction session at nine o'clock in the lecture block. Zoe isn't starting until nine thirty, but she's heading in with me. I'm leaving it to her to work out where the best place on campus is to get coffee.

"Good luck, Vi," she says, pulling me into a huge hug.

"Oh Zo, I can't believe we are really here."

"Knock 'em dead," she says. Then she pulls back out of the embrace to give me the kind of grin that only she can. "Not literally, obviously."

"Zoe!" I tap her shoulder in a playful gesture. "Not even funny."

"Go. Go on, you'll be late."

"Good luck too."

I smile, I nod, and I head to the lecture block for my first day as a student midwife.

By the time I get to the classroom, the world feels like it is moving in slow motion. It doesn't seem real. It's as though I am a character, stepping into a dramatisation of someone else's life.

I always try to sit somewhere in the middle of a class. At the front it feels too confrontational and exposed. I don't want the lecturer to direct every question at me; I don't have the confidence to give answers when I know so little. At the back I wouldn't feel engaged enough in the class. I want to be a part of it, but not too much so. I guess that sums me up. I take a seat next to the wall about half-way down the room. Everyone here so far is dotted about in isolation. There are no identifiable friend groups yet. This is the beginning; we all have a clean slate.

I pull my notebook and pen case out of my bag and place them neatly on the table in front of me. I love stationery, and I was glad to have the excuse to pick out new goodies to bring with me. Having these treats makes me feel a little more relaxed. I focus upon my floral pencil case, rather than letting myself get lost in my negative thoughts. I am so focussed that I don't notice when a girl with a short blonde bob and floral dress sits herself down next to me. It's only when I finally look up that I realise she is there.

"Oh hi," I say.

She nods, and I'm sure she's almost trembling. She looks how I feel. I guess I have had a long time to perfect not letting my anxiety show through in public.

"Hi," she says, in a soft, quiet voice. "I'm Sophie."

"Violet," I say. "So many people. Scary, isn't it?"

She smiles a little and looks away. I give her

a moment, and she turns back.

"It's all a bit surreal. I can't believe I am finally here." So, I'm not the only one. It's always a relief to know that whatever anxieties I have, that I am not alone in my thoughts.

"Same," I say. "I can't wait to get started."

There are twenty-two of us gathered in the classroom by the time the lecturer arrives. She is a short, round woman with wild curly hair. Her shirt is a bright purple Batik print, which she has paired with leggings and oxblood boots. Somehow, she looks exactly as I would have imagined a midwifery lecturer to look. I suppose *we* all look exactly like students, which evens the score. She drops her bag onto the chair at the front of the room and stands next to the lectern. We lower our chat to a polite silence, and she begins to speak.

"Welcome to your first day as future midwives."

An excited hum passes through the room as everyone turns toward the strangers sitting to either side of them, beginning to build shared bonds.

The lecturer lets us have this moment and pauses before continuing.

"I'm Zita Somerville, Programme Lead for Midwifery Studies. I'm also the module leader for the anatomy and physiology class you'll be taking this term. I am going to tell you, right now, on this very first day: this is not an easy course." We all start to mumble to each other again, but this time she carries on. "You will learn all of the theory that you need to know to enter the workforce as skilled novice practitioners, but," she pauses again, for effect this time, "the real learning will take place when you are with women."

She turns and writes the words 'with woman' onto the whiteboard. The marker pen squeaks against the board as she forms the two words that give the literal definition of midwife. *Midwife: with woman.*

"In France, we would be called a sage-femme, which means 'wise woman'. In days gone by we would have been called witches. I know what I prefer. With woman. That is what this, your vocation, is all about: being with a woman. Supporting her. Being by her side throughout the most intimate, emotional, challenging period of her life."

"What about men?" a male voice says from the left of the room.

"Simon, hello," the lecturer says. "The role of the midwife goes far beyond simply caring for a woman, and you will learn a lot about relationships, sociology psychology...a little bit of law, and a lot of ethics. You'll need communication skills, diplomacy, mathematics..."

There's a small but noticeable groan at the mention of this, and a laugh in response from the rest of the group.

"I'll be sure to keep an eye on you when you're calculating your drug administration," the lecturer smiles. "We have a role in protecting and promoting the health of communities. You may have days when you feel more like a social worker than a midwife. This job will make immense demands upon you." She pauses again. "You will rise to the challenge, and you will succeed. You will succeed for every woman and baby, for every husband..." Another pause. "Or wife." She is working the crowd well. "So, Simon, you are going to be a male midwife, and yes, you will support the women and you will do that by supporting their wider family, by identifying their individual needs, and by doing everything you can for them. When you can't do any more, or when you yourself need support, you will find it, and you will build your own toolkit. You will never stop learning. The three years that you are here are merely the beginning of the journey."

Sophie has been scribbling in her notepad the whole time that Zita has been talking. When the speech is over, she finally looks up from the paper, and smiles at me.

"Inspirational," she says. "I feel a bit better now."

"It's going to be a lot of hard work." I'm fired up by Zita's words too, but there is so much to this course, so much to learn.

Sophie tilts her head slightly and looks at me. For a moment I wish I hadn't said anything. I don't want other people thinking that I can't do this. I feel terribly vulnerable until she puts her hand on mine and says, "It is. But we are all in it together now."

I break into a huge smile and let go of a wave of tension within me that I didn't even realise I was holding. Looking around the room, I can see the same shared looks, whispered words and the seeds being sown of support, of friendships, of a real community.

At the front of the classroom, Zita sits in

silence and watches.

"This is a three-year course, and it is a marathon, not a sprint. Remember that. You are not going to do everything all at once. You have walked in here today as novices, but you will learn and develop throughout your three years, gradually and steadily. When you complete your course, you will continue to learn. Every day that you practice as a midwife, for the rest of your careers, you will continue to learn. You will never know everything."

This also feels like a relief. When I think about how much I need to learn it makes me nauseated. The impossibility of knowing everything is terrifying, but of course nobody can know everything. I like Zita. She knows what to say. She is realistic. She is keeping us grounded.

She clicks on the computer and brings up a copy of our practice documents on the display screen. A copy for each of us is circulated around the room. I receive my heavy coil bound A4 slab and place it on the desk in front of me. It stares at me intimidatingly.

"In your placements, you will work on completing the competencies required to pass the practical elements of the course. Everything is set out in your PAD, your Practice Assessment Document. Make sure you read it carefully. Your placement mentors will support you to make the most of your experiences."

I browse through the list of competencies that run over page after page. I start to feel dizzy thinking about the huge amount of work that this will entail. There is one list that grabs my attention.

**Advising of pregnant women, involving at least 100 antenatal examinations**

**Supervising and caring for at least 40 women in labour**

**Performance of episiotomy and initiation into suturing**

**Personally carrying out at least 40 births**

**Supervising and caring for 40 women at risk during pregnancy, labour or the postnatal period**

**Supervising and caring for (including examination) at least 100 postnatal women and at least 100 healthy newborn infants**

**Active participation with breech births (may be simulated)**

**Observation and care of the newborn requiring special care, including those born pre-term, post-term, underweight or ill**

Half of my time will be spent in university, and half on placement. Wondering how I am going to manage to fit in all those activities makes my head spin.

Zita is still talking.

"Try not to worry too much about getting everything done," she says, as if reading my mind. "I guarantee that the students who graduated this year all had the same thoughts when they were sitting where you are now. Every one of them achieved their competencies with time to spare."

"They weren't me," I say quietly.

"You'll be fine," Sophie says. "Really. It's going to be okay. We can do this."

I try to smile, but the words and numbers on the page stare up at me accusingly. She's trying to reassure herself as much as she is attempting to comfort me though, I can tell by the way that her fingers tremble slightly as she flicks through her pages.

"Read through the module guides. Familiarise yourself with your PADs. The sooner you start filling in your competencies the better. You don't want to be starting your final year thinking that you have time to complete eighty more antenatal checks, or you're going to find yourself struggling."

A hundred antenatal checks. A hundred postnatal checks. Forty births.

The room feels so hot and stuffy, I need to get outside. I need to breathe. I don't think I can sit here for the rest of this session. The heat is rushing through me like a tsunami. My cheeks are burning, my palms are sweaty, I'm going to...

"Violet? Violet?

Sophie is tapping on my arm, her voice getting louder. I snap myself back into the room.

"Ugh, I'm okay. Thanks." I'm not okay. Not really. My head is still swimming. I need some fresh air. The clock shows we only have five minutes left of the lecture; I think I can make it.

"Are you alright, Violet?" Zita calls over from the front of the room.

"Uh, yeah. Just hot, sorry."

She nods and flicks a button on the desk. "Air con should kick in shortly, give it a minute. Just let me know, anyone, if you need more air, more light, anything, okay? These are going to be long days, and I want you all to be comfortable." She looks back over to me to check that I am alright, and I give a feeble nod in return.

I'm going to have to get a grip on myself; I can't carry on like this every day. I consciously measure my breaths and tell myself to keep it together.

At the end of the session, I stuff my book into my bag, relieved that the class is over. We have an hour and a half until the next introductory slot. I text Zoe.

**What time do you get out of there? xx**

She replies almost immediately.

**Noon. How was it? xx**

It's eleven thirty now.

**Exciting! Where are we meeting? xx**

Again, her reply is rapid.

**Bradley's. Back of the library xx**

I'm still standing in the classroom, tapping away at my phone. Everyone has left apart from Zita. She walks down the aisle to the door and stops to talk to me.

"Are you really alright, Violet?" she says.

No point in hiding anything from her. Maybe being honest and open will help.

"I get anxiety attacks," I tell her. "I'm mostly used to them, I mean, you know, they are awful, but I have had them for a few years now. Sometimes," I shrug, "they overpower me a bit."

"Sounds tough, I'm sorry. Well, if you ever need to leave the room, you just walk out and take a breather. We can always have a catch-up afterwards if you need to. Let your mentors know too." She tugs in her bag, pulls out a leaflet and hands it to me. Student Support Services. "Give them a call, or pop in. They are really good."

"Thanks." I have had all kinds of support before, and nothing has helped to eradicate my anxiety. "I appreciate that."

"And talk to Deb Cross, she'll be your link tutor. She's lovely."

I smile. "Thanks."

We walk to the door together, and I slip the leaflet into my bag.

"How did you find it, apart from," she waves her hand instead of completing the sentence.

"I'm looking forward to getting stuck in. I can't wait."

We smile at each other, and head in our separate directions.

Bradley's is a small, strange shaped building tagged onto the back of the library. The counter area and its glass-fronted unit, brimming with cakes and sandwiches almost fills one end of the room. The rest of the space spreads out towards tall windows, comfortably allowing around a dozen round tables. We haven't discovered anywhere better on campus yet, so this, for now, is us.

I don't have to wait long for Zoe. She gets her usual extra shot, extra hot mocha and drops into the seat next to me.

"Sheesh!" she says. "You should see the size of our practice portfolios. There's so much paperwork!"

"Same." I nod to my bag, which is being held open by the A4 coil-bound PAD. "And I nearly had a full-on anxiety attack so that was, er, fun."

She puts her hand onto my shoulder, almost instinctively.

"Nearly? Are you okay now?"

"I think I was a bit overwhelmed by it all. There's so much to do and I...I don't know if I can do it." She's about to speak, and I raise my hand to stop her. "I know. You don't have to say it. It's just my stupid brain making me feel like this."

She rubs on the place where her hand sits upon me.

"You remember that, Vi. Next time your brain starts being a dick to you. Promise you'll remember that."

I nod and take a sip of my drink. I feel a lot more relaxed now. This place is ideal, Zoe did well. It's quiet. We can talk here. I can think.

"So, tell me about your morning," I say, and we chat, animatedly and excitedly, full of optimism for the future until the end of our break.

# Chapter Four

I settle into lectures far more easily than I
expected. I have a regular pattern of classes,
with Wednesday afternoons off. That's when
the academic staff have all of their meetings,
and we can get stuck into the social groups that
we signed up for in Fresher's Week. Zoe has
managed to go to two yoga classes, but I
haven't stepped foot on an allotment. I have a
slight suspicion that I may have been drawn to
sign up by the vaguely attractive student behind
the stall, rather than any real green-fingered
aspirations.

By the end of the first month, the upstairs
room at Tangiers Court has remained
mysteriously empty. When Zoe and I agreed the
lease on the rooms, we were told that there
would be two male students moving in with us,
but only Luke has arrived. It means that we
have a little extra fridge space, more room in
the cupboards, and that I can take a bath pretty
much any time I want to without feeling bad for
blocking the room. It also means that we have
invented a fourth housemate.

"Who's left this mug and plate in the sink
again?" I shout through to the living room.

"Must be Andrew," Luke replies.

"Oh, of course." I laugh and clean them for him.

"Whose turn is it to buy milk?"

"Um, I think it's Andrew's," says Zoe.

Luke heads down the road to the corner shop and comes back with a communal pint of semi-skimmed.

Basically, Andrew has become the scapegoat for anything any of us want to avoid doing. Don't get me wrong, on the whole, we are working well as a mini team. Despite his sometimes reluctance to wash up behind himself (he says it's because he never had to at home) Luke is fairly handy around the place. He's the only one who hoovers, and I am sure that it is Luke who is responsible for squirting green stuff into the toilets on a semi-regular basis. Either that or it's Andrew.

Luckily, we pay rent for each individual room rather than having to split the rent for the house between three of us rather than four, so Andrew's absence is a blessing rather than an inconvenience.

Today it's Andrew's turn to make dinner, so we end up ordering takeaway.

"How's your course going, Luke?" Zoe asks,

reaching over for another fried chicken ball.

"Mmm-mm," Luke nods through his mouthful of crispy chili beef.

"Enlightening, thank you," she laughs.

"Do you have any lectures at all?" I ask. "I'm basically in Monday to Friday, and Zoe seems to live between lectures and library now."

He's studying accountancy, which seems to mean he has approximately two lectures per week. Either that or it seems that way because Zoe and I have such full timetables.

"Bah, you get Wednesday afternoons off, just like everyone else," he laughs.

"I never see you go to uni though."

"Don't you worry, Miss Violet. I fully intend on getting the education that I am going to be spending the next ten years of my life paying for."

"And the rest!" Zoe says.

"Maybe you'll have to find yourself a rich husband to pay off your student loan then," Luke smiles, and plucks the final spring roll off Zoe's plate.

"Oi!" she says, thrusting her chopsticks towards him playfully.

He raises his eyebrows.

"Fight me for it. Chopsticks versus

chopsticks."

"Alright, settle down!" I say, but they don't hear me; they are having a bizarre fencing match with the wooden implements. I shake my head and twirl my noodles.

"Yes!" Zoe shouts. I don't think there were any set rules for the chopstick battle, but Zoe is claiming victory.

"A fair fight. Well won," Luke says. "You can have Andrew's spring roll."

"I'm sure it was mine," Zoe says. Still, she pulls it apart and splits it half each with him.

"Very sporting of you. Thanks ma'am." He stuffs it into his mouth, and Zoe eats her portion just as greedily.

"I think it was Andrew's turn to wash up," I say, as we finish up the last of the meal.

Zoe raises her eyebrows and shakes her head at me.

"You might want to check the rota there, Vi," she says. I know it's my turn. At least there's no cutlery to wash today. I gather the plates, and Zoe starts to stack the takeaway cartons.

"Thanks mate," Luke says. He leans back in his chair, stretching, and his t-shirt rides up exposing a slightly flabby, furry belly. I look away, but I notice that Zoe does just the opposite. She catches my glance and her face prickles red.

"Go and pick us a film to watch," I suggest as I head to the sink.

Luke lets out a belch.

"Lovely," I call back. Zoe laughs, and pulls him into the living room.

# Chapter Five

One of the worst parts of studying is group work. There's something about being thrown together with people that I don't really know yet and being expected to create something fantastic that fills me with dread. Worse still, the fantastic thing that we have to create is my worst nightmare: a presentation.

It might not seem like something that I should be afraid of. Getting up and talking in front of a class of twenty or so like-minded classmates is hardly wrestling a pit of angry snakes, scaling a tall building without a safety harness or plucking a spider out of the shower because Zoe has been screaming at it for the past five minutes. I'd rather do any of those things than give a presentation. *Preparing* a PowerPoint is fine. I can do the groundwork, pull everything together and make it look perfect with pretty pictures and detailed diagrams. Stand me up in front of a class though, and I turn to jelly.

Ironically, this module is colloquially known as 'FUN' – the Fundamentals of Midwifery Practice. As you can imagine from the name, it's meant to lay out the basics that we need to prepare us to step into our practice placements. Each week we will be given a topic to read up on, do our research in a group and then feed back to our course mates. Each week. Yes. Once every week, I will go through this trauma. On the upside, the other part of this module will involve skills lab sessions where we can get some hands-on experience – albeit on each other and on mannequins.

It makes sense that the lecturers want to know that we are safe and knowledgeable about the basics before we are launched into our community placements, but surely there must be another way. Even without my anxiety attacks I can't imagine that I would ever enjoy public speaking. Is it really public if it's the closed confines of the classroom? It's far too public for my liking, I know that much.

I enjoy working alone. I like to get an assignment, focus all my attention and energy onto it at my own pace, make my own decisions. I want everything to be perfect, or as perfect as I can make it, every time. I don't know if I can count on other people, other students that I barely know, to put in the work. Group work. Presentations. Ugh.

We've been part of a class together for four

weeks, and the only person I have had the chance to talk to at any length is Sophie. I mean I suppose I could have made more of an effort, but we have sat together during every class so far, and everyone rushes off in their own directions, with their own little groups, during break times. Of course, I go to find Zoe; perhaps it is my fault that I don't know my course mates better.

The lecturer has thrown us into groups rather than leaving us to choose for ourselves, but luckily, she did it according to where we were sitting in the classroom. I'll be with Sophie, and the two students that were sitting on our row at the time: Simon and Ashley.

Today's morning session was a lecture on antenatal physiology; this afternoon we are starting our group work. Each group has to describe one aspect of the physiological changes experienced during pregnancy. Our topic is 'describe the effects of placental hormones on the woman's body'. We have to use articles, textbooks, and the internet to pull together all of the information to present to the rest of the class. After lunch, we gather in one of the small, dark study rooms in the library.

It's a quiet place to get our thoughts together, close to the resources that we will need.

"I hate this," is what I want to say. Instead, I take a seat and smile at my group buddies. "Where shall we start?"

We spend a couple of hours picking out the key points. Ashley has an artistic eye, so she types everything into the PowerPoint, and adds a few appropriate images. Simon has the sharp suggestion of adding all our blurb into the notes section.

"If we forget anything when we're presenting at least it will all be there."

It sounds like a great idea, but the very mention of the word 'presenting' sends chills through me. I know that we are drafting a document that we will use as a presentation, but I've tried to dissociate from that fact. I'm trying to see it as gathering information with the team, trying to make sure that we have covered all the bases. I've pushed the thought of having to stand up and make a presentation to the corner of my mind. If I pushed it any further, I might be able to drop it out of reality. I can't though. I know I can't.

"Do you want to run through it?" Simon asks,

as Ashley saves the file to our shared drive.

Sophie and Ashley both nod enthusiastically. Whatever the opposite of that is, that's what I do. I'm silently, steadfastly unenthusiastic.

"You don't think we need to?" Simon's voice isn't unfriendly. I think he has misjudged my fear for overconfidence.

"I should have probably mentioned this sooner," I say, "but I hate presentations." I put my hands over my face and rub at my eyes. "Ugh. I'm not very good at being in front of people. I don't deal well with pressure." I drop my hands and look Simon in the eye. "I have terrible anxiety attacks." I shrug. There's no other way of saying it. "I don't think I can do it."

Sophie smiles at me and says, "We can do the talking. You've done your share of the work, it's okay."

I'm about to accept with a whoosh of heartfelt appreciation, but Simon is shaking his head.

"It's better for you to try to get used to this now. We have presentations every week this term while we are in uni. You're not going to be able to skip it every time."

Sophie opens her mouth to cut in, but Simon

raises a hand to silence her.

"Really. It's a good skill to learn, and you can do it. When we are in practice we are going to have to talk to a lot of people about a lot of difficult things. Being able to articulate our thoughts and explain things clearly is crucial."

The explanation makes sense. I don't get the feeling that he wants to be mean. I would still rather sit it out and let these three do the presentation instead though. I can already feel the blood thudding in my temples, and the familiar knot has tangled itself in my stomach. I don't even know if I can run through a practice presentation in front of these three.

"We are here, okay? We are a team now," Ashley's voice is so soft and calming. She is going to be amazing at talking to women when we get out into practice. Everything about her tone fills me with confidence. "Try. Okay? Just try this week. Try this time. We all know all of the presentation, so if you need to sit out, you nod at one of us and we will take over for you." She looks at Simon, and says, "*This time*. As long as you promise to try."

"I know that anxiety attacks are awful, Vi," Sophie says. "My sister has them, and I've seen how hard they are. We aren't going to push you.

We want to help."

My mind is flipping between grateful thanks for their support and abject fear at the thought of stepping out of my comfort zone. These three people who hardly know me are prepared to step up to give me the time and support that I need so that I can do the best that I can do. That means a lot to me. I can't let them down.

I nod timidly.

"Okay?" Simon says.

I force a more resolute nod, and he smiles.

"Phew." He relaxes. "I'm not good at being firm like that. I thought I might have pushed it too far." He laughs, and I relax enough to join in. "You can do it though, Violet. You've got this."

"Sure. I've got this."

They don't make me stand up to do the run through. I sit in my seat and click through my section of the slides. We've split it between the four of us, so there's not actually that much for me to present. Three slides. That's all I have to get through. Just three slides.

As soon as I start to speak aloud, I feel like I have lost control of my mouth. It's like I am chewing a huge ball of gum. My tongue won't form the sounds. My lips flap, my cheeks glow.

I shake my head.

"Sorry, guys," I say.

How can I not even be able to do this? I'll never have the confidence to stand in front of class if I can't sit with three people.

"It's okay," Ashley says. "Be calm."

I want to say that I would love to be calm, but that's rather difficult when I'm on the edge of an anxiety attack. I don't. I give a weak smile and read the words on the screen silently to myself.

"Tell you what, we will pop out for a minute, so you can practice on your own. Read it out to yourself. Get familiar with it. Alright?" Simon seems to know a lot about dealing with what I am going through; this sounds like a good idea.

"Sure," I say. "Thanks."

They leave the study room, Sophie patting my arm supportively on the way past, and I am left alone.

I'm too hot, my breathing is too fast, the words are spinning around my head. *Be calm, be calm, be calm.* I repeat it to myself, slowly and gently, trying to get a grip on my feelings.

One final deep breath in and out, and I focus my attention onto the laptop screen. I can do this. I must learn how to do this. I can do this.

I'm going to have to stand up in class, so I get to my feet. I imagine the rest of the cohort there in front of me, all interested in what I have to say. Focus. Focus. Think only of the words, the explanation, the presentation.

I start to speak. I let the text on the screen guide me as I describe antenatal blood volume changes, and how they affect the pregnant woman. I start off stiff, trying to hold my body still, trying to keep it under control. By the end of my section, I am loose, gesticulating at the screen with my arms, almost relaxed into the moment.

When I come to a stop, I look over to my right and see the three of them in the doorway.

"That was perfect," Simon says. "I knew you could do it."

"Brilliant," Ashley nods. "I think you even added some things on that I missed from the slides. You were spot on."

Sophie grins and claps. "Awesome!"

I feel like I have achieved something, like I have taken the first steps. I have to repeat this in front of the class though, and that thought still terrifies me.

# Chapter Six

Zoe doesn't start her placements until February
and she barely has any practice time this year
compared to me. I feel a little bad for her,
because I'm finding it difficult to stop myself
from enthusing about my rapidly approaching
community visits. I love my course, I love our
home, and I love university life.

I'm not sure that I am having the same
experience of university as my course mates.
Living with Zoe makes a difference. We live
within a bubble here at Tangiers Court. Zoe and
I haven't spent much time in the student union
bar since we arrived. Not that the first night and
the sickness that ensued put us off completely, I
suppose it is more that Zoe and I are already a
tight unit. If I was here on my own without her,
I might feel the need to socialise, to go out to
the bar, to actually attend the clubs I joined
during Fresher's Week, but instead, most of our
spare time is spent self-contained within the
sphere of our friendship.

Some nights Luke stays at Tangiers Court
with us, and he fits neatly into our group. Not
like a puzzle piece that we were missing, more
like a bolt-on, an optional extra. The house is

comfortable and even more spacious with the ongoing absence of our fourth housemate; we definitely got lucky with our residence.

Thursday night, the evening before my presentation, what I should be doing is sitting in my room running through my lines like an actress going up for her big-time audition. I should practice and repeat until what I am going to say is fixed in my mind, and I have no room for self-doubt anymore. If I can recite it by rote, I don't need to feel anxious about it, that's my reasoning anyway. Still, even the thought of this starts familiar prickles of panic.

I say that's what I should be doing, because it is not what I am actually doing. Instead, I am sitting at a table in the student union bar with Zoe, Luke and three lads that I have never met before, but who are, apparently, Luke's best friends. The occasion that persuaded me to leave my books and come to the union, despite my presentation? It's Luke's birthday. He invited us, and I really couldn't say no, so here I am. 'Bros before presentations' doesn't work quite as well as I would like, but the sentiment is there.

Ten o'clock and two hours into our session, I

am pacing myself well. Instead of the usual gin and tonic that Zoe is still throwing back, I have switched to diet cola, with a gin every third round. Surprisingly, this has still led to me feeling lightheaded and on the cusp of inebriation. Luke's friends are from his accountancy course. Damon, blonde, not yet over his teenage acne and from somewhere up North by the sounds of his accent. Rajesh, who must be at least six and a half feet tall and swears like a docker. Florin, who has a strong Eastern European twang to his voice, which is becoming more pronounced the more lager he drinks. Apparently, these guys are who Luke spends his time with when he is not with us.

I don't want to appear impolite, with it being Luke's birthday, but I have my phone on the table, and I keep glancing at the time.

"Have to be somewhere?" Florin asks.

I shake my head. His breath is thick with alcohol, and he has to lean in far too close towards me to make his voice audible over the noise of the bar. He's dangling precariously over the pint glasses on the wooden table between us.

"No. I have a thing tomorrow." I don't feel like explaining further, but I don't have to. He sits back up as Rajesh announces that it's Damon's turn to go to the bar.

Zoe is nestled on the opposite side of the table from me, in between Luke and Florin. I was sitting next to her, where Flo is now, but I popped to the toilet about half an hour ago and there was a change around. I don't mind too much. I'm on a stool, facing the three of them. If I want to say anything to Zoe, I have to shout over to her. This is another reason why we haven't really spent much time in the student union bar – neither of us particularly enjoy it.

From where I am sitting, I can't hear what Zoe and Luke are saying, but he leans in to speak into her ear, and she smiles in response; they switch so that she can reply.

Would it be rude for me to pick up my phone and refresh myself on my presentation? I can read through the notes here. It wouldn't take long, and…

Before I can even reach over for my phone, let alone open it, and start to read, Rajesh plops himself down onto the stool next to me.

"How's your course going?" he says. Standard conversation at the union bar.

"Yes, fine, thanks." I'm not one for small talk, and my mouth dries up just as the conversation does.

There's a heavy silence, or as near as there can be to a silence in a bar as loud as this, then he speaks again.

"Luke says you're going to be a midwife."

I think for a second before answering. This can go one of two ways. I can give him the short, sharp answer, or I can start to enthuse about my life dreams and how I can't wait to start my placement. He's drunk, and only being polite. I love talking about my course, but now isn't the time.

"Yes." I hope I don't find it as painful to talk to the women that I meet on my placements. I am terrible at this. I never know what to say. I either say too much or too little.

This is why I find it hard to make friends.

This is why I hardly ever go anywhere.

This is why, or one of the reasons why, it has always just been me and Zoe.

I don't think it is the two gins that are making my head spin. I need to get outside; I need some air. My throat. My mouth. Everything has dried up. I feel like my airway is clamping shut. I flash my eyes at Zoe, but she is still leaning in towards Luke, deep in conversation. I need to get out of here now. I think I'm going to –

There's a man in a black shirt and trouser combo standing over me. I can just about see the badge that shows he is campus security as the room starts to come back into focus. It's still loud, too loud, but it's not as busy anymore, at least not around me. There's a bare circle radiating out from where I am lying on the floor. I am the epicentre. I have clearly thrown everyone out of my path with some previously unknown superpower. Either that or the more likely explanation: security have cleared people back from where I am splayed out to keep them from treading on me.

Damon is still sitting on the opposite side of the table. Luke and Zoe are to either side of me; Zoe is squatted on the floor by my head, and Luke is standing to my other side, talking to the security guy.

"I don't think she needs a first aider," I hear him saying. "She's coming round. She's going to be fine." He leans down to me. "Are you okay?"

I use all the energy I can muster to nod.

Zoe bats away a student that walks past, leaning in too closely to me. "Get out of it. It's not a performance. Get lost." She strokes my hair away from my face. "Maybe the bar wasn't a good idea tonight," she says. "Let's go home."

I frown. "You...stay...with Luke." I sound pathetic, trying to push the words out, but my brain feels like mushy peas. Did I really only drink two gins? Two singles? I was feeling fine. I've not left my glass all night, so I know there's no chance that it's been spiked. I must have lost count, either that or I had doubles instead of singles and, well, the end result is this. Anxiety plus alcohol is not a good cocktail.

"I'm not leaving you here," Zoe says. I knew that she would insist on coming home with me.

"Really, get..." I take a deep breath. "Get a taxi and I'll go home to bed. Probably for the best anyway." The words are coming more easily now. I need to get back to Tangiers Court though.

"No way." Luke says from above. "We are getting you home. No argument."

"Luke, no. You stay with the lads. It's your birthday," Zoe says. "We will be fine. I mean I will be fine with Vi, and she will be fine."

Luke is resolute. I see him turn to his three friends, and although I can't hear what he says to them from here, I can see the disappointed expressions on their faces. I have a deep sinking feeling. Violet the party-killer. I ruin everything. My anxiety ruins everything. I should probably stay away from other humans that are trying to have a good time.

Zoe is on the phone now, calling a cab, making the arrangements to get me home. I want to sit up, get back on the stool and carry on the evening like a normal person, but as soon as I start to move, I want to vomit.

Luke kneels to my left. "Hey. Do you want me to carry you?" From his earnest expression, I can tell that he is completely genuine in his offer. I can't accept though, even if my whole body would be grateful for the excuse not to expend any energy right now.

"No thanks. But thanks. Really. And you don't have to leave. Zoe will look after me." Just like she does every time. It must be draining to be my friend sometimes. Here she is, having drinks like any normal student would do, and her stupid friend has to go and balls it up.

My father was right. I always make a mess of everything I do. I always bring down anyone that I spend time with. I'm a waste of space. That's all I am.

Zoe has stood up, and I can see her

exchanging worried glances with Luke. I've ruined his birthday. I've ruined her night. That's what I do. I ruin everything. Tomorrow I am going to mess up my presentation. The room is getting dark.

"Violet!" Zoe reaches down and places her hand on my forehead. "She's clammy."

The security guard repeats his suggestion of getting the first aider, but I am with it enough to be able to shake my head.

"She has panic attacks," Zoe tells him. "She will be alright in a few minutes. Honestly."

I do need air though. I need air and I need my bed.

Zoe looks at her phone and then at Luke. "The taxi is here," she says.

Luke reaches down and hooks his arms beneath my armpits. I haven't had my moving and handling training yet, but I am fairly sure this isn't standard. He pulls me to my feet, slowly and gently, and looks at me for a few moments, assessing me.

"Can you walk?" he asks.

I step forward, and then take another step. I feel woozy, but I'm going to make it to the street.

"Good," he says. "Sorry to cut it short, guys,"

he tells his friends. "We'll have a double session at weekend to make up for it."

"It's not your birthday then, so we won't have to buy your drinks," Rajesh says. He's sitting back at the table, Damon has come back from the bar with their drinks, and it looks like the three of them will be fine without us.

"Fair enough," Luke says with a smile.

"I'm sorry." I look at Luke and try to hold back unexpected tears.

"Hey. It's fine."

"Oh Vi." Zoe slips her arm around me and guides me towards the door. The crowd parts to let us through and I feel the weight of everyone's eyes upon us. They probably think I'm just another silly girl who can't handle her drink. I wish that were the case.

# Chapter Seven

I had planned to leave the party early and get home in time to run through my presentation. I did leave early, that's for sure.

I mustn't have set my alarm for this morning, because Zoe comes in to give me a shake awake.

"Eight o'clock, dozy duck. How's your head?"

It's too bright, too loud. I want to stay asleep. I pull the covers over my face in protest.

"Come on," Zoe says, not taking my avoidance for an answer. When I don't reply the second time, she tugs the covers down to look at me. "Are you alright to go in today?"

This is the perfect excuse for me to duck out of the presentation. I can send my apologies, explain, and everything will be fine. I give her a bleary-eyed groan.

"We should have stuck to singles," she says.

I know really that a hangover is not a good enough reason to miss class. I'm surprised the drink hit me so hard, but it has been a while. Add to that the whole anxious anticipation of today; I suppose my body is trying hard, but my brain can't quite handle it.

I hate myself right now. I knew I should have stayed at home and prepped for the presentation. I have three full hours in the skills lab this morning, no time at all to run through my lines. Maybe Zoe will listen to me over lunch. The thought of food starts to make me feel nauseated. Today is not a day for breakfast. It is, however, a day for wearing my student uniform. That is one tiny shred of positivity in the puddle that is my day ahead: the skills lab practice is my first actual opportunity to wear my uniform outside of the confines of my home.

Despite feeling rotten and terrified by the prospect of this afternoon, the skills lab session does manage to excite me a little. The atmosphere in the corridor as we wait for the lecturer to arrive is filled with an excited buzz.

We are all dressed in the grey tunic, navy trouser combinations of our student midwife uniforms. Of course I have stood in front of the mirror back at Tangiers Court, admiring myself, staring at my reflection in disbelief that I have made it this far.

Rather than taking away our individuality, wearing these uniforms only serves to unite us as a group. We have an identity and a shared purpose. We are working together to achieve our own individual and joint goals.

As I chat to my classmates my hangover starts to settle. My anxiety is still there, lying in wait, but it's a distant rumble rather than a deafening noise now.

"Feels kind of weird," Sophie says. Her eyes are sparkling, and I can tell she feels the same buzz that I do.

"Good weird," I say. "Here, let's get a selfie before Zita arrives." I angle my phone, and she leans in toward me, face gleaming in a natural smile. "Perfect!"

I know that I will be wearing this outfit here for these sessions, and out on my placements, many times over the next three years. Today, dressed like this for the first time with the rest of my cohort, the thrill makes my heart hiccup.

Zita Somerville arrives bang on time and unlocks the door to let us in.

"Don't you all look fabulous in your uniforms?" she says as she pushes the door open.

The skills lab is a large room, set out in part like a hospital ward, and in part like a clinical suite. The walls are white, the wall-mounted cupboards are white; the strip lights on the ceiling cast a harsh glare onto every surface. There are three hospital beds, each with the same kind of faux-wooden over-the-bed tables and side cabinets that I would expect to see in a real ward. There is even a nurse call bell, along with an emergency buzzer by each of the beds.

To the other side of the room is a platform with an overhead heater, and a plastic goldfish bowl type unit that I understand to be a hospital crib. Everything about this room is exactly what I expect I will find in the wards, when I finally get there. The only things missing are the patients.

"Today you will be practicing your skills on each other," the lecturer says. "We are going to run through the standard physical assessments that you are likely to perform regularly as midwives. Blood pressure, pulse, urinalysis." She pauses. "And then we will try out some abdominal palpation on our simulation models."

It's almost enough to make me forget about the presentation that I am going to have to give this afternoon. Almost.

"Into pairs, please." She does a quick head count to make sure there are an even number of us. I'm next to Sophie, so the two of us work together.

Somerville runs us through what we need to do, but when I try to listen to Sophie's blood pressure, I hear nothing. I watch the needle on the dial skip from a hundred and eighty, down through all the numbers to zero without catching any noise.

I shrug.

"Sorry, you don't have a blood pressure," I laugh.

Sophie grins. "Did you find the right place on my arm to listen in to?"

"I guess not. Shall I get Zita to show us?"

"No, let me help you." Sophie presses her index and middle finger onto the bend in her arm, and then guides my hand. "Here."

I place the end of the stethoscope onto the spot where my fingers meet her skin, and I try again.

This time, I hear the dull thud, thud, thud of her heartbeat. I am so impressed that I have found it that I almost forget that I am meant to be watching the dial as the marker moves.

"Fit and healthy. Sounds great. Thanks, Soph."

She smiles, and then we swap over.

She checks my pulse first, two fingers on my

wrist palpating my radial artery. Her eyes focus on the clock as she counts.

"Is your heart rate always this fast?" she asks.

I thought I was calm and in control. If my anxiety was making my pulse quicken before, it must be even faster now that she has mentioned it.

"Is it bad?"

"I was only joking." She smiles, and I try to smile back. "Hey, really, it's fine. You're worried about this afternoon?"

"Yeah. I feel like I am going to let everyone down."

"Impossible," she says. "It's the first presentation for all of us. We *are* all in this together. Look around. Everyone is doing new, scary things."

She waves her arm around the lab. In pairs, in every available space, my classmates are trying to put into practice the new skills that we are all starting to learn. None of them look fazed by it; everyone is helping each other.

"Maybe my blood pressure will be too high, and you'll have to send me home." I try to find something humorous to throw back to her.

She puts the stethoscope in place and listens carefully.

"You're fine," she says. "Perfect."

I shrug. "Good news is I have perfect blood pressure; bad news is I guess I have to stay for the presentation."

Zoe lets me read my presentation to her over and over while she drinks her mocha and eats a sandwich. I manage a latte, but I can't bear the thought of food. I still feel that woozy mix of nervous energy and last night's borderline excesses.

"Does it sound right?" I ask, as I finish my fifth run-through.

She shrugs. "I have no idea if what you are saying is correct, but you make it sound as if it is. I don't know the first thing about oestrogen and progesterone, apart from the fact that I hate it when I get PMT and one of those hormones is probably to blame."

I smile through my haze of anxiety.

"Something like that. Thanks for listening. I know I am probably boring you."

"Not at all! I'm always happy to help. Besides, by the end of your course I will probably learn a lot about pregnancy and birth too."

She gives me a final good luck hug as I drag

my feet up to the afternoon's classroom and prepare myself for the moment of doom.

We sit in our workgroups, and chat while we wait for Zita. My lines were fresh in my mind when I walked into the room, but as soon as we start to talk, I feel them fading away.

Simon is talking about something completely unrelated to the presentation, and part of me is grateful for the distraction. A larger part of me can't think about anything else.

"Good afternoon," says the lecturer "How did you all get on with your workgroups?"

There's a mass hum of responses before Zita indicates a girl in the front of the class.

"It was interesting looking things up. I think we found it useful to help us learn."

It was. I can't disagree. I like the research side of study, finding out new information, pulling it all together.

"Simon?" she asks.

He looks at the three of us before speaking. "I just want to get the presentation out of the way," he says.

There's a quiet burst of laughter throughout the class.

"Would you like to go first?"

He looks at us again. Do I want to get it over with, or put it off for as long as possible? I think I am going to be sick. My empty stomach tumbles like a washing machine. I nod.

"Sure," he says. "Let's get it out of the way."

The lecturer smiles. "I used to feel the same about presentations when I was a student," she says. "And now I'm doing this. It gets easier. I promise." She addresses the class. "I want you to take notes, and if you have any questions, wait until the end of the presentation, alright? Remember it will be you up here next, so lots of support and no talking during the presentations."

Collective heads bob up and down.

Simon gets up first and walks over to the computer stand. He taps on the keys and brings up the presentation. I didn't even think to email it or bring a memory stick so it's a good job someone was focussed enough to do the practical things. I try to get to my feet as Ashley and Soph go to join him. That swimming feeling in my gut threatens to turn to a drowning feeling. Sophie reaches out her hand to me.

"Let's do this," she says. Her voice is full of confidence and warmth.

"Okay," I say. My voice is quiet, uncertain, and timid. I clear my throat and repeat. "Okay."

"That's it." Sophie holds my hand, literally and metaphorically.

We walk to the lectern, and the four of us stand, ready to give our presentation. Looking out into the classroom, I see only supportive faces. I take a deep breath, let it out, repeat, and begin.

It's nowhere near as bad as I had expected. In fact, it all passes by so quickly that we are sitting down again before I know it, ready to watch the other groups.

Sophie pats my arm.

"That was great, well done."

"Thanks. I didn't stop to think. When I was up there with the three of you, it felt like I switched to autopilot."

Zita shoots us a look from the front of the room and puts her finger to her lips. The next group are taking their place at the lectern. On the outside I give the impression of focussing all my attention on the speakers, but inside all I can think about it the warm glow that is filling me, knowing that I did it. I gave my two-minutes-worth of presentation without messing up or falling flat.

Zoe is waiting outside the lecture block for me when I tumble out at the end of the afternoon.

"So how did it go?" she asks, looping her arm into mine.

"Apart from the part where I said *pic-turitary* instead of *pituitary*, it was fine."

"Well, it's an easy enough mistake to make," she says. "Not as bad as you thought then?"

"I don't think anything could have been as bad as I thought that presentation was going to be. Even if I had my dress tucked into my knickers, it wouldn't have come anywhere close to as bad as I imagined it. I'm an idiot, aren't I?"

"You're not an idiot. You have anxiety. Sometimes anxiety has you. Anxiety is the idiot. I'm glad you got the better of it today. Maybe this is the beginning of you kicking its arse?"

"I hope so!" One small victory is a tiny step towards winning the war. My anxiety has been a part of me for so long that I can't begin to hope that one success means that I will overcome it, but today feels good. I feel good. Perhaps I really can do this.

# Chapter Eight

Tangiers Court isn't exactly the most spacious of homes, even with the absence of Andrew. Still, when Luke asks whether it's okay for him to invite Florin, Rajesh, and Damon over, Zoe and I don't think twice before agreeing.

"We're going to have a poker night," he says. "You two are welcome to join in."

"I've never played before," I say. "I'm sure I would be terrible at it."

"It's not strip poker, is it?" Zoe grins. "I want to know what I am getting myself in for if I say yes."

"With those three? You think I want to see them strip?" He lets out a sharp laugh. "I don't think so. It's just a bit of fun. Damon has some cards and chips."

I pop my head out of the living room and look towards the kitchen.

"I guess the table is big enough," I say, despite having no idea how much space we would need to play poker. It's a card game. How difficult can it be?

"And will you be expecting us to provide the refreshments?" Zoe has a lot of questions, but I think we have both already made up our minds to join in.

"We are going to order pizza and have a few beers," Luke says. "So, is this okay with you two? We can go to Rajesh's if you    "

"No, it's fine," Zoe says, quickly. "Sounds like fun. Vi?"

"Sure. As long as there's no real money at stake, count me in!"

I have time to read up on the basics before Friday night, when Luke plans to host his game night. Maybe Zoe and I can even have a little bit of a practice. We haven't had houseguests since we moved in, and it seems like a good opportunity to show Luke's friends that I am not always falling on the floor drunk.

By Friday evening, Zoe and I have watched three YouTube videos and had a hilarious heads-up practice session. We are, as I predicted, terrible poker players.

Despite Zoe's show of not wanting to be responsible for the refreshments, she has been to the supermarket to gather a range of snacky foods and a bottle of gin for the two of us. Considering my resolve to show myself in a different light tonight, I should really not drink too much of that. Damon came back from uni with Luke and they are up in Luke's room, probably discussing tactics.

Zoe is emptying bags of crisps into little bowls, busying her way around the kitchen. I pop a cheese puff into my mouth.

"Do you need any help? Might just stick to the diet cola tonight, Zo."

"Keep a clear head for the game?" she says, batting my hand away from the dishes.

"Something like that." I back off and sit down at the table.

Luke has laid out a green felt cloth from Damon's poker set. It's like a tablecloth but marked with a line across the middle for placing the community cards. I've learned something this week, at least. We all get two cards, and then others get dealt onto the table. Whoever has the best hand wins – unless someone bluffs, that is. I am a horrendous liar, so I am hoping for good hands.

When she has finished prepping the snacks, Zoe pulls me upstairs so we can both get changed. It's game night at home but, as we don't get out much, it's more than enough of an excuse to make a little effort. She puts on some subtle make up and runs the straighteners through her usually wavy hair. I manage some mascara and a swish of lip-gloss and throw on a plain green tea dress.

Rajesh and Florin arrive together at just gone half past eight. Rajesh is playing the part with a Vegas t-shirt and one of those plastic visor-headbands. Florin has his sunglasses on top of his head. Luke and Damon have come down to join us in the kitchen and are both on their second cans of lager by the time the other guys arrive.

"Hey! Grab some snacks, come and take a seat," Luke says.

We gather around the table, Damon slides a stack of chips to each of us, and we are ready to begin.

It doesn't take long for everyone else to see that poker really isn't my game. Every time I see a pretty card (one of the ones with a picture instead of a number) I put chips into the pot. Apparently, this is not a good strategy. Rajesh and Damon both have some previous experience of playing, by the looks of their stacks. They keep scooping the pots towards them, whilst Zoe and I see our stacks shrinking with every hand we play.

By the time the pizza has arrived, I am

already out, but I don't mind too much that I get to sit on the side lines and watch. Zoe has a lucky double-up when she puts all of her chips in with a pair of eights ("my lucky number") and gets lucky against Florin's pair of Kings. I chew on a slice of ham and mushroom and try to follow the game.

From where I am sitting, I can see both Luke's cards and Zoe's. He peels up the corner of his carefully, trying not to reveal them to anyone else, but I am at the right angle to be able to see them anyway. Zoe lifts her hand up so haphazardly I'm sure that any of the guys would be able to see them if they wanted to. So far, they are being very sportsmanlike and avoiding looking at what she has.

Zoe is down to her last few chips. Luke is by far the chip leader. He has most of the chips that I started with, as well as a fair proportion of everyone else's. There's no prize for winning apart from bragging rights, but he is certainly giving it his all.

Zoe lifts her cards to show two Jacks. Two picture cards has to be a good hand, I know that much. She looks at the others, and says, "I raise".

"How much, Zo?" Luke asks. He has been

prompting her gently throughout the game, in a helpful rather than condescending way.

"Ten," she says. It looks like she has about sixty-pretend-dollars of chips left. If she doesn't win this one, she's probably going to be out.

"Okay," Luke says. "Ten dollars from the lady. Florin, it's on you."

Florin shakes his head and pushes his cards forward.

"Not for me," Rajesh says, folding his hand.

Luke hasn't looked at his cards yet, or at least I haven't seen them.

Damon is in the small blind position; he already has one-pretend-dollar in the pot. "Not with this rubbish," he says, and lets his hand go.

I lean slightly to see Luke's cards as he peels up the corners.

A red ace.

And another red ace.

I may not know much about poker, but I know this is not good news for Zoe.

Luke clears his throat in the worst example of not giving away any information about his hand that I can imagine.

"How many chips have you got left there, Zoe?" he asks.

She puts her hands up as a barrier around her

stack, shielding them from his view.

"You can't have them. I have a very good hand. I think you should fold. The other guys have done exactly the right thing. I'm not bluffing."

She is deadly serious, but it's obvious that she is trying hard not to let any emotion show through in her words.

Luke smiles. "I know you're not bluffing, but I am going to have to raise you," he says. "How much do you have?"

Zoe makes a show of looking behind her hands. "Not many. Not enough for you to worry about. I have sixty dollars total. Ten there in the pot and fifty here. I could buy something nice with these pretend dollars. A new pretend bag, or maybe a pretend dress."

We all laugh, but I know that Zoe is in trouble here. She's not going to be pretend buying anything.

"I'm going to make it thirty dollars." Luke counts out the chips and puts them onto the green felt.

"Thirty dollars? That's half of what I've got left."

"That's quite right," Luke says. "You're on the wrong course. You should definitely come over to accountancy with us."

Zoe raises her eyebrows. "I don't think so, mister. Are you trying to bully me? Would you bully a poor girl, just starting out her poker life?"

She thinks she is winning. I can see it in her face. She genuinely thinks that he is trying to get her to throw away her hand.

"Well, I really am not bluffing, so I am going to go all in," she says.

She moves her hands and counts her chips out one at a time into the middle of the table. "– forty, fifty, and sixty. Sixty dollars, all in."

She has dropped the 'pretend' now. This has suddenly become very real.

Her cheeks have started to fill with the red blush of excitement. She turns around to me and makes a little thumbs up gesture. I don't imagine this is a particularly good way to play poker, but she looks so happy right now.

Luke sees it too, that glow in her cheeks and the sparkle in her eyes. He slowly looks at his cards again, first one, and then the other, and finally looks back at Zoe, still facing me. I see a smile cross his face as he watches her. He runs one hand through his hair and taps the forefinger of his other on his cards.

"I have a big hand here, Zo," he says.

"Me too," she says. Her voice trembles slightly, but still I believe that it is the excitement of winning rather than the fear of being beaten. "You should fold. I'm winning this one. You don't want to get lucky and make me sad, do you?

Luke leans back in his chair. "Well, that wouldn't be fair at all, would it?" He looks at his cards one last time and says, "You've got me this time. Well played."

He slides his cards into the pile of discards and pushes his chips towards Zoe.

She lets out an excited squeaking noise and flips over her two cards. "Jacks!" she squeals. "Told you I had it."

Luke nods, smiles, and gathers the cards for the next hand.

When the game is over, the guys have gone home, and the three of us are cleaning up, I think about whether I should tell Zoe about what happened. Part of me wants to let her know that Luke did something sweet for her, but then again, she is so happy about having won a few hands that I don't want to burst her bubble. Maybe it means nothing. Maybe he was just being kind. I decide to bite my tongue, for now, and let her enjoy the evening for what it was.

# Chapter Nine

Monday, week seven, first term. The time has finally come. Before I settled down for an early night, I set four separate alarms to make sure I didn't oversleep, but I still wake up before any of them sound. No lying in bed, scrolling through my phone this morning. I jump up and head straight down to the shower.

All I can think about while I am washing my hair, running the scrunchie over my body and scrubbing my face is that today I will get to put on my uniform for real. Today it's not just about being in the skills lab with my course mates. Today I will finally meet patients. My mentor, Stacey, is picking me up and taking me out on her day of visits. Today, tomorrow, the rest of the week, five days a week until Christmas break. No more classes, just this: practicing to be a midwife.

I hear the beeping of a car horn outside and look in the mirror one last time before I head out of the house. My first day on placement. My first day meeting pregnant women, postnatal women, and whatever else comes our way.

Zoe is in the kitchen, and she runs into the hallway to meet me before I leave.

"I'm so excited for you," she says. "I wish I could start my placements too."

"Not long, Zo," I smile.

We share a hug and then she makes a show of wiping her hand over my uniform, straightening me out.

The car horn beeps again.

"I'd better go! See you tonight."

"Have an awesome day," she says. She stands in the hallway as I leave.

I dash to the door, and out onto the pavement. Stacey is sitting in a smart looking blue car, writing in a thick book that's propped precariously on her steering wheel.

I tap gently on the window. She leans across the passenger seat, pushes the door open, and calls out to me.

"Violet? Hi. Get in."

I drop my bag into the footwell and slide down into the seat.

"Hi," I reply, and smile through my nerves. "Sorry I was just coming downstairs."

"No worries," she says. "We have plenty of time."

Stacey is dressed in the standard community midwife uniform of navy polo shirt and matching trousers. I was expecting a middle-aged woman, but the driver can't be any older than thirty. She's got long blonde hair, pulled back into a tidy ponytail, and she lifts her glasses up onto her head as she puts her diary away.

"Alright? Nervous?"

I nod and grin. "Looking forward to it though."

"We have a visit to go to, then we can stop off in the office, look at your paperwork and have a chat before we really get going." She smiles and puts me completely at ease.

I buckle my seatbelt over my grey shirt, and we set off towards the beginning of my first placement.

When we pull up at the side of the road, I feel the butterflies in my stomach begin the flutter. Part nervousness, part excitement, I fiddle with my hair, look into the mirror on the drop-down visor and try to focus.

"Hey," Stacey says. "This is a routine postnatal check. Nothing to worry about, I'll introduce you, and all you have to do is watch. Okay?"

I was hoping that my anxiety didn't show, but either I am completely transparent, or Stacey is really good at reading people.

"Thanks," I say quietly.

She pats me on the arm, reaches to pull her bag from the back seat and gets out of the car.

As I step onto the pavement, I hear her open and close the boot, and she hands me a large black bag to carry.

"Throw this over your shoulder," she says.

"Sure," I smile, happy to have a purpose.

I follow Stacey up the path to the front door of the house. The garden is small and tidy, and there are a pair of trendy potted olive trees, one to either side of the entrance. I have already started to form an impression of the family who must live inside, and I wonder how many times I will do this. Is it wrong to make a judgment before I even meet the woman, or should I be picking up information in a Sherlock-like way?

Stacey knocks, and a voice from within shouts, "Come in, it's open."

She pushes the door and we both walk into the house.

The hall leads straight into a smart living room with polished wooden floorboards and two chunky, deliciously comfortable looking beige sofas. There's a large mirror over a fireplace that houses a wood-burner. On one of the sofas, breastfeeding, is Sally Jeffries, the woman we have come to visit, the first mum I have met as a student midwife.

Stacey heads straight over to Sally and peers in at the feeding infant.

"You've got it cracked now," she says. "No more trouble?"

"It still hurts a little on the other side," Sally says, completely indifferent to the fact that a woman is staring at her exposed breast. "But I think that's because he wasn't latching properly there at first. Much better now though, thanks."

"Good, good," Stacey says. She heads to the other sofa and sits down. Aware that I am still standing in the doorway, she beckons over to me. "This is Violet. It's her first day today."

"Hi, Violet. Do sit down. How's it going?"

Sally looks so comfortable feeding and chatting, it's hard to believe this is her first baby. She seems confident and in control.

"Good thanks. This is our first visit, so…I haven't had time to do anything wrong yet."

"Oh, bless you," Sally says. "I'm sure you won't do anything wrong. Stace will look after you. She's great."

"I pay her to say that," Stacey says.

She picks up Sally's notes from the table, and

starts to write in them. I sit next to her and lean across, looking at what she is writing. Effortlessly, Stacey carries on chatting to Sally, making notes as she goes along. It doesn't even sound like she is running through the check boxes that are listed in the notes, but she is gathering all of the information that she needs to assess the baby's sleeping, feeding, bowel moments and micturition (or urination for the non-medical), checking on his general wellbeing.

"Are you getting enough rest?" she asks.

"I'm fine, yes. I have tried to sleep when Caleb sleeps, like you said. Takes a bit of getting used to, but I'm doing a lot better now." Without further prompting from Stacey, she says, "I've had a poo now too."

"Oh, great," Stacey says, and makes a mark in the notes. I suppose that this kind of conversation is my new normal. "How was it?"

I make an involuntary noise at this, and I have to apologise. "I'm so sorry."

"Not used to the toilet talk yet," Stacey laughs, and Sally joins her.

"You soon will be," Sally smiles. Caleb has finished his feed, apparently, as Sally tucks her breast away and brings the baby over to us.

"Do you need to have a look at him?"

"I was going to weigh him today," Stacey says.

"Sure, I'll undress him. I was going to change him anyway."

Stacey nods to me to get the scales out of the big bag that I carried in. I pull them out of the case and skilfully drop them onto my foot. They aren't heavy, but I feel the heat bloom in my cheeks as I blush.

"You okay there?"

"Fine," I splutter, trying to sound fine.

"Better not let you get your hands on Caleb just yet," Stacey says. I am mortified, but Sally laughs again, and I relax a little.

"Sorry!" I step back and let Stacey continue. She lays a soft blanket onto the scales and sets them to zero before laying the naked baby onto them. I would probably have put him straight onto the cold plastic and made him scream. There seems to be so much that I have to learn.

"Great, he's started to put on weight already," Stacey says. "A lot of babies, especially breastfed babies, can lose weight in the first few days. He is already up on his birthweight."

"That's brilliant," I add, trying to think of something helpful to say. I don't want Sally to

think of me as just the ditsy student who can't
do anything right.

Sally smiles proudly and starts to dress Caleb
again. Nappy, Babygro, blanket, and then into
the Moses basket at the end of the sofa. He
doesn't make any kind of fuss, and I reflect that
he is probably setting an unfairly high standard
for all the future babies I will meet.

"Do you mind if I check your tum?" Stacey
asks.

Sally lies on the sofa, and folds down the top
of her trousers in a way that makes it clear she
has done this many times before.

Stacey nods for me to join her and I stand by
her side.

"I'm feeling for the top of the uterus, to make
sure it is going back down as it should be
doing."

I nod and smile at Sally. She doesn't seem to
mind me looking at her, and she smiles back.

"Do you mind if Violet feels?" Stacey asks.

"Of course, no problem. I think I am fairly
safe here," she laughs,

 I smile and nervously edge to her side.

"So, start just below the umbilicus there, with
your hand like I had mine. You'll need to press
in a little, gently, but firmly. Okay, now, move

down slightly towards the top of the pubis."

I follow her instructions carefully, fearful that I am going to use too much force, and hurt Sally in some way. At first, I feel only the gentle flab of the postnatal abdomen, completely normal, and then I reach the top of the uterus. I smile as I palpate it. I have practiced this on mannequins in the skills lab, and now here I am, on my placement, doing this for real.

"Here," I say to Stacey. "I can feel it."

Sally smiles at the excitement in my voice. "Bless you," she says. "You're going to make a great midwife; I can already tell."

My smile broadens, and Stacey rests her hand onto my shoulder.

"Good job, Violet. I think Sally might be right there."

By the time Stacey drops me off at home we have made two more postnatal visits, eaten a remarkably good meat and potato pie each from a little bakery she knows behind the clinic, gone through my paperwork, and carried out two antenatal booking appointments with women in early pregnancy. It's been a whirlwind of a day, and I'm happy to get into the living room and flop onto the sofa. It's gone four o'clock, but it seems I am the only one in the house. I make tea, turn on the television, and promptly fall asleep.

When I wake up an hour later, I see that I have been covered up in a thick brown fleece blanket, and my cold tea has been taken away. My mouth is dry, and my neck is sore from lying in an awkward position, but at least I am warm and cosy.

"Zoe?" I shout. There's no answer, so I rub my eyes, stretch, and get to my feet.

There's no sign of her downstairs, and she's not in her room or the bathroom on our floor either.

"Zoe?" I call again. Nothing.

"She's popped to the shop," a voice calls down from the top floor.

"Oh. Okay. Thanks." I look at the blanket that I have carried up. "Uh, thanks for this."

"No worries." I hear his feet hit the floor above and he comes down the stairs to meet me. "You feel okay? How was your first day in placement?"

I am about to answer when I hear the front door open.

"I guess she's home," Luke says

"It was great," I smile. "I'm knackered

though."

He gestures towards the staircase and we head down to meet Zo.

She greets me with a massive hug.

"So?"

"It was fine," I say, trying to keep my face straight.

"Yeah, nothing special, I guess," she says. "Same as any other old day."

"Totally. I don't know what all the fuss was about."

"Uniform looks pretty sweet though."

"I met an adorable baby, and some great women too. My community mentor is just amazing. Oh, she's so cool…" I can't keep up the play façade any longer, I have to gush about the day I have had.

Zoe sits attentively, listening to every word, nodding in all the right places, and listening to everything I have to say. Luke has given up and headed into the kitchen. He's turning out to be an absolute sweetheart, but that doesn't mean he has to listen to the ins and outs of my day spent cooing over babies. Zoe, on the other hand, is stuck with me.

We have fallen into a routine at Tangiers Court.

I'm still on day shift hours until next term, and the others are around most evenings. Zoe has managed to go to a few of the yoga classes that she signed up for, and Luke hangs out with his three friends sometimes, but apart from that we have fallen together as a group.

We take turns in making dinner – unless it's Andrew's turn, and then we have takeout. We have a rota for cleaning, and we work well as a team. Zoe and I have always been a dynamic duo; it's always been just the two of us. I never thought that anyone else would fit into our mini-team, but somehow Luke manages to fill a gap that we didn't even know was present.

# Chapter Ten

My community placement flies by. Before I know it, it's mid-December. I'd like to be looking forward to the end of term. I love Christmas, what with all the sparkling lights and mulled wine. I also adore being able to shop for other people; it's the most amazing kind of guilt-free shopping. That's especially true when I'm shopping for Zo, because I am pretty much buying things that I like too.

I can't relax and get excited about it yet though. I will have a three week break after the end of my community placement, before the beginning of the next trimester, but first I have to hand in two assignments. I've been so caught up in placements that have hardly thought about my coursework.

I haven't been onto campus while I've been on placement, it seems strange to think that I was there for all of those weeks at the start of term. Not being on campus also means that I have been nowhere near the library. I've got a copy of *'Myles Textbook for Midwives'* and *'Fundamentals of Midwifery'* but that's as far as my textbook collection runs. There's a huge selection of texts on the university's online catalogue, apparently, but I haven't gotten near to starting yet. I'm going to have to put some work in if I want to get these papers finished and handed in on time.

I'm sitting at my desk, laptop open, mug of tea and two chocolate digestives to my side. I'm ready to get stuck into it.

That's when Zoe comes to my door.

"Hey," she says, in a voice that is not quite her usual tone.

"Come in," I say, nodding towards the bed, for her to sit down. "You alright?"

She nods and sits. "Sorry, were you...?"

"I haven't started yet. I was about to actually read my essay questions."

"Tell me about it. I have some waffle about pedagogy to write by the twentieth."

"Peda- what?" My brain runs a quick calculation. "Something about children?"

"Kind of." She seems restless. I get the feeling that she isn't here to talk about her essays.

"We can work together on them later if you like?"

"Study buddies!" She smiles, but there's something going on beneath. I wait a beat, to see if she wants to start talking or if I need to ask. She opens her mouth, and then stops. On the second attempt, she speaks. "I need some advice."

I get up and turn my chair around properly, so that I am looking at her face on.

"It's Luke," she says.

"What about him?"

"Do you think it would be a terrible thing to, you know, try to start something with him? I mean we all live together, and I don't want things to be awkward for you, if we are, I mean if...well, you know what I mean."

"Oh," I say, without thinking. "Luke?" I pause to consider this, all the time watching Zoe, taking in her expression. She looks nervous, like a girl asking her father if she can date the boy next door. "You don't have to ask me, you know. If you like him, then of course you should go for it. We will be fine. I mean all of us, here; it will be fine."

"Vi, I know I don't need your permission. I...I suppose I was just...oh, I don't know."

"But you do know that you and I are always going to be there for each other, no matter what. We've dated people before; it never came between our friendship."

"I was worried more because, you know, now

we live together, I don't want it to be all up in your face and..."

"Is this because I am not showing an interest in dating anybody? Do you feel bad that you have someone you like and I'm on my own?"

She breaks eye contact. "I guess, a little bit," she says.

"You don't have to worry about me. I told you from the start, I'm not here to meet someone. I want to pass my assignments." I gesture at my laptop. "I want to be a midwife. Anything else is a bonus. Or an interruption, depending on how it goes."

She doesn't say anything.

"Look, if it makes you feel any better, I will start dating Andrew. He's just my type anyway."

This raises a small laugh from Zoe. "He is very quiet."

"Strong silent type. Perfect. Won't make too many demands on my time..."

"I can't see him taking you anywhere exciting for a date though."

"Well, we enjoy our own space."

We both laugh, and it feels good. Seeing Zoe glow with excitement like this makes me feel a warm thrill inside too.

"I like how you just assumed he will be interested in me," she says.

"Who wouldn't be? You're the best. Beautiful, clever, funny…actually I'm surprised Andrew hasn't snapped you up already," I say. Again, I think about mentioning poker night, and how Luke let her win, but again I decide against it. I can be supportive without taking that victory away from her.

"Andrew never does his share of the housework," she smiles. "Thanks Vi. Same back at you. How about I make us both a brew and we can start on these assignments?"

"Sounds like a plan. And Zoe…of course he likes you. I've seen the two of you. You have fun together. It will be amazing, I'm sure."

She gets up and flings her arms around me, giving me a firm, swift hug. "Thanks Vi. Good luck with Andrew." She winks and runs downstairs.

The rest of the evening is split between poring over the finer points of our essay writing, trying to work out how the Harvard referencing system works and how Zoe should approach Luke. That's seemingly easier than deciding whether we can use what someone said on Twitter as a valid argument in our essays, if we add the link to the tweet in the reference list.

We have a week left of term, which means a week left of my placement, a week to hand in this assignment and a week before Luke goes home for Christmas break.

"The way I see it, you can do this one of two ways," I say, my mind still half-thinking in academic arguments. "Some would argue that the most effective method would be to directly approach Luke and express your desire to..." I look at Zoe. "I was going to say date him. I assume you do want to date him, not just the, er..."

She digs me gently in the ribs, raises her finger to her lips in a 'shush' symbol and giggles.

"Okay, express your desire to bang him and date him. Others may use the seasonal festivities as an opportunity to fabricate a conducive environment where alcohol, music and the Christmas spirit could influence the outcome of events..."

"What does the great scientist Violet Cobham think?" Zoe says, her voice as serious as she can make it through her laughter.

"Much as I think that getting drunk and festive is a great idea, I also believe that asking

102

him when he is sober would be a better plan if you want more than just the banging. Imagine you have a drunken romp and then neither of you know where you stand; then it does all get kind of awkward around here."

"I think you're right." She taps a few final words onto her laptop and sits back. "You know, I've never been interested in one-night things. I don't want him to think that's all I want now."

"Talk to him. You have all week."

"All week. Sure." She smiles and mimes biting her nails in a faux-terrified movement.

"We managed to get our essays written. I feel like we can achieve anything," I say.

"I'll reserve judgement until I get my grades back," she replies, "and until I find the guts to ask him."

With the last of my coursework out of the way, I settle into enjoying the final week of my community placement. Between that first day, stepping out of the house in my uniform, and now has already felt like an incredible journey. It's only been four weeks, and I have a long way left to go.

I have started to fill in some of my PAD, and

today Deb, my personal tutor from university, is coming out to meet Stacey and me after clinic to see how I have been getting on. We have our regular visits in the morning, three postnatals and an antenatal blood pressure check, and then it's back to the office for lunch.

Stacey is trying to chat to me about my plans for Christmas, but all I can think about is the impending meeting with Deb.

"We always go to his mother's of course, what with her being…" She pauses midsentence, mug in one hand, sandwich in the other. "Are you alright, Violet?"

I haven't touched my lunch. Stacey knows me well enough by now for this to concern her. I'm usually the first to put the kettle on, make tea, get my food out and tuck in.

"Mmm," I say. "It's nothing. I'm fine."

"When people say that something is nothing, it is still a something. What's up?"

My stomach is turning over, and I'm afraid that if I eat my packed lunch, I will be bringing up the cheese salad. I don't feel hungry at all. Quite the opposite.

"Just a little nervous about the meeting," I say. "I'm being silly, I know."

"Nothing to worry about," Stacey smiles.

"You have been great on this placement. Deb coming to see me is a formality. It's what they do. They like to check that you are okay, and that *we* are okay supporting you. Alright? Nothing to be scared of."

I nod slowly and try to believe. Logically, of course I know that it is the truth, but my niggling, doubting brain still wants to have me believe that my tutor is coming to tell me that I am not good enough.

I nibble at my sandwich and raise it to show Stacey. She smiles again.

"Honestly, it's all fine. You do worry."

I do. I always do.


Deb Cross arrives bang on time at 12:45 and we leave the break room for the privacy of the consultation room. I feel like I am being interviewed all over again. The room feels smaller than it usually does when we are working in here, and it's making me claustrophobic. There's only one small window, and it doesn't let in enough light or air. Why have I never noticed this before? How could I have expected women to sit in this room and discuss their pregnancies with me when I can't bear to be in here myself? The thought makes the nausea throb harder within me.

"Such a lovely clinic," my link tutor says. "How have you been getting on? Do you like community?"

Stacey looks at me supportively. My hands are starting to feel clammy, so I slide them beneath my thighs and semi-sit on them.

"Yes," I say. My voice comes out like a shaky squeak. I clear my throat. "I've been really enjoying it."

I can almost hear Stacey's thoughts, willing me to have the confidence to keep talking. I can feel the warmth radiate from her.

"It feels like I have been out here for months, not weeks." I stop, and then I add quickly, "But I know I have so much to learn." I don't want to say the wrong thing. I don't want Deb to think I am cocky or overconfident. That is probably even worse than a lack of confidence.

"That's good." Deb writes some notes in her file. "What kind of things have you been doing?"

"Do you need to see my PAD?" I hand it over. "I've started to get some of my competencies signed off. It's been a mixture really. Antenatal, postnatal, and baby checks."

The tutor skim reads the contents of my

document. "Great. You've seen a lot already, that's super." She turns to Stacey. "Sounds like it has been a good learning experience?"

"Violet is so good with the women and their families. She's a natural."

I feel my cheeks flush red, and I look away. I don't know if I find it difficult to hear positive things about myself because I don't believe them, or if it is just a natural response to feel this way.

"I'll miss having her with me."

I'll miss being with Stacey too.

"Will I come back here on my next community placement?" I ask.

"We do try to keep students out in the same areas, yes. As long as Stacey is able to take you, you'll come back here. It probably won't be until either the end of this academic year or into next year though." She runs a finger down the page in her planner. "You'll have postnatal or antenatal next, and then the delivery unit."

"Postnatal next," I say. "I got the email through."

She nods and makes a note. "You know before I do," she smiles. "So, yes. Chances are you'll be back."

"I'll look forward to it," Stacey says, and I

know how much I will too.

Every placement is going to be full of new experiences and learning opportunities, but this has been special. I love being out on the road, visiting women in their own homes, helping out in the clinics. I could see myself choosing to work in community after I qualify. That's a long time away.

When I get back to Tangiers Court, Zoe is already home, sitting at the kitchen table, chatting to Luke.

"How was it?" she asks.

I pull the biscuit jar out of the cupboard and take a bite out of a Jammie Dodger.

"Yurmh," I say. I swallow and repeat myself. "Yeah. It was fine. Unsurprisingly I was stressing about nothing."

"The great triumvirate?" Luke says. "It sounds like an ancient Roman firing squad."

"I'm not sure the ancient Romans had guns, Luke," Zoe laughs, leaning in towards him.

"You can have a firing squad with, uh…" He pauses, racking his brain. "Tridents? What the heck did Romans use?"

"Who knows?" I say. "Whatever. It was fine anyway. And it's *tripartite*," I say. That's what the university calls it when the three of us meet to discuss my placement. Link tutor, placement mentor and student: three parts.

I eat the rest of the biscuit in two bites and hover at the edge of the table, looking at them. "So…"

Zoe shakes her head in a subtle move that Luke doesn't catch.

"Right," I say. "Okay."

He gives me a look, and I try to think of a new subject. "What's for dinner?"

"Andrew's turn," Zoe smiles.

"I wonder if he will show up after the holidays?" Luke says. "It would be nice to have another man around the house."

"Hey! What's wrong with us?" Zoe says in mock indignation.

"I'm surprised you even have to ask." He says it with a deadpan tone that can only be interpreted as a joke.

Zoe feigns offence, turning her back and raising her nose into the air. I hope she gets on with asking him soon. The tension is enough to make me want to push them together. It also makes me feel something that I haven't felt for some time. Ever since my last relationship I have been quite happy to be on my own and single. I mean, I'm only eighteen still. It's not like I have been on my own for years, falling into a pit of spinsterhood. Seeing Zoe, the way she is around Luke, and now that I think about it, the way he is around her, it makes me…well, it makes me think that maybe I would like someone like that in my life too. I can barely keep up with coursework, placements, and day to day existence, but I could possibly find space in my life for the right person. Who knows?

Zoe is scrolling through takeaway options on her phone. "Pizza? Indian? What do you guys fancy?"

"We only have a few days left here. Do you fancy going out to eat tonight?"

This could be an opportunity for Zoe. I open my mouth into an exaggerated yawn and stretch my arms above my head. I never was all that good at drama, but I am doing my best. "You two go, I think I'm going to shove something in the microwave and have an early night."

"Not much point just the two of us going out," he says, and looks over Zoe's shoulder at the food options. "Let's order pizza?"

"I quite fancy it now Violet's mentioned it," Zoe says. I know she is probably trying to sound cool and act naturally, but I can hear the flirtation in her voice. I almost smile and nudge her, but I hold it back.

"You should go. Really. Don't worry about me. You know what I'm like. It's been a tough few weeks. I fancy a bath and some chicken ding."

*Chicken ding* is what we have come to call any ready meal that consists at least in part of chicken and is reheated in the microwave. Ding! It's ready.

There's a slight pause, and then Zoe and Luke both start to speak at once. She begins with *"it doesn't matter if.."* and he is about to say *"we can go…"* but both of them get tangled up at once and there's an awkward exchange while they try to decide who should say their words first. I'm not sure if the tension between them is so obvious to me because Zoe has told me how she feels, or if it is just blatantly evident. Luke must be able to tell what she is feeling, surely?

I rub my temples melodramatically. "I'm starting to get a headache," I say. "You two go ahead. I'm going to run the bath and chill."

"Let me get you some paracetamol," Luke says. He leaps over to the cupboard, and Zoe flashes me a sharp, nervous glance.

"This is it!" I mouth, making sure I don't say

anything loudly enough for Luke to hear.

She makes a silent movement, gripping her fists together, and miming a squeal of excitement and I let out a tiny laugh.

"You okay?" Luke hands me two small round tablets and a half glass of water.

"Thanks, er yeah. I'll…" I stop myself from talking before I end up saying something stupid. I make my way upstairs, alone. I don't really have a headache at all, so I drop the painkillers onto my table and knock back the water. It's going to be a long night.

I sit alone in my room, flick through social media for a while and then pick up the book I have been slowly reading. I was doing the right thing for Zoe by faking the headache and coming up here, but I should probably have thought about bringing some food with me. I read about three pages before I hear someone coming up the stairs.

"We're getting pizza after all," she says. Her eyes tell me everything I need to know about how she is feeling.

"Oh, I'm sorry, Zo. I thought that if I got out of the way you might have some time alone together, maybe go out…"

"I know and thank you. Thanks for doing

that, but once you came up here, I don't know, it was like he didn't want to talk anymore."

"Ugh. Really, I'm sorry. I don't know what to say."

"You might as well come down. We'll get some food, and," she shrugs, "enjoy our last few days of term, I suppose."

"And what are you going to do about Luke?"

"Hope the right time presents itself. Flirt a little. Be my usual wonderful self until he falls desperately in love with me."

We both laugh. Why wouldn't he fall for her? Zoe is the best.

Before I know it, it's Friday. The end of the first trimester has come around more quickly than I could have imagined. Last day of term, last day of placement; for me, and for Zoe too.

At breakfast she prods at her toast and sips at the coffee that she usually guzzles down. There are only twenty minutes left before Stacey will arrive to take me to our last visits of the term, but I hate leaving Zoe like this.

"Want to talk about it?" I ask.

She shrugs and breaks a piece off her toast. Instead of eating it, she tears another piece, and then another. All her concentration is centred on creating a pile of cubed, crumby bread on her plate. More accurately, all her concentration is elsewhere, and desiccating her breakfast is what she is absent-mindedly doing instead of focusing on eating.

"Shall I make you something else?"

She shakes her head, without looking at me.

"Okay. Well." It's one of those moments when I know that she has so much that she wants to say, but she doesn't know where to start. I've seen this before. I know her mind must be filled with so many issues.

"Holidays? Uni? Luke? All of the above?"

This time, she nods, picks up one of the decimated pieces of her breakfast and sticks it into her mouth.

"Oh Zo. I'm sad that term is ending too. We have so much more to do after the holidays though. Do you not want to get home, have Christmas, see your folks?"

"Of course," she mutters, almost too quietly for me to hear.

"There's still tonight if you want to, you know, talk to Luke."

This provokes a heaving sigh.

"It's too late now. I don't want to start something up on the last day. I don't think I

114

could bear to get close to him now and have to leave for three weeks. Better to wait and…" She trails off. "I don't know. Not now though. I left it too late."

"He'll be back in January, just like us." I stop sharply, as Luke's footsteps thunk down the stairs. Zoe rolls her eyes and starts to chain-eat the rest of her toast.

Luke looks over her shoulder as he passes towards the cupboard. "Morning," he says in a voice that sounds much more awake than he appears.

"Hey," I say. Zoe waves her hand in a greeting gesture, her mouth full.

"Last day, eh? I finish at lunchtime. Probably going to set off for home this afternoon," Luke says.

Crumbs fly out onto the table as Zoe coughs out her toast.

"This afternoon?"

"Yeah, some of the gang back home want to go out tonight to celebrate. Pre-Christmas thing, you know. Don't want to miss that. Hey, are you alright?"

Zoe is still coughing, so I pass her my water, and nod at her to drink.

"Should I slap you on the back?" Her face is

deep red, but she raises a hand to me, and inhales deeply.

"I'm fine," she says, still breathless. "Fine."

"I have to go in a few minutes, Luke. We didn't even get to say goodbye properly," I say.

"I would have thought you two would be sick of the sight of my ugly mug by now, ladies." He puts his bowl of cereal on the table and sits between us, thrusting his spoon into what appears to be a mixture of chocolate crispies and corn flakes. "Couldn't decide which to have," he says, by way of explanation.

There's the beeping of a car horn form outside. All I can do is give Zoe a helpless look.

"Well, that's me. Uh, have a great Christmas then, Luke and we'll see you next year."

"If I come back," he says, with a wicked smile.

From the look on Zoe's face, I think she is close to coughing her toast up again, but she manages to hold it together. "I'd better leave too," she says. It's earlier than she needs to set off, but I guess she doesn't want to be here with Luke this morning. Not like this.

When I stand up, Luke reaches out to give me a hug. "Happy Christmas, Vi."

I pat him gently on the back. "Thanks, mate."

Zoe scuttles to her feet too and reaches out to him expectantly, and possibly a little too eagerly. He grabs hold of her and lifts her slightly off the floor as he squeezes her tightly. She's about a foot shorter than he is, so it's quite easy for him to swing her up.

I can't see her face, because it's buried into his chest, but I know that her expression will be somewhere between agony and ecstasy. I wait for him to release her, and when she turns away to walk to the door with me, she looks close to tears. I link arms with her and pull her close to me.

"Plenty of time," I say quietly, "Plenty of time."

And that is how we end the term. We finish our final day in placements, and when we return to the house afterwards, Luke has gone.

# Chapter Eleven

If the weeks at university passed more quickly than I expected, the Christmas holidays feel like months rather than weeks. Despite being my favourite time of the year, before we even get to Christmas Day, I am itching to get back to Tangiers Court, to lectures, and to my next placement. My agitation is nothing compared to Zoe's though. All that stuff about absence making the heart grow fonder is working for her. I can't help but wonder if it is having the same effect on Luke too. Apart from a few texts on Christmas Day though, neither of us hear from him.

On the first weekend of the new year, we bundle our bags into Zoe's Corsa and make our way back to uni.

Classes start again on Monday, and I am more than ready to get stuck in. This term we have three weeks of lectures and then I am rostered for my first rotation onto the postnatal ward. I had hoped that I would get the delivery suite as my next placement, but I won't have my slot there until April. Those four months seem a long way into the future. I have to assist in the delivery of forty babies while I am a student. I'll probably have finished my first year before I even get to see a baby being born.

I'm prepared for the start of term, everything laid out ready for the morning. Zoe and I have decided to have a chill night and binge watch Netflix rather than going onto campus for the Returners' Party in the SU bar.

It's Sunday evening, gone seven o'clock, and there is still no sign of Luke. It feels strangely quiet with just the two of us. Although we have been best friends since we met as toddling three-year olds, and even silence between us has never felt completely empty, it feels like there is something missing. I hadn't realised quite how much a part of our lives Luke has become until now. I'm sure Zoe must be feeling that even more acutely than I.

"He is coming back, isn't he?" Her face bears a deadly serious expression.

"Of course," I say. "He was laughing when he told us he wasn't coming back." He must have been joking, surely. "And he would have said something when he texted, wouldn't he?"

She nods and reaches out for the cushion on the sofa next to her, pulling it in front of her and cradling it in her arms like a hug.

"You could message him?" I suggest.

She buries her face into the cushion.

"Or I could?" I say the words even though I don't really want to be the one to message him. I will do it for Zoe if it is going to make her feel better. He is coming back though; he must be.

"No!" She almost shrieks the word. "Don't. He'll be back."

I smile. "And when he is? What are your plans?"

"My plan is that he will tell me how much he has missed me while he was away and declare his undying love for me." She waves her arms out in a melodramatic gesture and I can't help laughing.

"That sounds like an excellent plan."

Despite three weeks of lie-ins and lazy days over the holidays, I am up as soon as my first alarm sounds on Monday morning, and I'm out of the door with Zoe bang on time.

At nine o'clock, the hubbub in the lecture room is drawn to a sharp cessation by the arrival of our module leader. New term, new lecturer.

"Nice to see you all back and ready to learn," she says.

The lecturer is a tall, stern-looking brunette.

Her hair is short-bobbed, and its sharpness emphasises her dark eyes and prominent cheekbones. She must be close on six feet tall, even in the ballet pumps she's wearing with her no-nonsense pencil skirt and blouse. It is almost as though she is the polar opposite of Zita. I gently nudge Sophie and raise my eyebrows.

"Seems strict," I mouth, and she nods subtly in collusion.

"Now you are all settled into the course, we are going to start on this year's real work. Last term you all had FUN?" She says it as though it is an accusation, and throughout the class students turn to each other creating a susurration of whispers. The lecturer picks up the dry wipe marker. "This term we are going to be having…"

I expect her to utter something terrifying, but instead she says, "FUN too!"

She writes *FUN2* in bold, curvy letters on the centre of the board.

"I know. They could have thought of a more creative name for it." She smiles, and it is as though we all let out a collective breath that we were holding.

"Welcome to Fundamentals of Midwifery Two!"

She pulls out the sign-in sheet and passes it to one of the girls at the front of the class to circulate.

"I'm Rachel Rogers, and I will be your tutor throughout this module."

I settle into my chair, pick up my pen, and focus. I get the feeling that this is going to be a great class.

"Before we make a start, have you all had a chance to read through the module guide?"

Most of my classmates mumble variations of 'yes', and I nod along.

"Good. Then you will know that this term you will have your first OSCE." She pronounces it 'oss-kee', but my mind flits to the name, 'Oscar', and I can't help but think about a glitzy award ceremony.

From the sighed groans throughout the room, it's evident that the OSCE this term is not going to be glamourous in the slightest.

"OSCE," she repeats. "The Objective Structured Clinical Examination. Basically, it's a role play, but a role play that you are going to be assessed on. This is, as the name suggests, an exam. You need to pass this exam to continue with your course."

Suddenly this feels less like FUN and more

along the lines of the terror that I had first imagined. I had heard of the OSCE before we got to class, but my trepidation about the examination hadn't struck me until she said its name out loud. It's almost as though it didn't feel real when it was only letters that I had read on a screen. Rachel has conjured up the OSCE monster, and now it is looming in the not-too-distant future.

Rachel is still talking. "An actress plays the role of the patient, and the student, which will be you, will work through a scenario, making clinical decisions and behaving exactly as they would in a real-life situation."

The room has fallen into a stunned silence. Rachel clicks her heels over to the computer. "The first year OSCE is meant to be the easiest," she says.

My hands are clammy even at the thought of the assessment. It sounds like my idea of hell. I thought that presentations were my worst nightmare, but this is a new low. I've never had to do anything like this before but being critically observed while I am trying to act naturally, professionally, and safely fills me with a stomach clenching dread. I have three months to get it together.

"You will prepare for six scenarios. We are going to work through them in class, and they will be experiences that you are likely to encounter in your practice placements. There is nothing to be afraid of. This is basic midwifery care." She sounds so matter of fact.

I look at the letters that I have written onto my notepad, 'FUN2', and I scribble them out, obliterating them in a cyclone of black ink.

When I get back to Tangiers Court, I find Zoe, sitting on her bed, with her knees hugged up to her chest. She's got her headphones on, and hasn't heard me coming up the stairs, so she jumps a little as I peek around the door into her room.

"What's up?"

"Just chilling," she says, but the words are flat and empty.

"Have you eaten? Do you want a drink or anything?"

She shrugs and puts her headphones down on the bedside table. Our rooms are essentially the same, just laid out differently. The head of her bed faces towards the window, so she can sit exactly as she is now, and look out into the garden. I wonder how long she has been here, huddled up, doing just that.

"I'm fine," she says. "Really, I'm okay."

I perch on the edge of her bed.

"He's not back?"

She shakes her head.

"His stuff is still here," she says, nodding her head towards the door and the stairs up to the top floor. "So, he must be coming back."

"Unless he doesn't care about his stuff. Or unless something has -" I stop myself from completing the sentence. I don't want to think anything bad has happened, and I definitely don't want Zoe to think it.

Zoe finishes my thought anyway. "Happened to him?" She pulls herself into a more upright sitting position, flattening her legs out on the bed. "Do you think…? Has something…?" She frowns. "No. No."

"Hey, I'm sure that he is fine." I put my hand onto her ankle, making contact, trying to calm her. "He probably had something to deal with at home. He loves his course almost as much as we love ours. He's never given any indication that he doesn't want to be here."

"Leeds is a long way away. If something has happened maybe he can't get back here to get his stuff. Or perhaps it's down to someone else to come and collect it and they have other priorities." She takes a big gulp of air. I can hear that her breathing has become faster, and she is trying to get a hold of herself. "He never messaged over the holidays -"

"He sent us both a text on Christmas Day," I remind her. She waves the comment away.

"Apart from that. I mean, he didn't exactly keep in touch. I thought he would be back over the weekend, but the first day of term is over and he's still not here. He can't love his course that much."

I don't know what to tell her. A part of me is equally as confused as she is. Then again, how well do we know him? We have shared a house for three months, sure, but how long does it take to really get to know somebody?

"I'll message him," I say. It's the obvious thing to do. I'll check if he is alright. Zoe perks up at the suggestion.

"I was going to," she says, "but I don't want to come across as...well, you know."

I nod and smile. "I know. And it's fine for me to message because I don't want to..."

She tilts her head, raises her eyebrows and I don't have to finish my sentence. We both know what she wants to do with him.

My phone is in the bottom of my bag. I take it out and tap in a simple message:

**Thought you'd be back by now. You okay?**

I turn the screen to Zoe, and ask for her approval.

"Do you think that sounds like we are checking up on him? Should we change it to something less, I don't know, accusative?" she says.

"You think it sounds accusative?"

"Maybe. A little." She smiles a tiny smile, trying to keep light-hearted.

"I don't know how to ask without it sounding like that," I say. I delete what I have written and type:

**When are you coming back?**

That sounds worse, so I delete it immediately, and stare at my screen, hoping for inspiration to strike. Finally, I grin at Zoe and enter:

**Andrew is asking to swap rooms with you. Should we let him?**

Zoe gives that the thumbs up, and I send the message off into cyberspace, to Luke, wherever he is.

Zoe shuffles along the bed to sit next to me, and we both hunch over my phone, anticipating an instant reply. It doesn't come.

"Maybe he hasn't seen it yet, or he could be busy. Let's have dinner and see what happens?" I put my arm around her shoulder and give a little squeeze.

We cook, eat and clear away dinner. I want to talk to Zoe about the OSCE, but my mind is full of Luke, and I don't want to interrupt her with my worries. He hasn't replied to my message, and I don't know what to make of it. Maybe he's not into texting. I mean, in all the time that we have been here, apart from the *Happy Xmas* texts, we have only exchanged messages when one or the other of us has wanted something from the supermarket.

We live together, and texting seems superfluous when we are in the same building most of the time, but perhaps it's just not something he does. Zoe and I, on the other hand, do text each other quite regularly, even when we are in the same room, never mind other parts of the house. Is it a girl thing, or a best friend thing? Are we both expecting too much of him if we expect a reply?

I'm starting to worry about him, so I can't imagine what Zoe must be thinking. One thing I do know - she must tell him how she feels.

# Chapter Twelve

Despite not hearing back from Luke, when I drag myself, less than enthusiastically, out of bed on Tuesday morning, I run into him on the stairs. He's on his way up, I'm going down for breakfast.

"You scared me to death!" I yelp. It actually does sound like I am yapping at him, but I really didn't expect to see him here right now.

We stand on the staircase, which is the most cramped and ridiculously tight area to have a conversation.

"Sorry," he says, "I literally just got back."

I don't know what to say. My look must convey my disbelief, because he smiles and tries to give me an explanation.

"My lectures don't start until this morning, and I…" He stops before finishing the sentence, and when he talks again, I assume that he has changed what he was going to say. "I had some things to do back home."

"You've driven from Yorkshire overnight?"

He nods.

"Do you want to get past? I need a shower, then I'll come down and chat, if you have time."

I look at the clock on my phone screen.

"Sure."

I move to the side, and he heads up to his room.

I stand on the stairs briefly, trying to make sense of it. Something feels off, but I'm not sure what it is.

I turn and head back up to the landing.

"Zo?" I tap lightly on her door.

She takes a few moments to walk across her room and pop her head out. She only opens the door a crack; by the way she is gripping her duvet I can tell she isn't dressed yet.

"Was that Luke?" she asks. Although she's still half asleep, her excitement shows through in her voice.

I bob my head in a nod. "Yep. He's back."

"Why didn't he answer your message? Where has he been?" Her voice is a loud whisper, designed for me to hear and Luke not to.

I can only shrug. "Get dressed. He'll be down soon."

"Okay," she says, and ducks back into her room, pulling the door closed behind her.

By the time Luke comes downstairs, showered and dressed, Zoe and I are both at the kitchen table. She's hardly touched her breakfast.

"Alright?" he says, flopping into his usual chair, and plopping his bowl of chocolate crispies down.

"Where were you?" Zoe's tone is harsh and accusing. It's not really what I would have recommended if she is still trying to ingratiate herself with Luke.

"Woah!" He lifts his hands up in mock offence, at least I hope it's *mock*. "Sorry girls, I didn't mean to miss the sign-in." He says it with a smile and starts to tuck into his cereal.

I breathe a little relieved sigh and flash Zoe a look that's as sharp as her voice.

"Sorry," she says. "We didn't know where you were."

"Andrew was really worried," I add, trying to keep it light.

Luke angles his spoon upwards, pointing to where Andrew would be if he were in bed. And if he existed. "He wanted to muscle in on my room as soon as I was a day late back. I'm not sure I trust him anymore."

I pull a playful tight-lipped smile and give him a nudge that almost sends his crispies flying off his spoon.

Zoe seems to have been struck mute.

"So…where were you?" I ask, mimicking Zoe's tone, trying to turn it into a joke.

There's a moment of silence while Luke finishes his mouthful. Before he refills, he pauses, puts both hands palm down flat on the table and addresses us in a bold, serious voice. "I was with a girl."

The temperature in the room feels as though it drops five degrees in that moment. Zoe picks up her phone from the table, pretends to look at the time, and clatters to her feet, almost knocking her chair over.

"I've got to go," she says. She turns, nearly walking into the doorframe, and hurries out of the house.

"Is that the time? Gosh." I know that I am a terrible actress, but it's the best I can do under the circumstances. I scoop up my bag and chase after my best friend, leaving Luke looking in bewilderment at his bowl.

# Chapter Thirteen

Five weeks into term, the mornings start to feel a little brighter. February brings the promise of coming spring. There are daffodils trying to sprout in the tiny front garden of Tangiers Court, little yellow buds on dancing stalks of green. It's warmer too. We have already started to discuss getting an outdoors table for the backyard so we can breakfast out there, and sit under the stars in the evenings when it's warm enough to enjoy it. When I say we, I mean Zoe and me. We are the ones poring over Pinterest, getting excited about pictures of cups of coffee on delicate white metal tables, but I assume that if we set it up, Luke will happily join us.

Information about Luke's female friend has been non-existent. Neither Zoe nor I want to ask for further details, but in our conversations about the mysterious woman we both speculate and secretly hope that he will reveal more about her of his own volition. Zoe reasons that if she asks too many questions, she will risk showing him her true feelings, and now they seem "a bit bloody pointless". I can't help but agree.

February also brings my first in-hospital

placement. We are randomly allocated to antenatal, postnatal or delivery, and I am on my way to the Margaret Beresford Unit – St. Jude's Hospital's postnatal ward. Despite this being another new environment to adjust to, I don't have the apprehension and anxiety before starting this placement that I did with my community visits.

I expected that I would; I thought that the night before I started, I would be sitting on my bed, filled with dread and self-doubt, but it didn't happen. Instead, I am heading to the afternoon shift, for my first day in the hospital, full of the joys of (coming) spring and unfaltering optimism.

My mentor for this placement is Geri Smith. All I know before I meet her is her name. I phoned up last week to find out what shifts she is, and by definition I am, working. As much as possible we are encouraged to work to the same shift pattern as our mentors. I've no reason not to work the same days, nights, and weekends as Geri. This shift pattern is going to be my future, I may as well start getting used to it.

The postnatal unit is an old-fashioned set-up. The midwifery office is at the centre, opposite the entry door, and the ward itself stretches off to the east and west. The arms of the unit are Nightingale style, beds separated only by curtain from neighbouring beds, and one central gangway.

Closer to the midwives' office are a cluster of side rooms, which are allocated to women who have the greatest need of them. That might be due to a prolonged stay due to maternal complications, infection requiring isolation of mother or baby, or a mother whose baby is on the neonatal intensive care unit. The side rooms have en suite bathrooms, and there are shared toilet and shower rooms for the other women on the ward to use.

To the direct left of the midwives' room is the Head of Midwifery's personal office. Next to that, the kitchen. It's for staff use only, as the women have their nutritious and not so delicious hospital meals delivered to them from the main hospital kitchens.

There's a storeroom, a medicines room, a linen room, and a sluice. Luckily, the sluice is far away from the bed spaces and from the midwives' office, because that's where the bedpans are emptied, and the rubbish is sent down the chute in colour-coded bags.

It's all very new to me. I've never been a

hospital patient, apart from a quick visit to accident and emergency when I was in primary school. I was trying to give someone a piggy-back and fell and cracked my chin on a sharp desk corner. Seven stitches and a sugar-free lolly; that's my only experience of being a patient. I had never entered a ward until I walked onto the Margaret Beresford Unit.

After handover, Geri pulls a chair up next to where I am sitting in the midwives' office.

She eyes me in the way a lion might look at an antelope. Not that I think she is going to eat me, but her gaze makes me shuffle uncertainly in my seat. I put my hands beneath my thighs to keep them from shaking.

"You've done postnatal checks in the community," Geri says: a statement, not a question. "A lot of what you will do as routine here is pretty much the same."

I smile and let out a relieved breath before she continues. She's to the point, but her voice is soft. I can feel my heart rate steadying itself.

"A lot of it will also be very different. We have women who have been transferred after Caesarean sections, so there is a lot of post-surgical care. You're not a nurse, are you?"

I shake my head. Some students have done their nurse training first, before converting to midwifery, but clearly, I have not.

"Hmm, okay," she says. I'm sure I can hear a trace of judgment in her voice, but I try to ignore it. I can do this just as well as anyone else at my level. I know I can. Still, her words do nothing to help my nervousness about the new placement.

I say nothing, and when she gets up and starts to walk, I follow Geri down the ward.

We are looking after four women and their babies this morning. Two of the women have had Caesarean sections within the past week. One of the other women had a forceps delivery, and the final patient is a first-time mum who has been having some breastfeeding support.

Geri stops next to the first bed we come to.

"Morning, Fran," she says, smiling at the woman who is sitting up in the bed.

"Hi Geri," she replies.

"This is Violet, she is a student midwife working with me today. I'm going to get her to check you over, if that's okay?"

"Fine, no problem," Fran says. "Do you need my belly first?"

She's clearly used to the postnatal checks; she's lifting the sheet back to show me her Caesarean wound before I have time to even get to the bedside.

"Looks like it is healing well," I say, trying to sound professional. "Very clean."

I run through the rest of her check, but when it comes to reading her blood pressure, I pause. I've done this before, countless times, in the community, but always with a manual blood pressure monitor – a sphygmomanometer. Here, I am faced with a blue machine on a pole next to Fran's bed. Turning it on is easy; there's a button that says POWER. After pressing that, I stand and look at Geri.

"I haven't used one of these before," I say, hoping that I don't come across as incompetent to Geri or to Fran.

"That's okay. Fasten the cuff around Fran's arm, like with a manual sphyg." I wrap the blue band around her arm and look at Geri again.

"Just press that button, and it will record the blood pressure and pulse," she says.

I'm sure I hear her sigh, but I concentrate on what I am doing, and try to shrug off the idea.

I push the button that she is pointing to, and the cuff starts to inflate. Fran sits, watching, as though this has become a natural part of her life now.

The machine beeps softly and flashes up a result, which looks fine.

"All good," I smile, take off the cuff and jot down the reading before I forget.

Geri doesn't smile, or at least she doesn't smile at me. Instead she gestures to the tube poking out from beneath Fran's sheets.

"Check the catheter," she says.

I look at her blankly. Check what? Check it's there? Check what it's doing? It doesn't look like it is doing anything. There's a bag at the end of the tube, and there is definitely urine in the bag, but that doesn't give me many clues as to what I am meant to be checking.

My uncertainty must show in my hesitance.

"Check the catheter, Violet," Geri says again.

"I don't know what I do," I say. "I haven't looked after anyone with a catheter before."

"This is why you students should be nurses before they train as midwives," Geri says, but she speaks to Fran rather than to me. She steps in front of me, practically pushing me out of the way. "Watch," she tells me.

I want to learn, and I want to watch, but my head swims in embarrassment - and the feeling that I am completely useless.

Fran doesn't seem to have picked up on my ineptitude. Her baby has started to stir, and her focus switches to the cot.

Geri completes the rest of the check herself. "You'd better just watch from now on," she says. "Until you start to learn."

I gulp and nod impotently. I am here to learn, that's true, but I am not sure that destroying my confidence is the best way for Geri to teach me.

It's an arduous shift. Even with only a few patients to care for, my placement mentor keeps me on my toes, and indeed on my feet for the full seven and a half hours. At the end of the day, Geri stops me before I leave.

"Violet," Geri says. "You have a lot to learn, especially seeing as you have all of the basic nursing practice to catch up on, but I think we can get you through."

A tight ball catches in my throat. That was definitely a back-handed compliment.

"T-thanks."

"See you tomorrow afternoon," she says.

She walks away leaving me standing at the front of the maternity block, wondering exactly what to expect from this placement. I'm here for six weeks. I want to learn. I want to love this, but can I get through the next month and a half?

I catch the bus back from the hospital to Tangiers Court with tears in my eyes that I refuse to let fall. I won't be beaten. I have to push on; I have to show Geri that I can do this.

# Chapter Fourteen

I spend the rest of the night up in my room. When Zoe knocks on my door, I don't even want to answer. I need some time.

"Hey," I shout, not getting up.

"You okay?" She stays outside the door. She must sense that something is wrong. I could count on one hand the number of times that I have closed my door since we have been here.

"Yeah," I say, but I am not convincing anybody, least of all myself.

"Shall I come back later?"

"Okay," I say, just loud enough to be heard.

Something about today has sapped me of all my energy. I've tried my hardest, done my best, but perhaps I lack the knowledge and skills that I need to succeed. Maybe I will never be able to be a midwife.

Zoe pauses outside my door for a little longer, even though I am silent. I know she is there. I listen for the sound of her feet moving away but hear nothing. She waits, and gradually I pull myself to my feet and head over to the door to let her in.

As soon as I see her, I can't hold back my emotions any longer. I reach out to hold her and collapse into a wave of throbbing sobs.

She says nothing, stroking my hair and holding me close for what feels like an eternity, the two of us standing there on the tiny landing between our two rooms.

"Hey," she says, eventually. "It's alright, it's alright. Come on, let's sit down and you can tell me what happened."

I nod, and step back. My face is soggy, and I need to blow my nose. I tug a tissue out from the box by my bed before we both sit, and I tell her about my shift.

"She sounds awful," Zoe says. "What's wrong with her? Treating you like that. Awful."

"It could be me. The way I took it. I mean, on the surface, she didn't say anything wrong, but…"

"I think she meant it, from what you said. Don't make excuses for her."

I've been used to being told I am wrong, that I am not good enough, that I can't achieve anything. I have heard that from my father for so many years. I don't know why I thought that I could ever be a midwife, I don't know why I thought I could ever do this.

"Hey," Zoe says to my silence. "Stop thinking. Okay. Stop it."

We have been through this, or at least situations like this, before.

"I can't do it though. I can't, can I? I'll never be able to…"

"Stop it, Violet." She takes the tissue off me, and wipes at my eyes.

"Ugh!" I protest, but she wipes, and sets my face straight, then she pulls me upright.

"Come on. This isn't you. You're not that person anymore. You're not scared now. That's all behind you."

I thought it might be, I thought I could have left that behind, but it seems I was wrong. All the self-doubt I have ever felt has come back.

I don't know what to say to Zoe. I want to be strong. I want to be able to nod and agree and pick myself up and get it together and…I can't.

I let out a tearful sigh.

She tries a different tack.

"My placements have been tough too," she says. "I have to stand there in front of all those teenagers with their attitudes and, well, you know how they are. They are like us a few years ago, but worse."

She manages to make me smile a little.

"Remember Jenna Ford from school?"

I nod. She was an absolute nightmare to the

teachers. Always in the remove room. I never went there, of course, but I pictured it as the secondary school equivalent of a padded cell.

"Half the class is like her. And I am a first-year student teacher. You think they listen to me?"

"Even we wouldn't have listened to you." I manage a smile.

"Exactly. But Vi, this is what I want to do. This is what I have always wanted to do. You know that."

Again, I nod. These are our dreams. This is why we are here.

"So, no matter how many challenging students I meet, I am going to do this. Nothing is going to stop me."

"I'm not you, Zoe. I can't just…"

She cuts me off mid-sentence. "You are not me, but you are Violet Cobham. You are my best friend. You are going to be a midwife. You have worked your ass off to get here. *You* are not giving up on *my best friend's* dreams. Not now, not ever."

I snort a big snotty breath and give her a weak, tearful smile.

"You really do overrate me," I say. But every word she says makes me bloom inside. I can feel the warmth of her feelings blossom inside me. So what if Geri thinks I am incapable of succeeding. Zoe, my best friend Zoe, whose opinion matters to me more than anyone else in the world, she thinks I can succeed. No. She knows I can.

"I was going to ask to be given a different placement. Or a different mentor," I say. "But not now. Zoe, I'm going to show her. I am going to show her that I can do it."

"That's it. Put your big girl pants on and *show her*."

She reaches over and hugs me, and I try not to wipe my face onto her. When we break free, I dry my eyes again, and face her.

"Is your placement okay then? Will you be alright?" I ask her.

She waves the idea away. "Nothing I can't handle," she says. "Really, it's fine. They are just like us. I mean, a little bit worse, but I remember feeling frustrated and not wanting to be told what to do. It's tough, isn't it?"

"What is?"

"Being a teenager."

I huff a tiny laugh. We are both still eighteen. What we don't know about the world we can make up for through what we know about ourselves, and how much we care about each other.

"It is," I say. "It is."

# Chapter Fifteen

The next afternoon, back on my placement, I follow Geri as we check in on the women after handover. I remember how to use the blood pressure machine, and I am sure I do everything she asks exactly as she asks me to do it. Still, her voice is harsh when she talks to me.

The nursing assistant, Ivy, is stripping down a bed in the space next to our final stop of the ward round, and she looks up at me and smiles, giving me a little 'chin up' motion as Geri barks at me.

I want to show my mentor that despite anything she might say to me, I am here to learn, and I am here to succeed. I will do my best until she sees that I am capable and competent. Instead of putting me off, she is driving me to work harder, do better and achieve the very best that I can.

When we have finished the first ward round we go back into the midwives' office. She picks up the heavy steel teapot and pours herself a mug. I am about to sit down next to her when he holds up her hand in a stop sign.

"Go and help Ivy make the beds. You won't know how to fold hospital corners yet, will you?" She doesn't give me a chance to reply. "Now's a good time to learn."

I wouldn't mind a cup of tea too, but instead of protesting, I say "sure" with a smile on my face and I walk back onto the ward.

In principle, there is nothing wrong with being asked to make beds, and it's true that I need to learn. I still can't help thinking that this is some kind of test or even a punishment. Geri doesn't like me, that much is clear. Whether it's because she doesn't want to be held back by having a student midwife trailing around after her or because I didn't train as a nurse first, I don't know. Either way, it doesn't matter. The fact remains.

There are no other students on the ward. I have no one to share my feelings with. I was looking forward to being here, in the hospital and on the unit, but working with Geri is already feeling emotionally draining.

"Sent you to help, did she?" Ivy asks, as I join her next to the bed.

"We've seen all the ladies," I smile. "Everyone is happy, so I've come to learn how to make a bed."

Ivy hacks out a two-packs a day laugh. "Geri always finds me a helper," she says.

I tilt my head, and wait for her to say more.

"She likes to put her students to work, that's for sure."

It's not just me then, that's almost a relief.

"That's what I'm here for," I say, and as I let the words out, I realise that they are true. What's so wrong with wanting me out here on the ward rather than sitting in the office eating too many biscuits?

Ivy holds out the edge of the clean sheet to me, and I take a corner.

As I make the beds and chat with Ivy, I decide to give my all to this placement. I decide to learn how to work with Geri, and to reflect on what I can gain from working alongside her. If working with Stacey on community taught me the beginnings of the basic skills I need to be a midwife, my placement with Geri can offer me a new depth of understanding. Midwifery is hard work, but being part of a team, learning how to get along with and respect other members of staff is essential.

I've never been afraid of getting my hands dirty, but I will be the first to volunteer when the beds need making, or the bedpans need emptying. I will make the tea at the start of the shift, if no one has beaten me to it, and I will make time to talk to everyone, from consultants to cleaners. Everyone has their role here, and we couldn't work as a whole without each of the unique elements functioning together.

When I return to the midwives' office, there's a mug of tea waiting for me, and Geri hands it over with a smile that I didn't expect.

"Thanks, Violet," she says.

I look at her, accept the tea, and nod.

"It's all part of the learning process." I smile back at her, and I know that everything I do can help me to become a better midwife, even if that might not seem obvious to me at first.

# Chapter Sixteen

After six long but rewarding weeks on the postnatal ward, we have a final two-week block in university before Easter break. The excitement of seeing my course mates and catching up on stories from our practice placements is tempered only by the fact that this Friday we will have our first OSCE.

I hope that my scenarios are related to postnatal care. My mind is fresh with the experiences I have had on the Margaret Beresford Unit. If I get a scenario that I have been through in real life, I am sure that I will be fine remembering all the details under examination conditions. If it's something I am less well acquainted with, that will be a different story. The thought of assessors watching my every move, trying to single out anything and everything that I do wrong, is terrifying.

Sitting in the first class of the week, I can already feel the first signs of anxiety starting to bite away at me.

"Practice, practice, practice." Rachel Rogers writes the word on the board as she repeats it. "This is your first OSCE. It is the easiest. That's not to say that it is *easy*, but approaching this test with a positive mindset, after preparing well, will set you in good stead for the remaining OSCEs throughout your course. You can do this. There is nothing in any of the scenarios that you have not been taught about. There are no trick questions. You should behave exactly as you would do in a real-life situation."

"I'm bricking it," I whisper to Sophie. I hope that she is going to echo my feelings, but instead she gives me a gentle smile.

"You'll be okay, Vi. You know your stuff."

She obviously does, because she doesn't look at all worried. I wish I hadn't said anything. I feel even worse now.

We have gone over the six scenarios exhaustively, and I mean exhaustively, I'm absolutely drained now, and I wish we could get the examination over with. I've got the postnatal placement on my side, half the topics that we have covered are based on postnatal situations. If I get one of those, I will be much more confident.

*Behave as you would in a real-life situation.* If somehow I can trick my mind into believing that I am on the ward, with an actual pregnant or postpartum patient rather than an actress, maybe I will be able to be the calm, confident student midwife that so far I have managed to be on my placements.

Our exam is on Friday; on Thursday evening I persuade Zoe to stand in as a new mum for me so that I can practice, practice, practice. I've promised her that there's a bottle of gin in it for her afterwards, but tonight we are both keeping a clear head.

I've given Zoe one of the mock scenario sheets that the lecturer posted on the online learning pages, and she is getting into the part with aplomb. She told me to wait outside the bedroom door while she prepared herself, and now it's time for me to enter.

"Hi, Miss Colebrook," I say. It's hard to keep a straight face. Zoe is in the chair next to her desk with one of her pillows stuffed up her t-shirt. It's a very unconvincing fake bump but seeing her like that makes it difficult to control my giggles.

She gives me a stern look.

"You can call me Zoe," she says. She's channelling her inner teacher, and I wonder whether this is what she is like on her placement.

I try my best to straighten up and take this seriously. She is doing me a huge favour, and I need to make the most of this opportunity to practice.

"Thanks, Zoe. So, how are you?"

I ask all the right questions and respond appropriately to her answers. She lies on the bed for me, and even lets me palpate her super-flat tummy. Zoe has always been slim; my chubbiness could pass for a tiny baby belly. It's a good thing she isn't feeling my abdomen. It's difficult to get pregnant when you haven't had sex in...however long it has been.

"Concentrate!" my pretend patient says.

"Sorry, just your tummy is so flat. Hard not to be jealous," I smile.

She bats away the compliment. "So, student midwife Violet, is my imaginary baby growing alright?"

"There's definitely not a baby in there," I say, before snapping back into the role play. "Uh, I mean, yes, Zoe. Everything feels exactly as it should."

She's a great help. I don't know what I would do without her, but even though we spend the rest of the evening practising, there is still that undercurrent of fear that I just can't shake. I know what I am meant to do, I know what I am meant to say, but the thought of performing under exam conditions fills me with dread.

# Chapter Seventeen

We have all been given a time slot for our examinations, and unfortunately, I have to wait until afternoon for mine. Zoe is on her placement, but I have come onto campus early anyway. Better to sit in Bradley's and panic than to sit at home and do it; there's better coffee here.

Sophie and Ashley both had their assessments this morning. They were straight onto the group chat, each with their own take on the exam. Ashley thought it was a breeze and took it all in her stride. Sophie forgot her own name when she introduced herself but got into the swing of things once she warmed up. That's *almost* reassuring.

I can't decide whether it is best to read and reread the notes I have made on the scenarios or whether I should take a break now. Can I try to push too much information into my head? Am I going to get study fatigue? Is that even a thing? I feel like I have learned everything that I am likely to be able to learn now. I still have an hour before the dreaded OSCE. I buy my second latte, then lean back in my chair, stretching my arms and legs, trying to get my blood flowing to them instead of my anxious brain.

All I have done for as long as I can remember is study. My brain is fried. I wasn't planning on sharing that gin with Zoe, but perhaps I will be ready for it after I've finished today. The lecturer told us that learning the scenarios like this is meant to help us to prepare for facing these issues in practice, if we haven't already done so. We will know exactly what to do when we are in real-life situations. I can see where she is coming from, but I wish there were an easier way.

At two fifteen I make my way to the skills lab to wait for my turn. Five minutes early: I figure that's the right balance between not being anxious about getting to the lab late, and not being anxious about having to stand around in the corridor for too long. Either way, by the time I get to the lecture block I can already feel the familiar bubbling of fear in my gut.

When I first started to get anxiety attacks, around seven years ago, my mum took me to the GP. I don't think she knew what to do with me, my mum, that is, not the GP. The GP knew; I suppose they see people like me all the time:

panicky, stressed out teenagers who can't keep it together. Of course, I wasn't a teenager then. I was a child, an eleven-year-old child. Instead of putting me straight onto the drugs, I went through counselling and CBT. They didn't help. And then the drugs didn't help either. I didn't feel like myself when I was on them, I felt like I was somewhere else, outside of my body. It was like being a mannequin, just like the ones in the skills lab. I was so tired, but worse than that, I felt empty, dead inside.

And that is why I am standing here now, with sweaty palms and a galloping heartbeat. I choose not to pop the pills that make me feel numb, so I must live with the anxiety that makes me feel petrified.

The door opens and one of the other students walks out. She's smiling, and I take that to be a good sign.

"Good luck," she says, as she passes me.

"Thanks," I just about manage to say. My voice has shrivelled. I need to get back on track before I get into the lab.

"Violet?" Rachel pops her head out of the open door to summon me in.

"Yep." I intend it to sound confident and bold, but it comes out like more of a burp.

"Leave your bag by the door inside and come over to the desk."

She smiles at me; I take a deep breath and walk into the skills lab.

There are a series of cards laid out on the desk, all with their plain sides up. It's a random choice which scenario I will get. Everything is down to me now, which decision I make, and how I handle the scenario that follows. Everything that happens rides on me. I am responsible, I am the only one who can do this, I am going to be sick. I need air. I need to get out of here.

I reach one hand out, meaning to pick up one of the cards, an arbitrary selection, but instead I wobble slightly, and put my hand down on the table instead to stabilise myself.

"Get it together," I say, beneath my breath.

I look around, over my shoulder. Rachel and one of the other lecturers are sitting patiently, waiting for me to make my selection. They say nothing. I turn back to the table. I only have to choose one of these for now. Choose one, play it through, come back for the next. I'll be out of this room in an hour. That's all. I only have to make it through that long.

I can't believe that when I first came into this skills lab, I thought it was just like a hospital room. It has none of the atmosphere, none of the sounds, none of the smells of the ward. There's no undercurrent of chatting, babies crying, phones ringing. There's no baby bath scent, no wet nappy aroma, none of the wafting of hospital meals being delivered to hungry women. Everything feels as false as it actually is. I need to get myself into the right mindset, trick my brain into thinking that this is real.

"Are you ready, Violet? Just choose whichever you like," Rachel calls over.

If I don't get on with it, I'll make the next student late. I would be annoyed if someone had made me wait out there any longer than I had to. I must do this. I have to get on with it now.

I pick up the top left card, and without looking at it, I go over to the lecturers.

Rachel turns it over, and nods. "Lactation and infant feeding," she says. She offers the card back to me, so that I can read the scenario, but the words swim in front of my eyes.

"We will start the examination here, and then move on to the other stations," Rachel says, pointing over to the other side of the skills lab. I can see tables laid out, but my mind can't focus on what they hold.

I stand in front of the woman, smile,
and…and nothing. My mind is completely
blank. My eyes dart around the room,
frantically looking for something, for anything,
to prompt me into action, but there is nothing. I
am completely frozen.

The woman looks at me with a calm, patient
expression as I search for the words that I know
I should be saying.

"I…"

Nausea hits me like a punch in the stomach.
I'm churning inside. I can't think, I can't think.
I can't do anything.

"I'm sorry," I say.

"Take your time, Violet," Rachel says.

Nothing more. No prompts, no hints. I don't
need them anyway. I know everything I need to
know to pass this examination. I know the
basics of infant feeding. I have revised for this
scenario, I have seen and heard and advised
women on my placements. I know what I
should do and what I should say, but when I try
to act, I am statue-still. Everything else is
spinning. I feel like I am on a merry-go-round,
the room swirling around me, the lecturers, this
poor woman who has probably never seen

anyone react to her like this before, all of it, all of them, everything.

"I…I have to go," I say. "I can't."

"Violet? Are you okay?"

I must look as bad as I feel. I sway a little and put my hands out onto the side of the fake-hospital bed to steady myself.

"I need to go. I'm so sorry."

Rachel is getting to her feet. I wave my hand.

"Really. I'll be okay. It's just…"

I feel so stupid. I don't know what to say. There's nothing I can say to make this any better. All I can do is get out of here.

"Do you want to sit down?"

If I sit, I don't think I will ever get up. I will burst into tears and make even more of an idiot of myself. I shake my head.

"Really, I'm sorry."

I let go of the bed, and without making eye contact with anyone, I walk out of the door.

As soon as I am on the corridor, I break into a run. I don't want my tutor to follow me, to try to make me go back in there. I know that this will mean a big fat fail, but I can't do this. I can't do it. Not now. Maybe not ever.

I can't do it; I can't do it.

I feel deflated, totally drained.

Zoe will still be in her afternoon classes. Part of me wants to message her and ask her to get up, leave her placement and come home with me. I can't do that to her though. It's more than enough that I am messing up my own course, without me ruining her chances of success too.

When I break out of the lecture block into the cold fresh air of the afternoon, I look over to the building that Zoe is usually in. I imagine her sitting at her desk, taking copious amounts of notes, knowing the answers to ever question the lecturer asks. It has always been this way. She has always been the clever one; I've always been the one that messes everything up. Why does she bother hanging around with me? I'll never understand it. I don't deserve her, and I'm sure I don't deserve to be here. There must have been a mistake.

I want to run, to be as far away from here as possible. Being on campus is making my head spin. Why do I have to be so completely useless? When I am on my placements, everything feels so natural. I know what to do. I can talk to women and their families; I can talk to doctors. Working with Geri showed me that I can talk to my superiors, even if they might think that I am only a student, or if they might not appear to value my worth. I felt so good coming out of my postnatal placement, and now, all of that, everything I have learned seems to count for nothing. Now I am back to being the useless, hopeless failure that my dad always told me that I would be.

I thrust my hands deep into my pockets and start to make the walk home, alone. I can feel tears pushing their way into my eyes, but I can't let myself cry here. I'm sure everyone is already staring at me, the sad-faced student moping about on her own. I can't cry. Not here, not now. No matter how much I want to.

# Chapter Eighteen

By the time Zoe gets home and runs up to my room, I have had two hours to stew in the thoughts of my failure.

I've changed into leggings and a t-shirt: my lounging-around-feeling-sorry-for-myself outfit. I rarely ever wear anything other than dresses and tights, so as soon as Zoe sees me, she knows that my choice of clothes is not a good sign.

"What happened?" she says. Her eyes are filled with concern. A pang of guilt hits me, like an ice bolt to my heart. I don't want to make her feel bad for me. "You should have texted!"

"I messed up." What else can I say? "I totally bottled it."

"Did you do something wrong, or –"

"I didn't do anything. I stood there and turned to jelly. My brain went to mush, and I couldn't think of a single thing to say."

Zoe frowns and shakes her head. "You were so good in our practice session yesterday. It's not that you *can't* do it."

"Well, obviously, I can't." The words come out far more bitterly than I mean them to. Zoe ignores my tone though.

"You can. You did everything right last night," Zoe says.

"Last night didn't matter. Today mattered." I practically spit the words. I feel awful about talking to Zoe like this, but I can't seem to stop myself. She is doing her best, I know she is.

She looks down at her feet. I suppose she is trying to think of something reassuring to say to me. There's nothing that can make me feel better.

"Look, I'm going to run a bath and stew for a while, okay? I appreciate you're trying to help, but I think I need some time alone to get my head around things."

She nods and doesn't speak.

"I'm sorry for being an idiot," I say.

"You're really not, but okay," she says. "See you downstairs later?"

"Yeah."

I don't know whether I will feel like company, but it's always reassuring to know she is there for me. It's not often that I want to be alone. I don't like big crowds, or having a lot of people around me, but it's rare that I don't want to be with Zoe. It's not her personally that I don't want to be with; I need to be alone right now. I've messed up something that is incredibly important, and I only have myself to blame.

Before she turns to leave, she says, "Don't beat yourself up about this. It's going to be okay."

I don't know what else to say, but she hovers in the doorway until I give her a tight-lipped, obviously fake smile. I hate feeling like this. I hate being like this.

Hiding in the bathroom was one of my coping strategies when my mum and dad used to argue. Even if I were in my bedroom, their fights would always escalate to the point where I would be dragged in, like some kind of referee, or someone to cast the deciding vote.

"What do you think, Violet? Is your mother lazy?"

"Do you think she does enough around the house?"

"Are your friends' mothers like this?"

And, of course, that all time classic:

"Would you rather be with your mum or me?"

My dad. It was always my dad saying those things. Mum would stand looking embarrassed; I suppose she always knew that it was wrong to involve me in their fights. She wasn't strong enough to get out and get away from them though. Not then, at least.

If I ran a bath, locked the door, and lay in the tub, I would be left alone. They never disturbed me there. It was like a sacred place. I always felt safe in the bathroom, I suppose it still is my safe place. It's where I go to be alone, to relax and unwind.

I know that I have my own bedroom here, and I can shut my door and ask for some time or space or whatever, and Zoe will respect that, but I feel awful turning her away, or shutting her out. If I am in the bath, she knows not to disturb me; it's an unwritten rule of our friendship. I come in here and lock the door, but I am locking myself in rather than locking her out.

Slipping beneath the warm water, my mind begins to clear. I have to find a way to deal with my anxiety. If it is going to affect my course like this, I have to start to consider my options. Should I go back to the GP? I don't think I could handle medications again; all they did was make me feel a different kind of bad. There are probably different therapies that I could try, but last time was awful. The thought of it turns my stomach. I can't do that again. I was practically a zombie; I certainly wasn't myself.

Counselling then? Cognitive behaviour therapy? Self-help? Isn't that what I have been doing? Getting through by helping myself? By having Zoe help me? Perhaps it's time to see a professional, or at least talk to my tutor, the support services or someone. All of those options though, they make me feel like a failure, like I am not strong enough to deal with my life on my own. They make me feel like a failure. I don't think I am ready to label myself. Can I get through this on my own?

When I finally make it downstairs, I run through my thoughts with Zoe.

"You're not on your own," she says.

It's only eight o'clock, but I'm in my pyjamas, in the living room. Zoe and Luke are both on the sofa. I wasn't sure whether I should discuss my anxiety in front of him, but I guess he is my friend now, he may as well know the real me.

"I know," I say. "I mean without professional help. Or drugs. That kind of alone."

"They were pretty crappy when you took them before." She shudders as she speaks.

I'm sure Zoe remembers as clearly as I do what happened the last time I took the meds. Perhaps she remembers even more clearly, having been on the outside looking in.

"What happens now? About your exam?" Ever practical, Luke brings us back to the fundamentals.

"I got a message from Rachel, the module leader. I have to go and see her on Monday morning." It's my turn to shudder now. I have no idea how I am going to make myself go to her office.

"You have two full days to think through your options," he says. "Try to be logical and pragmatic."

"Us girls are emotional and unpredictable, Luke. Being logical and pragmatic is too difficult for us." I tilt my head as I deal out my snarky response.

He doesn't bite at the bait. "It's a good thing that you have another viewpoint here then. If you keep thinking about how you messed up, or how bad you think you are - and Violet, you really are not - you're going to drive yourself nuts over the weekend. Make a plan. Decide what you are going to do. You can't change what happened today, but you can change what you do in future."

"You think I should get help then?" I say, still on the defensive.

"I'm not saying that you should do that, no. I'm saying that you should decide what you want to do. Think about the pros and cons."

Zoe looks at me and shrugs. "That seems like a sensible suggestion."

I ease back into the armchair, starting to feel more relaxed. Having control of my future and starting to get control of my anxiety would be a step in the right direction, that's for sure. Maybe Luke is right.

# Chapter Nineteen

On Monday morning, the last week of term, I am standing outside Rachel's room. My mind is racing, trying to work out what I should say to her. Is there any way I can mitigate the way I acted in the examination? I cannot think of anything I can tell her that will make this any better.

She calls me in and gets straight to the point.

"You need to pass the resit to get through to the second year. There is no way around it. There's no way to substitute grades from another module or take an average mark forward." She looks at my file and nods her head. "You have achieved excellent grades so far. Your assignment results in the first term were all above sixty percent. That tells me that you are capable. What happened?"

"I clammed up. I had a massive anxiety attack and…" I throw my hands in the air. There's no way of explaining how I felt that she will understand.

"Do you have any medication, or have you received any support for this?"

"No. When I first started getting the attacks my mum took me to see someone, I mean my doctor. They gave me some tablets, but they didn't help. I stopped taking them. Why take something if it doesn't make you feel any better?" I'm bored of going over this now. I don't particularly want to talk about it again, but I understand why she needs to know.

"That makes sense," Rachel says. "But this is your future on the line. I want to make sure that you are as prepared as possible for your resit. It might be worth you contacting the Learning Support Service, and maybe you should ask your GP for some advice?"

I gulp, but the lump I feel in my throat remains firmly in place.

"Okay." I say the word quietly. I really don't want to take drugs again. I am not sure that it will help. I have to pass this module though. Without getting through the resit, I can't continue.

"If you don't mind sharing your details, there is another student in the group that needs to resit, and it might be worth the two of you running through some scenarios together to practice."

That sounds like a solution that I can get behind. My voice is firmer when I say *"okay"* this time.

"Chin up, Violet. You are not the first student to fail the OSCE and you will most certainly not be the last. See it as an additional opportunity to review your skills and knowledge."

An opportunity. It didn't feel like that at the time. Can I really put myself through that again? The bottom line is that I must if I want to continue.

I want to continue.

I have to do this.

I did think things through, over the weekend. I went over and over it in my head. I know that everyone only wants what is best for me, and that Zoe, Luke, and Rachel, all my mentors, everyone, they all want me to succeed. I have never had so much support before. I don't deserve all these lovely people backing me. What I do know is that having their support makes *me* want to succeed. I want to beat anxiety and although it might be a ridiculous thing to think – I want to do it on my own. I don't want the drugs that deaden me; I don't want therapy. I want the satisfaction of beating this.

"*Make a plan,*" Luke said.

That's what I have done. I have thought it

through all weekend, and my plan is to kick anxiety's butt. I can do it. I have to. I don't get those feelings when I am on placement; when I have my uniform on and I'm in the heat of the action I know what to do and when to do it. That must mean that I am capable, I am able to beat this. I'm going to give it my best shot.

# Chapter Twenty

Returning to uni after Easter break is bittersweet. On one hand I am finally about to start my first delivery suite placement. On the other hand, the prospect of resitting my OSCE is looming over me like a dark cloud. I'm trying to be positive, but If I don't pass, this is the end for me. No third chances, I will be out. I can't let that happen.

It's mid-April, my resit isn't until the second week of June. I wish I could do it straight away, get it over with. I wish I hadn't failed in the first place.

I have all this term's work to do in addition to my resit. I need to focus. Everything I have dreamed of rides on passing my OSCE. Nothing else matters. It's the final term of the first year. If I want to make it through to the second, I must pass.

Sunday evening, the day before start of term, the mood in the house is ice-cold. Zoe and I arrived back this afternoon, and, just like after the Christmas break, there's been no sign of Luke.

"Must be with that girl again," Zoe says.

"Hmm. Yeah." I should be more supportive, I

know, but my thoughts are elsewhere.

"Should have expected it, I suppose." She's curled up on the sofa, I'm in my usual armchair. We have so far managed to eat dinner and binge watch half of a new series that's based on a book we both read last year. Neither of us is motivated to do much else, it seems.

"Yeah," I say again. I can't remember anything I just watched on the television. Snap out of it. Come on. I look at Zoe. "I'm sorry," I say. "I know you really like him. I don't know what –"

Before I can carry on with the sentence, I hear the footfall on the stairs that can only mean one thing. If Andrew hasn't turned up, Luke must be home. He's been here all along, and neither of us realised.

Zoe and I pass a shared look of surprised confusion. I click pause on the remote, and we listen, waiting for him to come in and join us. There's a thud of footsteps heading into the kitchen, the clunk of the fridge opening, and another as it closes, and then the steps head back, through the hall and up the stairs.

He must know that we are in here; neither of us has been particularly quiet. The television has been on, and we weren't exactly listening quietly.

"Maybe she is with him?" Zoe says in a loud whisper. Her face is stricken; she sits up.

"Do you think so? I guess that would explain him not coming down."

"Oh no, oh no. I don't want to…" she trails off. "Vi, I couldn't."

All thoughts I had of the forthcoming stressful term fade away as I turn my focus to my best friend. I can't bear seeing her like this.

"Zo, I'm so sorry that things haven't worked out the way you wanted them to," I say.

"I should have said something before Christmas. I shouldn't have waited. I'm such an idiot."

"You thought you had time," I say. "Everything was going so well between you. Taking it slowly is the best way, right?"

I don't know if that's true or not. I know so little about relationships that it is impossible for me to give Zoe any real, practical advice. My last relationship was six months ago, and it only existed for two months. What do I know?

Jared Clarke. Tall, dark, and useless, as it turned out. Before that there was Charlie Nunn, my first, and only, love. I don't still love him, he's not my only love in the one-true-love of my life sense. He's my only love because he is the only man, boy, that I have ever loved. Yet. Eighteen months on, I know that I will find someone else. One day. When I am ready. Right now? I couldn't care less. My world is uni, and Zoe. I don't need anything else.

"I thought that if we kept getting to know each other then things might naturally progress." She runs her fingers through her long red hair and lets it fall over her face like a veil. "I'm so stupid."

"He's stupid not to have snapped you up," I say. I don't know what else I can do to make her feel better.

"What if he brings her down to introduce her to us? What then? I think I'll probably flip out." She tosses her head in a melodramatic flounce.

"You will do what you always do. You'll be cool and calm. You'll politely say hello and you will probably end up making friends with her, because that's the kind of person you are. You can't dislike anyone. Not really. You're too nice, Zo."

She smiles at this and gestures at me to restart the television programme.

"Let's not think about bad things," she says. "Let's watch the end of this and then break out the gin."

"A sound idea, Miss Colebrook." I smile.

"That's what the kids call me." She laughs, and we both settle to watch Netflix and try to not think about bad things.

When we don't see Luke at breakfast, we agree that our assumption was most probably right. I give Zoe a hug before we part company for our separate lectures, but I still carry with me the sadness that she is feeling.

Ashley has been to a midwifery conference over the Easter break and she enthuses about it from the moment I sit next to her to when our lecturer arrives to start the session. I try to concentrate, but my thoughts keep turning back to my friend, and what I can possibly do to help her.

I decide to make Zoe's favourite dinner to cheer her up. By six o'clock, two bowls of steaming pasta with a hashed-up tomato type sauce sit on the table. A glass of wine each. A loaf of piping hot garlic bread. I cooked, and Zoe opened the wine. It seems like a fair deal. We are just about to get stuck in when the door opens, and Luke comes in.

"Smells great," he says. Just that. No hello, no explanation of where he has been or what happened yesterday. Certainly no sign of a girl. His voice isn't quite its usual chirpy tone though; something seems a little out of sync.

"There's more in the pan, if you want some." Zoe nods her head in the direction of the hob. There's no trace of emotion in her voice. I'm impressed with her control.

"Thanks." Luke's voice is dull and flat, like cardboard that has been left out in the garden.

"You okay?" I ask. I think about leaving it there, but I bite the bullet and continue anyway. "We didn't want to disturb you last night."

He raises his head in a little jerk. "Yeah." He walks over to get himself some of the pasta, giving Zoe and I the chance to look at each other, sharing a bewildered exchange of glances. Something is going on, that's the only thing of which I am certain.

I lift my fork and start to eat, but it tastes bland now.

Luke hovers by the table and I think for a moment that he is going to take his food and go upstairs. I kick his chair back slightly, hoping it will encourage him to sit.

Throughout, Zoe is silent. She has taken a

large swig of her wine though.

Luke puts his bowl onto the table and stirs the pasta and sauce together. Without looking at either of us, he scoops some into his mouth, swallows, and repeats.

"Lovely dinner Vi," Zoe says. I nod; I'm forcing myself to keep eating. "Thanks for this."

The atmosphere hangs thick like fog, and I almost wish that Luke hadn't joined us. The three of us eat on in silence as the ambience freezes.

I leave it until I have almost finished my food, but I can't take it anymore.

"Do you want to talk about it?" I say. I put down my cutlery and look at Luke. "I'm not sure I can bear this silence. What's happened?"

Zoe coughs and almost chokes on the piece of garlic bread that she is chewing. I hand her wine to her, and nod at her to drink.

Luke looks from me to her and then back down into his bowl.

"I don't want to talk about it. No." He drops his fork, pushes himself back from the table and walks out, up the stairs, to his room.

Zoe raises her eyebrows. "Well done, Violet."

"Oh, what was I supposed to do? That was painful. You didn't want to ask because…" I stop myself. I don't want to get into an argument with Zoe, but we both know the reason that she didn't want to ask Luke what was wrong. "Forget it," I say. "I probably had too much wine." The truth is, I haven't touched a drop yet.

# Chapter Twenty-One

Community, postnatal and antenatal are all as much a part of maternity care as intrapartum, but there's something special about delivery suite. When I first started to dream of being a midwife it was being present with women during childbirth that drew me in. I wanted to be a part of something emotional, intimate, and intense. I wanted to support women to have the best experiences of that time that they possibly could. That was my starting point. As I became more aware, read more about midwifery and found out as much as I could about the career, I realised that what midwives do during the antenatal and postnatal periods can have a massive effect upon women's emotional and physical wellbeing too. Every action matters. Every interaction matters. Even today, coming to the end of only my first year of training, I know that.

Still, today is my first day on delivery suite, and if I told you that this is just the same as any other placement, I would be lying. I desperately want to see a baby being born. It's hard to explain what an amazing experience that will be. I have sat in class with Ashley, Simon, and

Sophie, and heard stories from their placements.
Simon was present at a birth in the first term; he
got lucky when his community placement
mentor was called into delivery suite. Ashley
had her delivery suite allocation last term, so
she has already seen five births, and helped with
two deliveries. I feel like I am lagging already.

Instead of anxiety, my chest flutters with
excitement as I push open the double doors of
the delivery suite. The long corridor stretches
past closed doors to the midwives' station, and
behind it the staff room. Am I meant to leave
my bag somewhere? Are there lockers for my
coat? Where do I find my mentor?

The last question is the first to be answered.

"Violet?"

I nod. I must stand out as the newbie, turning
up in my grey and navy, fresh and eager to be
here.

"Hi," I say.

"I'm Jade." She holds out her hand, formally.
"I'm your mentor."

"Hi," I say again. I realise that I am repeating
myself and superfluously add "Hello". I must
be bright red; I can feel it in my cheeks.

"Let me take you to the locker room quickly,
then we'll get into handover. We have a few

minutes. I'll show you around once the night shift have left, okay?"

I try to speak, and my voice comes out like a mouse squeak. Jade leads me along the corridor, past a further line of closed doors, and around a corner into a locked changing room.

"You can wear theatre blues on the ward if you want to. It can get a little messy at times." She waves to a set of shelves stacked with neat piles of azure blue tops and pants in various, labelled, sizes.

"Okay," I say. "Thanks." I'll stay in my uniform today though. I want everyone to know that I am a new student and I have no idea what I am doing. If I wear my uniform, I hope I won't be asked to do anything or fetch anything that I haven't a clue about. I don't want people to rely on me just yet, not while I am floundering around like a fish out of water.

There is a line of lockers, and Jade pulls one open for me so I can put my bag inside.

"Leave your coat on any of the hooks. It will be fine here. No mobile phones on the ward. Make sure it's turned off and placed in your locker."

I reach back into my bag and slide my phone off. It will be weird not having it by my side, but perhaps the break will do me good. I can live without social media for a few hours, and Zoe will just have to wait to hear about how exciting or how terrible my day is. I hope that it will turn out to be the former.

We go back up to the staff room in time for handover. On the wall is a large dry-wipe board, with nine rows outlined in what appears to be black tape. Down the side of the board is a column listing the initials of the doctors on call, the obstetricians, the paediatricians, and the anaesthetic team. I recognise some of the names from my spell on postnatal. It's reassuring to have at least something recognisable, because everything else flashes around me in a blur of new and unfamiliar.

There are three women's names listed in the rows, and beside each name are a string of numbers and letters. I don't need to try to decipher them, because the midwife in charge starts handover, and everything quickly becomes apparent.

"Angela Flint, thirty-two years old primigravida. Thirty-eight weeks. Induction of labour for pre-eclampsia." She reels off Ms Flint's vital signs, the medication she has had so far, and the general plan of care.

The other two women are Naomi Whyte, who has come in for a check in 'query early labour' and Michelle Staples who thinks her waters might have broken. Neither of them is in established labour yet, and the midwife in charge seems to think they will be discharged home soon.

"There's another induction on antenatal ward, nothing happening yet, and we sent a multip home a couple of hours ago. She came in with irregular contractions, didn't phone first." There's a collective sigh. "Not in labour, but who knows? She knows to phone and come in when she needs to. Okay, nothing else to report."

The midwife taking charge of the afternoon shift writes on the board and then looks around the room at the staff who will be joining her. She directs her attention to me.

"So, it's your first shift?" she asks, and I nod. "Okay, well Jade, you and Violet take room three."

The induction. I can't hold back my smile. I don't focus on the rest of the allocations; my mind is already on the possibility that I might see a birth on my very first shift on delivery.

After the midwife in charge finishes speaking, a brown-haired midwife with cute glasses comes over to talk to us.

"Hi Violet. Welcome to delivery suite. I'm Emma. I was looking after Angela this morning."

"Hi Emma," I say. My voice seems to be getting back to normal now that it has had time to settle, or now I am getting my excitement under control.

Emma directs most of what she is saying to Jade, but occasionally glances at me to keep me included. I like her already. "Her blood pressure has been fairly stable." She opens the notes to show the chart that tracks all the vital signs during labour. Midwives call this the partogram. I like the name. I like the not-so-secret language that we share, the language of childbirth. We have words and phrases that we would not usually use outside of the maternity world.

Primigravida, a first-time mother, also known as a primip (short for primipara). Multip, or multigravida, someone who has been pregnant or given birth before. Pre-eclampsia, well I wish we didn't have to know that one. It's a pregnancy disorder that is characterised mainly by high blood pressure and protein in the urine. If left uncontrolled or untreated it can lead to eclampsia, hence the name. Eclampsia can be lethal for mother and baby, so the trick is to spot it and treat it before it escalates.

"She's having a few contractions, but nothing regular yet. CTG has been fine."

CTG, there's another midwifery term. The cardiotocograph – a recording of the baby's heartbeat and activity of the mother's uterus. I haven't used one of those yet. In clinic we listened to babies' heartbeats through a handheld electronic machine called a Doppler, or the old school way, using a wooden cone called a Pinard. It's amazing how many tools of the trade there are for something as natural as childbirth. Once you start to introduce drugs to start contractions in an induction and add continuous monitoring with a CTG machine, things really aren't all that natural at all anymore. I wonder how many births I will attend that are 'natural' in the way that I think of it.

Emma leads the way into room three, and Jade and I follow behind.

Mum-to-be Angela is sitting up on the bed, dressed in an oversized nightshirt and covered from the waist down with a thin white sheet. Her brown hair is pulled up into a messy topknot.

There's an IV line connected to a cannula in her left hand, and two wires pop above the sheet and connect to the cardiotocograph monitor by the side of her bed that is providing a trace of the baby's heart rate.

"Hi Angela, this is Jade, and Violet, a student midwife, who will be looking after you this afternoon." Emma smiles, and I say hello.

As she finishes speaking, Angela's expression starts to change. Her face tightens, and she reaches down to grab the bar on the side of the bed.

"Contraction?" Emma asks.

Angela nods rapidly. Jade walks over to the side of the bed, but before she gets there the contraction has ended.

"They aren't lasting long," Angela says. "It's fine."

"Is your husband with you?" Jade asks.

"He's at work," Angela shrugs. "I'm okay. He's not far away, he can come at short notice."

"I'm going to leave you with Jade and Violet now," says Emma. "I hope you get going soon and have an easy labour.

"Thanks for this morning," Angela says. "Come and see us when we make it upstairs"

"I will," Emma smiles and leaves the three of us.

I don't know what to do or say, so I stand, trying to look friendly, calm, and approachable.

Jade seems completely at ease. She runs through a series of checks.

"We need to have a baseline at the beginning of the shift," she says, showing me everything that she is doing and chatting to Angela at the same time.

It seems almost automatic to her, yet there is nothing conveyer belt like about her approach. There's such a lot to take in. I wonder if I will ever be able to appear this comfortable and confident. All I can do today is whatever I can to make Angela's birth day as positive as possible.

# Chapter Twenty-Two

By the end of my first shift on delivery suite I haven't seen a birth. Jade and I supported Angela throughout the day, but by the time our shift finished at half past nine Angela was five centimetres dilated. Her contractions were strong and regular, and she was in established labour, but delivery was unlikely to happen until well into the nightshift.

I spent most of the shift chatting to Angela, not as a patient, not discussing only baby names and birth plans, but talking about life the universe and everything. I felt like I had a purpose, above being a student midwife, there to watch; I felt like I was learning more than how to listen to the baby's heartrate and monitor contractions. Still, a part of me is disappointed that I didn't get to see Angela's baby come into the world.

Tuesday's shift comes and goes with no sign of a delivery; I'm trying to be patient; I know that midwifery is about more than catching babies – even on delivery suite. I'm on a late shift on Wednesday. Zoe is out on her placement, so I have the morning to kill at Tangiers Court without her.

I'm so used to getting up early now that I don't even bother to plan a lie in. My schedule involves breakfast, a long, hot bath and then a little bit of reading before I get ready to go to my placement. As with all the best laid plans though, things are not turning out as I had expected.

I'm waiting for the kettle to boil for my first coffee of the day when Luke stumbles into the kitchen.

"No lectures today?" he asks.

"Placements," I say. "First week on delivery suite."

"Nice. Have you delivered any babies yet?" He walks over and pulls a mug out of the cupboard and puts it down next to mine.

"Not yet. It's my third shift today. They don't let us get stuck in straight away."

"See one do one?" he smiles.

I put a spoonful of coffee granules into his mug. "See five, do one, but you weren't far off."

"How hard can it be?" he says. "People in Africa give birth in the bushes, don't they?"

I've heard this before, unsurprisingly. "Well,

yes. And a lot of them have some serious problems."

This gets his interest, but I'm not really in much of a mood to start a discussion about potential pregnancy and birth complications right now. He looks at me expectantly.

"You'll have to switch to my course if you want to find out more," I say.

"I don't think that they allow a straight swap from accountancy to midwifery, but I could ask."

I tilt my head and smile. "Sure," I say.

"Men don't study midwifery, anyway, do they?" he asks.

"Not as many men as women, sure. We have a future male midwife on the course though."

A look of surprise crosses his face. "Not sure why a man would want to be a midwife."

"I'm not sure why a man would want to be an accountant, but there you go." I like teasing him; he's a fun target.

He picks up the spoon and bops me gently on the forehead with it. "Round one to the scientist."

The kettle clicks and I make the coffee. Luke passes me the milk from the fridge and puts it away again after I have added a splash to each of our cups.

"Teamwork," he says.

Luke appears to be in a much better mood than he has been since he came back from Leeds. I take a sip of my coffee. The text on the mug says, *'I'd agree with you but then we'd both be wrong'.* The drink's too hot, and I withdraw sharply.

"Careful there. What are your plans? Want to watch TV or something?"

"We could just chat if you like?" I gesture towards the chairs at the little round table.

He pauses, considering the idea carefully. It is as though I opened a window; a cold chill passes between us.

"Okay," he says, simply. He takes a seat, and I sit beside him.

Looking at my mug, reading the humorous slogan over and over, it seems like forever before he speaks.

"We're friends, aren't we, Violet?" he says.

It's not what I expected, and I start a little in surprise.

"Uh, of course, yes. Why?"

"Well, this isn't the sort of thing I talk about. I mean, I know men aren't known for discussing their emotions and all that, but I don't have any friends that I could talk about them with if I wanted to. I have friends, of course I do, but apart from you and Zoe they are all guys. And we really don't talk about feelings."

There's a heavy lump in my throat. Countless thoughts flash through my mind as I try to imagine what he is about to tell me. Feelings? What kind of feelings? About whom? Why would he talk to me about feelings?

"I'm a good listener." I smile and carefully take a small sip of my coffee. It's started to cool. "You have to be in my line of work, right?"

He nods but doesn't return the smile.

"Okay," he says. "I'm not sure that I am a good talker, but I'll try."

I shuffle around in my seat to get comfortable and give him my full attention, and then I am silent as I let him speak.

"The girl I was seeing, back home. It's all turned out to be a bit of a disaster."

I take another sip and say nothing.

"I didn't really want to go into it all with you two. You don't need to hear about my, er, issues." He runs his hand through his dark, unruly hair and continues. "I used to date her back in college. Over the summer, we agreed that a long-distance thing wasn't going to work. I mean she decided, and I couldn't persuade her otherwise, so I had to agree really. It wasn't what I wanted."

"First love?" I ask, trying to make my interest sound like nonchalance.

"Kind of. I'm not sure I know what *'love'* is yet, really. I liked her a lot though. I thought we had a future. We were together for eight months. December to August, okay, nine months. Then one day she says that we need to talk, and I know what's coming. I'm going to Wessex University, she's going to Aberdeen, and it's a long way between the two." He pauses again. "I told her I could get a plane up or something. We could have made it work." He looks genuinely crestfallen.

"So, you split up, and came here."

"Yeah. I tried to put her behind me. I got on with my studying and thought about her as little as possible."

"Then you saw her at Christmas?"

"Then…yeah. I was out with my mates, and she showed up. More beautiful than I even remembered her. She really is a stunner, you know. All curves and curls and…I don't want to think about that." He shakes his head, as if trying to shake the image out of his mind. "We had a few drinks and she asked me to go back to hers." He looks at me, with a sheepish expression. "What was I meant to do?"

I raise my hands in a tiny shrug gesture.

"Well, I said no, actually." He smiles at me, as if he has tricked me into thinking badly of him. "I told her that I couldn't do it. I wasn't prepared to get hurt again. I sound stupid, don't I?"

"Not at all. It sounds far from stupid." I say.

"We met up the next day and talked everything through. She told me how much she missed me, and it seemed too good to be true. She'd made a mistake letting me go, she said. Couldn't go on without me, all that stuff."

"So, you got back together."

"So, we got back together. Only after she promised that this was it, that she was committing to make it work and she wouldn't bail on me again. I told her that I couldn't go through that, Violet."

I never imagined that Luke could be so sensitive and vulnerable. I haven't seen this side of him before. Six months we have lived in this house together, and I know so little about him.

"I understand," I say.

"I couldn't wait to get home for Easter. All I could think about was seeing her again."

I frown. "What happened?"

"I hadn't been home more than an hour; I hadn't even had chance to go round to see her. Her sister turns up on my doorstep."

I must look very confused at this point.

"I know her from visiting Kelly, of course. That's her name. Kelly. I know her sister, sure. And when I saw her standing there, I got a sick feeling in my gut. I knew it wasn't going to be anything good."

"Kelly. Is she okay? Is…"

He stops me talking with a dark laugh.

"She is absolutely fine. Her sister wanted to let me in on a few home truths before I made a complete fool of myself. *'Kelly has been carrying on with someone up in Aberdeen,'* she told me. No wonder Kell didn't want me to go up there to visit her. She texted me, we did all the naughty phone stuff, but as soon as I mentioned going up to see her, she told me to wait until Easter, wait until we could be together again. All that time, she was with some other guy." His expression is a mix of anger and pain. I put my hand onto his wrist.

"That's awful, I'm sorry, Luke."

"I wanted to be home so much. I wanted to see her, be with her, but after that, all I wanted was to be back here, as far away from her as possible."

"Did she try to, I don't know, lie about it? Cover it up?"

"Not once her sister told me, no. At least she was honest after she got found out. I don't think she's thanking her sister for telling me though."

"No," I say. "Her sister did the right thing though, for whatever reason."

He laughs. "She said that she wanted Kelly to do the right thing too. Is that what it was? It didn't feel right. Nothing about it did."

"It's really rubbish. Sorry, Luke."

We look at our mugs, not speaking.

"It feels good to get it out though," he says eventually. "Thanks."

I nod. "Sure. Sorry I can't say much helpful."

"There's nothing that can help. I learned a lesson. Never trust anyone."

"I'm not sure that is your take home message from this." I frantically think of something to say to change his mind. Things might not have worked out with Kelly, but now there is a chance for Zoe. If there's anything I can do to keep his faith in womankind alive, I have to do it.

"She's not every woman, she is one woman. Just because she did this to you doesn't mean that every woman will."

"Well, I don't believe in second chances. I won't be seeing Kelly again. I don't think I want to see anyone. Not for a while."

"Hmm." I can't stop myself from nodding. "I know that feeling."

"Something similar happen to you?" he asks.

I think for a few moments. "Not similar, no. Someone broke up with me, and then wanted me to take him back when he felt like it. I said no." I shrug and drain the rest of my coffee. "I thought that being alone was better than being unhappy with someone."

"Tangiers Court. Home of the Singles Club." He manages a smile as he says it.

"Andrew is probably off in a harem somewhere, living the life for all of us."

"Ah. Let him have it. We have books, coffee and…actually, yeah. Pretty sad, aren't we?"

I start to laugh along with him. It's kind of funny, but somewhere inside, I do feel that there might just be some truth in what he has said.

# Chapter Twenty-Three

As I take the bus to the hospital for my afternoon shift, I send Zoe a text message.

**Had a chat with Luke. Lots to tell you xx**

I expect a rapid reply, but then I check the time and realise that she is likely to be in class, and away from her phone. On one hand, Luke is single and available now, on the other, he seems to be resolutely done with relationships for the time being. I don't know that this is going to feel like good news to Zoe. Still, at least she has a chance now.

I have to put my belongings in the locker again when I get to the ward, so there's no possibility of continuing our conversation until break time. When I am working my mind never has the opportunity to miss social contact. I focus on the women I am caring for or the tasks that I need to carry out. Still, today I wish I could talk to Zoe.

On my lunch break I pop back into the locker room. I sit on the wooden bench, between the hanging jackets, and turn my phone on. It takes a few seconds to glow back into life after its morning of sleep. When the data signal kicks in there are three messages from Zoe. It's half past twelve now, she should be on her lunch break too. I click on the notifications and read her messages.

**Can't leave you alone, can I? :) Tell me everything xx**

Ten minutes later

**You're on the ward, aren't you? This is agonising! Message me as soon as you read this! xx**

Immediately followed by

**Unless it is bad news. I don't want bad news. Tell me something good! xx**

I have to put her out of her misery. I try to think of the best way to phrase things in a quick text message.

**He's split up with the girl. She was no good. Will explain all later. Could be your chance! xx**

I re-read the message and click SEND. It will do for now. There's only so much you can say in a message. Much as I love texting, sometimes it feels so limited.

I sit a little longer, the overhead strip light buzzes softly to itself, and being here in the locker rooms feels like I am in a cocoon. It's a pod of calm in an otherwise hectic and noisy ward. I make a mental note to come and sit here again in future when I need some space. I've settled into the peacefulness when my phone buzzes in my hand. I almost let it slip through my fingers, but I grasp it just in time.

**WHAT? TELL ME EVERYTHING! XXX**

All capitals. Extra kiss. Yep, she is definitely excited.

**Be home before you. Coffee shop when you finish? xx**

It's not a conversation I want Luke to walk in on. There's a cute indic coffee shop on the high street that we have never quite managed to stop by, and I feel like today is the day.

By five o'clock we've got home, changed, and excitedly bustled our way into Blackheath's café. It's a super-cute boutique coffee shop with mismatched chairs and heavy old wooden tables, a far cry from the franchised chains that seem to have invaded the town centre. Latte for me and a mocha, extra shot, extra hot for Zoe. We find seats in the corner and I can finally start to tell her about my conversation with Luke.

I spill everything that he told me, and watch her expression turn from curiosity to compassion to confusion.

"Where does that leave me?" she says.

"I really don't know." It's the truth. I hope that the two of them will somehow get it together now, but if he is intent on staying single, should she try to persuade him otherwise? Should I even encourage her? She's Zoe. She's my best friend. Whatever she wants, I will always support her.

"I was kicking myself after Christmas for waiting too long and letting someone else snap him up," she says. "I don't know if I can be patient and let that happen again."

"Snap him up," I laugh. "Like he's a bargain in the January sales."

She smiles and nudges me. "You know what I mean."

I do, of course.

"As you know very well, I am far from an expert on these things," I say. "Asking me about love is like asking an atheist about religion. I have no idea. I don't know anything about how men's brains work."

"I have trouble understanding how my own brain works some days," she says. She holds onto her coffee cup, staring into it as if the answers to all her questions are somewhere in the milky drink.

"You can either tell him how you feel or wait and see what happens. If it's meant to be, it will be, right? I mean, you both get on so well, and…"

"You and he get on well too. We are all friends, aren't we? That's the thing. Maybe he is just a nice person who gets on with everyone, and I am wasting my time dreaming about being with him."

"Newsflash, Zo. You are a really nice person who gets on well with everyone too."

"You have to say that; you're my best friend."

"Well, yes, you've got me there." I give her a wink.

It's all true though. Zoe isn't simply my best friend, and my favourite human that I have ever met, she is genuinely a great person that everyone likes. Everyone. When we were in school together, everyone talked to her, from the cliques to the geeks. There's something about her that people seem to be attracted to. I just float along by her side being my wobbly, anxious, imperfect self.

"Well, if he's plumping for the bachelor life for a while, I probably don't have to rush anything." She lets out a light sigh. "You must have had enough of me going on about him."

"It's fine, really. Not like I have anyone to go on about, is it?"

"If you wanted to meet someone, I know that you would. You've never had a problem finding gorgeous guys to fall at your feet."

"Hmm." I put my mug down and stare at it. "Gorgeous but brainless."

"We are at university. If you want brains, you came to the right place."

I shudder slightly. "Yeah. No. I mean, not yet. It'll happen when it happens."

Meeting someone is still very close to the bottom of my to-do list. At the top is getting through the year, passing my resit, and seeing Zoe happy. If those things happen, life will be perfect.

# Chapter Twenty-Four

I'm not having much luck on delivery suite. I
know that I am not here to simply witness
births, and eventually start delivering babies,
but two weeks into my placement I have yet to
see a baby being born. Either the women that I
care for don't get anywhere near to delivery
during my shifts, or there aren't any labouring
women on the unit when I am here. The excited
buzz that I felt when I started this placement has
settled to a flat feeling, like the bubbles have
been let out of my bottle.

I'm trying to focus on the positives. I have
had some experience of being with women and
their partners during labour. It's something that
I hadn't anticipated being quite as emotional as
I have found it. Seeing couples together like
that, men supporting their partners, there's
something about it. It's hard to explain if you
haven't experienced it. Of course, there are
women who don't come in with a man, but so
far, I have only met couples, and male-female
couples at that. My experiences have been
extremely limited, but even without having seen
a birth, I am still enjoying every day here.

The postnatal ward was busy every day.

There was always something to do, especially seeing as Geri loved to keep me on my toes. Here on delivery, there are long lulls where no women's names are written on the board. Today is my tenth shift, I have a very small sample size to work with. I've spent the first hour and a half today going through my PAD with Jade.

I'm walking up the ward, carrying a tray of empty mugs and a huge metal teapot when I hear the phone ringing. Chloe, the midwife in charge of today's shift is at the desk, chatting to one of the junior doctors. She scoops the handset up and answers.

"Delivery suite, Sister Brookes, can I help you?"

I set the tray down in the staff room and keep an ear on the phone conversation. Incoming calls can lead to incoming patients, and I hope that, eventually, incoming patients will give birth. I flick my eyes up to the clock. I have another six hours on the ward today. That's plenty of time. I can hear Chloe talking.

"Can I speak to your wife? I know, but if she can talk to me, yes, that's great thanks. Elizabeth? Hello. So, what has been happening? Okay. And how often are these pains coming now? Right," I can hear the scratch of her pen against the paper in the call log. We write down the details of every phone call that comes in. "And how long are they lasting? Are you getting a pain now? Good, keep breathing, that's it."

The woman on the other end of the phone is definitely contracting then.

"Have you had any loss down below? Any blood or water? Not yet. Okay, that's fine. And it's your second baby, your husband said. Thirty-nine weeks?"

There's a slight pause whilst the woman answers and Chloe makes a note of the rest of the details.

"Any problems that we should know about? No. Okay. And you feel like you need to come in now? Yes, that's fine, Elizabeth. Do you have your notes there? I'll need your hospital number and address, so we can get your file. Great, thanks."

The ward clerk is already on her feet and walking to take the details from Chloe so that she can collect Elizabeth's main file. All patients have hand-held maternity notes so that they can carry them personally, but we also have a central file containing all of the patients' hospital records here on site.

Chloe comes into the staff room, and announces, "Elizabeth Foster, term, second baby, on her way in. All normal so far. Contracting every four minutes. Membranes intact. Violet."

I don't expect to hear my name and I splutter my tea. Luckily, I don't splash it over my uniform.

"Can you prepare a room for her, please?"

"Sure." I hold back my grin, but I share a quick glance with Jade. She makes a thumbs up sign. I lean to put my mug down on the table.

"Finish that first," Chloe says. "She'll be quarter of an hour, minimum, and you might not get the chance for another drink once she's here."

"I hope not!" I say. I expect that once I have qualified as a midwife and delivery suite shifts become routine, I will be less enthusiastic about the prospect of six hours on my feet without a brew. Today, I want to care for this woman in labour. I want to support Elizabeth and her husband, and I want to finally see a birth.

True to Chloe's estimate, the ward's door buzzer sounds twenty minutes later. Elizabeth's husband speaks into the intercom and Chloe lets them in. Jade looks at me.

"Ready?" she says.

"Absolutely!" I reply.

We walk down the corridor to meet the couple. Elizabeth has made it about six feet into the ward and has had to stop due to getting a contraction.

"Hi," Jade says. "Elizabeth?"

Her husband replies for her. "Hi. I'm Richard." He hands his wife's notes over to Jade and returns to leaning over by her side.

"We'll wait for this contraction to go and then get you into your room."

Elizabeth manages a nod.

"Was that a strong one?" Jade asks, once Elizabeth starts to straighten up.

"They all are now," she says. She is trying to smile, despite her pain.

"Okay. Let's get you to your room. This is Violet, she is a student midwife, working with me today. Do you mind if she watches?"

"I don't mind if everyone in the hospital watches, I just want to get this baby out now."

I can't help but let out a little laugh as we open the door into the delivery room. I'm not sure that I would be able to keep my sense of humour if I were in labour, and it makes me like

Elizabeth instantly.

Jade checks Elizabeth's vitals, listens to the baby's heartbeat and runs through the same questions that Elizabeth answered over the phone. How often are the contractions? How long do they last? How is she coping with the pain?

The pregnancy has been routine, and last time around Elizabeth had a straightforward delivery.

"I only had gas and air," she says. "I thought I was going to need an epidural. I was ready to have just about anything and everything, but it wasn't all that bad."

"And this time? How do you feel?" Jade asks.

"I'm okay so far."

Richard joins in. "The contractions have been getting more painful though. She's gripping my hand harder now."

Jade nods. "Let us know if you do need anything. The gas and air is right here if you want it." She points to the tubing attached to a mouthpiece, waiting by the bed.

"I need this baby to come out, that's what I need." As Elizabeth speaks, another contraction grips her. She bends over, pushing her hands into the mattress. Richard stands by her side and place his hand over hers.

"You are doing great, Liz," he says.

"It. Doesn't. Feel. Great." She speaks the words as she tries to control her breathing.

As she reaches the peak of her contraction, she lets out a guttural groaning noise. Jade's expression changes immediately.

"Do you need to push?" she asks.

I'm amazed at how she can deduce that from the nature of the noise coming from Elizabeth.

"I need to poo. I need to go to the toilet."

"Okay, Elizabeth. After this contraction I am going to listen to baby's heartbeat, and then, if you don't mind, I want to quickly examine you and find out what's happening. I think you might be getting on in labour."

"I need the toilet," she says again.

Jade explains, "I think it might be baby's head pushing down that is making you feel like that. Have you been to the toilet recently?"

"She went at home, before we came out," Richard says.

"Is it okay if I examine you quickly, and then you can pop to the toilet if you need to?"

Elizabeth shuffles out of her leggings, and clambers onto the bed whilst Jade washes her hands.

"Get my nightie out, Rich. Not the one with the bear on, that's for after. The striped one, get that. Thanks, love."

Jade speaks to me whilst Elizabeth gets changed. "I won't ask if you can repeat the examination this time, Violet. I think she is ready to push, and we won't have much time. I might need you to get me a delivery trolley. You remember where everything is?"

On our quiet shift yesterday, Jade showed me where everything is kept, and luckily, I paid attention. I nod. "Sure."

"Looks like you are finally going to see a birth."

Jade sits at the side of the bed next to Elizabeth with her gloves on.

"Okay, just relax and let your legs fall apart and I will be as quick as I can," she says.

Elizabeth has clearly been through this before, as she drops her legs apart and holds onto Richard's hand as Jade examines her.

"Yes, you are fully dilated," Jade says. "Baby's head is well down. Are you getting a contraction now?"

Elizabeth's voice changes as she squeaks, "Yes!"

"I'm going to keep still, alright. Keep breathing. Let me know if you feel like you want to push," Jade says. She turns to me and says, "Violet, get the trolley, please."

I pull the delivery pack from the cupboard and get everything ready on the trolley, just as Jade showed me yesterday.

"I need to pooh!" Elizabeth yells.

"You need to push," Jade says, much more softly. "Hold your breath and push down into your bottom."

I wheel the trolley next to Jade so that she can reach everything that she needs.

"That's brilliant, Elizabeth," I say.

"Keep it coming," Jade tells her.

Elizabeth lets go of her breath and inhales deeply again.

"That's it, Elizabeth. Use all of your contraction to push now. Push against that pain." Jade's voice is so calm and reassuring.

"Is it coming?" Richard asks. He's up next to her head but craning down to see if he can catch sight of anything below.

"I can feel baby moving when you push. You're doing really well. See if you can get three big pushes in with every contraction, and baby will soon be here."

Elizabeth closes her eyes and takes a few deep breaths between contractions.

Jade points at the heartrate monitor, and I press the transducer gently against Elizabeth's abdomen. The machine pounds out a solid, steady heart rate of a hundred and twenty beats per minute.

"That sounds perfect," Jade says.

"It's coming again," Elizabeth says.

"Alright, you know what to do. Take a big breath in and push right down into your bottom. Let's get baby moving."

I stand at the bottom of the bed, next to Jade, and watch. As Elizabeth pushes, the birth canal gapes open slightly, and I can see my first glimpse of the baby's head.

"I can see your baby. You're pushing so well."

"Keep going, Elizabeth."

"Well done, Liz."

With the second push of the contraction, the baby moves even closer towards being born. I can see a five-centimetre diameter of the top of his head now. This is a lot quicker than I thought it would be.

"Nearly there, that's it."

When she pushes for the third time, the

baby's head is almost bursting from the birth canal, and as the contraction ends, the head remains in sight.

"That stings," she says. "Can you get it out?"

"Soon *you* can get your baby out," Jade says. "I'm going to get you to pant with your next contraction, and let your uterus do the work. We're going to take it nice and slowly, and try to make sure you don't tear. Concentrate on panting, and listen to my voice, okay?"

"Okay," Elizabeth says. She sounds breathless. I wonder how it feels to be so close to giving birth, and to have the baby's head pushing against you like that.

The contraction soon starts to build, and as it does, baby's head slowly moves forwards.

"Pant, now. Pant."

Elizabeth takes tiny, short breaths and pants them out. Jade's hand is on the baby's head, controlling it as it crowns.

"Nearly there. Keep panting, keep going."

"Shit!" Elizabeth shouts as her baby's head is born.

"It's okay. You're alright. Baby's head is out now. You're nearly there. Just relax, wait for the next contraction now."

Richard hands his wife the plastic tumbler

and she takes a quick sip of water.

Jade is reaching her finger into the birth canal, feeling around the baby's neck in case the cord is wrapped around it.

When the contraction builds, she tells Elizabeth, "Push now. Let's get baby out."

Elizabeth gives one huge shove, and Jade assists the baby up and out of the birth canal, and into the warm delivery room.

"There you are," she says. "You were amazing."

She takes a quick look at the baby and then passes his up towards his parents.

It all happened so quickly. Elizabeth was controlled and calm, and now, as I watch her look at her newborn baby with tears in her eyes, I can't help letting out a few tears of my own.

# Chapter Twenty-Five

Even though I still have the stress of the OSCE resit hanging over me, once I have finally seen a baby being born, I feel like something has changed. I was already enthusiastic, of course, this is what I have wanted to do for as long as I can remember, but being at the birth has given me an extra push. No pun intended. I can't wait until I can be the one holding out my hands to receive a baby into the world.

I feel like I am settling into university life. Even though I haven't taken any professional support for my anxiety, I feel lighter, more able to cope with whatever life throws at me. It seems I'm not the only one to notice this.

"You're full of the joys of spring," Luke says.

He finally caved and agreed to chip in with the table and chairs for the garden. It's looking great out here. Zoe and I have strung some outdoors fairy lights around the trellis against the wall, and Luke helped us to set up a bird table. At first, I shook out the crumbs from the bottom of the bags when we finished our loaves, but the more birds came to the table, the more I wanted to give. I've started making an extra slice of toast in the mornings just so I can pretend that I can't manage it and bring it out here for our feathered visitors.

Today Luke is taking the role of head chef. We've got a few sausages and burgers and a disposable barbeque on the go. It would be difficult not to be full of those joys today.

"Things are going pretty well right now," I tell him. "Delivery suite has been great; I've passed all of my written assignments so far. All I have to do now is –" I leave the sentence hanging. We have an unspoken agreement in the house that we won't mention my OSCE. Not until I am ready to talk about the resit, anyway. It's getting closer; I've been reading every night, trying to take in everything I need to so that I can pass this time. I have got to start thinking about something else.

It seems to have become cloudier since I started to let my mind focus on my exam. When we came into the garden there was bright sunshine. Zoe is wearing a yellow strappy dress and these amazing cork wedge sandals that she picked up in town last week. I'm, as always, rather less glamourous in a floral sundress that I have owned since I was sixteen. There's a small hole on the hem where the stitching has come loose, but I figure that no one is going to look closely enough to see it. Zoe knows it's there anyway.

Zoe's hair is pinned up into a chunky top bun that looks effortless, but I know that she spends about half an hour achieving that look. She's sitting next to Luke as he flips the sausages, drinking Budweiser straight from the bottle. I used to think that Luke must feel like a third wheel being around the two of us, but now sometimes it feels like I am the piggy in the middle.

It's May bank holiday. The end of the month; the end of my delivery suite placement. There are four weeks in uni coming up. In less than two weeks tine I will be resitting my OSCE.

It seems that no matter how hard I try to keep smiling and not think about it, the resit creeps into my thoughts.

A large wet splat falls onto the concrete in front of me, and I look up at the sky. Above, where there had been clear skies, is now a heavy grey blanket of cloud.

"Rain," I say flatly.

"You sure?" Zoe says. I don't think she even noticed that the sun had gone in.

I hold out my hand and let a few thick

droplets of water pad down onto my palm.

There's a loud crash of thunder, and the sky opens.

"I am now," I say.

"Sod it." Luke puts the tongs down onto the tea towel by his side. My mind is so used to thinking midwifery thoughts that for a moment I picture them as forceps. I haven't seen them used in practice yet, but Jade let me hold some. They are strictly for the doctors to use, and I am relieved that I won't ever have that responsibility.

"Are we going in then?" Zoe is up on her feet, holding her cardigan over her head.

"Go on. I'll bring this indoors. Or I'll bring the food inside anyway." Luke makes a shooing motion with his hands, and the two of us push the door and go back into the kitchen.

Although I know it's a ridiculous thought, a part of me thinks for the flash of a second that I caused the weather to turn by thinking about my exam. I was happy and smiling and we were all having a great time, until my mind started to wander. I am not superstitious, but after bottling it in the last exam I feel somehow cursed. I said it was ridiculous.

"What's up?" Zoe says.

The two of us sit at the kitchen table, waiting for Luke to gather up the food from outside and bring it in.

"Nothing."

I can see him sliding the burgers off the grill onto a plate.

"Sure," she says. "I know it's not just the fact that we can't sit outside and eat our burnt food. Is it me?"

"What? Why would it be you?"

"Talking to Luke. I mean, am I talking to him too much and not talking to you?"

This has come out of nowhere. It's been six weeks since we came back here after Easter, and as far as I can tell Zoe has still not made her move. The two of them seem no closer to being together than they did before the Christmas holidays.

"Do you think you were?" I ask.

"So, you do," she says. "You *do* think that."

"Not at all. I didn't say that. What I mean is, do you feel like you are talking to him too much? Is that how you feel?"

"I don't know," she says. "At first, maybe. I get so self-conscious now. Like I want to impress him, or say the right thing, or at least not say the wrong thing. I feel like I am waiting for something to happen."

He's putting the sausages into a pile, waving one hand over his head in a futile attempt to bat away the falling rain.

"Do you think it's time to make something happen?"

She waves her hands in a dramatic shrug. "I don't want to rush things. I don't want to spoilt things happening naturally."

"This is what you said before Easter, and you were mortified when you thought you had lost him."

"It's not like he is out every night looking for women. He spends his evenings either with us or with the lads, and Raj, Flo and Damon are hardly womanisers."

If there's one thing that can distract me from thinking about my exam it's Zoe's prevaricating. I have often wondered if one of the reasons that I wanted a job in a caring profession is that while I am helping and supporting other people, I don't have time to worry about myself. I don't stress out and panic while I am focussing on being there for others. It's only when I stew on my own problems that they start to eat away at me. Anxiety can only hurt me because it overpowers me; it consumes my thoughts, replacing everything else.

Zoe picks up her bottle and picks at the label. I guess she is trying not to think about the thing that is stressing her out too. Actually telling Luke how she feels will be a massive step, I understand that.

"All I am saying is that I think you should be sure about what you want. And if you are sure, then don't let him get away."

She nods wordlessly and tips her head in the direction of the door to alert me to Luke coming through. Each of his hands is carrying a plate piled high with the food he was cooking.

"That went well," he says.

Luke grins, and I can almost hear Zoe sigh next to me. His hair is plastered to his head now, and his t-shirt is clinging to his chest.

He puts the food down on the countertop then he says, "I'd better dry up and get changed. I guess we can cook this here and just pretend we are having a barbie."

Zoe pushes her chair back and gets to her feet. "I'll put the oven on and stick these in. You go and sort yourself out."

He reaches out to ruffle her hair, and then stops awkwardly, his hand in mid-air as he realises it's a tough job with her bun pinned up as it is. Instead he ends up patting her gently and she taps her hand against his wet chest in a mock *'get off me'* gesture.

Not that I know anything about relationships, but I am fairly certain that this is flirtatious behaviour on both sides. Awkward and badly co-ordinated, but flirtatious all the same.

# Chapter Twenty-Six

My placement ends on the last day of May, and I have the weekend blocked out to focus on revision. I may have tried to stop myself from getting worked up about the exam until now, but the circle that I have drawn on my calendar is glaring out at me from the moment I get out of bed.

The plan is this: Zoe and Luke are going into town for the morning. Whilst they are out, I am going to go through everything I have learned about my scenarios. When they come back, Luke is going to play act the patient, and Zoe is going to be the tutor. Of course, I asked Zoe to be the patient again, but she had this gem of an idea.

"Someone should watch to check you are saying all the right things, covering all the bases and that," she said.

It made sense.

"And if someone else is there apart from me the stress of the situation will be more real for you. You're hardly going to be shitting yourself if it's just the two of us. You need to practice how you are going to behave, not just what you are going to say."

That made even more sense.

What I should have done is call up one of the girls from my class, or Simon of course, and ask them to come over and help me. I could have done that. Zoe has been so helpful though, and I kind of want to do this for her. I want her to see how much she helps me. Not just by supporting me and letting me practice with her, but her general presence. She is a calming influence. I only wish she could be there at the exam with me.

I was going to ask one of my course mates to come and be a mock patient for me, but Luke overheard Zoe and I talking, and that's how I ended up with a six-foot-tall man with stubble as my pretend pregnant woman.

I make coffee and then sit at my desk and focus. This is my last chance to nail it before the test this week. I would rather have had the exam first thing Monday morning instead of having to get through the week of lectures.

I read through all of the sections in Myles Midwifery that relate to the possible scenarios. I check through my lecture notes and flick through the slides on the virtual learning environment. I turn away from the desk and speak into the empty room, telling my bed and the door what I would do in each of the potential role play situations. The thing is, I know all of the information that I need to know. I have the facts indelibly imprinted in my brain. It feels like basic, fundamental knowledge to me now. When I first stood outside the skills lab waiting to go in to take the exam, my mind was blank. Now I can't imagine everything that I have learned by heart being so difficult to access from my brain. It's not that I don't know what to do or what to say. The problem is staying calm for long enough to be able to do and say it.

When the others get home, I run downstairs to meet them. Zoe hands me a takeaway cup from Blackheath's containing a still-hot latte.

"We went there last," she smiles.

"You went there without me!" I say.

"I don't even like coffee, but that's a great place." Luke is carrying two bags of groceries and he squeezes past to get to the kitchen.

"Anything exciting happen?" I ask when he is out of earshot. Zoe shakes her head, and I shrug and smile. I don't know what else to say right now.

"How did you get on with the cramming?" she says.

"I think I have stuffed all of the info into my tiny brain," I say. "Now I need to find the secret formula for getting it out again when I need it…without letting anxiety mess it up for me."

Luke rests his hand firmly on my shoulder.

"I'm ready to be your patient," he says. "The things we do for friends, eh?"

"Thanks," I say. "I appreciate this. I owe you one."

He smiles. "When I need someone to act as a client for an accountancy role play, I will let you know."

Somehow, he always manages to lighten the atmosphere. I can see why Zoe likes him. Fortunately, we have never been attracted to the same type, but I am glad that he is my friend.

We go into the sitting room to run through our role plays, or at least Zoe and Luke go in, and I stand in the hallway. It's the anxiety that I have to get over. The worst part for me will be standing in the corridor, waiting to go in for my exam, taking the card, and getting started. When I get going I will be able to trick my mind into thinking that I am in a real clinical setting, I know I will, and when that happens, my anxiety won't be able to hurt me.

I asked Zoe to let me wait in the hall for a couple of minutes before we start. I want to feel the build-up, and train myself to cope with it. Even here, at home, knowing that I am going into my own living room to work through a scenario with my two friends, my pulse is pounding. The bottom line is that I know how important this exam is. I know what is at stake. I practice slowing my breath, focusing my thoughts. I feel that nervous twitch gripping my body, the creeping cold of anxiety thundering through my veins. I let it build. I let myself feel the anxiety that I know I will feel in six days' time when I have to do this for real.

And then

I let it go.

I breathe deeply.

I concentrate on the tension in my body.

I focus on my heartrate, commanding myself to be calm, to relax.

Negative thoughts flood my brain. I can't do it. I'm going to fail again. I'm going to fail the year.

And I think

No.

Not this time.

I can do this.

Those four words, *"I can do this",* sound so similar to the words that I have told myself so many times before. Until now, it has always been the reverse, the negative. *I can't do this. I can't.*

Not this time.

I know that this isn't the end of anxiety for me, but as I push open the door, it isn't fear that I feel, it is self-confidence.

I pick up a card from the coffee table, and I run through the scenario.

I *can* do this.

# Chapter Twenty-Seven

If I was worried about the week dragging, I need not have been. Friday morning comes around in a flash. There's only one other student resitting apart from me. No waiting around for my turn, no time to stand in the corridor letting the anxiety bubble within me.

Rachel comes to let me in.

"Good morning, Violet. Leave your bag by the door and, when you're ready, go and choose your first scenario. Bridget Brody is the second marker today. I don't think you know her, but she will be leading one of your second-year modules."

Second year. If I make it through.

I nod, silently, take a deep breath and go through the door. I allow myself one look over to where the other lecturer and the actress are sitting.

The woman playing the part of the patient isn't the same as the one who was here last time. I'm thankful for that. I don't know if I could have handled seeing her again after I messed up so badly before. The tutors have seen other students in other years struggle through this exam, but having a stranger, someone from the outside world, see me like that was mortifying.

There are six cards face-down on the table, just like last time. However, this time I don't spend minutes trying to decide which card to take. This time, I reach out, let my hand fall upon whichever scenario fate decides to give me, and I turn it over immediately.

Antenatal. Okay. That's got to be good. The woman is thirty-six weeks pregnant, and I am seeing her for an antenatal appointment. It's her first baby, everything has been normal so far, but today her blood pressure is 145/100.

High blood pressure. I can do this. I close my eyes for a few moments. I'm trying to imagine myself in the antenatal clinic, trying to picture Stacey, way back in those first weeks, showing me the basics. Blood pressure checks are routine. Knowing what to do when the results are abnormal is a basic midwifery skill. I can do this.

I open my eyes, focus upon the woman, and walk over to where she and my two tutors are waiting.

Rachel checks the scenario that I chose and shows it to the woman and the other tutor. Both of them nod.

J.E. ROWNEY

"I have some additional information here for you," Rachel says. She reaches onto the table beside her and hands me some paperwork. There's a partially completed pregnancy record, and a chart that we refer to as a MEOWS chart. It's nothing to do with cats; it's a Modified Early Obstetric Warning Score, used on maternity wards to record vital signs and physiological observations. They are similar to the notes and charts that I have been working with on my placements. They feel recognisable and the familiarity is comforting.

I can feel my own pulse pounding, and my blood pressure may well be as high as the subject in the scenario by now, but I breathe, and I focus. Even though my skin is prickling, and my mind is racing, I bring myself back to the present moment.

Rachel has a concerned expression; perhaps she thinks I am going to mess this up again. We both know what is at stake. I can't fail.

"Are you ready to begin?" she asks.

I suck in a breath, look at the scenario, and at the paperwork in my hand, and then nod.

"Yes. Let's go."

As soon as I start the mock-assessment of the

238

patient my instincts take over. I can feel my heart beating double time, thudding against my chest wall, but as soon as I become aware of it, I concentrate on slowing my breathing, calming myself, focussing on the scenario. There's no room for self-doubt. I have to give this everything I have got.

I greet the actress as though she is really my patient, and I carry out the observations just as I would if I were with Stacey out in community. As I am talking to the woman, I feel my fear slipping away. The more I concentrate on what I am doing the less chance my anxiety has to wheedle its way in.

I write in the notes, detailing and documenting everything to the letter. I know exactly what I should do, and I do it.

I'm sure that the lecturers are meant to remain impartial, but I am aware of Rachel smiling at me and nodding as I fill in the MEOWS chart and sign my name.

When I have completed the second scenario and it is time to leave, I know that I have done my best and I am as confident as I can be that I have passed this time. I have studied and I have rehearsed, but most of all I have learned something about myself. I have learned to listen to my body, to listen to my mind, but more than that, I have learned to not always believe what they tell me.

I can do this. I can.

# Chapter Twenty-Eight

With the OSCE behind me there are six weeks left of term. I have two assignments to hand in, and a four-week placement on the antenatal ward. I already feel like I am starting to wind down for the year. I won't actually get my OSCE results until the end of the month, but I don't need to see the number on the screen to know what I need to know. I have passed. Rachel as much as told me that before I left the skills lab. I guess she didn't want me to have to go through any more stress about the exam. I can forget about the OSCE… until we have our second next year. Right now, I feel invincible.

Zoe has placements until the end of term. Apparently it's a good time for her to be out in school. The Year Elevens are finishing their exams, the Year Tens are excited about coming back for their final year of GCSEs. I don't remember being quite as thrilled as Zoe describes it, but I am feeling something of that buzz now. I have made it through the year; I can't wait to start again in October. Now that I have made it through the resit, I can relax and enjoy the rest of term.

My antenatal placement begins at the start of July. From the outset, I feel like I am winding down towards the two months of summer holidays. I'm not sure what I am going to do with myself for all of those weeks away from here. Tangiers Court feels like home now. That said, it's not a certainty yet that we will return to the house that we have come to love.

I am sitting on the sofa, with Zoe next to me, her legs stretched across my lap, Luke is on one of the armchairs. It's a standard evening here: television, coffee, and conversation.

"Not that I don't want a holiday," Zoe says, "but being back with my parents is going to be weird."

"Your parents are down the road," Luke smiles. "You could go home every night if you wanted to. If you think that is going to be weird, try spending the summer in Leeds."

"Sounds exotic," I say. I've never been any further north than Bristol, so in a way Yorkshire *is* exotic to me.

When we first came here I thought I would be on the phone to my mum all the time, driving her nuts by wanting to go home every weekend. She and I were a team, the two of us, through all of the crappy times she had with my dad. Leaving home and coming here though, I feel like it's given us both the space we needed. Mum's socialising now, always telling me about the book club she's joined or the friends she is meeting up with from work. She never did any of that when I was at home. Perhaps I am going to be in the way when I go back.

"Do you girls have anything exciting planned?" Luke asks.

That phrase 'you girls' instantly makes me think of my father, and the way he used to talk down to Mum and me. It feels like I have been burying my thoughts of home and of the past few years while I have been here, kind of out of sight and out of mind. Now that I am thinking about going home, they are all flooding back.

"Spend some time with my mum," I say.

"Yeah, and catch up with some of our friends who are off at uni all over the place, hopefully," Zoe adds.

There aren't that many people that I am bothered about seeing, but Zoe always had more friends than I did. She likes to keep in touch, whereas I tend to let go. I'm happy spending my time with Zoe, I don't feel the need to keep up with anyone else. I wonder if

Luke lives somewhere else next year whether I
will lose touch with him too.

"Are you planning on living with the lads
next year?" Zoe asks. She slips in the question
like it means nothing to her, but I know that it
means so much.

He shrugs and takes a drink from his mug.
"Haven't thought about it," he says. He doesn't
make eye contact when he speaks. I wonder if
he is telling the truth.

Zoe flashes me a look, as if looking for
backup, but I really don't know what to say.
Her plan of waiting for things to happen
between them doesn't seem to be getting her
anywhere. They obviously get on well, and I am
sure that he flirts with her just as much as she
does with him, but perhaps that's just the kind
of person he is. If she isn't going to make a
move, maybe nothing will ever happen.

"We haven't started looking yet," I say. "I'd
like to stay here, I think."

I try to make it sound casual, but Zoe and I
have spoken about it at length. Our ideal
scenario sees Luke, Zoe and I staying at
Tangiers Court, and the fourth bedroom staying
empty. Not that I wouldn't like to see some
geeky-but-gorgeous guy move in with us, but I

think I would rather have the extra space in the house than the extra complication in my life.

Luke nods silently and focuses on the television. As we have been talking throughout most of the episode that's playing it feels like he is avoiding the topic rather than actually watching the programme. Zoe chose this one; it's some cookery competition where the guests have to try and make their creations look, and taste, like the ones that a professional has made earlier. They always come out looking like abominations, but that's what makes it fun. I can identify with those bakers, and a part of me probably identifies with the cakes too: always trying to be what I am *supposed* to be, but never quite getting there.

The three of us sit without saying another word until the end of the episode. Then Luke gets to his feet.

"Anyone want another drink or anything while I'm up?"

Zoe and I both shake our heads.

"Be back in a minute then. Start the next one if you want."

He leaves the room, and walks down the hall to the bathroom. I watch him go into the room and close the door, and then I speak to Zoe.

"Are you going to say something, or –"

"I don't want to spoil things," she says in a hushed tone. "This is all so perfect. I feel like if I say something and he's not into me, I'm going to mess everything up."

I tighten my lips and frown. "It's up to you, but what if this is it? What if he moves out next month? You'll hardly see him. You might never see him."

"You really think he isn't going to stay here? You saw him, just as clearly as I did. He says he hasn't thought about it, but I think it's pretty obvious…"

Luke's footsteps pad back down the hallway; I put my finger to my lips to hush Zoe.

He settles back into his chair.

"I'll message the landlord and see if this place is even available for next year," I say. "Just let us know when you decide what you want. I mean, what you want to do."

I feel Zoe give me a little kick of her leg against my thigh and Luke looks over at me.

"Sure," he says.

I'm not convinced that trying to be subtle is going to prompt either of them to make a move, but sitting on the side lines, watching them, I feel like I have to do something.

# Chapter Twenty-Nine

I settle into my antenatal ward placement easily. I think, in part, it's because I don't have the worry of university work to think about. So far, I have had the option of following the night shift pattern of my mentors or plumping to stick to daytime and working with someone else. With only two weeks left of the academic year, all my coursework handed in and nothing planned on my social calendar it seems like as good a time as any to volunteer for the night shift.

I can't imagine that much exciting happens on the antenatal ward at night. Most of the women with pregnancy complications have the same sleep-wake patterns as anyone else. By the time we have taken handover at half past eight, conducted the routine observations, circled the ward with medications and again with bedtime drinks and snacks, almost everyone is settling down to sleep.

By ten o'clock the lights are dimmed, and my mentor, the second and only other midwife on shift, Caroline, and I are sitting in the midwives' office, mugs of tea in our hands.

It's a good opportunity for me to go through

my PAD, making sure it's up to date, and having Becky sign off some of my competencies.

A call bell buzzes out from the darkened bays.

"I'll go," I offer. Becky nods, and I get up and walk out into the ward.

I have to look for where the call is coming from. The first bay to my left is dark and silent. In the second, one of the women has her lamp on, reading a Kindle, but she smiles as I pass by. At the bottom of the ward, I find two women sitting together; Jackie, a third-time mum with high blood pressure that we are monitor is rubbing her hand on the lower back of Carla, a primip who came in leaking fluid this evening. It looks like her waters have definitely broken, but up until now she wasn't getting any pains.

I silence the buzzer.

"Are you okay? What's happening?"

Jackie speaks. "She's getting contractions. She didn't want to bother you, but I told her to buzz. They are regular now. Every three minutes."

Carla nods, but says nothing. She's eighteen, single, and she looks terrified.

"It's alright," I say. "It's going to be alright. When did they start?"

Jackie starts to answer, but I nod towards Carla.

"I don't know," she says. "They started getting stronger, more regular after I lay down. I tried to ignore it and go to sleep, but they're…"

Her sentence is interrupted by the onset of another contraction. Jackie runs her hand in circles on Carla's back.

"Can I feel?" I ask. She nods, and I place my hand, softly, onto the top of her uterus, palpating the contraction. I feel her abdomen stiffen beneath my palm, the tight grip of the contraction hard against my hand. "Breathe slowly, deeply. In and out. Nice and easy. Okay, that's it." She is doing a great job of staying calm, but I can see the discomfort in her face.

"Do you need some pain relief?"

She shakes her head briskly and resolutely.

As soon as the contraction has passed, she takes a few more deep breaths and then says "I wanted to go without. I don't want anything."

"Okay," I say. "You can ask for some any time that you want to." She nods. "How about a couple of paracetamol for a start? It sometimes helps with the early pains."

"No." She says it sharply, and then adds, "Thank you."

"That's fine." I say. "Can I have a quick listen to your baby's heartbeat, please? Check how he or she…"

"He," she smiles.

"Check how he is getting on with these contractions."

"Sure," she says.

Jackie stands up, but Carla grabs out for her hand and pulls her back. "Please stay," she says.

Jackie looks to me for approval and I nod. "Of course."

Carla lays back so that I can palpate her abdomen and find the position of the baby. His head is well down. He's lying with his back to Carla's side. Everything is normal. As I am about to put the fetal heart transducer onto her abdomen she starts to have another contraction.

"Would you feel better sitting?" I pull her up, and Jackie resumes her support. I unobtrusively listen in to the baby's heart rate while Carla breathes through the contraction.

It's slower than it should be.

Instead of the rapid thudding that I should

hear, the heartbeat thuds away at around a hundred beats per minute. I try not to show my concern, and I reach up to palpate Carla's pulse rate, to check that it's not her heartbeat that I am auscultating.

As the contraction eases up, the heart rate speeds back to a normal rate. One hundred and twenty-five beats per minute. That's more like it.

Carla is sitting on the edge of the bed again now. That dip in the heart rate. It isn't normal. I need to fetch Becky to listen and check her over. What do I do next? It feels like the OSCE all over again, but this time for real. I don't panic though. There's not a shred of anxiety.

"Carla. Baby's heartbeat slowed down a little but when you had your contraction then. I'm going to pop and get my supervisor to have a listen, okay?"

I don't want to start talking about all of the reasons that a baby's heart rate might drop. It could be position, it could be compression of the umbilical cord, there could be something more serious at work. I don't have the knowledge or confidence yet to make this judgement, so I do exactly what I should do, I ask Carla to lie on her left side, and I hurry to fetch Becky.

My supervisor comes immediately and confirms the details that I have gathered.

The contractions are strong and regular.

Becky talks to Carla in a reassuring tone. "If it's okay with you, I want to check how far dilated you are, and listen in to baby. If you're in labour, we'll get you upstairs to delivery suite. If your baby's heartrate keeps dropping with the contractions, you're going to need to be transferred up so we can keep an eye on him and get one of the doctors to find out what's going on."

"Do you want me to go?" Jackie asks.

Carla shakes her head. She looks scared, but she lies back on the bed so that Becky can examine her.

I don't ask whether I can practice my skills too. It's not the right time.

Becky washes her hands and puts on her gloves. She sits at the side of the bed and slicks her fingers with lubricating jelly.

"Bring your legs up and let them flop apart at the knees," Becky says.

Carla keeps her eyes focussed on Jackie, up the top end of the bed.

"Okay, okay. Let me know if you get a contraction and I will keep still." Becky gently slides her fingers into the birth canal, and there are a few seconds where a look of concentration fixes upon her face, as she feels for the cervix. "Are you starting to get a contraction now?" she asks.

Carla nods and starts to breathe deeply, blowing out her exhalations. Her left hand is gripping Jackie's, her right is grasping the bottom sheet.

"Are you getting any pressure in your bottom?" Becky asks. My eyes widen at the question. Is she this far on?

Carla frantically bobs her head. "Yes. I think I need to go to the toilet."

"It's baby's head pressing down on your bottom. It's okay." Becky nods towards the heart rate monitor in my hand and then to Carla's abdomen, and I take the hint. The heart rate is still dipping.

"Baby is on his way," Becky says. "The heart rate is dropping because he is getting squashed on his way down. Sometimes the cord can get trapped a little bit so it's more difficult for baby to get all of the oxygen he needs." She withdraws her fingers. "Violet, ask Caroline to call the junior obstetrician; tell her what's happening and bring a delivery pack."

"Don't I need to go upstairs?" Carla says.

"I think you are too far on for that. We'll get a doctor down, just in case. And I need to pop you on the monitor. Baby's heartbeat is picking up between contractions but…"

I'm on my way to the office so I don't hear the rest of the explanation. This wasn't what I expected for my first night shift. Caroline is looking through a magazine at the desk and looks up sharply as I run through everything that I must remember to tell her.

"Thanks, Violet," she says. She picks up the phone to call the obstetrician.

On the way back to Carla's bed, I pick up the delivery pack from the storeroom. Should I ask Becky if I can deliver the baby? I've seen my quota; I could do this. On the antenatal ward though? There's not a proper delivery bed. These are the flat, regular hospital type, they don't have electronic risers to lift the backrests, they don't come apart in the middle so that you can sit between the woman's legs as you prepare to catch the baby. Are those things necessary?

I wheel a trolley over and start to open the

delivery pack for my supervisor.

"I can see the top of baby's head when you get the contractions," Becky says, giving Carla a reassuring smile. She's managed to link the cardiotocograph machine up to measure the heart rate and contractions, and I can see the short, sharp deceleration of the heart rate on the tracing with the contraction. As soon as the contraction ends, the heart rate picks back up to a regular, variable beat within normal limits.

"Caroline is letting the doctors know, and she's told sister on delivery suite too."

Becky nods. "Thanks." She turns to Carla. "You're nearly there, okay? You're doing so well."

I'm amazed at how little noise Carla is making despite being so far advanced in labour. I don't think I would be able to be this quiet.

"Violet is at the end of her first year of training," Becky says, and I know what is coming next. I feel a flushed thrill through my body. "Would you mind if I supervised her to help you deliver your baby?"

Carla shakes her head. "No." My thrill thuds to a full stop but then she adds. "No. I don't mind."

I can't control my grin. I pull a pair of gloves

from the bottom of the trolley, and quickly head to wash my hands so that I can prepare.

I set up the equipment, and Becky moves from the edge of the bed to allow me to sit.

"It's not going to be much longer, Carla. Are you feeling that urge to push?"

"Yes. Really bad."

"When you get your next contraction, take a big deep breath in, and hold it. Use that to push right down into your bottom."

"I might poo myself." She laughs nervously.

"I think I pooed myself with both of mine," Jackie says. "They've seen it all before." She indicates Becky and me, and I smile.

"It's all normal. If you do, it means you must be pushing well. Try not to think about it. Definitely don't worry about it."

She doesn't have time to say anything else, because the next contraction starts.

"Big deep breath," I say. "And push. Hold it as long as you can. Perfect." The brown hair on top of the baby's head moves closer to me. I'm sitting back, watching the baby, watching Carla, watching the heartrate. No dip this time. I look at Becky and point to the monitor. She nods and makes a mark in Carla's notes.

"Well done, Carla, that's great. And again."

She grits her teeth and gives it everything she's got. All my focus is directed upon the present moment. I don't have any thoughts of my own feelings, all that exists in this instant is Carla, and her baby.

"One more push before your contraction ends," I tell her, and she does it. She pushes in one extended effort, and when she lets it go and flops back into the pillows the baby's head stays, more of it visible now.

Becky has a towel ready at the side of me. Before the next contraction starts, a head pops around the corner of the curtain around the bay.

"Hi, I'm on call tonight," the doctor says. "How are we doing?"

My supervisor turns to talk to him and fills him in on the details. He looks at the heart rate tracing and nods.

"Looks like baby is ready to come out, Carla," he says. "I'm going to stay here a little while, and see what's happening, but I think as long as you push him out soon everything is going to be fine."

Carla is in no position to have a conversation right now.

"Okay, Carla?" I say. "Everything is fine.

You can do this. A few more pushes like the last ones when you get your next contraction. Are you comfortable? Do you need to sit up more?"

She has slouched a little in the bed, it's not so easy with these flat bases as it is with the beds on delivery suite to help her into a comfortable position.

"I'm okay," she breathes.

Another contraction starts.

"Go on, Carla," the doctor says. "Show me how well you can push."

I want to keep leading the delivery, but I feel less confident with the doctor and midwife both watching.

"That's it," I say. I start to get caught back up in the birth. "Perfect, Carla. Big breath. Push. Hold on to it, keep it coming. Amazing." I don't have to think of the words because they come out easily. She is amazing. This is amazing.

Three more tremendous pushes, and the baby's head is almost crowning. When Carla relaxes at the end of the contraction, I pat her on the hand to make sure I have her attention.

"Next time, I need you to give me a big push again, but I need you to listen to me carefully. Baby's head is nearly out, and I am going to tell you when to stop pushing, and just breathe in shallow, tiny pants like a dog, okay?" I demonstrate. "It's going to help baby to come out more slowly, so that you don't tear."

She nods quickly. "Okay," she says. "I need a drink."

Jackie passes her the plastic cup from the bedside unit. She takes a few quick sips, and then it is time to concentrate on one of the final contractions.

I have my fingers on the top of the baby's head now, flexing as I have seen done by the midwives before.

Becky leans over me, putting her hand over mine, feeling to make sure that I am doing everything as I should. "That's great," she whispers to me. "You're doing great. You okay?" I nod and smile and focus on Carla.

"Big push. And…okay stop pushing, just breathe now. Tiny breaths. Pant, pant, pant."

The baby's head moves slowly into my hand, and suddenly in one bursting movement, the whole head emerges from the birth canal.

"Head's out, Carla. Well done. Just relax now. Wait for the next contraction, and baby will be here."

The baby's face is all squashed up, his lips

puckered, eyes tightly shut. He's covered in blood and fluid, and I gently reach down by the side of his neck, feeling for any sign of umbilical cord around his neck. I feel it. A shiny smooth loop wrapped around him.

"There's cord around his neck," I say to my supervisor.

"Slip your finger between the cord and his neck," she says, and I do it. "Good. Now slide it up and over his head. That's it."

It slides easily and I smile in relief. "No problem, Carla. That's probably what was upsetting him a little earlier."

The contraction comes more slowly this time, and it feels like an age that I am sitting, looking at the baby's head, waiting for the contraction that will bring the rest of the baby into the world. Finally, Carla grunts, and starts to push.

"Guide the shoulders, Violet," Becky reminds me.

I gently assist the baby through the last stages of his journey into the world. His shoulder passes easily beneath Carla's pelvic bone and with one last huge push, she becomes a mother.

A perfect, healthy baby boy lies on the towel in front of me. Pink, soft and a little goo-covered, but absolutely perfect.

I look up at Carla through the emotional tears that I can't hold back.

"Is he okay?" she asks.

"He is awesome." I wrap him loosely in the towel and pass him up so that she can press her son against her skin.

"Good work ladies," the doctor says. He signs his name on the CTG trace and backs out of the bed space.

"Well done, Carla," Becky says. She looks at me and mouths "Well done, Violet."

All I can do is grin. "I didn't do anything," I say. "It was all Carla."

# Chapter Thirty

Catching the bus back to Tangiers Court the morning after my first night shift, I am barely able to keep my eyes open. It's only the last waves of excitement rippling through me that keep me focussed. The bus is hot and full; there are a mixture of hospital staff leaving work and making their way back home, to their beds, mostly as tired-looking as I am, and day workers heading into town for their nine-to-fives. I'll probably never know what it is like to live that life. I will always be heading to or from work at unsociable hours, waking up at six in the morning or six at night, working weekends when my friends are partying, putting in evening shifts when Zoe is at home watching television.

It strikes me that she might have already left for the day by the time I get back to the house. I need to sleep, but I want to spill out all the details about how I, Violet Cobham, have delivered a baby. It's a massive, emotional milestone, and I want to share it with Zoe.

I check my phone. It's nearly eight o'clock. Her first alarm will be going off on the hour; I'm sure it's not too early to text her.

I tap in a message

**I did it! I delivered a baby!!!! xx**

I'm about to press SEND when I change my mind. I want to tell her in person. I want to see the look on her face when she hears my news.

I rest my head against the window, and smile to myself, and I don't care who sees me do it.

Ten minutes later I bundle through the front door, throw my keys into the bowl on the table and race up to her room.

"Zoe! Zoe! Zoe!" I sing the words as I take the stairs two at a time.

I burst in through her bedroom door and find her, still lying in bed. I can't stop myself though. I launch myself onto her and wrap her up in a huge hug.

"I delivered my first baby!"

Zoe lets out a whooping noise and throws her arms back around me.

The two of us lie side-by-side on her bed making excited sounds, while I try to share the whole story with her.

Luke is on his way downstairs, and he stops to pop his head into the room.

"Oh yes?" he says, with a smile. The two of us snuggled up on Zoe's bed must be quite a sight.

"She delivered a baby!" Zoe shrieks.

"Nice work, Violet," he says. "Do I get to join in the hug too?"

"Maybe not on my bed," Zoe says. I wink at her, and she starts to blush.

"Come on," I say, getting to my feet and reaching my arms towards him.

Zoe drags herself up and joins in, and we spend the next five minutes wrapped up in the best group hug that I have ever experienced.

The curtains in my room are thin, and the excitement pumping through me is intense. It's hard to get to sleep, but once Luke and Zoe have left for the day, I finally drift off.

By the time Zoe gets home at just before five I've slept a few hours, but probably not quite as many as I would have liked. As soon as I hear her, I sit up and throw my feet onto the floor.

"Zo!" I call out into the landing.

"Vi, Vi, Vi," she shouts as she runs up and throws herself into my room.

More quietly she asks, "is he home?"

I shake my head. "Just us."

She grabs hold of me and we hug again.

"You delivered a baby!" she says. "How

amazing. Tell me all about it. I thought you were on antenatal. What happened?"

I stumble downstairs in my pyjamas and sit at the kitchen table with her. She makes her dinner and I have my breakfast. The future is going to be filled with days like this, but I can't imagine that any of them will be quite this exciting.

I didn't feel the tiniest trace of anxiety. I focused on Carla, on the baby, on what I had to do to make sure she had a positive, happy, safe delivery. That was all that mattered to me. It wasn't like I was running on autopilot, I'm far too inexperienced for that, but something powered me on, leading me through everything I had to remember, everything I had to do. If I was on autopilot, I might have parroted off the words that I thought I should say, but I didn't.

Everything about the birth was natural and easy, not just for Carla, but for me too. Becky supported me to do my best. I knew she was there, but she didn't intrude, she let me take the lead. I make a mental note to tell her tonight how much I appreciate that. The silent support meant so much.

It's getting towards the end of year, it will soon be time for the holidays, three long months before I return. Seeing a birth has been an amazing climax, but now I don't want the year to finish.

# Chapter Thirty-One

I wrap up the final chapter of my first year as a student midwife with one last three-way meeting between my antenatal mentor and my link tutor. It's the last week of my placement. I'm flicking through my PAD, reading through the comments that I have left along the way and the notes made by my sign-off mentors.

It's amazing how much I have managed to pack into one year. Looking back to that first day in class, months ago when I walked into the lecture block. I hadn't even got my uniform. All I had was excitement, tinged with fear and apprehension, and laced with a little of that self-doubt that is my signature ingredient. But despite everything, the ups and downs of the year, I have made it through.

I finish my shift and Becky and I head into the office to meet with Deb.

"Good to see you, Violet. How has it been going?"

I'm all smiles. I've enjoyed every placement this year, but antenatal has turned out to be my favourite. Not necessarily because I got to deliver a baby, but I feel like I have had time here to talk to women, to spend time with them and make a difference to their experience. Isn't that what my motivation has always been?

"I love my antenatal placement," I tell her. "I think I have learned a lot."

Becky nods. "It's been great having Violet here. The women have given a lot of positive feedback." I can feel my heart pounding, not with anxiety, not now. This is pride. This is the flip side of fear.

I have learned such a lot this year. Not just about starting to become a midwife, but also about myself, and about what I can achieve if I put my mind to it.

When I get back to Tangiers Court, Zoe runs to meet me. I can see from the look on her face that she has been waiting for me to get home.

"Did you get a text from the landlord?" Zoe asks.

She's almost jumping up and down with excitement.

I did get the message. He wants to know whether we want to renew the contract for the next academic year. The house is available, it's up to us whether we stay. Tangiers Court feels like home now. It's ideally located for the bus ride to my placements, and not far for Zoe to travel to hers. Uni is a ten-minute walk. I can't imagine that we would be able to find anywhere better. It's roomy, comfortable and, well, it's our home. Of course, we want to stay.

"Yes! Good news! I'm so glad we get another year," I say.

"I love it here." She grins and takes both of my hands in hers. "I'm so glad we get to stay."

We jump up and down like excited kids. When we settle back to our seats, I ask the million-dollar question.

"What about Luke?"

She shrugs.

"I haven't asked him yet. Has he said anything more about it? He hasn't said anything to me. He might have had enough of us. He might want to go and live with Rash, Florian and Damon." Her voice is an excited garble.

It's possible though. Just because we have lived together this year doesn't mean that he will necessarily want to keep living with us.

"I'll ask him," she says, and that seems like the most straightforward approach. "I want us to all stay here, to be just the way we are right now. I want to carry on doing placements, and, well, I don't really care about lectures, and I particularly don't care about assignments, but apart from that, I don't want anything to change. I want this. This here. Just this."

The words spill out of her in a fast, furious deluge, and she stops at the end, breathless.

"Oh Zo. I want that too."

As I finish speaking, Luke's key turns in the lock and he calls in from the hall.

"Have you told him we are staying?"

Zoe looks at me, and beams.

Luke comes straight into the living room and sits down next to Zoe.

"We were just talking about it," Zoe says.

"Yeah, I thought you might prefer to move in with the cool boys rather than hang around with us two for another year."

"As if I would choose to live with a bunch of accountants when I could be with you," he says.

I wonder if he always knew that he would stay, or whether he was waiting to see what happened with Zoe? Or whether his friends asked him to live with them? I really don't know.

"I'll check with Andrew if he is staying too." I laugh, and then I stop myself. "What if someone does move into that room next year? I mean, they must, someone has to move in, surely?"

"The landlord won't keep it empty for two years," Zoe says. "He must be losing a lot of money."

The thought hangs in the room like an unwanted visitor.

"He'll get used to us," Luke says. "Whoever moves in will have to take us as we are."

There will be less space, more sharing, and no one to act as a convenient excuse when we want to skip the washing up or order takeaway. Then again, if we hadn't moved into a multi-occupancy house, we would never have met Luke, and I'm sure that's a world that Zoe doesn't want to imagine.

Who knows, perhaps the new housemate will turn out to be the man of my dreams. Who knows, maybe next year Zoe will finally get around to telling Luke how she feels.

# love

# lessons

## je rowney

## the lessons of a
## student midwife

BOOK TWO

# Chapter One

By the beginning of October, Zoe and I are desperate to get back to Tangiers Court. All we have been able to talk about for the past week is coming back, starting our second year at Wessex University, and settling back into our life here. We could have returned sooner; the house has been empty, waiting for our arrival.

One day, a couple of weeks into August, Zoe drove us up here. We spent the afternoon in Blackheath's cafe, drinking latte (me) and mocha (Zoe) and dreaming of the start of the new academic year. We passed down the street and paused for a few moments outside number twenty-one. Our home. We both had our keys with us, but we didn't stop, we didn't go in. What would be the point? It wouldn't be the same. No lectures to prepare for. No Luke.

At the beginning of the holidays, Zoe talked about Luke non-stop. It's become better over time, but only because she has learned to stop herself. I find it funny now; I don't mind all that much. Not really. It's not like I have anyone to rabbit on about. I love her romantic streak; I don't think I have one of my own. Perhaps when I meet the right person everything will change.

So now, here we are.

If there was one take away learning point that I picked up moving in here last year, it was that carrying several bags full of clothes and general bits and pieces down the road is hard work. I learned a lot of other things too, of course. I learned that anxiety is a beast, but that every so often I can tame it. I learned that other people can appear to be challenging (to put it politely), until you take a step back and see the bigger picture. I learned that I can do things that I never thought I would be able to achieve. Now I'm back, and I want to learn more.

I've borrowed my mum's suitcase on wheels, and I'm pulling it up the street towards Tangiers Court. It's an ugly blue plastic monstrosity, but at least my arms aren't aching. Zoe has plumped for a rucksack. Well, a rucksack and two suitcases; she doesn't know the meaning of travelling light.

"You want a hand with some of that?" I ask her.

She shakes her head, but she pauses again, redistributing the weight of her cargo.

"No, no. It's fine. We're nearly there now."

I stop beside her and reach out to take the

smaller of the cases.

"What have you got in this one anyway? It weighs a tonne."

"You know. Stuff. The stuff you always borrow from me. You've probably only got less clothes because you borrow half of what you wear from me!" She's smiling when she says it.

I wish it were true. Zoe is a slim size 8, and I'm a curvy 14 on a good day. She does have a few sweet sweaters and cardigans that I have maybe, possibly been known to squeeze into, but I could never borrow most of what she wears. We are different shapes, different sizes, but so what? She's my best friend. Always has been, always will be.

"I wish!" I grin back at her and hoist the case up clumsily on top of mine. It forms a double-decked stack that I can just about pull with the rickety metal handle that rises from the top of Mum's case.

"I should have got one of those," Zoe says.

"Next year!" I say, but I know she will have forgotten by then, and I will forget to remind her.

I pull the luggage behind me, but Zoe's case wobbles from precariously on its unstable foundation, and I can't trust it to be out of my

3

sight. Instead, I turn the cases around gently, get behind them and - very carefully - start to push.

"I hope we are here before him," she says.

I know who she means, of course.

"You've waited all this time to see Luke, and now you don't want him to be here?"

"I want him to be here *soon,* but I want to get changed, freshen up, make myself look human." She gestures at her hair as though it's a wild bush. She's wrong though. It's perfect.

"You look amazing already!" I say. She does. Her flame-red hair is brighter than ever in the Autumn sunlight. Her skin is clear, and slightly less pale than usual after sitting out in the sun over our break.

She brushes the compliment away.

"Did he say when he would be back?" I ask.

We started off a group chat last **year for important conversations such as "Pick up some more toilet roll when you're near Wilko x"** or "**If you don't get out of bed soon, you're going to miss Cooking Queens xxx**". I haven't paid much attention to the conversation over the summer, but every now and again I see a notification pop up that Zoe or Luke have added a message. Not like she couldn't just text him privately, of course, but I guess using the group chat must have felt threatening.

"Today," she says. "He didn't say when though."

It's around three o'clock now. Luke lives in Leeds when he is not at uni. It's a good four and a half hours away; I doubt he would be here much earlier than this.

Nonetheless, as we approach Tangiers Court, and Zoe puts her hand into her pocket to fish out her key, I put my hand out to stop her.

The door is wide open.

"Hello?" Zoe calls in.

She drops her remaining case in the hallway and starts to shrug the rucksack off her shoulders. There are two angry marks on her skin where the straps have been digging into her. I knew it was too heavy.

I stand behind her, peering into the house.

"Luke?" I shout. "Are you home?"

The door to the living room is closed; the door ahead of us, that leads to the kitchen - the one we have never once closed since we moved in last October - is also shut.

There's someone in there though.

"Luke?" I call again.

Zoe turns and whispers to me. "I'm sure it's

fine. It must be Luke."

I shrug. It's broad daylight. I can't imagine that anyone would have broken in, left the front door open and decided to raid our very empty kitchen.

I lean the stacked cases against the wall, with the intention of walking down the hall. I've taken two steps before both cases tumble to the ground in a clattering crash.

Behind the frosted pane of the kitchen door, I see a shape moving. A six-foot-tall shape reaches for the handle and opens the door.

It's not Luke.

"Er, hi?" It's not a question, but the way it comes out of my mouth definitely makes it sound like one.

"Hello," the man says.

The three of us stand in the narrow hallway, looking at each other.

He's holding a knife, thick with a blob of peanut butter. I can't seem to take my eyes off it.

After what feels like an age, Zoe says, "We, er…we live here."

He nods and licks the peanut butter off the steel. When he has finished, he says, "Good."

I wonder for a moment if he is not English, or

at least if he doesn't speak English, if it isn't his first language. His complexion appears to be that of a fairly standard Englishman, with pale peachy skin; there's nothing about his looks that would back up my suspicion. I'm only on guard because he is not talking to us.

Zoe and I look at each other.

"I live here too," he says.

"Oh," I say. "Oh, right. Yes. The spare room."

"Not anymore," he says. "My room now."

He can speak English after all. He is English. He doesn't appear to have a lot to say though. His tone is flat, and I wouldn't exactly call it friendly.

"Right," I say.

We stand silently again until the awkwardness begins to overwhelm me.

"I'm Violet. This is…"

"I'm Zoe." She holds out her hand to him in an excruciatingly uncomfortable motion. He passes the butter knife to his other hand and shakes hers. After she lets go I notice her subtly wipe her hand onto her skirt. I decide not to offer mine.

"Carl."

Carl. A man of few words. Our new

housemate.

Last year Tangiers Court felt fun, it felt
spacious, it felt like home. I have only been
back for ten minutes and I'm already starting to
feel the change. I'd hoped that the spare room
would remain empty, but at the back of my
mind I suppose I knew that it was too much to
ask. We had a good year here, Luke, Zoe, and
me. This year though? Who knows?

Carl turns and goes back into the kitchen
without saying anything else, leaving Zoe and I
standing in the hallway, equally at a loss for
words.

# Chapter Two

When Luke arrives later the same evening, Zoe and I are sitting in the living room, in our usual positions. The final chair, the one we used to joke belonged to Andrew, our imaginary fourth housemate, remains empty. The best thing about Andrew was that he didn't exist. We could use him as an excuse for all the things that we wanted to do (like order takeaway because it was his turn to make dinner) or didn't want to do (usually the washing up or the cleaning). Now we have Carl, and we are going to have to learn how to fit around a real person.

As soon as Zoe hears the front door opening, she looks at me with a huge grin on her face. She spent the majority of our first year here crushing on Luke and not actually doing anything about it. Perhaps it is finally time for her to act on her feelings. The door to the living room is open, and Luke pops his head in.

"Ladies!" He sounds as excited to be back as we are.

"Luke!" There's no holding back. Zoe jumps to her feet and runs to launch a big hug at him.

I bring myself to a standing position and offer my arms out too. "Hey! Welcome back. Was your drive okay?"

"It feels longer every time," he says.

"Yeah, same," Zoe smiles. Then, in a hushed, conspiratorial tone she says, "Someone has moved into Andrew's room!"

Luke affects a look of feigned shock. "Have you told Andrew? Someone should let him know!"

Zoe pats him softly. "Silly! It's good to see you."

He pauses, then says, "You too."

I get a little warm flutter in my chest. I really hope they don't leave it too long before one or the other of them makes a move. It's like waiting for an inevitable storm to break, but a good storm, the kind you are waiting for when the days have been long and hot, and you need the relief of rain.

"Let me get this stuff upstairs and I'll come and have a drink with you. I assume you're not going to have a repeat performance of your first night here last year."

Zoe laughs. I'm sure she would rather that he forgot how drunk, and how sick, she was.

"Not for me, thanks," she says.

"I'll make us a brew." I smile, and head towards the kitchen, leaving Luke and Zoe standing together for a few more minutes, alone, before Luke goes up to his room.

Ten minutes later Luke comes back downstairs and sits on the sofa next to Zoe.

"Did you see him?" I ask, handing Luke his coffee.

"Thanks Vi. Andrew? I mean, Carl?" Luke says.

"Uh huh." As we didn't mention his name I assume that Luke *has* met our new housemate.

"Yeah," he says. "He was complaining that you two had the best rooms and wondering why I let you get away with it."

"What?!" Zoe almost knocks the mug out of Luke's hand, as she jumps upright. "He never said that."

Luke's expression remains unchanged.

"He did say that?" Zoe is wide-eyed. "Wow! We have been here a year and he walks in and…"

She brings the sentence to a close as we hear the sound of footsteps on the stairs.

We all look at each other. The atmosphere here has certainly changed.

The footsteps come to a stop outside the living room, and Carl looks in.

"I'm going to head down to the union tonight," he says. "Any of you want to come?"

If we say no, we are not going to make a particularly friendly first impression on our new housemate. On the other hand, I really do not want to go out and drink. I want to stay here, watch Netflix, and catch up with Luke. I want to start settling back into the life we had last year, the life that I have missed so much over the summer break. I want things to get back to normal, and with Carl here, I'm no longer sure that things are going to be the same.

"Not tonight," Luke says. "Sorry mate. We are fuddy-duddy housemates, I'm afraid. You'll find us with our hot chocolate and slippers by nine o'clock most nights."

I know Luke is trying to be friendly and joke with Carl, but the look that Carl gives him is neither friendly nor joking.

"Sure," he says. He looks to Zoe, and then to me. "I suppose the same goes for you two?"

"You're welcome to join us in here," I say, by way of a compromise.

He nods slowly, but his expression doesn't change.

"Sure," he says again, in the same flat tone. "Well, see you later then, guys."

With that, he is gone, out of the front door and off to the bar.

The three of us sit and look at each other.

"That was awkward." Luke says exactly what all of us are thinking.

"It must be difficult coming into a house where the other people know each other," I say. "What was it like for you last year? Zoe and I were already here, best friends all of our lives…"

"But Zoe broke the ice by throwing up and passing out on the floor," he says, and gives Zoe a cheeky wink.

Zoe raises her eyebrows and makes an over-the-top pouty face.

"Maybe we should have gone with him." The other two look at me in unison. "Okay, okay, I know," I say.

I'd expected us to have a chilled night, chatting about our summer holidays. Even though I thought that someone might possibly move into the empty room, I didn't think it would cause this much friction.

"It's early days," Zoe says. "Give him the chance to settle. We got used to Luke, didn't we?"

"I thought it was I who got used to you two.

Well, I got used to Violet, at least. I don't think I will ever get used to the girl who leaves her tights hanging over the shower rail to dry."

"It's the best place for them!" Zoe protests. I'm starting to feel like maybe I should have gone out with Carl and left them to it.

I clear my throat. "How was summer?" If I don't bring the conversation around I'm going to end up going to my room.

"It's never particularly sunny in Yorkshire, but there were a couple of days when it didn't rain." He settles back onto the sofa.

"We've been on the beach most days," Zoe says, "but you wouldn't have liked it. It was packed."

"The nearest beach to where I was must be an hour and a half away. Perhaps I should have stayed here."

"We did come past Tangiers Court once," I say, and Zoe throws me a sharp look. I don't know why she wouldn't want me to tell him that. It's not like he was in the house. "We went for coffee at Blackheath's and then…well, we didn't come in."

"I missed it too," Luke says. "I missed you too."

"And you," says Zoe.

14

The two of them look at each other for a few seconds before Zoe breaks eye contact.

"Anyone remember what episode of Scrap House we were up to?" She points the remote control at the TV and forces her attention away from Luke. Her face is glowing red though, and I'm sure he must have noticed it too.

# Chapter Three

I've kept in touch with my closest course mates over the summer break, but it is still a great feeling when I see Sophie, Ashley and Simon on our first day back. Their out of term addresses are scattered across the country, so none of them have seen each other over the break either. Sophie and Ashley have a house share together this year with a couple of students from the nursing course, so they have had time to catch up before this morning at least.

I love learning, and I love my lectures, but I know that on the first day of our modules we will be given our assignments for the term. It's a bittersweet feeling to be back. Our unit guides give us an overview of what we can expect to cover during the term. I like to look at each of the sessions and look forward to each topic we will be taught about. At the back of the document for each module is an overview of the assessment, what we have to submit for the course and when. I would rather be given that information later down the line, closer to the deadline time. I want to enjoy learning, without thinking that I have to prepare to be assessed on what I have learned. At least this term there aren't going to be any exams.

Last year, the focus of our modules was on learning about the normal parameters of maternity. We were taught about the fundamentals, and how to assess and recognise deviations from them. This year we move on to look at more complex issues, pathophysiology and medicines management. Midwifery isn't just about delivering babies, taking blood pressures, and feeling women's bellies. Being a midwife means bearing a huge weight of responsibility.

We have six weeks of classes before we start our first placements of the year. Today's first lecture is an introduction to the new module, 'Altered Health in Pregnancy and Childbirth'.

"You all came back," the lecturer says, as she looks around the room. "Twenty-three out of twenty-three. That's impressive. When I did my training, two of the girls dropped out over the summer holidays because they were pregnant. One of the occupational hazards of working in this profession, I'm afraid."

There's a low rumble of laughter. I can't imagine getting pregnant on this course, I would be surprised if I even had time to have a relationship.

"I'm Sarah. I work here part-time, and for the rest of the time I have an independent midwifery practice. I work with two other midwives, and we can have a talk about independent midwifery at some point."

A quick, quiet buzz passes around the room as the class turn to each other and make their hushed, excited comments. I hadn't even considered that there were options outside of working in a hospital, in the NHS. It's easy to assume that most babies are born in hospitals and so that's where I should work. I have another two years to think about what I want to do, and where. Two years. That's not long at all.

"This term, we are going to start exploring some of the things that can go wrong in pregnancy, or at least could go wrong if we don't identify them early and take the appropriate action. We will look at pathophysiology in this module, and your other module for this term will explore your role as public health practitioners."

Public health. I barely understand what the phrase means. I'm sure that I will before too long.

"Patho-physio-logy." Sarah says as she writes the word on the board, split into three component parts. "The Greeks have it all backwards, of course. 'Logos' means 'the study of', 'physio' – 'nature', and 'pathos' translates as 'suffering'. Essentially, it's the study of where suffering originates, but more simply pathophysiology is about looking at abnormalities and changes in body functions."

I write it down on my notepad, hoping that it will make more sense to me later. Sometimes it all sounds far more technical that it needs to. It's about when things go wrong. That's all I need to know for now.

Sarah is still talking. "This module will have a written assessment, but during the course I will also expect you to submit formative reports on the topics that we cover so that I can check that you are on the right track."

I thought the workload was steep last year. Now I will have placements, assignments for the other module, an essay to write for this, and all that extra work. It feels overwhelming already and we haven't even begun yet. I can feel my palms begin to sweat, and my attention is drifting. I try to focus and bring my thoughts back to the room.

Ashley, sitting to my right, has written on a piece of paper in the front of her new A4 pad, and she pushes it towards me. "At least there are no presentations this year," she has written, and followed it with a crudely drawn smiley face.

I'd almost forgotten how much I struggled at the start of last year. By repeating the process of preparing and presenting in front of the class, the process that caused me so much stress and anxiety at first, I managed to overcome my fears and gain skills that I never thought I would be able to. I had to be part of a group presentation every week, and I went from being terrified to being almost competent. If I were asked to stand at the front of the class and deliver a presentation now, as long as I had time to prepare it properly, I think I could get up there without any fear at all. Of course, that's not what is being asked of me this term. Now I will need to channel my time into writing reports: less scary, but less interesting. It's not that I found being terrified *interesting*, but I actually did start to enjoy myself once I overcame my initial fears. That doesn't mean that I have even got started on overcoming my anxiety though. I'm not going to escape it that easily, I know.

I give Ashley a smile, flick my eyes over to check that Sarah isn't looking in our direction and I write on the pad, below Ashley's message.

"So much work though."

I draw a circle, dot in the eyes, and draw a downturned mouth. It seems that we even add emojis to written words nowadays. I'm so used to conveying my feelings, or at least stressing my meaning, with the tiny pixel pictures.

Ashley forms a tight-lipped grimace and mouths, "Ugh." She's so smart though, I'm sure it doesn't bother her in the slightest.

"I'll be expecting a report from you every fortnight," Sarah says. "You can choose any of the pathophysiologies that we discuss to base your submissions on. You might want to reflect upon something you have experienced in practice. How many of you have met a woman with pre-eclampsia?"

Everyone in the class raises a hand, without exception.

"How many of you cared for someone with gestational diabetes?"

There are fewer hands lifted this time.

"I'm sure you can all think of someone you

encountered over the past year whose pregnancy was not straightforward. It is our role to identify those deviations as soon as possible and take the appropriate action. We have to know what signs to look out for, what they may mean, and how we should respond. We need to know when we should refer women for further help, support or treatment."

I feel like that is what I try to do for myself too. I watch for signs that my anxiety is building, I try to be aware of when my heart starts to race, when my mouth dries up, when my mind begins to lose focus. What I tend not to do is ask for help. Perhaps that is where I am going wrong. My thoughts are wandering now, but not in an anxious way. I'm starting to wonder whether I should try to take a hold of my own pathophysiology. How can I help other people when I can't even help myself? I bottled an exam and stressed about so much last year. I've struggled with my anxiety for such a long time, perhaps now it's time I did something about it.

This module might mean a lot of coursework but reflecting on other people's health may help me to think about my own.

# Chapter Four

At the end of the third week back at Tangiers Court, life seems to be pretty much the same as it was last year. Luke, Zoe, and I spend most evenings together chatting and watching television. Sometimes Luke goes out with his course mates, and it's just the two of us. Apart from crossing paths sometimes in the kitchen, I have hardly seen Carl. We may as well have kept Andrew as our fourth housemate, although I'm sure the landlord is happy that he now has a real-life paying tenant.

This evening, Zoe and I have been home from uni for about half an hour. She's in her room and I've just made coffee. It's coming to the end of October, but the evenings have been warm this week. Our plan is to sit out in the garden until the sun goes down and we get too cold to stay out any longer. I pick up our mugs, and with one in each hand, I use my butt to push the back door open.

I nearly drop the two steaming cups as I see Carl sitting at the little white metal table. It's almost like seeing a stranger or an intruder, his presence is so unexpected.

He looks up from his phone and sees me

almost stumble. Still, he doesn't speak, and he looks back down at the screen.

"Sorry," I say, but I'm not sure what I have to be sorry for or why I say it. I feel like I'm the one intruding or invading his space. I hover, uncertain as to whether I should carry on into the yard or turn back and put the drinks down on the kitchen table instead.

He nods his head, but his attention remains focused on his screen.

"I was, I mean, we were, Zoe and I were going to sit out here."

I can't believe how awkward I can be sometimes. He lives here as much as we do. He has every right to sit here in the garden. We don't have special privileges just because we lived here last year, and he didn't.

He waves his hand at the empty seats. There are four white metal chairs around the table, including the one on which he is sitting; there is room for all of us to sit. Now that I have almost been invited, I can do nothing other than take one of the free spaces, put the mugs down onto the table, and sit, uncomfortably, while I wait for Zoe.

I choose the seat opposite him. I might be able to sit at the table but taking one of the chairs next to him would feel even more weird.

I'm about to pick my mug up to drink, when I pause for a moment and ask, "Can I get you a coffee?" It's an icebreaker, I guess, but also common courtesy.

This time, he looks at me when I speak. It feels like he is appraising the situation, wondering whether to accept my offering. Perhaps he is shy. Perhaps he doesn't know how to mix with other people. Perhaps he just doesn't want to.

"Sure," he says. "Thanks."

He looks away after accepting, leaving me wondering whether I dare ask about milk and sugar. I also now have to shuffle back to my feet and go back into the kitchen to make his drink. Was there enough water in the kettle? I hope so.

I get up, leaving our drinks on the table. They will probably be cold by the time I get back out. I'm already starting to wish that I hadn't been so polite. It's not like he can't make his own drink. He lives here too, he's not a guest. He's never offered to make me anything since he got here. I don't think he's said more than twenty words to me. Still, I offered, and he accepted, so now I have to go back indoors to make coffee for him. It's my own fault for being so stupidly polite.

I'm in the kitchen, standing next to the kettle, waiting for it to reboil when Zoe comes down.

She looks at the single mug on the counter and reaches into the cupboard above me to pull hers out. I raise my hand to stop her.

"Yours is outside," I say, with a nod in the direction of the garden.

She looks confused for a second, before looking out, through the window, to see Carl at the table.

"Our mysterious housemate," she says. She makes a show of standing on her tiptoes to see out, and I hope that he doesn't notice. "That's for him?" she asks, pointing at the mug.

"Yep. I was being nice, and now our coffee is going cold outside, and I'm standing in here, glad that I don't have to make small talk."

"He's probably waiting for one of us to start a conversation, you know. It must be tough for him with us three."

"You go out then, and I'll bring this when I have finished."

She looks at me, as if I have set her a challenge, but then she shrugs, and goes out into the garden.

I force myself to look away from the kettle, remembering what they say about a watched pot never boiling. I want to get out there now; I don't want to leave Zoe alone. Steam starts to rise, and there's a reassuring click as the kettle turns itself off. I make the coffee quickly and almost splash the water over my hand. I curse under my breath, pour milk into the cup, and stir as I walk back outside.

I nudge the door open and see Zoe and Carl at the table. Zoe has taken the seat that I was in, so my only option now is to sit down next to him.

I hold out the cup and put on my best smile.

"Hope this is okay," I say. I'm never usually this subservient, but I feel like I'm still in the realms of making a first impression.

He nods. "Thanks."

He puts his phone down on the table. I guess he has been looking at it the whole time that Zoe has been out here rather than chatting with her. I look over to Zoe, and she smiles back at me, not giving anything away.

"I didn't know if you wanted sugar."

"It's fine."

The three of us sit, and I wish for a moment

that he would go back to doing whatever he was doing on his phone. At least I could talk to Zoe then without feeling quite so rude.

Zoe breaks the silence. "How's your course going?" she asks Carl. It's a very standard subject, it seems.

He nods slowly. "Good." He has both hands around his mug, as if keeping them warm. He raises it to his mouth and puts it down again before saying, "Thanks."

Zoe smiles. "What is it that you are studying?"

He looks at her as though he is terribly bored. There's something in his face that makes me wish that we had never come to sit out here, but this is our garden too. We bought this table, and these chairs. Heck, we even bought the coffee. I did offer it to him though. Why am I so socially awkward? He doesn't look like someone I should be worried about talking too. He's quite tall, probably around the same height as Luke's six-feet, his hair is a neat sandy-brown crop, and now that I am close up, I can see that his eyes are a cool blue-grey. If I were poetic, I would say they are like a winter sky, but I'm not the kind of girl to be poetic about a man's eyes. What am I even thinking? I turn my gaze away as soon as I realise that I'm staring, but it seems it is too late. Carl lets out a momentary laugh.

"I feel outnumbered here," he says. Still, he settles back into his chair, releasing his cup from his grip and leaving it on the table. "I'm studying psychology. What about you two?"

The laugh has warmed the atmosphere a little, but I know that I'm blushing, and now I feel even more awkward.

"I'm doing my B.Ed.," Zoe says. "Teacher training."

He nods in understanding, and then turns his gaze to me, expectantly.

"Midwifery," I say. My voice is weak and wobbly. I don't know what's wrong with me.

He keeps looking at me, even after I have finished speaking. There's something in his expression that I can't put my finger on.

"You know, you can come down and sit with the three of us anytime, Carl. I would have said something before, but I haven't seen much of you," Zoe says.

"That's okay," he says. "I keep myself to myself mostly." Zoe nods and he continues. "I have a few friends at uni, but well, you know."

No. I don't know, not really, but Zoe and I

both make the same "mmm" noise. That sound that means, *"yes, I understand"*.

"Or you can have dinner with us, or, well, whatever." Zoe really is trying hard to make him feel welcome. Her social skills have always been better than mine.

He nods again. "You see, you three are *'us'* and I'm not really part of that *unit*," he says. "I'm okay. Really."

I can see Zoe gulp, but if Carl notices, he doesn't acknowledge it in any way.

I still haven't spoken. I'm sitting between them, using my coffee as a reason to keep my mouth occupied.

Carl tips his mug, draining the last of his drink, and sets it back down on the table.

"I'm going out tonight, so, er, I'd better go and get ready," he says, getting to his feet. "I would ask you two, but I get the impression you don't go out much."

I don't know whether to take this as an insult or an observation. The whole interaction with him has left me feeling more confused than ever.

As he walks past us, into the kitchen, I hear another male voice from indoors. Luke is home.

I nudge Zoe's ankle with mine and make a

*"what the heck was that about"* gesture. She shakes her head.

Luke steps out to join us and stands waiting for one of us to say something. When neither of us does, he speaks. "You've finally had chance to talk to Andrew's replacement?"

Zoe and I look at each other and shrug.

"If you can call it that," I say.

I realise just how lucky we were to end up with a housemate like Luke last year. It already feels like having Carl around is going to be complicated. It's not Carl's fault, but I can't help but think that imaginary Andrew set the bar too high. Luke is easy going and fun to be around. Carl makes me feel awkward and uncomfortable. It's probably my social anxiety that's to blame. When things aren't quite right, it's usually my fault.

Maybe it will get better when we get to know each other. Maybe this is how it is going to be for the rest of the year.

# Chapter Five

Just as our lectures this term are shifting towards the study of pathophysiology, the skills lab sessions are also preparing us to recognise and deal with the complications of pregnancy and childbirth. It's no use being able to determine that someone is suffering from eclampsia if you don't know how to care for them when they start to have a fit.

I hope that it is not a situation that I will find myself in whilst I'm on placement, but I know that one day this knowledge can help me to save a woman's life. One day it probably will.

I'm not a nurse. I have no experience of nursing outside of the elements that crossover with my midwifery skills. Sometimes I'm acutely aware of this fact. Since my first-year placement on the postnatal ward, where I learned how important basic nursing skills can be (and how much importance some midwifery mentors place upon them), I have tried to focus upon being a good nurse as well as a good midwife. I think I have changed my perception of what it means to be a nurse. I saw it as caring for ill people, and because that's not something specifically that I want to do I shied away from the idea. If anyone referred to me as a nursing student my hackles would rise and I would defensively tell them that I'm a student midwife, thank you very much. Now I recognise that nursing skills are those that we use to care for women and their families, and that those skills are essential to midwifery care.

"Don't forget," the lecturer tells us. "This year you will need to undertake your SPOKE placements. If you have forgotten what they are, refer to your PADs and make sure you start to book them in."

PADs, SPOKEs. There is so much jargon to get my head around on this course. The SPOKE refers to a "hub and spoke" system. The hub consists of the essential midwifery placements that we started last year and will continue through to the end of our third and final year. The SPOKE placements are designed to provide us with additional experience in units, wards and environments that fall outside of the usual maternity areas but can still offer a lot of scope for learning experience.

The lecturer is running through some of the suggested areas that we can attend as part of our SPOKE experience. "You might want to visit a diabetic clinic, a cancer treatment centre, accident and emergency. As long as you have thought about your learning outcomes and discussed them with your link tutor there is time for you to explore several options. I strongly recommend that you visit at least one of the gynaecology-related placements that you will see on your list."

I have the print-out in front of me. Early Pregnancy Unit. Colposcopy. Genito-urinary medicine clinic. Gynaecology ward. Gynae theatre. None of them sound particularly appealing.

"If you want to arrange a SPOKE placement in a surgical or other medical unit, as long as you can justify its value, talk to your link and we will do our best to support you."

Throughout the lab, my classmates turn to each other and start to chatter about which areas they are planning to visit. In all truthfulness I haven't given it much though yet. Mainly because I know that it is going to trigger my anxiety. Going to a new unit, where I don't fit in, caring for patients when I know very little about their conditions or how to treat them makes me feel very inadequate and incapable. I don't want to let these people down. I'm not the best person to be with them, and if I'm not actually helping them I feel like I would be little more than a voyeur.

Sophie and Simon are by my side, talking about their plans.

"I was looking after a woman with gestational diabetes on the antenatal ward," Simon is saying. "I think I want to go to the diabetic clinic so I can learn more about it. I felt like I knew nothing."

I'm not the only one then.

Sophie nods too. "I want to learn about epilepsy. We were visiting a woman at the beginning of last year who had been epileptic all her life, and it sounded pretty complicated, you know, sorting her meds out, making sure that she was safe, but that the drugs weren't going to harm the baby. I don't know anything about the actual condition. Disease. Disorder. Whatever it is. I know nothing."

I try to think back over the year. Was there anyone with a medical condition or with a pregnancy-related disorder that I didn't know anything about? My memories swirl like a fog.

"I have no idea," I say.

I must have spoken too loudly, because the lecturer looks over at me and says, "For those of you who have *no idea* of where they are going to go, now is the time to start thinking. By the third term you will want to be focussing back on getting the competencies you need for your PADs."

Delivering 40 babies. Carrying out 100 antenatal checks, 100 postnatal checks. Other things that I can't remember without looking them up in my Practice Assessment Document. I know that the numbers are there, listed, waiting for me to carry out the tasks and have them signed off so that I can be approved as competent.

Maybe I will check what everyone else is doing and pick the best ideas from their placement options. The Early Pregnancy Unit at least sounds like it is related to midwifery.

"Your SPOKE placements are not formally assessed, but remember, whilst you are in practice, wearing your uniforms, you are representing the university, and you are expected to behave appropriately. These placements are not an excuse to slack off or avoid your regular maternity ward responsibilities. You will not be able to carry out the full range of duties on your elective placements, but you will give one hundred percent at all times. Is that clear?"

The students in the room, including myself, murmur a hushed agreement. It feels as though there must have been a past incident where someone did not do as the lecturer is suggesting.

"Make a list of the places that you want to visit and work out what you think will be most interesting and most beneficial. This is a learning opportunity. You are not likely to have the chance again, especially when you are qualified, so make the most of it."

Nursing isn't my dream, but I don't expect the placements to be a nightmare. I want to learn. I want to do everything I can to become a better midwife. I need to work out what it is that I need to focus on to achieve this. I have to use this opportunity to fill the gaps in my knowledge and experience that I will be able to use to support the women I care for throughout my career.

Right now, I have to start looking at the positives, or this year and these placements are going to be more stressful than educational. I stare at the list on the paper in front of me, and let my mind wander to the wards, units and specialist areas, willing myself to make the right choices, no matter how much my stomach

churns at the thought of stepping out of my
comfort zone.

# Chapter Six

Over the following few days, I start to pull together some ideas for my SPOKE visits, but my regular maternity placements are the ones that I'm really looking forward to. I'm back to the postnatal ward on Monday, and Zoe and I have decided to spend Saturday having a girlie day together.

Both Zoe's Bachelor of Education course and my midwifery degree are a mix of placements and blocks of university time. When we are in uni, we see each other every day. We walk to lectures together, and for the most part we walk home together too. We have our lunch together whenever possible, and when we are at home we spend our evenings together. Through all that, I never get bored of her; if she tires of my company she has never told me. I have absolutely no doubt that she enjoys being with me as much as I do with her. We have been inseparable since we were toddlers. I don't think it will ever change. I hope that it won't. Spending so much time with me probably isn't helping her to work out how to get with Luke. We are six weeks into this academic year, and she is no closer to having told him how she feels.

Over a latte (me) and a mocha (Zoe), I broach the subject.

"So…Luke." I'm about as good as getting to the point as she is.

"So, Luke," she echoes, and takes another mouthful of coffee rather than saying anything else.

"Are you ever going to…" I make a gesture with my hand and stop halfway through, not quite sure where I am going with the sentence.

She raises her eyebrows and then laughs, sending the foam flying from the top of her mug.

"I think we have established by now that I'm never going to…" She tries to mimic whatever it was I was trying to do and waves her hands in the air in exasperation. "If he were interested, he would have done something by now."

"He probably thinks that if you were interested you would have done something," I say. The two of them dance around each other, figuratively, like two people who want to dance around each other, literally. I don't know what I can do to help them to get there.

"He told you that he isn't interested in dating," she says.

It's true. He did say that, but it was months ago. Things change.

"That was last Easter," I say. "He had just split up with a girl who messed him around and played him like a fool. It was a long time ago. I'm sure he has moved on, or at least I'm sure he's ready to move on."

She makes a tiny, delicate shrugging gesture. "I don't want to make myself look stupid, and I don't want to spoil our friendship. If I say something and he isn't interested…well, we can hardly carry on like we have been. As friends, I mean."

"But he is interested. He must be."

"You are only saying that because I'm your best friend and you love me. Not everyone loves me, you know." She leans in towards me conspiratorially, almost putting her elbow onto her plate.

In fairness most people that meet Zoe do think that she is wonderful. She's the clever, funny, beautiful one. I'm the chubby, anxious, plain one. It's fine. I know my place.

I open my mouth to speak, and she shakes her head. "And don't go saying that they love me more than they love you. Don't start putting yourself down. You always do this."

I know that Zoe can read my mind. It comes with spending so much time around each other.

I take a breath and change tack. "How about the two of you spend some time alone together. Without me around."

"At home? Where would you go? How would we…" She trails off, as though trying to think of a scenario.

"Yeah, sure. I could go out. I don't know. I'll think of something. You could make a nice dinner, get drinks, set up something on the TV to get him in the mood."

"If I put on a romantic movie he will run a mile, I'm sure," she says. "Besides, he knows I'm not into that sort of thing. Maybe I should go for a horror film instead."

I laugh. "Maybe. It doesn't have to be a romantic film, does it? You can cosy up next to him watching Cooking Queens."

"Seems more his thing," she smiles.

This is the kind of television programme that the three of us watch every night that we are together in the living room. Cooking competitions, antique hunts, teams of middle-aged men and women sorting through scrap heaps looking for treasure. We watch television shows as background noise that we don't have to think about while we laugh and chat.

I'm trying my best to help Zoe, but I am not the expert in matters of the heart. I make my best attempt at sounding authoritative and tell her, "If you do…you know…if you get some time with him, well, if it's going to happen, it will."

She nods, but she doesn't appear convinced.

"What about Carl?" she asks. She says Carl's name in a sigh, as though the word is painful to speak. He still hasn't integrated into our group, and although he keeps himself to himself for the most part, he does come and sit with us, silently and awkwardly, sometimes.

"If he chooses that night as one of the nights he graces us with his presence then I think you're just unlucky," I say. I don't know what else I can say. Then I pause. It comes to me in a flash, and I speak without thinking it through. "I could ask him if he wants to come out with me."

"You and Carl? Spending time together? For me?" Her eyes widen and she stares at me, apparently lost for words.

It actually seems like the obvious solution, apart from the fact that I'm excruciatingly introverted, and I hate small talk. Sure, apart from that it seems like a great idea.

"I know," I say. "It's not going to be easy for me, and to be honest he probably won't even accept if I ask him to go somewhere, but I think it's the best way to give you and Luke the space you need."

She is nodding slowly, and I can feel myself starting to become restless at the thought of what I have offered to do.

"Pressure, though," she says. "Pressure. If you do this, and then I don't make a move, or if nothing happens, I'm going to feel terrible."

"No pressure," I say, but I can feel my fingers start to tingle and the thought of drinking any more of my latte nauseates me. "What will be will be."

She takes a deep breath and lets out a low wordless sound. "Okay," she says. "Let's do this."

When we get back to Tangiers Court, Luke is in the kitchen, sitting at the table scrolling through his phone.

"Good afternoon?" he says. His eyes are scanning the shopping bags that we brought back with us. "Did you get food?"

"Yeah," Zoe says. "I'm going to make pasta

tonight." We both know that Zoe's pasta is his favourite. His face lights up at the mention of it.

"Nice."

"Anything exciting happening?" I ask, nodding at the phone, and pulling up a chair next to Luke as Zoe starts to put the shopping away.

"Not really," Luke says. "Leeds lost again."

I don't particularly want to get into a conversation about football; I'm more interested in Luke's plans for the evening. I make a noise that I hope sounds like a vague show of interest.

"That's about it," he says, clicking his phone off and giving me his full attention. "How was town? Get anything good?"

"Apart from the pasta?" I say. "Not much that would interest you. We shopped, we had coffee, we came home."

"Veni, vidi, latte, eh?" He laughs out loud at his own joke, and I manage a smile.

"Something like that," I say. "What have you and Carl been up to? Planning a boys' night out?"

"He's alright, you know. He did come and have a chat with me earlier, but no. I don't think we are quite at going to the bar together stage yet."

"Maybe we should, you know, go out with him, try harder to be sociable."

Last year Luke did hit the student union with his course mates, but he has hardly gone out at all since we have been back. It's been once or twice at most, and strangely I hadn't even noticed until I thought about it just now.

He shrugs. "I've got lazy. I'm happy just chilling at home with you two, watching whatever trashy television series Zoe has discovered. I don't think I'm hardcore enough for Carl."

Hardcore? Is that what he is? He does seem to go out every Friday and Saturday, but I know that there are students, even on a course as demanding as mine, that go out every night. We are students, it's part of the stereotype. Just because Zoe and I have settled down into our comfortable old-maid habits, and Luke has happily joined us, it doesn't mean that this is what everyone else should do. Carl is probably trying to socialise with people who don't curl up with hot chocolate and a blanket by nine o'clock, or don't think that a trip to Tesco at midnight for biscuits is an adventure. We are different, that's all it is.

As if summoned by the mention of his name,

I can hear Carl coming down the stairs. He doesn't look dressed for a night out, but it's still early. He tends to wear jeans and t-shirts when he goes to uni and when he potters around the house; I've never seen him in the communal areas in sweatpants or pyjama bottoms. On Friday and Saturday nights he scrubs up, does something to his hair that makes it sit neatly in place rather than flop down onto his forehead like it does the rest of the week. When he goes out he wears one of a range of smart, ironed shirts. I don't think Luke knows how to operate an iron, but to be fair if I didn't need to press my uniform I probably wouldn't bother ironing either.

I've noticed a lot about him for someone that I barely speak to.

Carl nods at Luke and I as he comes into the living room and walks towards the fridge. Zoe is still putting our shopping away, and she steps awkwardly out of the way to let him in.

"Sorry," she says.

There's a very particular smile that she uses for strangers; it's an asymmetrical slant that looks like it is not quite sure of itself. That's the smile that she gives to Carl.

"No worries," he replies.

His voice is deep and firm. There's something about it that sounds more masculine than Luke's chirpy northern accent.

He reaches up towards the top of the fridge, to the shelf that we allocated to him because we tend to use the others communally between the three of us. As he stretches, his t-shirt rises slightly. I catch myself looking at the firm, tanned flesh for a few moments too long, and I turn my gaze back to Luke.

"Not off with Damon and the guys tonight then?" I ask.

"Damon and the guys? Why not Florin and the guys? Raj and the guys? Something you aren't telling me, Vi?" Luke is ribbing me, I know, but that doesn't stop me from glowing bright red. "Something special about Damon is there?"

"I was just saving the time of listing them all off, but" I shrug, "apparently that didn't work."

Without looking over at Zoe I know that she is hanging on Luke's answer.

"I'm not going anywhere when there's pasta here," he says.

"There might be enough," Zoe says.      I flick a look at her, and then look towards Carl so that she follows my eyes and takes the hint.

As if I should have to remind her what's riding on this.

I always feel like we are leaving Carl out when we start to talk like this in front of him. Apparently Zoe does too.

"Would you like to join us for dinner, Carl?" she adds.

I'm sure she is just being polite, but if he decides to stay in and have dinner with Luke and Zoe, it isn't going to be the most romantic meal.

Carl stops what he is doing in the fridge and draws back to look at her.

"Uh, thanks," he says. "I'm, uh, probably going to head out in an hour or so though."

Zoe nods.

I take a breath and try to sound natural. "Are you going to the union bar?"

"Something going on?" he says, and my heart almost stops. Am I that obvious? He carries on, "First you ask Luke, and then me. Do you need a drink or something?"

I let out a nervous laugh that I don't even have to fake, and then I add a sweet little shrug. "It's my last night before placements. I thought one of these guys might come out with me but…"

"I didn't sleep well last night," says Zoe, filling in the gap, quickly and unprompted.

"And it doesn't look like I'm going to drag Luke away from dinner," I say.

Luke gives me a curious wide-eyed look, and nods slowly. Does he realise there is something going on here?

Carl pulls a bowl of leftovers from his shelf in the fridge and turns to grab a spoon from the draining board before replying.

"Sure," he says, as though he has made a considered decision. "I'm going out at eight. If you're ready by then, why not?"

Part of me is regretting this plan already. A full evening on my own with Carl, and in the union bar on a packed Saturday night at that. The things I do for Zoe. I give her a discreet wink, and I hope with all of my heart that this is the nudge that she and Luke need to finally get together.

# Chapter Seven

In case I haven't made it clear, the student union bar on a Saturday night is not my favourite place to be. I keep reminding myself that I'm doing this for Zoe. I am doing this to give her some time alone with Luke, and that if the plan works out she might finally get together with him, after all this time.

Carl is dressed as he usually does on a weekend night out: smart and well groomed. He's never scruffy. Even when we are at home, I've never seen him without his hair brushed. He shaves every day, there's no sign of stubble. It's not that Luke is untidy, but I know for a fact that some weeks he wears the same t-shirt three days in a row.

I've done my best to try to look presentable. I borrowed Zoe's straighteners to get my hair under control, and I've even gone to the effort of throwing some make up onto my face. I have tried to match Carl's style, with a knee-length deep purple cotton dress and flat black Mary Jane shoes. I feel heavy and wobbly, and I throw a black cardigan over the top to cover my curves. This is far from being a date, of course, but I'm tagging along with a man I don't know very well on a night out that he didn't plan for me to be part of. I feel like I owe him something.

When we arrive at the bar I'm relieved that we manage to find a table. Apart from that positive note, the whole situation feels somewhat bizarre. Not only because I don't enjoy coming to the bar, but also due to barely knowing Carl. In the silence on our walk down here I reminded myself that he is our flatmate, and it's probably far more difficult for him to join our established group and start to get to know us that it is for us to make an effort to talk to him. We should have spoken to him more before now. I feel almost guilty about the way we have shut Carl out. Tonight could work out well for all of us.

I shuffle behind the table and fold my jacket onto the seat next to me.

"What do you drink?" he asks.

I sit open-mouthed, trying to decide what to drink. Gin? Coke? I don't want to get drunk and let my brain make an idiot of me. It wasn't all that long ago that Zoe and Luke had to escort me out of here after I had an alcohol-induced anxiety attack.

"Sorry," I say. "I try not to drink too much. I'll have a couple though, I guess. Gin and tonic, please." I smile nervously, but he nods.

I would be better off not drinking at all, but I think I'm going to need one or two to lubricate the conversation.

"No problem," he says. "I don't drink a lot either. I just like being around people."

My smile turns into a grin. Not because I like being around people, because I really don't. I grin because it's such a relief to know he isn't expecting me to have a drinking race with him.

"Thanks, Carl."

He nods, and heads to the bar, without even asking for the money for my drink. I guess I will be getting the next round.

As he walks off, I look around the room, trying to see if there is anyone I recognise. There are groups around tables throughout the bar, all wearing similar clothes, all at similar levels of drunkenness. It seems that Carl is probably the best-dressed man in the room.

Over by the windows I can see Sophie with three other girls that I don't recognise. She doesn't see me looking over, and it would take me a while to push through the crowd to get to her. Also, I would definitely lose the table, and possibly lose my jacket, if I get up now. I raise my hand to see if a wave will catch her attention, but still she doesn't notice me.

"Hey." Carl is back before I realise it, sliding a glass towards me. He squeezes onto the bench; my coat sits between us like a bright pink barrier.

"Thanks," I say, and pick up my glass.

"Cheers," he says, clicking his bottle against the rim of my glass.

I nod and take a sip. I forget when I don't drink for a while how good a cold glass of gin and tonic can taste. I let it dance around my taste buds before I swallow.

"Too good," I smile.

"Have you never been into drinking?" Carl asks.

I shake my head. "It probably sounds terribly square, but I have never really been into going out. Zoe and I are cosy night in types. Weekends back home we would just stay home and watch TV with our parents." I shrug and take another drink. "And I'm not good with strangers. Sometimes I'm not good in crowds."

He regards me for a few moments before speaking again. "I would say that you and I are probably strangers," he says. "This is probably the longest conversation we have had, and we have lived together for over a month."

His words make me feel a weird stirring of negativity that I interpret as guilt. We should have tried harder to integrate Carl into the household, or to get out of our comfort zones like I'm now. If it weren't for Zoe wanting to be alone with Luke, we would perhaps have carried on as we were for the rest of the year. Carl would possibly have thought that we were anti-social nerds. He would possibly have been right.

"I'm sorry," I say. "I forget sometimes what it is like. I mean what *we* are like."

"Luke probably only puts up with it because of his crush on Zoe," he says, as though it is nothing.

"What?" I stutter, almost spilling my gin, and settle my glass down gently on the table.

"She must have noticed. It was obvious to me within, like, a day." He laughs when he says it. He isn't judging or adding any negative inflection. "I thought she must have a boyfriend back home or something to not be, well, you know, with him." He drinks some more of his beer. "Or a girlfriend. Whatever."

The last words make me snort out a laugh

too. "Boyfriend, definitely boyfriend," I say. And then, "But she doesn't, no. She hasn't got a boyfriend."

"Good to know," he says, but it doesn't sound as though he means it.

"Are your friends out tonight?" I ask.

I haven't seen him talking to anyone else since we arrived, but I have always assumed that when he comes here that he is with people he knows.

"You're changing the subject. Okay. Sure, yeah, a couple of lads from my course are over there."

He points the neck of his bottle towards the area we came through on our way in. It's an open space, with pool tables and retro arcade machines. There's a clunky old pinball machine in the corner and a small crowd are standing around it. I can't see anyone looking in our direction, so his friends could be any of the many young men.

"Right," I say. "Did you want to…I mean, do you want to go talk to them, or…?"

"Maybe later, sure. I thought it was probably time I got to know at least one of the people that I live with though."

I'm drinking too fast; I've nearly finished the

gin that Carl brought over and it's starting to hit me already.

"Yeah. I didn't mean…"

I always say the wrong thing. My head feels fuzzy, and I'm not sure if it's the alcohol, the noise, or a rising tide of anxiety. He smiles though, and I relax a little.

"I know. You worry too much."

"Actually, I really do. I have quite severe anxiety." I might as well tell him now. If I do end up having a meltdown at least he will have been forewarned.

An expression crosses his face that I can't quite put my finger on. It's not concern, and I'm sure it's not derision. Somehow it's not sympathy either. It makes me uneasy.

"What's that like?" he asks.

I find the question as strange as his expression. It's not something that relative strangers usually ask.

"What's it like?" I repeat. "I'm better than I was."

"What's it like though? What happens?" He sits back, as if settling to hear a story from me.

"Like an anxiety attack," I say.

"I don't know anything about anxiety. Tell me what happens."

I pause, take a mouthful of my drink, and realise that I have drained the glass. I look at him for a few moments before I reply.

"It's not always the same. Sometimes it's just this inexplicable abject fear of…" I pause again, trying to get this right. "Fear of failure. Fear of the future. Fear that everything I do is going to be, I don't know, wrong, I suppose, but worse than that. It's the fear that I will just mess up everything I try to do. That's what happens in my head anyway. Sometimes it's what happens in my body that hits me the hardest though. I get dizzy, like I can't focus on anything. My heart feels like it's going to explode; it's all over the place, fast and thudding. I can't breathe properly. I feel sick, my stomach…it's like being drunk sometimes."

I stop to take a breath. I can feel my heart pounding now, even talking about my anxiety makes me anxious.

Carl is looking at me with an emotionless expression. His composure feels out of place considering what I have told him. There's something else though. There's still something else. That's what's unsettling me. There's something else, and I don't know what it is.

I expect him to say something, but for ten,

maybe fifteen, seconds he says nothing. We sit in silence looking at each other. I've probably freaked him out. I thought that being open was a good plan, but now it seems that I was completely wrong.

Finally, he says, "Another drink?"

I squint in surprise and look down at my glass, even though I know it is empty.

"It's my round," I say. My voice sounds like sandpaper.

"I'll get them, it's fine."

"Okay," I rasp. "Coke then, please."

He gets up without saying anything else and goes over to queue for the bar.

I wish we were sitting near the window; I need some air. Perhaps I wish that I were sitting near the window so that I could be with Sophie and her friends instead of here with Carl. Tonight is turning out to be a terrible idea.

The thought of 'tonight' reminds me of why I'm actually here. Zoe. I pull out my phone and check for messages. There's one.

**How's it going with Carl? I owe you one. xx**

I'd say that she owes me more than one. This is painful. I guess that I'm finding out why Carl doesn't mix with us at home.

I message Zoe back.

**Terrible. Anything happening there? xx**

I send the text and pause, wondering for a second whether I should pop a message to Sophie, and tell her that I'm here. She might come over and invite me to join them. What am I thinking? Carl has left *his* friends to sit here with me, I can't up and leave now.

Before Zoe has the chance to reply to the text, Carl is back.

"Everything okay?" He nods towards my phone.

Should I be honest? Probably.

"I was checking in with Zoe," I say.

"She wanted to know if I was behaving like a gentleman?" he asks.

I cough slightly in surprise. "No! I mean, I was checking what she was doing. I thought that Luke…well, we thought that if she had some time alone with Luke she might, they might…" I'm stumbling over my sentences, and I know I must sound like a clumsy idiot. It makes me feel more anxious, and I don't think I should say anything else. My brain is a mushy jumble of words. I hate this.

"You only came out with me so that they could do whatever it is that they have spent the last year not doing?" He looks offended and I get a heavy feeling in my gut as though I have swallowed a bowling ball.

"No," I say, speaking slowly and carefully. But it is the truth, isn't it? That *is* why I'm here. "Sort of." There's another awful silence before I continue. "Not just that. I want to get to know you. I do. It's silly that we live in the same house and hardly speak. It's like, you know, killing two birds with one stone." It's a bad metaphor for this situation. "Sorry," I say. "I'm sorry."

He shakes his head, but he doesn't stand up and leave. "It's hard being the new guy when everyone knows each other. I'm…" He pauses, as though it's his turn to think of the right words to say. "I'm not as confident as you might think I am."

It strikes me as a strange thing to say. I don't have any preconceived ideas about his confidence or lack of confidence. It has never crossed my mind.

"I find it difficult to talk to people," he says. "And with you and Zoe and Luke already so close and so happy, well, I suppose I didn't think that there was room for me."

He reaches his hand out across the table and places it on top of mine.

"I'm so touched that you could open up to me," he says. "It must be difficult to talk to someone you don't know very well about your anxiety. I'm sorry that I flipped out a bit there about you only coming out with me to help Zoe."

"You...you didn't flip out. Not really." I look at his hand, but I don't pull back. "It's fine."

"Thank you," he says in a calm, measured tone. "Thanks Violet. Now, shall we start again?"

Although I'm slightly puzzled, I smile, happy to be back on track towards at least a half-decent evening.

"That would be lovely," I say.

When he smiles back, I catch myself for a split-second thinking that the man sitting next to me, with his hand on mine, is actually quite attractive. Perhaps it's the gin. I haven't had this kind of thought about Carl before, but when have I taken the time to stop to look at him, or to even speak with him properly? I hope I'm not blushing, but I fear that my cheeks are starting to fill.

I'm here for Zoe. I definitely don't need to start thinking about anything else. I shake the thoughts out of my head and resolve not to drink any more alcohol tonight. I don't want to end up making a fool of myself in any one of the number of ways that I potentially could. No more alcohol, and no more thoughts about blue eyes and how I have been single for far too long.

# Chapter Eight

By the time we get back to Tangiers Court it's
almost midnight. I feel a little woozy, but I'm
not what I would classify as 'drunk'. Tipsy
maybe, but that's all I'll admit to. Carl was
actually very understanding about me not
wanting to drink much, especially after I'd told
him about the anxiety, and the way that alcohol
can affect me. It ended up being a decent
evening, all things considered.

I haven't heard from Zoe for the last couple
of hours. I want to assume that it's a good sign,
that she was too busy with Luke to message me.
When I walk past the living room though I see
her on the sofa, tucked under Luke's cosy fleece
blanket, curled asleep. He's in the armchair and
he puts his finger to his lips as I look in, as if I
can't see that Zoe is sleeping.

I turn to Carl and pass on the finger on the
lips gesture. He nods in acknowledgement, and
then points to the kitchen. As quietly as
possible, we pick our way down the hall, and
slouch down at the table. Luke is only a few
paces behind us.

He closes the kitchen door softly, so as not to
wake Zoe, and asks, "Coffee?"

"Sure, thanks," Carl says, and I nod my head too.

It feels strange, the two of them here with me and Zoe not with us. It's like there's an imbalance in the room. It also feels strange that I have no idea what has happened with Zoe and Luke tonight, and the one person that I want to ask about it is fast asleep. I know I can't say anything to Luke, not without speaking to Zoe first, but I'm itching to find out.

The whole room is shimmering, a haze of mild intoxication, when suddenly it hits me that I didn't tell Carl not to say anything about Zoe's feelings. I really shouldn't have mentioned it to him. I can't believe what a big, stupid mouth I have. I'm starting to panic; I can feel my forehead heating up and a clammy dampness rising through my skin.

"You okay, Violet?" Carl asks. He leans over the table to me and puts his hand flat against my skin. "You're burning up." He gets up and opens the back door, letting in the cool autumnal night. It feels fresh and welcome, but it doesn't make me feel any better.

"Uh, I might sit outside," I say, pushing myself up from the table and wobbling to my feet.

"Careful," he says. "Maybe you had a couple too many. We were pretty restrained though." He smiles, and it's such a gentle, caring smile. It does nothing to help me to cool down.

Carl gets up too and puts his hand on my arm to steady me.

"I can bring the drinks out," Luke says. He is still keeping his voice as quiet as possible, ever conscious of the sleeping Zoe in the other room.

I'm about to say that it's okay, and that I will be fine here, but Carl speaks first.

"Thanks, mate," he says. "I'll come out with you, Vi. I could do with some air too."

I pass a quick look to Luke and he raises his eyebrows, but only says, "Sure, fine."

In the garden, we sit at the pretty metal table. Fairy lights glow around the trellises like fireflies. The night is clear and quiet, and not as cold as it should be for November.

"Are you sure you're okay?" Carl asks.

I look over his shoulder and through the window into the kitchen, where Luke is pouring hot water into our mugs. "Yeah," I say. I lean towards him so that I can speak more quietly and still be heard. "I was worrying, panicking I suppose. I should have told you earlier, you know, not to say anything to Luke about how Zoe feels."

He smiles, but there's something cold about the expression, as though the smile is concealing his true feelings.

"Okay," he says.

"Okay?" I echo. His response is not helpful.

"Okay," he says again, flatly.

I look at him in a way that I hope conveys my confusion.

"Okay, really. Look, they obviously both feel it, if they are too dumb to get it together, well it's definitely not my problem."

"They aren't dumb," I say, defensively. "Zoe is my best friend. She isn't dumb. And neither is Luke. They are just -"

"What? What are they?" Before I can say anything else, Luke comes into the garden, and I'm forced to stop talking.

"Any better, Violet?" he says.

"Uh, yeah. Thanks. I was…I needed some air. Thanks."

"Did you have a good night?" Carl asks.

"We watched TV; Zoe fell asleep. The usual exciting Saturday night in Tangiers Court," Luke smiles. I watch his face, trying to work out if there was anything else that he doesn't want to talk about here, in front of Carl. He doesn't give me any sign. "What about you two? How was the union?"

Carl shrugs. "Same as ever."

"I know what you mean," Luke says.

If nothing else comes of tonight, I think it's a good thing that Carl is finally talking to us, or should that be that we are finally talking to him? Luke is chatting to him now as though he is a friend, rather than someone who has lived with us all this time and never bothered to have a conversation. I shake the thought away, reminding myself that it was down to us as much as Carl, if not more so. Tonight, at the bar, it was fine. For Saturday night in the union bar to be anything other than an ordeal is a plus for me. We chatted, we laughed, and now, here we are, sitting together in our garden, feeling like friends.

"I quite liked it," I say, although my thoughts are distant. It could be the drink, or perhaps the ambience, but I feel strangely peaceful. I'm drifting. I could probably close my eyes and -

"Oh, and I kissed Zoe," Luke says.

I snap back from my reverie.

"Nice," Carl says. "About time."

I want to shake him, ask what he's doing

reacting like that, making it obvious that he knew what was going on, but Luke laughs, and Carl joins in. Of course, it was clear to Carl, before I even told him, he knew there was something going on. Or at least that something should have been going on.

"About time," I repeat, and I smile at Luke.

"I'm not going to kiss and tell, so don't go asking me for details," he says. "Besides, I wouldn't want to deprive Zoe of the chance to gossip all about it."

I reach over and put my hand onto his arm. "I'm so pleased," I say. "I can't believe it took you both this long, but…yes, I'm so pleased that you're finally getting it together."

Luke looks at me, and I pause. A feeling of panic runs through me like electricity.

"You are, aren't you? Getting it together? It wasn't…I mean, it…you…?"

From the doorway comes a familiar voice, sounding happier than I have heard it in a long time.

"We are," Zoe says. "We are definitely, finally getting it together."

My body seems to have forgotten that a couple of minutes ago I was ready to drift off into a peaceful doze. I leap to my feet and rush over to her.

"Zoe!" I scoop her up into a hug, my arms wrapping all the way around her petite frame, lifting her slightly off the floor in my excitement.

She makes a happy squeaking noise, and under any other circumstances, with any other man, I would probably shush her, tell her to play it cool, and not look so excited in front of him, but this is Luke. This is different. This is perfect.

# Chapter Nine

I stay up way too late, talking to Zoe about what happened, or more precisely, how it happened. The bottom line is that she finally told Luke how she feels, and he said something like she shouldn't have waited so long to tell him, and boom, they kissed. I'm sure it was all very romantic and sweet. I'm happy for her, but I don't know if I will ever experience anything similar. I worry too much, I panic, I stress, I overreact, I'm over-protective of my own feelings. Zoe throws herself in, albeit after waiting around for months this time, but still, when she does it, she gives one hundred percent. I wish I could be like her. If I were as pretty, as smart, as likeable as she is, perhaps I could be. If I were less anxious, perhaps, perhaps.

This week I will be back on placement, which feels like perfect timing. I'm not around the house so much, as the shift pattern is a mixture of early mornings and late evenings. I won't be getting in their way. I try to shake that feeling out of my head as soon as I think it, but wasn't my presence what kept the two of them apart for so long? It took me going out with Carl to

encourage them to finally make a move. I want
Zoe to be happy, but what if she can't be while
I'm around? My shifts will give them space,
and I hope that's enough.

Being back on the postnatal ward means
working with Geri Smith again. Last year I
almost gave up on my placement with her after
the first day. She is strict, demanding and
doesn't accept anything other than one hundred
percent effort. She was exactly what I needed.
She pushed me to learn, to increase my practical
knowledge, and my nursing skills. I can't wait
to see her.

When I turn up to the ward on Monday
afternoon, there is a girl sitting in the office,
wearing the same student midwife uniform as I
am. I don't recognise her, so she's either a first
year or final year student. From her timid
expression I assume it's the former.

"Hi," I say, with a big smile. "I'm Violet."

"Shell," she says. She manages to smile back,
just about.

"Are you alright?" I ask. "Are you on the
morning shift?"

She shakes her head roughly. "Community,"
she says. So, she is a first year. "My mentor is

picking up some paperwork and she wanted to visit one of the ladies."

"You didn't want to go with her?" I ask, confused.

"I don't know her. The patient, I mean. It's my first day out. I haven't met her, so…"

I nod. "You can still go with your mentor though. What's her name?"

"The woman?"

"Your mentor."

"Oh. Of course." She blushes, and answers, "Sarah Godley."

She's in the same team as the community midwife I had my placement with this time last year. Did I look like this twelve months ago? Shell is like a rabbit in the headlights, wide-eyed and nervy.

"You'll have a great time. Look, can I get you some tea, or…"

I'm cut off by Geri coming through the doors, calling my name.

"Violet Cobham! My favourite student has returned!" Geri says. Favourite? Well, that is a surprise to me. Either that, or she says the same thing to everyone.

The timid girl curls even more tightly inside her shell. Shell. Her name seems appropriate.

"Hi Geri," I enthuse, and stand up to give her a gentle hug. "I'm happy to be back."

"Are you here too?" Geri barks the words at Shell. The poor girl looks like she is on the edge of tears.

I shake my head and answer for her, without thinking. "She's on community. Waiting for Sarah Godley."

"Make the tea, do something useful," Geri says to the girl. She brushes her hand in the air as though she is trying to waft away a fly.

"I was just about to get it," I say, "but I'll show Shell the kitchen."

"Good girl," Geri says with a big smile. She doesn't mean it to sound condescending, I know, having been here with her last year, but I'm sure that Shell is not getting the best first impression of my mentor.

When we get into the kitchen, Shell speaks. "Who is that? I'm glad she's not my mentor."

"She's fine," I say. I try to keep my voice pleasantly chirpy and stop myself from sounding defensive. I remember how I felt last year when I started on my community placement, and again when I first met Geri. "Honestly," I smile at her. "All of the midwives here are lovely. Don't worry."

Don't worry. I've dealt with anxiety and panic attacks since I was eleven and here I am telling someone else not to worry. Seeing this girl reminds me of who I was last year. I have achieved so much since then, academically and personally.

The girl nods, but stands rigid, her hands grasped in front of her, one inside the other, in a stiff, tight pose.

I fill the huge heavy teapot with boiling water and stack the mugs next to the milk and sugar on the tray. I have done this so many times before, and doing it again today feels like a kind of homecoming. I was on this ward for six weeks last spring, and I never realised how much I missed it until now.

"Do you always have to make the tea?" Shell asks.

"I always offer," I say. "Unless someone beats me to it." I give her another smile. She's going to think smiling is all I ever do.

Shell says nothing, but I feel her silent judgement. I don't care. She will learn what I have learned: being part of the team is more than fulfilling my midwifery duties.

I pick up the tray and gesture for her to

follow me back into the office. The other staff members have started to arrive for the shift by the time I place it down onto the heavy wooden desk.

"Violet!"

"You're back!"

"Nice to have you with us."

Voices come at me from all around the room, and my smiles turn into a grin.

Shell stands by the door, watching as I lift the pot and pour hot tea into the mismatching mugs.

"Want one?" I offer.

Shell turns to look down the corridor, I expect she is trying to see whether Sarah is finally on her way. She looks back at me, nervously.

"I'm sure it's fine," I tell her.

If Sarah is anything like Stacey, the mentor that I had in community last year, no doubt she will have a lot to talk about with the woman she has gone to visit. When you have got to know someone like that I'm sure there's plenty to say. I haven't had the opportunity to see someone through from antenatal to postnatal yet, but I hope that I'll have the chance soon.

I thrust a mug towards Shell, and then take my place amongst the postnatal ward staff for the afternoon shift. It's not a big office, and we are all crammed in, squashed onto desk chairs, low armchairs, and perched on tables. There's no room for Shell to sit, so she hovers in the doorway, clutching her drink and listening in.

I feel at home here now. Everything seems to be falling into place. I'm so much more at peace this year. Apart from the few occasional blips, I have rarely had the slightest glimmer of anxiety. When I have, it has passed quickly. I have dealt with it.

I feel like everything I'm learning as a student midwife is also helping me to grow as a person. I'm learning to help others, but in doing so, I'm helping myself. This time last year, I was the meek, timid girl that Shell is now. I was worse than that. I fled from my first practical exam because I couldn't even handle thinking about it when I was in the skills lab. I panicked about my placements; I was a mess. Now, I'm calmly making tea for all the midwives, trying to reassure this student, and feeling nothing but excitement and confidence for my placement.

Just before handover starts, Shell's mentor returns, and pops her head into the office.

"Hi everyone," Sarah says. She turns to Shell and asks, "Ready to go?"

Shell looks at her almost full mug of tea, and then back at her mentor.

"Yes, sure." Her eyes scan the room looking for somewhere to put her drink down.

"The tea is hot if you want one before you go," I offer. Last year I wouldn't have spoken to any midwife that I didn't know. Last year, I would have been the girl looking for somewhere to put her mug and run along with my mentor.

"Great," Sarah smiles. "Finish yours too," she says to Shell.

The corners of Shell's mouth turn up, and she raises the tea to her lips. I know that she is going to be fine. I hope that by this time next year she is offering kindness and tea to another new student. I wonder where I will be then.

# Chapter Ten

I'm on an early shift on Tuesday, and Zoe is on her placement at the school. We have agreed to meet up at Blackheath's cafe in the town centre after we finish, for a catch up.

Yes, we live together, and we can catch up any time that we want to, but sometimes it's good to have some dedicated girl time. No interruptions, just me and my best friend. Besides, Blackheath's has the best Bakewell slices in Wessex.

I've already drunk my latte, and my cake is only crumbs on my plate when I steel myself to bring up something that has been on my mind. Zoe and I have never shied from discussing personal issues, but now that her boyfriend is someone that we live with, somehow things feel different.

"You and Luke…well, you don't seem to be all that physical with each other. Not around me, anyway."

I feel awkward saying it, and I can't hold eye contact with her. It's not so much that I'm worried about how their budding relationship is progressing, I'm worried that I'm getting in the way.

She makes a tiny laughing noise, that sounds more like surprise than amusement.

"Well, what do you want us to be like? Would you rather that we were all over each other?" she says. I can't read her voice, even though I know her better than anyone else. I can't tell what she is thinking, not now.

I'm looking at my plate, pushing the last flake of almond around with the tip of my fork.

"No." I look up. "No. I mean, it's just, I don't know. I don't want you to have to rein it in or hold back just because I'm always around." I want to say, 'in the way', but as I think the words I realise how self-pitying they would sound, so I cut the sentence off.

She bats the words away. "Don't be silly. I want you around. I want you around, always. I do."

"He might not feel the same," I say. "Have you even talked about it?"

She pauses just long enough for me to realise that they must have indeed discussed it.

"You have?" I say. "And, what? What did he say?" Now I'm not looking away from her; now she has my full attention. I have to know what's been said. I start to feel that familiar rush of nausea as my anxiety floods my body.

"Hey, relax," she says, reading me better than I read her. "Nothing bad. Do you really think I would ever say anything bad about you?"

"Not you," I mutter, and this time I can't hold the pathetic words back.

"Luke?" She sounds incredulous. "You think that he would?"

I roll my eyes, at my own stupid thoughts more than anything else. Then I silently shake my head.

"Violet. I don't want things to be any different than they are. I don't know, maybe subconsciously this is why I didn't approach Luke for all that time. Maybe it's what stopped him too."

"Me? You both blame me for being in the way?"

"Violet!" She snaps my name this time, and then reaches out her hand, placing it on my arm when I look away. "I'm sorry. I didn't mean to be so sharp. What you're saying though, it doesn't make sense. I have never treated you like you're in the way, and I never will. Do you really think that?"

I sigh. "I'm just worried that you can't be natural with him, that you can't have the kind of relationship that you would if I weren't around."

"I wouldn't even be living here with him if you weren't around. That is what makes it weird for me, that I live with him. I always thought that I would meet someone, date for a while, six months, a year, more, and then maybe choose out somewhere to live together."

"We used to look at that block of apartments by the pier. You wanted to live there."

"And you were going to move into the flat next door to me. I remember."

We always shared our dreams, our hopes for the future. Being here at university is one of the goals that we have actually achieved. I don't know if I ever believed that training to be a midwife, living with Zoe, would actually happen. Sometimes when I picture something that I really want to do my brain tells me that I will never really do it, that I'm stupid for wanting things that I will never have. Did I really ever think that Zoe and I would live next door to each other in beachfront apartments in the town we grew up in? A part of me must have believed in it.

She gives me the tender, soft smile that makes me feel warm and safe.

"Instead we have moved into a cosy student

house, and I met the man of my dreams. Sometimes things just happen, don't they? I wouldn't have planned it this way, but I'm happy with how things are. I want you to be happy too, Violet."

Happy. It's an interesting word. I am content. I have every reason to be happy. I made it here. I'm getting through my course. I've met some great people in my classes, but I haven't really made friends. I adore my placements; being in my uniform, on the wards makes me feel something that I don't get from anything else. I love the little house that we have made a home. I get to see my best friend every day. But something is missing. I don't know what it is. Perhaps it is the way that anxiety taints everything I do. I can never actually relax and enjoy things, because at the back of my mind - and sometimes at the front of my mind - I feel like everything is going to fall apart.

"For the record," she says, "Luke was concerned about you. He said that he didn't want to make you feel uncomfortable or awkward."

"He's a good one," I smile. "He wasn't just saying that to make you happy, was he?" There I go again. I can't just accept things the way they are. I have to think about the negative side.

Zoe laughs, and I assume that she thinks I'm joking. Good. It's better that way. Better for her.

"You two should do some normal things. You know, go out for a walk to the beach together, take him to see a movie, I don't know, have dinner out or drinks, or -"

"Go on a date," she says.

"Yeah," I say. They seem to have skipped that part of the relationship and gone from just housemates to housemates-that-are-in-a-relationship without doing any of the fun things that people do at the start of a relationship. Not that I know much about it, but those are the things that I like. That 'getting to know each other' phase is my favourite. The thrill of the new. I don't much like the chase, that part where you are trying to work out whether someone likes you or not, but when you both work out where you stand, and start talking, exploring each other, that's the fun part.

Zoe is quiet for a few seconds while she thinks this over. It's as though I have suggested something ground-breaking, but it seems pretty obvious to me.

"It would do you good to have some time out

alone together. You can make out all you like, and not have to worry about making me blush."

This raises another laugh from Zoe. "I'm not sure that we are likely to snog each other's faces off in public, to be honest, but it would be nice to have a date. What about you though, what would you do?"

"Do?" I ask. "I could come along to carry your bag for you, I suppose."

She bats me with her hand. "Silly. I mean -"

"I know what you mean. You have to stop thinking like that. You aren't responsible for me. I can fill my time on my own, you know." I smile, but actually I don't feel completely confident that what I'm saying is true. I have never really spent much time in my own company. Not that I have had many relationships, but I have always had Zoe. Even when the two of us have dated people in the past, we have always had time together too.

"I'll ask Carl to babysit you," she smiles.

Perhaps I would spend more time talking to Carl if Luke and Zoe weren't around. I don't ever want to live in a world without Zoe, but I wonder how different things would be if she weren't here. If I had to do everything alone, would I even have got to university? I doubt it.

I don't respond to her joke. Instead I ask, "So, where will you go?"

She grins, and the two of us tumble into her bubble of happiness, thinking up ideas and making plans.

# Chapter Eleven

Luke loves Zoe's idea of date night, and dutifully starts to make arrangements. They go out for pizza for their first proper date, and I'm sadder about missing out on the food than I am about missing Zoe's company for the evening.

On their second date night I don't have any plans of my own, and I'm on my own in the living room. I could have thought of something to do; I could have gone out with Sophie, Ashley and Simon, or any combination of the group, but instead I decided to stay in and enjoy my alone time. Alone, that is, until Carl comes into the living room.

"Do you mind if I join you?"

The noise startles me, and I can feel my heart thundering. It doesn't take much to tip me onto the brink of a panic attack sometimes. I'm flimsy, I know.

"Uh, yeah, I mean, no, sure, come in." I try to gather my words, so I don't sound like a gibbering idiot.

Carl is dressed in a pair of black jeans and a white t-shirt with a faded print. His feet are bare, I notice as he flops into the chair and stretches his legs out in front of him.

"What are we watching?" he asks.

My mind goes blank for a moment. To be honest, I have been scrolling through my phone, and the Netflix show on the television really is just background noise.

"You can change it if you like." I toss the control into his lap.

"Okay," he says, and starts to read through the menu.

I suppose it's only polite that I put my phone down now, so I do. I feel a little disgruntled that I have been interrupted from my nothingness, but I remind myself that Carl lives here too and has just as much right to sit here and watch trashy television as I do.

"Salvage Den alright for you?"

It's the kind of programme that Zoe and I would choose.

"Sure. Anything."

He switches it on, and we both sit in awkward silence through the first five minutes.

I can't bear it much longer.

"Can I get you a drink? Tea, coffee? Beer?" I don't even know what he drinks.

"Fetch me a beer back, thanks," he says. I suppose he assumes that I was going anyway. I am now.

When I come back with the drinks he shows me a big smile. It seems a little forced, but maybe he is just trying to be friendly.

"Thanks so much, Violet," he says.

"No problem," I reply, and take my seat back on the sofa, with my brew.

Somehow I feel more comfortable with a prop. I can sit and drink my coffee and not feel like I should be chatting to Carl. Apparently, now that he has a beer, he thinks just the opposite.

"Zoe and Luke out tonight?" he asks.

"Um, yeah." It's fairly obvious, so he must just be making conversation.

"Anywhere nice?"

"Dinner, I think. I mean they weren't here for dinner, so, you know."

He nods and falls silent again for a short time.

He speaks again. "I feel a bit of a gooseberry down here with those two around, you know. I don't mean to be anti-social, I just, I don't know. I feel like I am in their way sometimes."

"I'm sure they don't mean to make you feel like that." I immediately jump to Zoe's defence, even though I can totally understand how he feels.

"I know. I don't think they do it on purpose." He laughs, as though I have made a joke rather than said something stupid. "I'd rather give them the space."

"It's your home too," I say.

"And yours," he nods.

"Yeah, I mean, it's not all about them. If you want to come in here and spend time, there's room for you. I mean, you are always welcome. No one thinks you're a gooseberry."

"I think I am. Do you never feel like that?"

I look at him. Do I admit to it, and possibly reflect badly on Zoe, or should I cover up my feelings?

"I think it's good for them to have some time alone together away from here," I deflect.

He laughs again. "You're very loyal to your friend. I like it. I respect that."

He has a deep, earthy voice, and his laughter is like soft shale. I find myself wanting to hear more.

"But you do know what I'm talking about," he says. It's not a question, this time. I don't give him an answer. Instead I shuffle in my chair and focus on the television.

Unfettered, he carries on with the questions. It's not like I'm engrossed in the show, but I'm not used to being interrogated. At least it's not small talk. It feels as though the questions he is throwing at me run far deeper than that.

"Do you not go out much?" he asks.

He's lived here with us for nearly three months; I'm sure he already knows the answer to the question.

"I'm more a bath and book type," I smile. I know I must sound terribly boring to him. He is probably used to far more interesting conversations with far more interesting people. "We do go out shopping at the weekend though. There's a great cafe in town and -" I know this wasn't the type of going out that he meant, so I shut my mouth. He looks at me as though prompting me to say more. "Well, you don't need to hear about it," I say, quietly.

"I'm trying to get to know you," he says. His voice is soft and gentle now, as though I'm a wild animal he is trying to approach and calm. I'm more like a pet hamster than a feral cat though.

"I know, I'm sorry. I'm not used to anyone wanting to get to know me," I say, and immediately wish I hadn't. I must sound stupid.

"I'm sure that's not true," he says with a kind, warm smile.

"Tell me about yourself. I hardly know anything about you." I ask, trying to deflect the attention onto him.

He shrugs and puts his beer bottle to his mouth, knocking back a deep gulp.

"Not much to tell. I come from Leicester, I'm studying psychology, I like football and going out with the lads. I don't think there's anything exceptional about me."

"Why did you choose Wessex University?"

He pauses before answering, and I see something cross over his face that I think could possibly be sadness. It's hard to tell, but his expression changes, briefly.

"I wanted to get as far away from home as I could," he says. "London was too expensive. Wessex is near the sea, and near the countryside, and I was told there was meant to be a good social scene. What's not to like."

I grew up half an hour away from here. I suppose I take for granted the things that people like about the area. Tourists flock here for the beach and the beauty spots, but I don't think I have even bothered to go down to the promenade in the past year. I could say that I don't have time, but I can make time. It's not like I have a hectic social life.

"Fair enough," I say. "Zoe and I come from Portland. It's half an hour down the coast."

"I thought you two must have been friends for longer than a year. You're too close to only have met as Freshers."

I nod. "I've known her all my life."

"That's why you're so defensive then," he says, more to himself than to me, "and so caught up in each other."

"Caught up?" I can't tell whether he means it as an insult or merely an observation.

"You follow each other around, always in each other's pockets. I've lived here for three months, and this is the first time that I have ever had chance to talk to you alone."

My eyes can't meet his. I know that it is true, but I have never wanted it any other way.

"It's fine," he says. "If you're happy, it's fine. I have been wondering though…" He stops mid-sentence.

"What?" I ask. He knows how to get my attention, that's for sure.

"Wondering whether it's good for you. You're kind of living in her shadow. It would be good for you to have your own friends, do your own thing." He stops, shakes his head, and drains the rest of the bottle of beer. "I've said too much."

Maybe he has. I'm not sure.

"I have friends," I say. "I know people on my course."

"Course mates. That doesn't really count. What about at home? Before you came here?"

I shake my head. "We know a few other people, sure."

"We," he echoes. "What about you?"

It's starting to feel very hot in here. The room is large enough for a sofa, two armchairs and the unit that houses our television, but right now it feels tiny. I'm getting claustrophobic in my own home. This is not good.

Suddenly, it's like there's a shift in energy in the room, like a switch has been flicked.

"I didn't mean to make you feel bad," Carl says. His voice is soft and sweet like honey. "You seem like an interesting person. I barely know you. I shouldn't make assumptions."

He's right. He's right about me being an extension of Zoe, or that we are extensions of each other. She is all I have ever known. Being her friend is all I have ever been. I have never questioned it, but now, with Luke taking up so much of her time, where does that leave me. Who am I without her?

I shake my head slowly. My face is burning, and I can feel tears prickling my eyes. I wipe my face, trying to look casual, and hoping that he doesn't catch on to my emotions.

"It's fine. Really. I appreciate your honesty." And I do. It's uncomfortable but refreshing. Carl says what he thinks, he just comes out with it, and what he has told me is true. "You're right," I say. "I have probably been too dependent on her."

It's a criticism of myself, not Zoe. She's not the one to blame.

Carl nods, and again he gives me that smile. It's friendly, reassuring and kind. Despite his words making me question so much about my life, I somehow feel safe here with him now. Those anxious uprisings are settling within me.

# Chapter Twelve

Shift work means early mornings, late nights, and sometimes overnight sessions at the hospital. The mornings start at half past seven, the afternoons finish at ten at night. Some staff work a full day which is, appropriately, called a "Long Day". Even though choosing Long Days means only having to work three days out of the week, I don't think I have the stamina to give my complete focus and attention for that long in one chunk. Geri works a regular five-day-week, so I follow her shift pattern. All of the midwives have their working days scheduled onto a planner referred to as the "off-duty", although it effectively tells you when you are *on* duty.

Looking on the bright side, after working Monday late and Tuesday morning I have Wednesday off before two afternoon shifts; then I'm on the rota for Saturday morning. As a qualified midwife I would be paid a little extra for the weekend shift; as a student, I do it because I need to experience what it is like to work the shift pattern. It's also useful to learn what happens differently on different days.

During the week, there are elective

inductions, where women come to the antenatal ward (or sometimes to the delivery suite directly) to have their labours started artificially. They are usually past their due dates, but there are other reasons for induction too.

There's a theatre list most weekdays, for women who need to be booked for elective caesarean sections. Elective makes it sound like they *want* to have the surgery, which isn't always the most accurate way to describe them. Planned caesareans captures it more precisely. Women who need to have caesareans for clinical reasons are booked onto the surgery list, and as there are more doctors available Monday to Friday, that's when the list runs.

There are, of course, women who were planning to give birth the 'normal' way and experience complications that mean they need to have caesareans - and that can happen any day, at any time. Also, women who have been planning caesareans can go into labour. Sometimes they can deliver vaginally, but sometimes they still need to have the caesarean they were booked in for, just ahead of schedule. What all of this means is that whilst some things are planned, and some things are expected, when it comes to the human body, you never really know what is going to happen.

On Friday, the domestic assistant has wheeled the dinner trolley around the ward, and I have just returned to the office after helping her to dish out the evening meal.

"There's a section coming up from Delivery," Geri says. She still slips into this habit of referring to women as 'a section', 'a delivery', 'a multip'. I'm not a fan. Reducing the person to their experience or their condition is rooted in the medical tradition that Geri, many of the other nurses, and all of the doctors have been trained in. I like to believe that I will never feel that way and will never treat anyone as a patient rather than a person. It's easy to use the word "patient" as shorthand, but they are women, first and foremost.

I nod at Geri and wait for her to give me further details. She's in the middle of eating a cup of soup, dipping thick white bread into the red tomato, like a swab into blood. My mind makes too many connections like that when I have been out on the ward for a few days. Strangely, it doesn't turn my stomach; it has become sort of normal.

"Fay Curtis. Uh, failed forceps."

An emergency caesarean then. She will have been in labour and got so far into her delivery that she was on the point of pushing the baby out, and something went wrong. I will read her notes when she comes up, but a caesarean for failed forceps usually means that the baby has been distressed, the heartbeat dropping, the blood becoming acidic. If the mother's cervix is fully dilated and the baby is low enough down the birth canal, sometimes it is possible to use forceps to help baby to be born. If that fails, it's straight into the theatre so the baby can be delivered quickly.

"It's her first baby. She wants to breastfeed." Geri dips her bread again, and a large splash drips back into the cup before she lifts it up to her mouth.

"Okay," I say. "How long?"

"They're just cleaning her up, and then bringing her."

I nod. "I'll get a space ready."

From theatre, women are usually transferred into a small recovery room for post-operative observations, and after half an hour, or sometimes a little longer if necessary, they are transferred up to postnatal. Regardless of whether they have had a general anaesthetic or a spinal (where they are given a local anaesthetic into the space around the bones in the spine), they aren't able to walk, so they are brought up on a bed, and we wheel one of ours out in a straight swap. I'll move the bed out of one of our bays, and the recovery midwife and theatre assistant will bring the bed with Fay on it to fill the space. Where possible, we try to allocate the post-operative ladies to side rooms, so I write Fay's name on the board in one of the appropriate spaces.

The postnatal ward runs on a pattern of routine. We have our handover at the beginning of shift, then it's the drug round before we visit every patient to check that she and her baby are fit and well. The assistants go around with refreshments, and the catering staff take the meals. For those women who are post-op, the loop of routine is doubled up with more frequent observation, and usually additional drugs.

There are checklists to cover every eventuality: daily observations for mother and baby, drugs charts, fluid balance, discharge sheets. Some days it feels like the ward runs according to paperwork and processes rather than patients.

Fay will come up from the recovery room; I will start the routine observations, checking her blood pressure, pulse, and blood loss. I'll make sure she's pain-free, and generally feeling alright. If she still has intravenous fluids, I'll make sure they are running correctly. Then there's the baby. Check he or she is pink, warm, and well. Hopefully, the baby will have fed in recovery, but if not, I'll make sure Fay tries to feed. If all of this sounds process-driven and nurse-like, that's probably because it is. This part of the job is about ensuring physical wellbeing, making sure that the patient is post-operatively well. No matter how much I think that I never wanted to be a nurse, or that I don't want to care for patients who are unwell, there are aspects of the midwife's role that need me to have those skills.

I have to know how to carry out the nursing basics. That's not to say that I lose the "with woman" side of the role. Midwife. With woman. That's what the word means, and every time I think about my role, I remember that. I'm not doing this just to carry out the checks and write in the paperwork; I'm here because I want to make a better experience for each woman that I care for.

When Fay arrives on the ward, I meet the
recovery midwife and the theatre assistant in the
corridor, before they wheel the bed down into
the space that I have prepared. Fay is tucked
under a plain white sheet and a light blue waffle
blanket. Just visible above the top of the covers
is her baby, cradled in her arms. I smile at her,
and peer to smile at her baby too.

"Hi Fay. I'm Violet. I'm a student midwife.
I'll be taking care of you this evening," I say, as
I walk down the corridor next to her bed.

"Hi," she replies. She seems alert. There's a
metal pole at the top of the bed, with a hook at
the top for her IV fluid bag. Just dangling below
the blanket at the side of the bed is her catheter
bag.

"She's exhausted," the recovery midwife tells
me, after she has wheeled the bed into position.
"It's been a long day."

Fay manages a weak smile and nods. "You
can say that again."

The theatre assistant sets up the drip onto one
of our free-standing poles and tucks the baby
into a cot by Fay's bedside. Meanwhile, the
recovery midwife runs through the handover.

"She's had some stitches for the forceps. The caesarean itself was straightforward when we got there. Record time, I think." She shows me the operation notes and pulls out the drug chart. "She's had the usual PR analgesia, and the drip is to stay up until this bag has run through, then you can take it down. Post op, everything was fine. Baby was a little slow to pick up, but we gave a little oxygen, and she was fine. No grunting. Had a little breastfeed, but not for long. Probably needs to try again before the end of shift." She pauses for a moment, as if running through a checklist in her head, trying to work out if she has forgotten anything. "Partner has been with her all day. He left about half an hour ago, but I told him that he can pop in and see her later."

"Thanks," I say, taking the brown folder containing Fay's notes. It's strange to think that a caesarean can be normal and straightforward, especially one that was performed in an emergency situation, but that's the way it is. Not everyone comes into hospital and has a natural vaginal birth, but I never thought that midwifery would be all catching babies and getting to cuddle them afterwards. Postnatal ward gives me plenty of opportunities for those cuddles, but it is also teaching me about how much nursing is necessary as part of my role.

I put the notes down onto the bedside cabinet as the midwife and assistant wheel the spare bed back to theatre and leave Fay in my care.

"Sounds like you've had a tough day," I say.

She looks exhausted. I can't begin to imagine what it is like being in labour all day, and then having to go through an operation. On top of that, having a baby to look after seems like an impossible task. Even though I can't imagine, I can empathise, and I can care.

"Do you think you can manage a cup of tea?"

Her face brightens up. "Am I allowed one? Oh yes, please." It's as though I have offered her something far more exciting than a simple drink. Sometimes it's the little things that make all the difference.

When I have made the tea, I will come back and talk to her, be with her, listen to whatever she wants to tell me about her birth day. I will support her to feed her baby, and I will make sure she is comfortable and well. Most of all, I will be with her, because that is why I'm doing this: to be with woman.

# Chapter Thirteen

Even though there are always lots of women and babies to care for, and I'm on my feet for most of the day, postnatal ward is not necessarily more tiring than any of the other placements, so far. Perhaps it is because there is a routine to the day that everything flows in a natural order. Still, by the end of the fourth week, I'm exhausted. Maybe it's working whilst trying to complete my assignments for the term. Maybe it's not just that.

Since Zoe and Luke got it together, things have felt different. I mean, I knew that it wouldn't be the same, it couldn't be, but I didn't know exactly what it was going to be like. I hope that now they are starting to go out on dates and act more like a "normal" couple that feeling might start to settle.

When I get home after my early shift on Saturday, I have the first chance in two days to talk to Zoe. I get home from my placement just after three in the afternoon, and I can't wait to see her. The house is silent when I open the front door, and when I look into her room it's empty. My disappointment feels like biting into a sweet, thinking it's going to be sugary in the centre and finding out it's sour. There's no Luke, and even Carl doesn't seem to be around. I make a drink, and pull two chocolate biscuits from a pack, think again, and take a third. Why not?

It's not often that the house is quiet and unoccupied; there's usually someone in the living room or the kitchen to talk to. Today, I make do with taking myself up to my room, and flop onto my bed to enjoy my snack and occupy myself with a book until Zoe gets home.

I'm not patient enough, and I send her a text.

**Home now. WUU2? xx**

I hate myself for using the shorthand for "what are you up to?" as soon as I've typed it, but I press send before I waste time rewriting.

I put my phone down on the bed next to me and get stuck into the book I'm currently reading. It's a distraction. I used to love to read, and I guess I haven't had much time since I've been at uni. Still, it doesn't feel like a pleasure, it feels like a pacifier.

I've read two and a half chapters before I hear the front door click open. I set down my book and try to focus, and work out whether it is Zoe, and if so, whether she's alone.

"Violet?" It's Zoe's voice.

As soon as I hear her coming up the stairs I leap off my bed and spring to open my door to see her. I feel like a puppy who has been left for too long by her owner. Perhaps I shouldn't think about myself in such a negative, needy light, but it's the truth. I have become used to having Zoe here with me, accessible all day every day, and I have loved it.

Back home, growing up, our homes were a ten minutes' walk apart. Even then, I would see her every day. I can't imagine a time when I won't be able to be with her. It's hard to explain without making it sound weird. It sounds like a cliché, but she truly is like the sister that I never had. It's not like the sentiment has been one-sided. Our bond runs both ways.

Yesterday she was up and off to her placement before I was out of bed, and I wasn't home until after ten. She was already asleep. Today it was my turn to be out of the house whilst she was still snoring. If this is what I'm like about time with Zoe, how am I ever going to have a *relationship* while I'm studying. How will I ever manage it when I'm a midwife?

Zoe manages to get to the landing before I throw my arms out and hug her.

"It's not been that long," she laughs, as she drops her bag onto the floor and joins the hug.

"Two days! And I have been waiting to hear about your date!" I have to laugh too, because the thought is ridiculous. How can I miss her presence after such a short time? I don't know, but I do. I always miss her.

"I texted you," she says, and it's true. We have messaged each other, but it's just not the same.

I shrug, and say, "Tell me everything! What have you been up to?" My voice is heavy with exclamation marks; if I really were that dog, I would be wagging my tail furiously, and probably licking her cheek. I manage not to.

We go into her room. She tugs her jumper off and throws it onto her chair, and then lets her hair out of the high ponytail that she favours for work. I don't think she has to wear her hair tied back, it's her choice. I have to keep my hair up and my nails short and unpolished. The sacrifices we make for our careers.

"Seriously," I say. "What's new? How's everything going with Luke?"

"You don't have to be serious," she grins. "There's nothing to be serious about. He is lovely. Just as you would expect him to be."

She starts to brush her hair. It falls in long, natural waves, shimmering like sunlight.

"Would I?" I ask.

"I suppose I imagined for quite a while what he would be like," she says. "And what I imagined is quite close to the truth." She pauses, before adding, "Which is great, because I thought that he was going to be wonderful."

That gets a big smile from me. She is positively radiant with happiness. I have never seen her like this before, and if Luke is the cause of this, then I can't be anything other than thrilled for her.

"Tell me about your date." If I don't have the time or inclination for my own love life at the moment, at least I can live vicariously through hers.

It's her turn to shrug.

"We walked into town and had dinner at that Mexican place opposite the park."

"The one with two-for-one cocktails?"

"You got it! But we had three cocktails each, I mean, why not, right?"

"Did you actually have dinner?" I take the brush from her and run it through her hair. This is something we used to do years ago. When we were younger we both decided that we wanted long hair, and our respective parents agreed to let us grow it out. I decided one day when I was about six years old that I was going to cut my fringe. I made such a hack job of it that instead of telling me off for it, my mum just felt sorry for me. Still, the only way to make me look half decent was to chop off the rest of my locks to match. After that I was fascinated by Zoe's hair. She told me that she would get hers cut short to match mine, but I insisted that she didn't. Keep it, I told her. Don't you dare spoil it just because of me. She would have though. She would have done that for me. Even though I knew how much she loved her long hair, she would have let go of it in a flash for me. I lost mine through my own stupidity, or since I was only a child, let's call it misadventure.

"Are you even listening?" she says, putting her hand up and stopping me.

"I'm sorry." I haven't heard a word that she has been saying. "For some reason I was thinking about that time I cut my hair."

She bursts into a peel of laughter. "You wanted me to cut mine too!" she says, in between her giggles.

I frown and shake my head. "No, I told you not to."

She pauses for a moment, trying to hold in her laughter. "Oh maybe," she says. "You looked pretty cool with short hair though. I was probably jealous and wanted to have the same hair as you."

I shake my head, and laugh too, but at what she has said, rather than at the memory of the situation. "I looked like a boy."

"Short hair is cute," she says. "I would look terrible with short hair. I would just be all freckles and silly little snub nose. I *need* my hair to be pretty. You are naturally gorgeous."

I hand her the hairbrush back, and smile. "I'm not but thank you. It's you that has the lovely boyfriend and gets to go on dreamy dates. Tell me again. I'm listening."

"You could have a dreamy boyfriend and go on lovely dates too if you wanted to," she says. "I didn't think you wanted that though."

I shrug and say nothing. I probably don't. I don't think I do. I don't think I could anyway.

"We had dinner, and then we walked back through the gardens. It was dark by then. The park was beautiful, with all the Christmas lights, and the smell of doughnuts coming up from the skating rink. It was busy, you know. Lots of teenagers around, hanging about in their groups, playing music though the loudspeakers on their phones. I don't know why they do that. Luke had his arm around me, and we were like a little bubble, like no one else mattered. There were so many people, but it could have just been us."

I can feel the warmth inside me, as though I can share the feelings of love that she is experiencing.

"It sounds perfect," I say. My voice is quiet and soft, like it is coming from far away. "Zoe, I'm so happy for you."

Now we *are* being serious. The laughter has stopped, and the two of us are sitting, looking at each other, understanding that what she has is something bigger than either of us thought it was going to be.

"Thanks," she says. "Thanks, Violet. Thank you for giving me the push to finally do this. Thank you for encouraging me to go on normal dates. Thank you for everything that you have done and everything you do. I know that things are changing, that things are probably going to change even more, but whatever happens, you are so important to me."

"Oh Zo." I don't know what to say. There isn't anything that I can say.

"I was thinking, maybe we should set some time aside that's just for us. So we know that we are always going to see each other, no matter what."

I'm about to say that it's difficult, with me being on shifts, but instead I think about all that she has done for me, and how important she is to me too.

"Yes," I say. "I'd love that."

"How about Mondays. Monday afternoon. We will commit to coffee and cake, and all the girlie chat that we can handle?"

I grin and nod. "All of my favourite things, with my favourite person. What more could I ask for?"

She holds her hand out, as if to shake on it, and seal the deal, but as I move forward, instead she grabs me, pulling me towards her, into another warm, deep embrace.

"I'll always be here for you," she says, her face buried in my hair. "I promise. Always."

"Me too, Zoe. Me too."

# Chapter Fourteen

My first official Monday meet-up with Zoe comes at the end of a morning shift for me and a placement day for her. I'm tired, but grateful for the chance to sit and chat. I have a lot on my mind, and knowing that we have this time set aside has made me worry about it a lot less than I might have otherwise. I don't want to stress about interrupting her and Luke, or being in the way, bringing them down with my problems when otherwise they are obviously so incredibly happy. This time together feels like a safe space to talk.

The main thing that's bothering me is planning my SPOKE placements on the non-maternity units. I'm not looking forward to any of them. I know that I should probably be more positive, but, as I have said, I never wanted to be a nurse. It sounds terrible when I articulate it, but I don't really want to work with sick people. I can't make that sound anything other than terrible. Even though I have obviously come to realise how important it is to understand about the nursing elements of maternity care, actually going into nursing units or nursing wards is making my anxiety bubble inside me. Every time I start to think about planning my placements I feel physically sick.

I try to explain it to Zoe.

"I'm dreading the non-midwifery placements," I tell her. I'm pushing a fragment of carrot cake around my plate absent-mindedly, slightly disappointed that they had sold out of the Bakewell before we arrived.

Zoe looks at me quizzically. "It will be good experience for you, won't it? What's worrying you?"

I settle my fork down, and Zoe swoops in like an over-keen seagull to take my leftovers. I look up at her and manage a smile.

"Ill people," I say. It sounds dreadful coming out of my mouth. I pick up my mug and take a mouthful of mocha, trying to wash away the bad taste of the words.

Zoe laughs for a second, and then stops. "You're serious," she observes.

"Uh-huh," I say. "Awful, isn't it?"

She starts to shake her head but turns the shake into a nod instead. "Maybe a little."

I fiddle with the fork, running my finger over the steel distractedly.

"Is it bothering you that much?" she asks.

Without looking at her, it's my turn to nod. "I

feel so bad for thinking it, but I never wanted to be a nurse. I don't deal well with sick people. I don't know; I just don't think I'm the best person to be caring for people that are, you know, ill."

"But you have maternity patients that are ill, surely. It's not all happy endings, is it?"

I sigh and say, "You're right. I know. I feel like it's a bit of a waste of time though. I don't want to be a nurse, I don't want to focus on sickness, I want to be a midwife. It's like sending you on a placement to…to…" I can't think of an equivalent example.

"To a zoo, probably," Zoe smiles. "Although that might actually be quite useful."

She always manages to make me feel a little better. Still, as much as I feel bad for thinking the things I do, I can't get around the fact that this is the truth.

"Where do you have to go, exactly," she asks.

"I have to choose relevant areas. Places that are going to help me to learn how to be a better midwife. I would rather spend more time on my actual maternity placement learning how to be a better midwife."

"Children's ward might be nice," she says. Then she stops to think. "Actually, no. It would probably be awful. I don't know. I pictured brightly coloured walls and clowns going in to cheer up the children and…well, I suppose it's not like that at all. Looking after children that are so unwell that they need to be in hospital is probably very demanding, isn't it?"

I nod again, slowly and silently. I thought something similar when we were told about the allocations, and it took me about the same amount of time as it did for Zoe to understand that it wasn't going to be a kids' party.

"Mental health?" she ventures. "That's not the same as a nursing ward. Could be interesting."

I shake my head almost reflexively. "Oh no."

I'm not sure what would happen in a mental health unit. The only experience I have is from television and the media, and I doubt very much that modern mental health treatment is anything like *One Flew Over the Cuckoo's Nest*. I hope it's not, anyway. I have my own mental health issues to deal with. How would I be able to support other people, patients that should be getting care from a trained professional rather than an anxious student midwife? I feel like I would be doing them a disservice by being involved in their care.

"I don't know how to look after people with those kinds of complex needs," I say. "I imagine it would be a ward full of people who are in need of a lot of support. It would be heart-breaking."

"Not as heart-breaking as being on a ward full of children with serious diseases without a cure," Zoe says.

I can feel tears prickling my eyes. If thinking about the placements is able to upset me this much, what am I going to be like when I have to start attending them.

"Listen," Zoe says. She wipes away the tear that's formed in my eye. "You need to try to get as much as you can out of these placements. Look for positives. Try to think of things that you can apply to midwifery. Think about those women that you care for that are going to be ill, and how applying yourself in these placements will benefit them."

"We have women with high blood pressure, postnatal haemorrhages, gestational diabetes," I say. "If I go onto the medical wards to look after people with raised blood pressure or diabetes I'll probably end up stuck with a bunch of old people..." I stop myself before I say anything else, as I realise what I must sound like.

"Ill people can be pregnant, and pregnant people can be ill though, surely." It's obvious when she says it.

"I don't see many of them. I mean, I haven't so far, but sure, of course that's true."

I've thought about everything from my own perspective. I don't want to be a nurse. I don't want to look after ill people. I don't want to look after old people. Nursing isn't my vocation. I'm sure that the women I will meet who have serious illnesses or medical conditions won't want to have them either. I need to look beyond what I want and focus on becoming the best midwife that I can be.

I know Zoe is trying to help, and I know she is trying to make me feel better about the placements, but I'm stepping out of my comfort zone, and as soon as I do that my anxiety starts to rear its ugly head. I've been so in control. I thought I was over it. I thought I could do this. Now, I think that I was deluding myself.

I can't talk about it anymore, so I smile and nod, and change the subject.

It's two weeks until the start of Christmas break. I don't know if it is too soon for Zoe and Luke to want to spend the holiday together. If it were me, I would think it was too soon. She hasn't mentioned it, though. I segue into the topic.

"I'll sort it all out after Christmas," I say. I add, as if it's an afterthought, "Have you talked to Luke about the holidays."

She acts as though it's a reasonable change in conversation, so I can't have sounded as clunky as I felt.

"He's going back to Leeds; I'm going home to the folks. Same as usual." She doesn't look at all upset by the prospect of their enforced separation.

"And you're okay with that?" I ask.

"Sure. It's early days. Family comes first," she says. Then she rests her hand onto mine and adds, "And friends."

Three weeks at home, back in Portland, with Zoe. The two of us alone together again. It really is going to be a good Christmas. Whatever happens next term can wait. I'm not going to think about it. I'm going to enjoy the holidays, and my time with my friend.

# Chapter Fifteen

Despite the extra time that I have with Zoe, being home for Christmas break feels different to any of our previous holidays. If it were Easter or maybe even summer, we might have stayed at Tangiers Court, Zoe, Luke, and I, but as she said Christmas means family, and family means home.

Of course, Zoe has been messaging Luke constantly over the holidays. It's not like she has been stuck to her phone the whole time, but every time her Samsung has pipped out its three little beeps, she has scrambled to look at the screen. I can tell that she has been trying hard not to let her budding relationship with Luke affect the time she has with me, but still it has. I don't think badly of her. If I had a boyfriend, or anything like one, I would probably want to be messaging him too. Especially if he happened to be a few hundred miles away.

Even on the way back to university, her phone has been ringing out the signal to herald more messages from Luke.

She's the driver; I still don't have my licence, but I'm a good passenger - I brought a bag of sweets for the journey after all.

"He should be there when we get back," she tells me.

I nod, and realise she is looking at the road and not at me. "Okay," I say. It sounds flat and disinterested, and I don't want her to think I'm bored. "You must be looking forward to seeing him. Have you got anything planned together?"

I want the answer to be no. Selfish as it might sound, I've had Zoe to myself for the past three weeks, and it has felt like things have been normal between us again. All the time though, I knew we would be coming back, and I knew she was going to be spending her time with him instead. When I think about it like this, it sounds awful. I have to stop this. I have to let her get on with her life, and more importantly, I have to get on with mine.

It's Friday afternoon. We don't have to be back at uni until Monday, but Luke is coming home today, and so we are too. Home. It's strange how I think of Tangiers Court as home now, rather than Portland, where I spent Christmas with my mother. I would have always called there *home* until recently. Portland is half an hour's drive from the university, it's not like I left home and travelled the world in search of adventure. Zoe and I moved away but stayed as close to home as possible. It's an adventure, but it's a safe one. They are, apparently, my favourite kind.

"I guess you'll be busy tonight then." The sentence comes out a lot harsher than I mean it to. I don't want to burst Zoe's bubble. I wished and hoped for her and Luke to get together, after all. I've had the luxury of having her to myself, if you exclude the phone calls and messages; now it's time to give her back.

She takes her eyes off the road for a split second and flashes me a look of concern.

"I don't mean -" I start to apologise.

She looks away, focusing on the duel carriageway ahead of us.

"I'm sorry," I say. "I've enjoyed having the holidays with you. I want you to be happy, you know that."

She remains tight-lipped and nods silently.

I turn my head and look out of the passenger window. The sky is a pale washed-out grey. The fields that we are driving past are a dull dark green in the winter afternoon light. Every so often the background is broken up by the occasional off-white dots of sheep. The whole scene appears depressed and dreary, but there is still an underlying beauty to it, which reminds me of why I would never want to live far from here. We head along the road in silence, and as we crest a hill I know that if I look across and through Zoe's window I will be able to see the slightest glimpse of the sea.

When I look over, I see a stream of tears on Zoe's cheek.

"Zoe. Zoe, what's up? I'm sorry. Gosh, really, I didn't mean anything. Please. Look, pull over, don't, please." Despite the January cold, I suddenly feel very hot. I want her to stop the car, I need it as much for myself as for her.

"I'm fine," she says. Her words sound fragile.

"You're obviously not. Zo, I'm so happy for you and Luke, I honestly am. I don't want to get in the way of -"

"You are not in the way. You will never be in the way."

She flicks on her indicator and pulls over into a lay-by, bringing us to a sharp stop. Then, she turns as far as her seatbelt will allow, and she looks at me.

"I have missed Luke so much, but I'm scared. I'm scared of not being able to spend as much time with you as I want to. I'm scared that, because Luke lives with us, I'm always going to be under some kind of pressure to be with him, to talk to him, to prioritise him - and most of all I'm scared because I don't want to do that. The past few weeks, I have felt awful when you and I have been shopping and he has phoned up, or when we have been in the coffee shop and he has texted. You know, all those times when it would usually just have been the two of us."

She is still crying, perhaps even more now. The tears are silent, but they are running down her face, through her light peach-coloured blusher, leaving thin grey trails in their wake.

"Zoe. It's okay. It's alright. We will work it out. It is going to be fine."

I nod my head towards the rear-view mirror, and she looks up, seeing her reflection. She sniffs a snotty laugh and reaches for a tissue.

"Can't be turning up looking like a sad clown, can I?" She tries to smile.

"Please don't worry about me, Zoe. Whatever happens, I'm always going to be around. I will always be your best friend. Always. Or at least for as long as you want me to be."

"I always want you to be," she says, and somehow this tilts her over the edge again. She honks out a deep sob and I reach over and wrap my arms around her. Anyone driving past would wonder what on earth we are doing here, but, as usual, when it comes to me and Zoe, I just don't care what anyone thinks. All I care about is us.

As Luke predicted, when we get to Tangiers Court just before three, he is already back. Not only that but he has picked up some food from the supermarket, and there is a box of donuts on the work surface in the kitchen next to the kettle.

"I brought the snacks, you can make the tea," he smiles, and scoops Zoe up into a welcoming hug.

"Or you two can hug and I will comfort eat them all," I say. I flash them my biggest grin so that they know I'm joking, but the chocolate-glazed treats do look amazing. "How was Christmas?" I ask, as Zoe nuzzles her head into Luke's chest.

"Great, yeah, thanks. Christmas can't be anything other than great, can it?" Luke says.

He doesn't say that he missed Zoe or couldn't wait to get back here. I don't know why I expected that to be his answer, I suppose because that is what Zoe would have said if I asked her. Christmas *is* always great, but she looks so much happier now than she has for the entirety of the past three weeks.

This is home now, and Luke is her happiness.

# Chapter Sixteen

Last term was a relative breeze. I was back in a clinical placement that I'd been to before, my assessments were all written assignments. I felt confident and competent. I think it was just what I needed to consolidate what I learned last year - not just about midwifery, but also in terms of my self-confidence and ability to handle situations. If I thought that I'd conquered my anxiety though, I was very wrong. Did I think that? Did I ever really think that?

The night before the start of my second term, Luke and Zoe are watching a movie downstairs, and even though I know I am more than welcome to join them, I feel like getting ready for my classes, and having some alone time. Carl is out somewhere, so I'm sitting on my bed with a stack of papers that I printed out on my mum's computer. I've got the module guides for this term: 'Pharmacology' and 'Complex Midwifery Care'. I knew this was coming. Complex Midwifery Care is the module that I have been dreading, for the assessment rather than the subject itself. This term I will have my second Objective Structured Clinical

Examination.

My anxiety spiralled out of control when I had the first OSCE last year. I ran from the skills lab without being able to carry out the assessment and failed without even trying. I can't do that to myself again.

If that's not scary enough, I also have a written examination for the pharmacology module. I'm not a mathematician, not by a long shot. My brain is scientific enough to understand the biology and biochemistry required of me for the course and for my future career, but maths is not my strong point. I know that it's essential that I can calculate the correct doses of drugs and administer them safely to mothers and babies, but this module is filling me with fear. I don't know how I'll be able to get through it.

I check through the module guide. There is no room for error with this exam. I have to answer every question correctly. That sounds incredibly harsh. How can an exam have a one hundred percent pass mark? Perhaps there has been some kind of mistake. I will have to ask the module leader. I keep reading. At least if I fail this exam I will be able to resit. Once.

My hand is starting to shake, and I let the

paper fall onto the bed. I feel sick. I shouldn't have started to think about these modules. Then again, it's better that I think about them and get this out of my system while I'm in the comfort and privacy of my bedroom instead of flipping out in the middle of the classroom.

I close my eyes, and bring my knees up to my chest, hugging them against me. Maybe I should forget about this for tonight and go and sit with Zoe and Luke instead. I could grab a cup of tea and some chocolate and switch my brain off. It almost feels like a possibility, but as I sit here, thinking, my thoughts keep flicking back to the OSCE.

I passed last year, but only on my second attempt. I could have messed up my entire career - my entire future - because of a stupid panic attack. I failed myself. I let myself down. That's what happened. The sickness in my stomach is rising through me now. I'm glad that I am sitting down already, because I feel like I'm on a rocking ship on a rough tide rather than seated on my bed. I haven't felt like this for months, and I sure as heck haven't missed this feeling.

No, I didn't think that I'd conquered my anxiety. I don't believe that I could ever be that overconfident. I managed to push it away into a dark corner for a little while, but it has still been there, waiting to resurface. Perhaps this is why I was tense and snappy with Zoe. It wasn't about coming back here and not being able to spend time with her; it was about knowing what was in store for me this trimester. I knew that the OSCE was drawing near. I know that it is - and it terrifies me.

I kick my legs and thrash them against the pile of paperwork, pushing the sheets onto the floor. I want them away from me. I don't want to think about it anymore. I can't. It's too much.

My face is burning hot, my cheeks on fire with the heat of anxiety. I pick up my phone from beside me and look at the time. It's only half past eight. Too early to sleep, but I don't want to go downstairs now. Zoe will know that there is something wrong, and she will stop watching her film, take me into the kitchen or bring me up here, and sit and talk me down until I'm feeling calm, in control, and terribly guilty about taking her away from what she is doing. I have to do this by myself. Zoe isn't going to be as available for me as she has been, and the sooner I start to deal with that, and accept it, the better.

I didn't realise how much that thought would affect me.

I pull in a long deep breath and let out a sob, then cover my mouth immediately. I was too loud. I don't want to distract her. I don't want to be any trouble. I'm terrible, I'm useless. Why shouldn't she be able to get on with her life without having me in the way?

I hear the living room door open downstairs, and Zoe shouts up to me. "Are you alright?"

I call back, "Yeah, thanks. I had my headphones on. I was getting carried away."

"Okay," she says. She would never usually have accepted such an obvious lie. She must be having a good night.

"I'm going to get in the bath," I shout. "Have fun!"

I hadn't actually thought about getting into the bath before I said the words, but my brain usually knows what my body needs, or vice versa.

"Alright." One word, and then she's silent.

I hear the downstairs door click closed again. I feel strange. Not just because of the anxiety that is bubbling inside me; I feel like something has definitely changed between Zoe and me. Before Luke, she would have run upstairs, checked on me and not taken my shouted words for an answer. She would have talked to me until I spilled all of my thoughts and feelings.

Perhaps I *have* been too dependent upon her. Perhaps this is actually for the best for both of us. I have to start learning how to deal with my thoughts. I have to get in control of my own life, and let Zoe live hers.

I stretch out my arms, throwing them as wide as I can, and then kick my legs forward again. It's kind of like a seated star jump; all I want to do is to push some of the stress out of my limbs. I also want to shout out, or maybe even scream, but given the circumstances, I control myself.

Instead, I get up, pull my robe off the hanger, and head along the corridor to the bathroom. If there is one thing I know for sure, it's that feeling hot water embrace me will make me feel at least a little better - even if it is only temporary.

This term is going to be tough, and I'm going to have to be tougher. More importantly, I'm going to have to learn how to do it without Zoe.

# Chapter Seventeen

The first day of term always seems to be a
jumble of emotions. There's the thrill of being
introduced to new modules and looking forward
to what I will be learning during the sessions,
and the excitement of catching up with my
course mates again after a few weeks away
from each other. On the other hand, new
modules mean more assignments to prepare for
and worry about.

I already know what this term has in store,
and there is not much that I'm looking forward
to. There's the pharmacology exam, the second
OSCE, and I can't even balance my dread of
these with the happy anticipation of my
placement, because I know that I need to get at
least some of my SPOKE sessions over with. I
probably shouldn't think of them like that. I
have been so negative about the external visits I
have to attend, but to me, they feel like
challenges rather than opportunities.
Psychologically, not having as much time with
Zoe is no doubt making all of my worries about
this term even worse.

Still, it's Monday. That means when we have
finished our lectures for the day instead of

heading back to Tangiers Court, we will go into town for our weekly mate date. Zita Somerville is leading the Monday morning module this term, but even though she is one of the most inspirational and engaging tutors, my mind is still wandering to this afternoon, cake and, above all, Zoe.

All the other students are full of passion and enthusiasm, but I'm starting to feel out of my depth. It's like I have been treading water, kicking my legs as hard as I can to try to keep afloat, but my head is starting to sink beneath the surface. I'm not as smart as any of my classmates. Everything comes so easily to them, not just retaining information and building on their knowledge, but their basic self-confidence far outweighs my own. I never put my hand up in class to answer anything because I'm terrified of being wrong, or more specifically, saying something stupid.

Zita is leading the pharmacology module, and she is currently standing by the side of the SMART board, talking us through the module guide.

"Why is it important for midwives to know about drugs?" she asks.

I instinctively look away from her. Not only

do I not want to raise my hand, but also I don't want her to make eye contact with me and single me out. I have some ideas as to what the answer is, but I don't have the confidence to speak up.

One of the girls on the front row responds. "So that we understand what doctors are talking about."

There's a murmur of laughter, but it's amusement at the comment; no one is laughing at the girl, no one thinks she is stupid. I'm sure if I'd given that answer, I would have sounded ridiculous.

Even Zita smiles. "That is certainly one way of looking at it. We need to know what drugs are being offered to or prescribed for the women in our care. As advocates for women, knowing about the drugs that are used will help us to talk to them about the risks and benefits, and the side effects. Anything else?"

"We need to know about dosage?" Sophie speaks from my right. Her voice is uncertain, and she phrases her answer like a question, but at least she has the confidence to say something.

"Especially if we are the ones that are giving the medication to the patient," Zita says. "In this module we will look at the most common drugs that are used, and you need to start making a mental note when you are in your placements, so that the usual dosages become second nature to you. There are many drugs that you will be able to give without them being prescribed by a doctor, because they are covered by the standing order for the unit. Make sure you know what is covered in your own hospital." She pulls a booklet from her bag and holds it in the air. "You will all need to read this document. You can access it online, and the address is in your module guides."

I recognise it. I've already read through it, but I know that I will have to revisit it several times before all of the content sinks in. It's the Nursing and Midwifery Council's *'Standards for Medicines Management'* guideline: the definitive principles from the midwifery regulatory body.

This all felt overwhelming when I was preparing for the term last night, and today it is almost too much for me. I know that I still have so much to learn about the clinical elements of midwifery, but at least I vaguely understand what I'm doing and why I am doing it. The principles of pharmacology and medicines management are far more difficult to get my head around. If I make even the slightest error it could have huge implications. I guess that's why student midwives can only ever administer medication under supervision. We aren't expected to be experts, at least not yet, but in order to pass this module, I need to know enough to pass the exam.

After class, I leave the lecture block and walk out into a torrential downpour of rain. Zoe is standing across the path, sheltering beneath the overhang at the front of the library.

I don't have a hood or an umbrella, so I try to pull my jacket up over my head, and dash over to join her.

"Typical," she says. She looks at me and her face registers concern. "You okay? What's up?"

I hadn't meant to let my feelings show through. I wanted our time together to be light and happy, but sometimes my emotions are too big for me to stuff them into a corner, out of view.

"I don't think I can do it," I say.

My face is already dripping wet from the rivulets of rain, and I could probably get away with letting my tears out, but still, I try to hold them back.

"You still want to go into town?" she asks.

"Uh, yes, of course." The very thought that I might have jeopardised our coffee date makes a heavy leaden feeling thud into my gut. "Don't you?"

"I mean, do you want to stay here and talk instead? We could go into the bar?"

"Oh, right." It's always my instinct to think the worst, but I should never jump to the conclusion that Zoe would let me down or not want to talk to me just because of my own stupid thoughts. I feel even more of an idiot now.

It's early. First day back at lectures, are there going to be that many students in the bar at half past four?

"If it's not too busy," I say.

She nods. "Hey. It's going to be okay."

I couldn't stop my tears after all. I give her a weak nod in reply, and wipe at my eyes.

"Come on. Let's go and find a quiet corner and a strong drink."

"Strong coffee is fine for me," I say. The last thing I need when I'm already feeling down is alcohol.

We both pull our jackets above us, making a run for the main university block that houses the union bar.

Five minutes later we are sitting in the almost empty room that I've previously only seen packed with boisterous students. It feels strange being here when it is so quiet, almost like we are trespassing. Still, I much prefer it this way. I would rather have made it to our planned destination and be sitting with a slice of something sweet and sticky and a latte that doesn't taste like instant, but at least I'm here with Zoe.

We've hung our coats up on the backs of two chairs, and we're sitting next to each other on two others. It's like we have two spaces reserved for friends who have popped out somewhere. Strangely it reminds me of the absence of the two house mates that are always around us these days.

"What's happened, Violet?" she asks, her eyes heavy with concern.

I shake my head. "I don't know where to start," I say.

"I thought everything was getting better. You haven't seemed at all anxious recently." She is about to blow onto her cappuccino - there are no mochas available in the union bar, apparently - when she stops and looks at me. "I haven't noticed, have I? You've been worrying and I haven't noticed. Oh, Violet. Oh…I'm so sorry." She puts her cup back down onto its saucer and reaches over for my hand. "I really am sorry."

"You shouldn't have to look out for me and worry about me all the time," I say. "It's not your job to be my minder. Or my carer."

"It's not like that. I didn't mean -" She stops again. "You know I don't mean that."

Objectively I know she would never mean that, but beneath my anxiety-tinted glasses everything looks dark. My brain can make me believe almost anything.

"It's all getting on top of me. Last term - I think it gave me a false sense of security. There was nothing big and scary, and I let myself get too comfortable."

She's giving me her full attention. I thought this was what I wanted, but now I feel guilty for my dependence upon her.

"Look," I say. "Let's talk about something else. I want to hear about what you have been doing. Tell me about your course. How is -"

She cuts me off. "You don't have to do that," she says. "Stop it. You don't need to hold back what you're feeling or worry about offloading onto me. We can talk about what I have been doing later. I'm fine. I'm great, in fact. Apart from one thing."

"What's that?" I ask. This could be my chance to give something back, do something for her for a change.

She smiles and taps her spoon against the edge of my mug. "I'm worried about you, silly."

I was wrong. There doesn't appear to be much I can do about that.

"So, tell me," she says. "What happened today to make you feel like this?"

"It's not just today. I have exams this term, and I keep thinking about how I messed up last year. Then there's the SPOKE placements. We've already talked about them though; I don't want to bore you with all that again."

"You never bore me," she says. I know that she is telling the truth, because her eyes are filled with a mixture of concern and compassion. "You passed your OSCE resit, remember. You breezed through it. You can do that again."

"Breeze through a resit?" I say, with the faintest hint of a smile. I know what she means, and I know that her intentions are good, but it isn't as easy as she thinks. "I fluked it. I somehow managed to have a good day and -"

"Don't do that." She narrows her eyes, and her voice is sharp and serious. "Stop it."

But I can't. I can't change the way that I think about myself, not just because she says so. Instead, I stop talking.

"Vi." She tries to get me to look at her, but my focus is transfixed upon the mug in front of me. If I look at her again I think I might start crying again. I don't want that. I don't want to do it to her. I have to start taking responsibility for myself. I'm nineteen years old. I'm not a child anymore. I shouldn't expect her to babysit me.

"Violet." She says my name again, firmly, commanding my attention.

Slowly, I bring my gaze up to meet hers.

"I need to do something about it," I say. "I have to get over this once and for all."

Her expression changes like a sharp snap. "You mean -"

She doesn't want to say it and I'm not sure that I do either. I have to though. I have to say the words to make them real.

"I'm going to make an appointment at the

health centre." Actually forming the words and releasing them feels cathartic. "I'm going to get some support. Some drugs. Some…anything."

I hope that she won't blame herself or think that I'm doing this because she can't give me all the time that she did before. It's not like that though. It's my anxiety telling me that. I know. Objectively, I know. I have to keep reminding myself, whilst I can still think objectively at least.

"I'm -" She pauses, trying to find the words. "I'm proud of you. I hope you don't take that the wrong way. I mean it in the best way possible. I know how difficult it must be. I know what it was like before, and I know how hard it is."

She does. She is the only person who does, because she has been there through everything. It's about time I was there for myself.

"If you want me to come with you, or anything, you know I will," she says.

"Thanks," I say.

I already know that I'm going to go alone. Having someone as dependable as Zoe has made me dependent. Now, I have to learn how to depend upon myself. The first step is to believe in myself and get my anxiety in check.

# Chapter Eighteen

I make the appointment straight away, so that I don't give myself the chance to change my mind. I've coasted along for so many years, avoiding facing up to the fact that actually, I do need help. Zoe has been a crutch, and now that she is getting on with her life, I need to learn to walk on my own.

The meeting with the GP is not what I expected. It's nothing like the grim discussion I had as an eleven-year-old child, being dragged into the doctor's office by my parents. Then, the two of them pointed the finger of blame at each other for the full length of my assessment session, each convinced that the other was at fault for my anxiety. Meanwhile, I sat in silence, becoming more and more anxious. Looking back, I think that one of the main reasons that I didn't engage with treatment - the talking, counselling side of the treatment - was that I couldn't bear spending that extra time listening to my parents fighting. It was bad enough at home. If they were going to let their hostility spill over into the waiting room, I had to do everything I could to avoid that.

Now, things are different. Now, I'm an adult,

and I can make my own decisions. I can make
my own appointment, and I can look for support
on my own terms. It's almost as though I'm
actually too confident now to need help with
my anxiety. Almost. I am confident enough to
know that I need help.

So, here I am, face to face with Doctor
Fisher, one of the three GPs that work in the
campus health centre.

She starts with the standard questions about
why I have come to see her. It feels strange
being the patient. I'm starting to get used to
being in the role of the professional, even
though I'm still only at student level. I'm used
to asking the questions, taking the history,
thinking about what steps I need to take. Now,
I'm giving my own history. I'm self-conscious;
I feel like my every word will be judged.

"I should have seen someone sooner," I say.
"I have suffered too long. I mean, it's been
going on for too long. Eight years now, more or
less. I started having anxiety attacks not long
after I turned eleven. Things were bad at home,
between my parents." She is watching me,
nodding, saying nothing. "They didn't do
anything to me. They didn't hurt me. Nothing
like that. At least, you know, they didn't

physically hurt me, or neglect me or anything. But -" I pause again.

I don't know what to say. They argued in front of me every day. My dad, in particular, said terrible things to my mother. She sometimes responded, but after he hit her a few times she stopped arguing back. I don't want to talk about that though. I don't want to talk about the reasons that this started, I want to look for a way to make it end.

"They're divorced now. I live here, not at home. I don't want to blame them for what happened then. I want to stop feeling like this."

Doctor Fisher nods. "Why didn't you get help before?"

"I wasn't ready," I say. The words come out without me having to think about them too much, and I believe that they are the truth. "I didn't think I needed help. I thought that I would get better. But I haven't. I could have a better life if I didn't feel the way that I do. I want to pass my course. I want to be the best I can be. To do that I need to try to fight this."

Do I blame them? Do I really blame my parents for making me feel this way? I always thought that I would miss my mum awfully when I started university. I'm all that she has now that she and Dad have divorced, but still, I barely even message her. I see her at holidays, but I'm always eager to get away again. I don't want to feel like that. I don't want to enjoy the distance between us. Perhaps I also blame her for my inability to hold down a relationship. I'm too young to know that yet, to know it for sure, but I have the sneaking suspicion that I'm building a wall to protect myself, and to keep everyone out.

I don't want to be a Rapunzel in a tower, waiting for someone to come and rescue me. I would rather be Snow White, having a long nap in a glass case. I realise that still means not letting anyone get too close.

"You tried drug treatment in the past?" Fisher asks.

I nod. "I don't want that again. At least, not what I had before."

"Side effects?"

Again, I nod. "I felt out of it all of the time. It was horrible. I preferred the anxiety to the apathy."

"Okay," she says. "We can try something different. Not everyone experiences those side effects, and not every drug will make you feel like that." She taps a few keys on her computer and turns back to me. "What are your thoughts on counselling?"

"Does it help?" I ask.

"Some people, yes. Many people. You have to want to do it. If you can commit to the process, then, yes, it can help."

I think it over for a silent minute.

"Maybe," I say.

If I'm finding it strange being a patient here in this setting, how am I going to feel sitting with a counsellor for an hour every week. Besides, I know what is wrong with me, don't I? I know when this started and what caused it. Is rehashing all of that going to help me to feel any better?

"There's a waiting list, unfortunately. It's around twelve weeks at the moment. We have a lot of students who need support, and the service is stretched, I'm afraid."

I nod. I understand what it must be like. That's the other side to working in the health profession, you soon realise how the balance of supply and demand doesn't match up. People need services, but the services either don't exist, or the waiting list is so long that the treatment or support isn't much use by the time they get it.

"I could go on the list," I say, "and start the drugs now?"

"I would recommend that, yes," she says.

She seems like the sort of person that I can talk to. She is warm and caring, and she is talking to me on her level. I hope that I come across like this to the women that I care for.

"Okay," I say.

It's a no-brainer. I came here to get help, and if the help that is available now is drug treatment, then I have to give it a try. I can't carry on the way I have been. I have to do this now. It's for the good of my future. It's what I need.

I wish I'd accepted Zoe's offer of coming with me, sometimes just the moral support of having her by my side can make all the difference. She has Luke to think about now. I can't spend my whole life hanging around her neck. This is what is best for me, what is best for her, what is best for everyone. It is time.

# Chapter Nineteen

Doctor Fisher warned me that the medication might not start working straight away, but I want to feel the effect as soon as possible. It took me this long to make the move and see a doctor, now I want to keep the momentum going. I can't expect a miracle cure. I'm not going to take a few pills and be a different person, but I hope that the drug treatment, the therapy sessions, and my own positive attitude will be steps in the right direction.

My exams are looming, and if I can at least get my mind under control and not flip out over them that will be something.

By the time I get back to the wards, two weeks after I start my meds, I can't decide if they are making any difference or not. My allocated placement for this term is antenatal ward, but I know that I have to start fitting in my SPOKE placements. On the first day with my mentor Becky, we sit over lunch and discuss the options available to me.

I have a shortlist of units and wards that I think are likely to be useful. Becky reads through them as we sit in the office with our sandwiches.

"We can definitely get you into the Early Pregnancy Unit," she says. "Doctor St. Claire runs a clinic there, so we can ask her when she does the ward round."

Melanie St. Claire is one of the more approachable consultants. We see most of the consultant teams every day, as they carry out ward rounds for the antenatal patients. Doctor St. Claire always makes time to talk to the women, and she always makes time to talk to me.

I nod and smile. "That will be great."

"Same for the genito-urinary and gynae wards. Should be easy to get you in there if there aren't too many students already."

The nursing students are allocated to the wards too, so I have to fit in around them, as well as trying to make the SPOKE placements fit around my own shifts here.

"Have you had any thoughts about other places you'd like to spend some time?"

My mouth is full of bread and ham, and I chew and swallow, giving myself the chance to prepare an answer. The bottom line is that I don't really want to be on a ward with sick people. It might sound terrible but spending time on a nursing ward does not appeal to me at all. I can learn all I need to through my maternity placements.

"Not really," I say, eventually. "Maybe A and E."

I've watched enough hospital-based fly-on-the-wall television to know that an accident and emergency placement will probably be exciting. It's not your standard kind of nursing ward, for a start, and it's one of those places, pretty much like delivery suite, that you never know what is going to come through the doors.

"Okay," Becky says. "What do you think you will learn there to help with your midwifery?"

I shrug. "I just thought that I would see a lot of different things." I'm not sure this is a good enough answer, so I add, "And it will be useful to see the how the staff manage, you know, with all the patients, and such a range of, er, problems."

Becky nods. "It's not a trick question. I'm sure it could be useful. What else?" She writes A and E onto my list.

I've covered all of the pregnancy related units and wards, and I added in the only other place that I thought might be interesting.

"Er, maybe family planning? Is there a

contraception clinic or something?"

One of the conversations that midwives have in community before we discharge patients to health visitor care is about what contraception they are planning to use. Some of the women look at us as though they think they will never have sex again - bear in mind this is usually between a week and two weeks after they have given birth - but some of them are already asking when they can resume normal services, as it were.

Becky nods and writes.

"I have a suggestion," she says. "I know it's not your specialism, but have you considered going to the mental health unit?"

I let my expression hit my face before I can stop my feelings showing. Even though I don't want to spend time on a general nursing ward, I would prefer a month there to spending a day on a mental health unit. Not because I don't care, or because of any prejudice, but more because of my own mental fragility. I'm scared that I will see myself and my own anxiety reflected back at me. I'm not sure that I am strong enough to look at it.

"What's the matter?" Becky asks. She places her sandwich on top of the lid of the plastic box she brought it in, using it as a makeshift plate. Wiping her hands on a wet wipe, she reaches over to me. "Hey, what's wrong?"

I must look even more concerned than I thought.

"I don't know. I don't think I would be much good there. I would rather not go."

She nods slowly and looks at me. Her eyes are fixed on mine, as though she is trying to buoy me up.

"There's a mother and baby unit at the Linden Unit. I know that they take some of our students, and it really would be a good opportunity for you. You don't have to do a placement on the main unit, if that's what's bothering you?"

"I'm what's bothering me," I say, beneath my breath. I know she won't be able to hear me, and when she asks me what I said, instead I say, "I don't know what's bothering me."

She looks at me as though she doesn't quite believe me but isn't going to make a big deal of it.

"You could go for one or two days?"

"Can I think about it?" I ask. I don't feel hungry anymore, and I put my own sandwich back into its bag.

"I was a patient there," Becky says, out of nowhere. "After I had my first."

"I didn't realise," I say.

I feel terrible. What must she think of me? She must feel like I'm dismissive of the unit, and how will that make her feel about having been a patient there. Still, she is telling me this voluntarily.

"They saved my life. They helped me when I was at my lowest point. I don't think I would have been able to be a mother without the care and support that I got in the unit."

"It must have been awful for you." I don't want to pry too deeply or ask for any more information than she wants to give me.

"It was. For me, and for my family. I think everyone was terrified. No one knew what to say to me. No one knew what to do."

I don't know if I would know either. Mental health is not exactly something I'm good at dealing with, my own especially. I'm trying though, at least I'm trying.

Perhaps Becky is right. If I spend some time in the mother and baby unit, maybe I will be able to make the difference to a woman who really needs the unit's help and support. If I can say that I have been there and seen for myself what is available, I will be able to reassure someone that I need to refer. I would never have thought about this unit as an option, but it is already starting to make perfect sense. Still, I need to know that I'm strong enough. I want to be able to give a hundred percent.

"I think it would be useful," I say, quietly. "I need to think about it, but yes. I think you're right. Thanks, Becky."

"Now eat your lunch. I don't want you fading away halfway through the shift," she smiles.

# Chapter Twenty

When I get home, I sit at my desk and make a shortlist of contenders for my SPOKE placements. I'm trying to think about the positives, and the experiences that I might be able to have, but I still have that undercurrent of fear that I won't be any use to the patients. I don't want to be a burden on the staff or a liability to patient care. I'm going to start phoning around the units after my shift tomorrow, so I have set myself the task of making this list final today. It's more difficult than I thought.

Zoe is out with Luke this evening. The house is quiet, but the lack of company and the silence is distracting me. I don't want to sit here with my own thoughts, even if I do need to concentrate. Outside, the evening is still light. It's coming up to eight, but it's warm enough for me to throw on a sweater and take my list out to the garden.

Looking for inspiration, I send a text to the group chat I have with Ashley, Simon and Sophie.

Where are you going for your SPOKEs?

The last messages we sent in the chat were

about some television game show that Simon had discovered. I still haven't watched it, but Ash and Sophie seem to think it's the best thing ever. I should get more involved, make more of an effort. The only messages I have sent have been about coursework or placements. I hate to imagine what they must think of me.

I'm lost in my thoughts when the back-door swings open and makes a thucking sound. I shudder a look in its direction and see Carl standing in the opening.

"Mind if I join you?" he says.

It's weird. We are halfway through the year and he still asks before sitting, even though we talk to each other now more than ever before.

"Sure," I say.

The paper in front of me still only has a few jumbled ideas scrawled upon it. I need to commit myself, but I would rather have the distraction of talking to Carl.

My phone buzzes on the table, jerking onto the paper, and I reach forward to pick it up.

"Are you trying to work?" he asks, leaning over to look at what I have written. That word, 'trying' feels like it is loaded with meaning, the implication being that I'm not getting far at all. The scrappy note is evidence that I can't get away from.

"Uh, sort of."

There's no point in asking Carl, he can't help me make the decisions I need to. The text is from Simon, giving me a brief list of his choices. The truth is, I already know where I should be considering, I'm stalling because I don't really want to go anywhere but the maternity placements.

"I can be quiet, if you like?"

He's seated himself next to me, and now he's craning to see my phone screen.

"No, it's fine, really." I let out a heavy breath. "I have to choose some elective placements. Not long ones, just a day here and there, but -"

"You don't want to." He finishes my sentence, making me aware of how patently obviously my feelings must be.

"Yep. I mean nope. I mean, I don't want to."

My words are starting to jumble because my brain is losing its focus. Trying to plan these sessions is making me more anxious than I have felt in days. I thought the tablets would have started working by now. I'm not meant to feel this way.

Carl straightens himself up, and tilts his body towards me, turning all his attention in my direction. "Tell me about it."

"About what?"

"Whatever you like. Whatever is bothering you about the placements."

I wrinkle my brow. "Really? Why?"

He prods the note, and says, "You're not getting far, and it's obviously bothering you, so…" He shrugs rather than finishing the sentence, and then he adds, "And I'm not doing anything. Go ahead."

I never imagined that talking through my worries with Carl could be so therapeutic. Even though he doesn't know the first thing about the practicalities of my course or my placement, he listened attentively. He asked me about how I was feeling, and what I was thinking. It's the first time in a while that I have felt listened to.

Zoe is still not home by eleven, and I have another early shift tomorrow. I have to go to bed without talking my final choices through with her. Thanks to my chat with Carl, I'm *almost* happy about my decisions, and I'm definitely feeling a lot more positive in general about the placements.

Although we are free to choose the SPOKE placements that we want to attend, there is some

guidance in our practice documents to make
sure that we are including everything that we
should. One of the required SPOKE placement
visits is to spend time with a specialist midwife.

St. Jude's hospital, where I have my clinical
allocation, is lucky to have several specialist
midwives. There's a midwife who specialises in
bereavement care, one who is an expert in
domestic abuse, one whose focus is teenage
pregnancy. I know that I can learn so much
from all of them, and I'm sure that eventually
each of them will be able to give me insight and
experience.

For my placement I'm going to spend the day
with the mental health specialist. I hope that I
will be able to visit the Linden Unit and the
mother and baby unit with the specialist
midwife. I don't think I could face going alone,
but this could be the ideal compromise. I want
to learn, but I can't risk letting myself be
overwhelmed. I can't risk letting patients down.

# Chapter Twenty-One

My routine settles back into its cycles of shifts and study. From the messages in the group chat, I can tell that I'm not the only one who is daunted by the non-midwifery placements. Sophie and Ashley have both been dithering equally about where to opt for, and even Simon is nervy.

I feel a lot better about the SPOKE placements now that I have actually made my mind and started to arrange them. I'm calmer than I have been for some time, and I can't help but believe the tablets are actually starting to help me.

Most mornings when I'm on late shifts I come down to an empty house. Luke has taken to going into uni to study even when he doesn't have lectures. I guess he wants to get it out of the way so that he can spend his at-home-time with Zoe. She's out of the door by eight while she's in the school, so that only leaves Carl. I don't see much of him in the mornings. I tend to treat myself to a lie in and lounge around in my room.

Today I went down to make tea and toast

and found a distinct lack of milk. I've just bundled back in from my trip to the shop and flicked the toaster on when Carl hovers in. I say hover, because he is standing beside me in the kitchen, saying nothing, but looking at me like he has something on his mind and doesn't know how to start.

"Uh, morning," I say.

I'm not sure whether to prompt him or let this go and take my breakfast upstairs as I had planned.

"Just about," he says. The clock on the microwave says 11:50. I didn't realise it was so late. Still, I have a couple of hours before I have to leave. Plenty of time to do the whole lot of nothing that I was going to do.

"You okay?" I say the words without thinking, and that's it, I've committed to a conversation.

"I feel really bad," he says. I believe him. He's shifting his weight from one foot to the other, looking anywhere but directly at me. He's usually so confident, but now, he looks nervous.

He continues. "The other day, I went into your room. I'm sorry. I shouldn't have. I had a cracking headache and I needed paracetamol. I thought you might have some."

I can't imagine what is coming next, but I feel my cheeks starting to glow.

"I saw something. Do you mind if we, er, talk about it?"

I have a terrible sense of unease. My stomach is trembling like a jelly. I can't say no, although I feel like I should.

"Uh, sure," I say. My inflection makes it sound like a question, but really it's an uncertain agreement.

"Shall we sit outside?" he asks.

"Okay." My voice remains hesitant and uncertain. I don't have a clue where this is going.

I look into the toaster, wondering whether to ask him to wait until I've made my breakfast, but somehow I'm swept along, and I hear the pop as I go out of the door.

Out in the garden, he pulls back one of the chairs for me, and when I'm seated, he takes the chair beside me.

He leans back, looking far more relaxed than I'm feeling right now.

"I know that we aren't very close friends," he says, "but I'm worried about you."

My mind is racing, trying to work out what it

is that he saw. What could possibly have
happened to make him worry?

"You don't need to be. I'm fine," I say.

"Remember before Christmas, when we went
out for drinks."

I remember, but it isn't at the forefront of my
memories. It's not like it's something I have
gone over and over in my brain. Is he - does he
have some kind of feelings that I haven't picked
up on?

"Yes," I say. I want to leave the talking to
him.

"You told me something. I don't know if you
remember. You were, I mean you weren't really
drunk, but you were drinking, and I thought
maybe you could have forgotten that you had
said anything."

What does this have to do with him going in
my room? Did I say something I shouldn't
have? Did I tell him I liked him? I mean he's
not *bad* looking, and he seems -

"You have no idea what I'm talking about, do
you?" he laughs. There's no meanness in it;
he's not laughing at me. "It's okay."

He leans closer towards me, closer to the
table, and reaches across, taking hold of my
hand. It feels reassuring rather than awkward,

like he is trying to connect with me. I'm not a huge fan of physical closeness with people I'm not emotionally close to, but this somehow feels fine. It's calming. I almost like it.

"You told me about your anxiety. That you have trouble with it."

Of course. It all starts coming back to me. There was hardly anything else personal that I told him about myself. I was trying not to make a bad first impression, if you could call it that after we had lived together for weeks before talking to each other properly.

I nod my head and instinctively look down at the table. My embarrassment at the subject makes me shut down. I'm going to have to talk to a counsellor about it soon though, I have to get used to opening up. Can I open up to Carl though? To my housemate that I barely know?

"When I went in your room, I promise I wasn't snooping around. If I wanted to root through your drawers I'd do that when you were out of the house, right?"

He smiles, and after a tiny pause I smile back.

He continues, "I saw a packet of tablets on your desk. I thought they might be what I was looking for at first. Then I recognised them because they're the same ones that my mum used to take. They're for the anxiety, aren't they?"

"The anxiety? Yeah."

I feel relieved that all he saw in my room were my meds. He didn't read through my emails or check my internet browser history. Come to think of it, though, there's hardly anything shocking in either of those places. I'm a fairly straightforward, vanilla kind of girl. I'm not thrilled that he went into my room, but I believe his explanation. It makes sense.

"Violet, I know that anxiety is really tough, I know how bad it can feel, but you don't need those tablets. They are no good for you."

My forehead corrugates into a frown.

"I've struggled for a long time," I tell him. "I've suffered with this ever since I was eleven years old. It's stopping me from doing my best at uni. I need to get a grip of it."

As I talk, he nods. This is definitely good practice for talking to a counsellor.

"Those tablets *are* really bad though," he says. "They...well, I didn't want to say anything, but you haven't been the same recently. When I first met you, I..." He stops and looks away from me.

"What? What is it? You can tell me." It's my

turn to be concerned now. He pulls back, letting go of my hand, and I reach over towards him. I don't even think about it, my hand darts out and rests upon his arm.

"I shouldn't say anything." He shakes his head and looks back at me, his eyes meeting mine. He doesn't pull away from me.

"No, please. When you first met me, what?"

"You were…different. You were more light-hearted." He pauses again before saying. "You were more *alive*."

I let my grip on his arm loosen, but I leave my hand resting on his cool skin. This hits home, and it feels like a slap. I know what the tablets did to me last time. I don't want to change like that again. I haven't had Zoe keeping an eye on me, watching out for changes. Perhaps Carl is right.

"Do you think I have changed, then? Recently, I mean?" I can hardly get the words out. My breaths are shallow and fast. This is why I need the tablets. I'm sure I need them.

"You're…" He stops again and looks deep in thought. He puts his hand on top of mine, sandwiching it between the two layers of his flesh. "You're more like a cardboard cut-out of yourself, of the girl I first met. It's like your soul has been flattened. Deadened, maybe. Look, I'm sorry, I probably shouldn't have said anything, but I saw this happen to my mum and I wanted to warn you. I wanted to stop you before you got hooked on them."

"Hooked?" I say it without thinking, but after I have spoken the word, it starts to consume me. Is that my future? Am I going to become a zombie-like addict? I don't want that. I want to be me. This is exactly what happened before. This is why I have avoided these drugs for so long.

Carl nods his head slowly, and never takes his eyes off mine.

"I think you can do this without the tablets, Violet. I know that you are stronger than you think you are."

I haven't been. Not so far. I have tried, and there have been good patches, but on the whole, I am anxiety's slave. It can do whatever it wants with me - and it does. I want to get up and leave. I need the toilet. I think I do, anyway, perhaps my body is just telling me that so that I have an excuse to run away. I want to be away from this conversation. I can't do this.

"I can't," I say.

He pats my hand softly. It should feel

condescending or patronising, but strangely it doesn't.

"Really, you can. You are so full of life and energy, usually. Isn't that who you want to be? What good is it getting over your anxiety if the result is this?"

I didn't realise that I was so bad, that I was so useless now. He must see it. He lives with me. He sees me every day.

"I shouldn't have said anything," he says, suddenly pulling away again.

He sits back in his chair and I get a strange sensation of feeling too far away from him. It's disconcerting how these thoughts enter my mind without any conscious decision on my part.

"I'm sorry. I was out of line," he says. "It's nothing to do with me."

"No. No. It's fine. Really." I want to reach over and pull his arm back, for some reason, the physical contact between us felt good. I don't know why. It was somehow grounding me, I think. I felt like we were connecting, that he was listening, that he was actually interested in me. "I'm glad you said what you did. I would never have noticed the change in myself."

"And Zoe is wrapped up in Luke now," he

says, echoing the thought that I had earlier.

I nod in acknowledgement.

"I tried the drugs before. Not these exact ones, different ones. When I was younger." I'm speaking in rapid, short snatches; my breathing pattern is still too fast and too light. "It did what you said. It changed me. I was scared. I mean, I haven't tried them again until now because I was scared."

"You don't need them," he says again. "You should be you, not the person that the tablets turn you into."

"I'm on the waiting list for counselling," I say. It sounds defensive, I know as the words come out.

"So that you can sit and talk to someone for an hour every week about how terrible life is?" He snorts a short, sharp laugh. "It's no good, Violet. You don't need that."

"What else do I have? I have to get on top of this. My course means so much to me, and I can't keep messing up because of my anxiety."

"Have you messed up though? Have you really?"

"You weren't here last year. I had this exam, a really important exam, and I couldn't even start it. I ran away before it even really began."

"And you think it was your anxiety?"

I stop dead in my tracks. Of course it was anxiety. What else could it be?

"Well…"

He tilts his head and looks at me. "Are you anxious when you are on your placements?"

"Uh, no. I know what I'm doing then. I get on with it and -"

"You get on with it," he echoes. "How about if you tried to do that in your exams? When you're feeling anxious, push those thoughts away and get on with it."

He has obviously never had an anxiety attack. I wish I had the words to explain to him that it is not as easy as he is making it out to be, but I don't know where to start.

"What's the next thing that you are going to do that you are feeling anxious about?"

"I have a pharmacology exam, two weeks from now."

"Okay, so how about you revise for your exam, make sure you know everything there is to know, and if you start to feel anxious, come and talk to me. Let me help you through this. I know that you must have relied on Zoe before but she's not here for you right now…"

"She's always here for me," I protest, without

arguing about the other suggestions he has made.

"She's not available for you all the time now," he says, without backing down. "I want to help you. I want you to stop taking those evil tablets."

"They could help me," I say, but I already know that I have to stop. If they are creating such a change in me that Carl has noticed, they must be bad.

"Try it? For me?"

"Why would you even want to do this? Why do you want to help me? Because of your mum?"

He nods but stops himself. "That, yes, but also, I like you. I like the person that you were, and I don't want her to go away. I don't want that fun, vibrant, exciting girl to get lost."

The blush is rising to my cheeks again. I don't know what to say. He is trying to lock eyes with me again, but I turn my head.

Carl reaches across the table and puts two fingers gently upon my cheek. He tilts it in his direction, making me look at him.

"I like you. I mean it. I want to do this."

I don't know what I want, and right now, I don't know what I feel.

# Chapter Twenty-Two

The pharmacology exam is on Monday afternoon, bang in the middle of my placement block. It feels weird going back in for the day, but I'm used to arranging my Monday shifts so that I can have my meetings with Zoe. The exam is at two, so I should be finished in plenty of time to get to Blackheath's and meet her.

I ought to be worrying about the exam, but I'm not. I'm thinking about seeing Zoe, talking to her about my meds, and about Carl. I've revised well for the exam, thanks to having a lot of time alone in my room. Not that I can't sit in the living room with Zoe and Luke, but even if Carl doesn't mind being a gooseberry, it still doesn't feel right to me.

Carl. I've thought about him a lot since our talk. He's been more supportive than I could possibly have imagined, but is there more to it than that? When he touched my face, it felt like there might be something else. I'm not sure. I'm probably reading too much into it. A man does something nice for me, and my brain starts imagining all sorts of things.

I will be glad to have this exam behind me, and out of the way. If I pass, that is. Last year when I failed my first OSCE, I felt like it was hanging over me the whole time between the failed attempt and the resit. It was like a constant pressure weighing down upon me. I don't want to feel like that again. This year's OSCE is a week away. I can't start thinking about that now though.

Despite having stopped the tablets, I don't feel as anxious as I thought I was going to. I walk into the room, I take my place in my seat, and I look ahead to the screen at the front. I want to clear my mind. I don't want to think about anything. As long as I don't clear everything that I have learned about pharmacology and drug calculations, I'm going to be fine.

Twenty-three students sit at twenty-three desks. In front of each of us are a few sheets of paper, and an examination question sheet. We had to drop our bags by the entrance, only calculators and pencils are allowed on our desks. As soon as I look down at the paper, I have to put my hands onto my knees. I'm trying to keep them from trembling; I can already feel how clammy they are.

It's begun. I should have known that I wasn't going to get away from my anxiety that easily.

I'm worried that my pencil is going to slip straight out of my fingers and roll across the floor. Now my head is filled with numbers, equations, drug names, and everything that I have been practicing to help me to pass this exam. I need water, but we weren't allowed to bring our drinks in. I can't go back to my bag. I'm on the verge of putting up my hand, calling the supervisor over and asking to be excused. I'm burning up, I can feel it. I should have sat near the door. If I have to run, everyone is going to see me.

I take a few breaths and look straight ahead to the front of the room. I fix my attention on the supervisor. I try to focus all of my thoughts onto what she is saying. She runs through the procedure for the examination. Thirty minutes. Answer every question. Pass mark is one hundred percent. I don't need reminding.

I know that today I have to get everything right. I want to keep looking at the supervisor, but I can hear Ashley breathing to my right. She sounds almost as nervous as I am. I turn my head slightly, and she looks back at me. Her mouth forms a tiny smile, and I know that she is trying to reassure me, even though she feels awful herself. I move my hand slightly into view from under the desk and give her a thumbs up gesture. Good luck. Good luck to both of us.

"Turn your papers over," the supervisor says. All around the room a wave of noise ripples. The tapping of pencils being picked up and the swoosh of papers being flipped and placed onto tables. I'm probably the last to look at the questions. I take my time, not because I don't think I need every moment that I have allocated to me, but more because I don't want to drop my paper or my pencil onto the floor. My nerves are on edge, and it seems highly likely that I'm going to do something stupid.

I look at the writing on the sheet. There are a series of calculations, and some questions that I have to write out answers for. Before I even start, I turn on my calculator, distracting my mind from the thought of having to actually work on the answers for as long as possible. I look back to the sheet. I know how to do this. I can do it.

I tap the numbers I need into the calculator. I had to buy it especially for the test, we aren't allowed to use the apps on our phones. It feels almost archaic to use these big-buttoned pieces of equipment. Still, I know that on the wards the same technology will be right there by the drug cupboard when I need it. I don't have to get my maths completely right, but I do have to know how to make the calculations so that the calculator gets the maths right. Out in practice lives will depend on whether we work out the correct dosage.

I feel my anxiety nip away at me, and I try to push ahead. I felt it last night before I tried to sleep. I felt it this morning when my alarm blared out, and I hit the snooze button. I felt it on the walk into uni. I felt it when I was standing in the corridor, trying to appear like I was listening to Simon and Sophie talking about their weekends. I feel it.

Sometimes anxiety hits me like a truck. It slams into me, pushes my heartrate out of control, makes me feel like I can't breathe. Sometimes it's like drowning, as though I am thrashing my arms and legs about, trying to get to the surface, but my thoughts keep pulling me further and further down.

Today, every time the thought tries to enter my head "you can't do this" or "you're going to fail", I say "no". I try to tell that voice that it's time to shut up, because the voice has spoken to me and held me down for too long.

I don't know. I don't believe it can be this

easy. After all this time, I can't simply shut up the internal voice that I have come to believe, no matter how bad it has made me feel. Somewhere else though I hear Carl's voice. I hear him telling me that I can succeed. I hear him describe the girl that I was without the meds, the girl that I want to be. When I'm on placements I never worry - why do I need to feel anxious now.

"You don't," I hear Carl-inside-my-head tell me.

Someone who barely knows me believes in me. Someone likes me.

Whichever one of those facts is driving me on, it is working. I look down at the paper again, and I smile.

I know this. I can do it.

# Chapter Twenty-Three

With Zoe on placements, I miss our morning walks into uni together, and walking into town to meet her after my exam gives me too much thinking time. I start with the basics, wondering if I screwed up the exam, and if so, how badly. If I did, I did. It doesn't actually matter how much I screwed up this time. If I even got one thing wrong, I would have to resit. Strangely that thought helps me to focus and calm my mind. For the second half of the walk I'm consumed with what I'm going to say about Carl.

I'm not concentrating, and I almost trip over a dog lead that's trailing between a short squat sausage dog and the short squat man who is walking him. I don't wait for the man to chastise me. I mutter *"sorry"* under my breath and carry on.

If I talk to Zoe about Carl, and how my thoughts on him are changing, I will also have to tell her about stopping my anxiety meds, and she's not going to be pleased. It's my life, and my decision though. Maybe it's better if I don't say anything.

Zoe is already sitting at our usual table when I arrive. There are two cups on the table. I know one will have her extra-hot-extra-shot mocha, and one will hold my latte. Some things never change.

We make small talk for a while, while I dance around the things I really want to talk about. The fact is I don't want to talk about the important issues at all. I want to relax and enjoy being with my friend.

I think I have escaped, until Zoe returns from the counter with our second round of coffees.

"Now are you ready to talk to me about whatever's on your mind?" she says, without any trace of judgement.

I'm taken off guard, but I think quickly. "I have my OSCE next week."

It's the truth. It's not what has been on my mind, but it is the truth. In a few days from now I will have my OSCE, the scenario-based assessment that I have to pass to make it through to the next year of the course. Having failed on my first attempt last year, well, okay, having run out of the room before I had a chance to see if I could even pass, it would be understandable if I were terrified, especially with my crappy anxiety, but that's not how I actually feel.

I thought I would be dreading the OSCE. In reality, I feel strangely calm and resigned. I'm not used to feeling this way. I expected the sweats, the nausea, the inability to act. I expected to be chewing my nails off, but instead, I'm focussing on preparing and performing. I managed it for the pharmacology exam, I can do it again.

"Do you need me to run through scenarios with you?" Zoe says. Her face is full of concern. She knows how much this means to me.

I remember how she and Luke helped me last year. Him as a make-believe patient, and Zoe as a stand-in assessor. It seems that so much has changed over the past twelve months.

"I'm meeting up with Simon and the girls on Sunday afternoon," I tell her.

I made plans because I thought that she would be busy with Luke, but instead of looking relieved, a look of hurt flashes across her face.

"Oh," she says. "Okay. I could have, I mean, I would have…I'm happy to help, if you need me."

I nod and try to smile. "I know," I say. "I just

thought, I didn't want to, I -"

This is what it has come to, the two of us speaking in broken sentences to each other, tiptoeing around each other's feelings.

"Really," I say. "It's fine."

"I suppose they want to practice too," Zoe says. I don't know if she is trying to make *me* feel better, or herself.

"Yeah," I say. "We are like a little study group. And actually, I don't feel as bad this year."

"Probably the tablets. They must be working."

"Uh, yeah. I suppose they must." I should probably tell her.

I was wrong. *This* is what it has come to, and this is not what I want.

"Actually, I'm not taking them. I stopped."

Her eyes widen, and her mouth drops slightly open.

"I'm sorry, I don't know why I didn't tell you. I should have talked to you, but -" I don't want to say it. I don't want to make her feel bad about being with Luke and not me. I bite my tongue and leave the sentence hanging.

"Right," she says. "Are you sure?"

"I feel fine. I had my pharma exam and apart

from a few seconds of the sweaty palms I was fine. That's normal. Everyone feels like that."

"You don't have to get defensive. It's fine. I'm glad you're feeling better." She pauses before saying, "You didn't go for the counselling either then? Are you still on the list?"

"No. I mean, I haven't been. I don't think I'm going to go. My name is still on the list. It could take some time, so…I suppose it's my safety net."

"Won't they want you to have been taking the drugs that you were prescribed though? Do you not think you -" She stops and presses her lips together tightly. "Whatever you think is best, Vi. I'm just worried about you, that's all." She picks up her spoon and starts to swipe it through the chocolatey foam at the bottom of her mug, as though she isn't able to look at me anymore.

I look forward to our chats every week, but this time the atmosphere is tense and tight, almost claustrophobic. But this is us, this is me and Zoe. How can we feel like this?

"Want anything else?" I ask, gesturing to the counter.

It's quiet in here; we are the only people in

the coffee shop apart from a lady with a small white fluffy dog who is sitting in the window alcove. Her dog is on a little red pillow that the owner must carry around everywhere with her. Most days, I would nudge Zoe and point at the pup, and we would coo over it. The fact that we are not doing that thuds heavily in my chest.

"Thanks. I shouldn't, but...okay," she says.

For a second I want to smile, knowing that we will have more time together while we drink more coffee, but as I start to stand up, she pulls out her phone and looks at the time. Just that simple movement is enough to make me painfully aware of how limited our time together now is.

I know that I have to get used to this. It's ridiculous having these feelings of loss and wanting to be with her, when all that she is doing is having a normal life. Without realising it, over the years I have become completely dependent on Zoe. Now I'm trying to balance my need for her time with my need to become independent. I'm sure I shouldn't feel bad about reaching out to my other friends - my course mates - for help with my revision, but for some reason, I do.

The rest of our coffee date passes in a

subdued shimmer. I feel like we are skimming the surface of everything that we talk about, rather than actually discussing anything real. I avoid talking about my emotions, and for her part, Zoe steers clear of the subject of Luke. As these are the two main drivers in our lives at the moment, what results is a tepid, over-polite conversation that leaves me feeling empty.

Of course, I don't mention Carl.

We walk back to Tangiers Court through the park and arrive home to find Luke and Carl in the living room together, deep in conversation. I never considered that either Luke or Zoe spoke to Carl much - mainly because all their time is devoted to each other - but then I never stopped to wonder what Luke does on a Monday when Zoe and I have our coffee date.

"Okay guys?" Zoe grins.

She throws her coat over the back of the sofa and bends down to kiss Luke.

The change in her mood as soon as she sees him is palpable. It's not as though she was unhappy, spending time with me, but now that she is with Luke, she is glowing, back to her usual happy self. Instead of feeling put out by this, I stand in the doorway, looking at the two of them. His face is all smiles and he reaches up to embrace her, pulling her towards him, down onto the sofa by his side.

I want to be alone. Not to be out of their way, leaving them to each other's company, not that. Carl is here anyway, so it's not as though they have the place to themselves. I need some time to think.

"I'll just -" I move backwards slightly, stepping into the corridor.

"We were about to watch Salvage Den," Carl says. "Come and sit down. Don't leave me here being a gooseberry."

He has sat with the two of them often enough for me to know that he doesn't really have any concerns about being a third wheel. The look in his eye tells me that he wants me to stay. He moves his head ever so slightly, indicating that I should do as he suggests.

I can't think of a decent reason why I shouldn't, so I drop my bag in the hallway, throw my jacket over the bottom of the bannister, and go back into the living room to sit beside Carl.

Things are different now. I have to accept that. I can sit in my room on my own all evening or I can be here, with my friends, and start getting used to it.

# Chapter Twenty-Four

Although I'm on placement for the rest of the week, I feel like I can't concentrate on what I'm doing. All I can think about is the upcoming OSCE. I'm on the antenatal ward, and some of the scenarios are linked to antenatal care and pregnancy-related problems, so I'm trying to see my shifts as revision. I suppose it should always be this way. Everything I learn in class is designed to help me to be a better midwife when I'm on my placements. Everything I learn in placements must be able to help me do better in my assessments.

I don't have to worry about feeling bad at home, shutting myself in my room and going over and over the flashcards that I have written out. Zoe knows what happened last year, and so does Luke. They know how important it is that I pass this exam, for my course and for my own confidence. I cram and I cram. Occasionally Zoe brings a mug of tea and a couple of biscuits up to my room, and gives me an encouraging smile, but apart from that I'm completely absorbed in my revision.

The study session with my course mates is one last push to help me to stuff everything I possibly can into my brain. We spend the whole day running through every scenario, and it's reassuring to me that I seem to remember just as much as any of them do. I don't feel stupid. I don't feel like I can't do it. I feel normal. That's kind of a big deal for me.

On Sunday evening, when I get back from meeting Ash, Simon and Sophie, my plan is to put the books away and chill. I'm in my pyjamas by nine o'clock, acutely conscious that my exam is in twelve hours' time.

I've stripped my make-up, which doesn't take long as I barely wear more than foundation and mascara, and I'm smearing moisturiser onto my face when there's a quiet, short tap on my door.

I know before I say anything that it must be Carl. Zoe would just come in, and Luke would send Zoe if he needed me. That's just the way it is.

"Hang on," I say.

I have three big smudges of thick cream on my face, ready to be massaged into my skin: one on my forehead and one on each cheek. I can't let him see me like this. I reach for the nearest item I can and wipe my face over. My new Zara smock. I hope the cream doesn't stain.

I take a quick look in the mirror. My hair is pinned up in a bun, which I only ever do when I'm putting on or taking off my make-up, and my face looks pale and puffy.

"Er, I'm in bed," I call. I don't want him to see me like this.

"It doesn't sound like you're in bed," he says, with laughter in his voice.

I frantically unravel my bun and straighten my hair down with both hands as I stumble to the door. This is not a good look.

Carl doesn't look at all shocked or put out by my appearance.

I wave my hand at my face. "I was almost in bed. Getting ready for bed," I say, as an apology for my appearance, and for my lie.

"Okay," he says, giving me a look of amused puzzlement. "Zoe said you have an important exam tomorrow."

I nod. I have barely spoken to Carl this week. All I have thought about is the OSCE. I should probably have made time to chat with him, but –

"I wanted to say good luck. I'm sure you don't need it, but, well, you know."

Sometimes he comes across as confident and

191

cocky, but sometimes, like now, he appears nervous, shy even. He has come up specially, to talk to me, and I should be grateful rather than being worried that my hair is a mess and my skin is blotchy.

"Thanks, Carl. That means a lot. I really appreciate it." It sounds over-the-top as I say it, but he grins anyway.

"You all set? Know everything you need to know?"

We are hovering on the landing, him outside the door, and me within the threshold of my room. I feel like I should invite him in, but something is holding me back. I need to get to sleep soon, even at this early hour. I want to give myself every chance to pass the OSCE first time.

"I think so," I say. "I've studied hard, and I know everything I can know. Whether that's everything I need to know, well, I'll find out tomorrow."

"You are going to be fine," he says. "Better than fine. I know it. You're doing okay, aren't you?"

I know that he means the anxiety and not the studying.

"I am. Thanks, Carl."

"I knew it. You didn't need those drugs, you just needed to believe in yourself. I'm right aren't I? I was right."

There's a wave of excitement in his expression that makes him look like a child who knew the answer to an important question. It's really quite sweet.

"You were," I smile. "I really appreciate it. I'm sorry I haven't had much time –"

He shakes his head and cuts me off.

"It's fine, really. I know you have had studying to do."

I turn my head, looking into my room and wondering again whether I should invite him in. I'm only thinking about the two of us sitting down to talk, rather than standing here, but there still seems something wrong about having him in my room with me.

He must have noticed me looking, because he says, "I'll leave you to get to sleep now. I'm sorry I interrupted you."

"Thanks. And thanks for coming up. Things will be back to normal after the exam. I'll be downstairs more often."

He smiles again, his blue eyes shimmering. "I'll look forward to it. You'll smash it tomorrow. You can do it. I know you can."

I almost reach out and hug him, but I stop myself. Instead I step backwards into my room and wait for him to turn and walk down the stairs before I close my door.

I haven't had time to think about Carl, or about what might happen, everything has been about my exam. Still, he has had time to think about me and he thinks that I can pass.

A warm glow courses through me, and any tension I had left about tomorrow's OSCE slides away. I know everything I need to know. What is there to worry about?

Despite my increased confidence, this year's OSCE scenarios are going to be tougher than those I faced last year. I have had two experiences of doing this before, thanks to my resit, so I have to see that as a positive.

I have memorised every intricate detail. I know the scenarios inside out. I know that all of this will count for nothing if my anxiety overwhelms me again.

I try to focus on the image that fills my head - Carl telling me that I can do it. I picture myself back out in the garden, sitting in front of him, my hands in his, listening to him say that I'm clever and competent. All I need to do is believe in myself the way that he believes in me. Something about the way he talks to me, building me up the way he does, makes me feel a something that I can't describe. He's a good friend, that's what it is. I have only ever felt that warmth from being with Zoe before.

No matter how well prepared I am, the echoes of last year are reverberating through my mind, shaking my confidence, making my thoughts turn to swirling images, rather than the sharp focus I need. Still, I'm more determined than anxious, and every time the negative ideas spill into my brain, I try to replace them with positives.

"Violet," Zita calls me into the lab.

"You can do it," I hear Carl's voice. It's clearer than my own self-doubt. The words are sharp in my memory, and I tune into them. I can do it. I'm not going to bottle it this time, I'm going to ace it.

I fix Zita with a confident smile and I walk into the lab.

# Chapter Twenty-Five

With my OSCE behind me, the rest of the term starts to race by. On the morning of my SPOKE day with Helen, the specialist mental health midwife, she picks me up from home to take me out for whatever it is she has planned. In a way, this feels a lot like my community placement last year. We are sitting in Helen's car, going to visit women, in the same way that Stacey and I went last year when I started my course. It feels comfortable and known in a way, but I also know that today is going to be different.

"This morning we will go into the Linden Unit. There's just one lady in the mother and baby unit at the moment. She's been there a couple of weeks, and she's a lot better than she was, but…" She leaves the sentence dangling, and my mind tries to put together the rest of the words.

"There are two visits this afternoon," Helen says. "I try not to book any more than that, because I never know how long I'm going to be staying with any particular woman. I want to give all the time that any woman needs. Sometimes it's a brief visit, sometimes I will be there for hours."

I nod. I have no idea what to expect from these appointments.

"They won't mind having me along?"

"The ladies we're going to visit today know you're coming, and they're fine with that."

Helen doesn't wear the uniform that the other community midwives do. She's in plain clothes: a smart dark blue skirt and a navy and white striped tunic. I feel conscious of my uniform, but I know that I need to be recognisable as a student. Especially when we go into the mother and baby unit; I don't want to be mistaken for a member of staff and asked to do things that I have neither the knowledge nor experience to tackle.

The Linden Unit is a fifteen-minute drive out of town. I imagine the building has been a mental health hospital for many years. It's an old-fashioned building, a stark contrast to the modern styling of St. Jude's where I have my placements. Despite being a staff member, who must visit the unit on a semi-regular basis, Helen buzzes to be let into the ward. She says her name and adds mine as an afterthought. She looks up at the camera mounted above the door, as if to confirm that she's telling the truth about who she is.

I'm used to working on wards where security is paramount, so it comes as no surprise. There's a sharp buzz, and the lock is released.

Inside, there's a corridor, much the same as any other corridor in any other ward, with side rooms off to the left and right. Just before the nurses' office I can see what looks like a drug treatment room. There's a woman in the corridor, turning into a room as we walk along. The staff wear plain clothes; without knowing anyone, and not being able to see a name badge from here, the woman could be a nurse or a patient. I'm already unsteady about being on here, and the thought of not knowing who's who throws me further off balance.

Helen pops her head into a small square room where two nurses are sitting. At least I assume they are nurses.

"Hi. This is Violet. Student midwife. She's with me today, okay."

"Alright," says a chubby man in a sweatshirt and trousers combo. "Just going to see Meg?"

"Unless you have anything I need to know about?"

He shuffles through a large diary, then looks up and shakes his head. "No, nothing new. Did you come in yesterday?"

"Briefly, yes."

He nods, and mumbles through Meg's progress over the past twenty-four hours. I can feel my own anxiety rising. I'm starting to wonder whether it was such a good idea to come here. I can't try to avoid caring for women with mental health disorders just because I can't handle my own though. I have to get a grip. I have the swimming buzz of nausea and I know that if I don't get out of this room and get some air soon I'm likely to have my first major anxiety attack of the year. I was stupid to stop the meds. I was getting somewhere, I was -

"Are you ok, Violet?" Helen asks, putting her hand instinctively onto my wrist. I think she is trying to steady me, but then I realise that she is checking my pulse.

"Oh, yes. Yes I am. I'm fine. Sorry. I skipped breakfast. I'm just feeling a bit…you know."

She looks at me as if she doesn't know but accepts my answer.

"Okay. If you need to sit down, or get a drink or whatever, let me know."

I'm making a fool of myself in front of Helen and these two nurses. I have to snap out of it before I get to the patient.

I can feel my heart threatening to switch up to triple time, that familiar thumping in my temples and the churning of my gut. I was expecting this. I knew I would feel anxious here, the only surprise to me is that it has taken this long.

"Sorry," I whisper. "I'm fine, really."

Helen eyes me cautiously but turns to finish her conversation with the mental health nurse. By the time she is ready to go and see the patient, I have managed to settle myself sufficiently to tag along.

She bumbles ahead of me, giving me a brief tour of the ward as we walk. It doesn't look much different to the delivery suite, with its side rooms and lino corridors. There aren't any patients in sight, but I can hear a baby crying somewhere further down, in one of the rooms.

"We have space for women that have pre-existing mental health conditions and need extra support after childbirth, and we have patients admitted with postnatal psychosis, that kind of thing."

That kind of thing. Of course.

"There's just one lady here at the moment?" I ask.

"She has her baby with her, but the nurses who work in the mother and baby unit are there to monitor and support her."

I've met a couple of women with postnatal depression, it's a surprisingly common occurrence. I've never encountered anyone with any other mental health disorders though, not yet. Something about supporting women who have psychological needs...I suppose I can identify with it. I've had my own demons to fight for years. I have tried to do it by myself, I know what that is like. I know how it feels to not want to be labelled, to not reach out for help when I have really needed it.

When we get to Meg's room it is empty. For some reason, a feeling of panic kicks in. I think she has taken the baby and escaped. It's a ridiculous thought to have. Meg is a voluntary patient here; she wanted to be admitted, and she wants to receive support. I know nothing about her, and I have somehow made an assumption about her. It reminds me even more clearly about how I expect people would make assumptions about me if I told everyone about my own mental health issues. If I jump to these ridiculous conclusions, having battled my own issues, how can I expect other people to hold back their judgment?

"She's probably out in the garden," Helen says, calmly, as though this is a regular occurrence. She isn't at all concerned about Meg's absence. I shouldn't be either.

True enough, we make our way out to the small quad, enclosed between the blocks of the hospital, but apart from that a pretty, green, airy space, and find Meg sitting in the shade with her pram. The baby is sleeping, and Meg is absorbed in a book.

I don't know what I expected, but Meg appears completely normal. There's nothing remarkable about her manner or the way that she talks to us. Helen chats to her about the baby, the book, and life in general. It doesn't feel like we are doing anything clinical, and essentially we are not. The mental health nurses are providing Meg with the care she needs to recover. Helen is checking in, seeing what additional support is needed. Meg appears open and unguarded, and I can tell that the relationship that Helen has built up with her is strong and trusting.

We sit with Meg for just over an hour, until one of the nurses pops their head into the garden to let her know it is time for a session to begin. Again, I make the mental connection that it must be a therapy session, and again I'm wrong. It is baby massage. I have so much to learn about maternal mental health, and how to support women. I have so much to learn about the way that I leap to conclusions. I would never have come here if it were not for the SPOKE placements; I would never have experienced this. I'm already glad that I made this choice.

On the way back to town for our two afternoon visits, Helen tells me how lucky Meg is. The mother and baby centre at the Linden Unit is one of only seventeen in the country. I can't quite believe it. So many women experience some mental health issues in the perinatal period, I can't believe that these units aren't more widely available.

"Most places are lucky to even have a specialist midwife," she tells me.

"What happens in the other towns? What happens if there aren't any units, or specialists?"

"Then they are cared for by their regular midwifery teams, and whatever mental health services are available locally. If women need to be admitted, unfortunately a lot of the time that means separating them from their babies."

I shake my head. I can't believe that something so basic is so difficult for women to access. I suppose that mental health services in general can mean a long wait, just like the list I'm on for my sessions. I should take my name off the list, let someone else move up it. I can do this on my own.

For some reason, I expected both of the home visits to be with postnatal women. Even after a year and a half of training I'm green enough to think that maternal mental health means postnatal depression. The first woman that we call in to see is indeed one of the more than one in ten women that is fighting postnatal depression. Add to that all the women who go through the baby blues, and I'm surprised that I haven't already been taught about maternal mental health in more detail. I'm sure I will be. As Helen listens to the woman, exploring her feelings and giving support I feel completely out of my depth. I wouldn't know where to start.

The second visit hits me with an even greater impact. The woman that we visit is heavily pregnant. She had a stillbirth at term in her previous pregnancy and is suffering from anxiety far worse than anything I have ever experienced.

"It's a form of PTSD," Helen tells me. "The trauma from her last birth…"

I nod. She doesn't have to finish the explanation; I can put it together by myself.

"Sometimes in cases like this, women can become severely depressed. Especially coming up to the birth, as Kaye is. I'm meeting her weekly, but if she needs more regular contact, I will be here for her."

"I can't imagine what it must feel like. Having been through that and, well –"

Now it's me that doesn't need to finish the sentence. There is a lot that is intrinsically understood between midwives, and between them and their patients.

Even with the anxiety that I have lived with, I genuinely can't imagine what Kaye is going through. Her anxiety is rooted in experience. Mine seems flimsy in comparison. What basis do I really have for being so hard on myself, and so afraid of failure?

My day with Helen has given me a lot to think

about, both in terms of my developmental needs as a student midwife, and my personal mental health. I won't forget the women that I have met today. I have so much to learn about so many things. Perhaps one day I will train to be a specialist in maternal mental health. I thought the SPOKE visits were going to be a waste of time, but I have learned so much on just this one day. I understand how important it is to see the bigger picture, and now I want to learn more.

# Chapter Twenty-Six

After my day with Helen I feel inspired and yet drained. All I want to do is go upstairs, flop into a hot bath and shut out the world for an hour. Or longer, if I can get away with it. My head is swimming, I feel like I'm carrying so much of the day home with me. For once I hope that Zoe and Luke are out. I want to be alone. Of course, the one time that I want solitude, as I start to run up the stairs, Zoe calls me from the living room.

"Vi!"

It sounds like a question, but I know that she recognises the sound of my feet on the stairs, just as I would recognise hers. I can't carry on and pretend that I didn't hear her, but the thought does flicker through my head. I stop on the third stair, put my hand on the bannister and turn around, not moving.

"Yeah?" I call back.

"Come in here. Don't run off!"

I know she can't see me, but I still feel bad as I roll my eyes and sigh.

"Okay. Let me get changed. Be down in a minute."

I don't want to be in my uniform any longer

207

than I have to. I remember when I first wore it. I felt so proud, and so excited. Now it is only reminding me of everything I have seen at work. Today was so close to home. I know that's what it was; that's why it has affected me so much. I'm putting my own mental health under the microscope, and what I see is difficult to deal with.

I change and slowly make my way back downstairs. My evening does not get any better when I sit with Zoe and she starts to talk to me. She tells me she has something she wanted to bring up but didn't know how to. I can't believe we have got to this point. Still, I don't know why I didn't see it coming.

It should have been obvious.

She wants to spend the Easter holidays with Luke.

Of course, she would want to be with him. I suppose a part of me took for granted that Zoe would want to go home, visit her family, and that we would have three weeks together back in Portland.

"I'll drive you back though, of course. If you want to go, I mean."

It hadn't even occurred to me that she might

want me to stay here too. What do I have back home now though?

It feels awful to think that way, because what I have is my mum. I should have called her more often; I should have gone to visit her. It's half an hour's drive, so maybe an hour on the bus. I could have made the effort. Instead, I have been tied up in university, worrying about losing my closeness with Zoe, and wallowing in my anxiety. Now, going home alone would feel as though I was treating my mum as a fall-back, rather than respecting her for what she is. We were so close over the past few years, brought together by her and my dad falling apart. What happened?

"I'll think about it," I say. "I assumed I would be going home, but -" I shrug. "If you want me to stay…?"

"I want to be here, and I don't want to be without you," she says. "You're not cross with me, are you?"

"Cross? Uh, no. Not cross."

"Something then? What?"

"It's a surprise, that's all. I haven't thought about it. I hadn't thought about it, I mean."

There's a frostiness between us that I have never felt before. The two of us, at odds with each other. We are adults, young adults, maybe, but adults. Of course, one of us was eventually going to have an adult relationship, and of course it was most likely to be Zoe.

"I'm sorry," she says. "I should have thought it through. I didn't even think about the impact it might have on you. I'm stupid,"

"No. You're not. We have never been in a situation like this before, that's all. The boyfriends we have had before, they weren't serious."

"You thought Jared was The One at the time," she smiles.

I did, but I was sixteen. What did I know? What do I know now?

"I know now that he wasn't. Maybe Luke is your 'One' though. If he is then I want you to be happy. I don't want to be holding you back or stopping you from doing all the things that normal people do in normal relationships. Everyone in your situation would do exactly what you're doing. It's only because you have a ridiculous clingy friend who has nothing else in her life that it's even an issue."

She looks horrified. I didn't realise that my words would have such an impact upon her.

"Is that what you really think? Because I

don't think that. You're not clingy. Up until a few months ago it was you and me against the world. If it had been the other way round, if you had met someone, I'm sure I would have had just as much trouble adjusting. It's not you. It's nothing you have done, and it is nothing to do with the person you are. Tell me that you know that."

The tears are welling up in my eyes, and the dam is on the verge of breaking.

"Tell me, Violet," she says, insistent, her voice brimming with emotion.

"I'm sorry," I say. "I know. I do. Listen, give me time to think about it, okay?"

She nods, moving her head as though it is heavy and painful.

"We can make this work," she says. "For all of us. You will never not be important to me."

I juggle the double negative for a moment. "You'll always be important to me too. And it's important to me that you are happy."

I think I already know what I'm going to do. Being at home without Zoe is going to be tough, but she needs time alone with Luke. We aren't far away. I could come up for the day, or she can come down to me. I'm sure she will, but I need to go home.

# Chapter Twenty-Seven

Easter break is even more tough than I imagined it would be. I stay at home for the entire three weeks. Zoe comes down for the first weekend, to see her parents, and of course to see me. I get the bus up to our home away from home during the second week. Apart from that, we don't see each other. We carry on with the usual text messages, even more than usual considering our physical distance, but it's not the same. I thought about asking her to come for our coffee date last Monday, but it felt twee and ever so slightly emotionally manipulative. I don't know why. She's my best friend, inviting her out shouldn't feel that way.

Zoe arrives to pick me up at just after two on the Friday afternoon before term starts again. I have been packed and ready since ten in the morning. I couldn't settle. I've been pacing the living room, watching terrible daytime TV, waiting for her to come and take me back to Tangiers Court.

When I hear the triple beep of her horn, I scramble for my bag, throw my mum a hasty hug, and dash out of the house. Seeing Mum, having some down time with her has been nice, but it has made me remember how much I like living at university. I love her so much, but the two of us need the distance between us. Being in the house I grew up in, sleeping in the bedroom that once held my cot and still has my teenage posters on the wall is a weird experience.

I throw myself into Zoe's car and awkwardly reach across to hug her.

"It's not been that long," she says, her palms flat on my back, pulling me in.

"It felt like it."

"I told you I would have come sooner. You should have said."

"I had to do this. I had to have the time here alone. You understand, don't you?" I say the words, but I'm not sure if I really believe them. Did I need to be here by myself, or am I just being a martyr for her relationship?

She nods. "Sure. I think so. I kind of understand."

It's strange, heading back to Tangiers Court. I have always thought of it as home, since we moved in together, but now, I feel more like a visitor. It is Luke and Zoe's home. I don't know where that leaves me. I'm not sure about anything anymore.

Zoe is chatting away about what she has been doing during the week, and what plans she has for the weekend, but it sounds like a stream of words to me, I can't focus. My brain is too busy.

This feeling that I have of not fitting in is getting stronger the closer we get to Tangiers Court. It's a feeling of unease and unrest. I should be happy. I should be looking forward to being back, to seeing Zoe again, and to launching into the final term of the year. Instead, I feel a little lost.

"Really, are you okay?" she asks me, taking a break from her chatter.

"I don't know," I tell her. I can only be honest.

"I thought you'd be excited to come home," she says. Her eyes are focused on the road ahead, but she flicks a quick look in my direction, trying to assess me. "Are you not happy?"

I think about the question for a few seconds before answering. "It's not you, Zoe, really it's not. But –" The thought has only just come to me, and perhaps I should have considered it for longer before blurting it out. "- I think I ought to live somewhere else next year."

I'm glad she is driving. She has to keep looking ahead, she can't give me a look of disappointment or anger, or anything. I should have waited, it's not fair of me to say what I did, not here, not like this. As the words came from my mouth though, I knew they were true. It was a snap decision, in some ways, but surely the thought must have been there, bubbling away inside my mind for it to have come out like that.

I have been dependent on Zoe for too long. I've held her back, always making demands on her time. Maybe she would have had the kind of relationship she has with Luke before now if she weren't always stuck spending her time with me. It works the other way too. Perhaps without having Zoe as a constant crutch I would have been forced to overcome my anxiety and get myself together. I can't bear to think about it that way. She has only done her best for me. I don't blame her for caring about me, I don't blame her for loving me. Now, I think it's time that we gave each other space, and let each other go.

"I don't know what to say," she says. Her voice is quiet and hurt. "I don't want you to leave."

"I don't want to leave you either. But I have to. I was pathetically sad over the past few weeks. I should be able to spend time with my family, and with the few friends that I have back in Portland and be able to be happy. I wasn't. I missed being with you. I missed home." As soon as I say the word I correct myself. "I missed Tangiers Court; I mean. I missed there."

"It *is* your home," Zoe says. "Things have changed, I know, but it is your home. Please. I don't want this."

"I need it, Zo. I need to be stronger."

She shakes her head silently, and I can see the moisture of tears in her eyes that she is fighting to hold back. She keeps her focus on the road ahead and drives without speaking another word.

I'm grateful that our university is only a short distance from our old homes, because the silence makes every minute feel like an hour. I don't know where the thought came from, or why my stupid brain felt the urge to make me say it. It's time for a change, though. It's time for me to change. I just have to find a way to do that without losing Zoe.

# Chapter Twenty-Eight

After everything that has happened this year, the final term is almost easy. All my exams are behind me; I have a reflective assignment and another essay to write this term. I am heading back to delivery suite for my placement, and I can't wait.

Over Easter I made a pact with myself that I would try to engage more with other people. I want to try talking to my course mates more often, to get to know them better and to try to be friends with them, rather than just seeing them as people who are on the same course as me.

I'm going to try to go out more, to do more things that perhaps I wouldn't have been brave enough to do before. This change isn't only down to Zoe and Luke, it's also about myself, and who I am. My anxiety is at an all-time low; I haven't had an attack in as long as I can remember. I'm getting on top of it this time, I know I am. I feel great knowing that I am doing this myself, without the drugs.

I had a moment of weakness, when I went to see the doctor. That's all it was. I thought I couldn't cope without Zoe, but I don't need her to carry me every minute of the day.

Although I'm telling myself that I want to be more friendly so that I can have friends, I know that I have an underlying motive too. As much as I don't want to think about it, I'm not sure that I will be living with Zoe next year. Not that I don't want to, of course I do, but sometimes I feel like Andrew, the imaginary housemate that we had last year. I might as well not be around. I don't say that in entirely a self-deprecating, self-pitying way. What I mean is, I'm not needed anymore. It's a little self-pitying, I know.

A few classes into the new term I get the opportunity to make a start on my new resolution to be more sociable. When the session breaks for coffee mid-morning, I traipse along with my three course mates.

Sophie and Ashley are already deep in conversation by the time we get to the refectory.

"It's not that I don't like him," Ashley says, "but I don't want the same things as he does."

"He adores you," Sophie tells her.

I have no idea who they are talking about, so I stand behind them in the queue, and smile awkwardly at Simon.

"How's it going?" I ask him, for something to say.

"Yeah," he replies. "Good thanks. Glad to be back in uni."

"Oh?" I enjoy the lectures well enough, but I'd always rather be out on placement.

"Yeah," he says again. "I don't know. I'm not feeling it quite so much this year. I was so enthusiastic at the beginning."

"You were, I remember," I interrupt.

"Recently I've been finding it tough.

"The placements? What's happened?"

"Nothing specific. I don't know if it's trying to balance uni and shifts and trying to have a life, or what, but -" He shrugs, but I know what he means.

"That's exactly it," Ashley says, turning to join our conversation. Sophie has got to the counter, and she's ordering something with an extra shot of hazelnut syrup. "It feels like there is no time."

I don't have this problem. I have the opposite problem. I have too much time on my hands. I have endless evenings and weekends with no plans, no real friends (other than Zoe of course) and certainly no romantic interest. Well, maybe I do, but it's not like I have done anything about it. I suppose the grass is always greener.

Simon nods at Ashley. "Right. I've been trying to see this girl from the nursing course."

"Kayla, yeah?" Ashley says.

"That's the one. I didn't know you knew."

"We know some of the same people."

Simon and Ashley seem to have grouped off into their own conversation. My mouth has dried up, and it feels like my brain has too. I want to keep talking, but I don't know what I can add. I don't know anything. I don't have any relevant experiences to contribute.

Sophie's got her coffee now, and Ashley is next in line, leaving Simon open for conversation again. Still, I find myself standing in silence, unable to find any words. I find small talk difficult, which is strange because it comes so naturally when I am speaking to patients.

"What about you?" Simon says. "Are you seeing anyone? How are you finding it?"

Simon is a good-looking lad. He's not much taller than I am, probably around five foot eight or nine, and he has floppy blonde hair and great skin. He's not muscular, not out of shape. I've never considered him as anything other than my course mate. I would say that he is not my type, but I'm not really certain what my type is anymore. I only even think these things because he has asked whether I'm seeing anyone. It feels like an instinctive reaction. That and laughing, because that's what I do. I laugh.

"That bad, eh?" he says. "Well, plenty of time."

"I'm not really looking," I say.

"What about the hottie I saw you with in the union bar?" Sophie asks. She's cradling her mug in two hands, waiting for the rest of us to be served.

"What?" My mind goes into overdrive. When was I even in the bar? Not in a long time, that's for sure. And certainly not with any 'hottie'.

"It was a while ago. I was in with my girlfriend and some of our mates, and you were sitting at one of the little tables with a guy."

"Oh no!" I laugh again. It's a way of trying to cover my nerves, and I know it is probably irritating, but sometimes, I can't help myself. "You mean Carl. No. He's my housemate."

Having Sophie call him a 'hottie' doesn't really mean much, seeing as she is not interested in men, but I pause for a moment to consider.

"Now you're thinking about it!" Sophie nudges me, almost spilling her sweet-smelling drink in the process. "No laws against dating your housemate!" she says.

I know.

"What did I miss?" Ashley chips in. She's got a coffee in one hand and a small piece of granola bar on a plate in the other.

"Nothing," I say, turning to the barista.

I can hear Sophie and Ashley behind me, chatting and giggling. Simon has taken out his phone and he's occupying himself while the two girls gossip. The way Sophie and Ashley bounce off each other reminds me too much of how Zoe and I used to be. If I lived with the two of them, perhaps I would feel just as side-lined as I do now. It's as though I'm destined to be a puzzle piece that doesn't fit, like an extra tile that has no place of its own. I'd say this was my anxiety talking, but it doesn't feel like that. Social awkwardness, paranoia, I don't know.

I wanted to get to know my course mates better, to make more friends and try to fit in, but it's as though everyone already has their place in a group and there's nowhere left for me. Maybe I made a mistake coming here with Zoe, living with her, everything. I wanted us to fulfil our dreams together, but all of hers are coming true while I carry on sleepwalking beside her.

# Chapter Twenty-Nine

All I get from trying to socialise more with my course mates is the numbing realisation that I'm not going to be asking to move in with any of them next year. Despite my best intentions, I can't bring myself to spend Saturday nights in the union bar. I'm not sure I could even face sitting in a living room with them, forcing myself into small talk every night. I want a quiet life. It would seem terribly boring to some people, I'm sure, but it's who I am. Whoever I am, I'm not afraid to be myself.

That does leave me in the unenviable position of *still* having no idea what I should do about my living arrangements.

I hadn't considered asking Carl about what he intends to do, but the subject comes up anyway. The two of us are in the living room, me curled on the sofa, and him spread across the two armchairs in a position that looks rather uncomfortable. He's concertina-folded himself in a way that manages to squeeze his butt against the side of one chair while supporting his legs on the other. Even with only the two of us in the room, the space feels full.

Apropos of nothing, he says, "Are the three of you extending the lease for another year?" He asks the question casually, not looking up from his phone.

It hits me out of the blue. My living arrangements for next year have been on my mind constantly, but he can't know that. I haven't mentioned it to him. I feel a bit weirded out by the question, but then the realisation dawns on me that he must be trying to make plans for next academic year too. It's not only me that has to work out where I'm going to live.

"Uh, I don't know. I haven't decided yet," I tell him.

"Okay." His answer sounds clipped.

"What will you do?" I ask. I know that he has a lot of friends, but I wonder who he will choose to live with. It's a genuine question, I'm not just trying to sound polite.

He shrugs and clicks his phone closed, turning to give me his full attention.

"I was wondering if you were planning to stay. I thought I would find out and decide from there."

"What?" I cough the word out before I even think. "Sorry, I mean you wanted to know whether we were staying?"

"Whether you were, yes. Whether you all were." He adds the second sentence as if he doesn't want me to think that he is particularly interested in what I, personally, am doing. It makes me think just the opposite.

"Right." I don't know what to say, and to be honest, I don't know where to look, I certainly can't look him in the eyes. Then I sigh and decide to let it all out. "I don't know what to do," I say. "I love living with Zoe, of course I do, but things have changed. They're different now. She has Luke, and well, you know how that is. I thought it might be time I moved out on my own, maybe with some of my friends."

He raises an eyebrow. He has lived with me long enough to know that I don't have a heap of friends on standby. He's gentlemanly enough not to mention it.

"It's not ideal, living with a couple. I try to get on with my own thing," he says.

I've noticed how he doesn't seem to react to them being together. If they are hugging in the kitchen when he walks in, he walks around them, while I stand in the hallway, wondering whether I'll disturb them if I go in. If they are watching a film together, he's happy to sit in the living room with them, eating his snacks, chilling as if they were just two people. They are. Of course they are. They are still Zoe and Luke.

"I like living with you though," he says. "I like you."

I think about what Sophie said. The word "hottie" bounces around my head. Without wanting to look like I'm staring, I cast my eyes over him. He's focusing on the television, not me, even though we are having a conversation. He always seems distracted. Hot? Is he hot? He's attractive, sure. Am I attracted to him though? Everything about him tells me that I should be. He's tall, slightly muscular without being over-the-top beefy.

"Violet?"

"Sorry," I say. I'm not good at the not-looking-like-I-am-staring, it seems.

He smiles and shakes his head. I swear sometimes it feels as if he's reading my mind. I'm not sure whether I like it or not.

Whatever he is thinking, he doesn't appear fazed by my attention. He's already turned back to the television.

He *is* a good-looking guy. Good looking, caring, kind. I mean he's a bit untidy, and I haven't seen him cook a single proper meal since we have lived together, but as I'm far from perfect, I'm not in any place to demand perfection in a man. I can't believe I'm even thinking about this, especially not with him sitting across the room from me. I wanted to complete my course, focus on studying. I told Zoe right at the start of our first year that neither of us would have time for dating. Looks like I was wrong.

"I might stay," he says. "If you're planning on being here too."

I have no idea what to say. I want to get up and run out of the room. I feel like I've been put on the spot. My heart is fluttering, but not in a good way.

Or maybe it is.

Maybe I've been too caught up in myself to have noticed what's been happening. Carl has been there for me. We have got to know each other, talked, and laughed. I'm so unused to seeing the signs, I suppose I have stopped looking for them.

Could I stay here next year if Carl stays too? Would we be more than friends? Am I only considering this because Zoe has Luke, and I am alone? I'm so confused. I have no idea about the answers to any of these questions.

# Chapter Thirty

My next chance to talk to Zoe doesn't come until the following day. When I get home from uni, I run up the stairs, determined to discuss this with her. It's time I told her how I feel. As I get to the landing, I can hear a scrabbling noise from Zoe's bedroom.

"Zoe?" I say, as I get to the landing outside her door.

"Hang on," she shouts.

Hang on? When have I ever had to 'hang on' for Zoe? What could she possibly be doing that she has to hide from me?

"Are you okay?" I'm suddenly worried. This is not like her. I put my hand onto the door.

"Wait!" she calls, her voice trembling a little as I push the door slightly.

I stop, my hand still pressed against the wood, but not moving. I'm waiting for her to say something else, but I don't know what to expect. Then it hits me. I swear, I'm so slow sometimes. I suppose it's because, even though Zoe and Luke have been together for six months now, I am only rarely aware of any physical intimacy between them. It's almost as if she doesn't want to do anything in front of me, like I'm a child that she has to protect from seeing her with Luke.

"Oh. I'm sorry," I say, stepping backwards. "I didn't think. I didn't mean to interrupt –"

"You're not. It's fine." I can hear her moving around, pulling on her clothes.

"Really. I can talk to you later."

The door opens, and Zoe stands in the entrance. Her usually perfect hair is a tousled mess; she's wearing sweatpants and a t-shirt that I have never seen before. I didn't know she had any clothes that I wouldn't recognise. I stare without thinking.

"You okay?" she asks. "What's up?"

Behind her, I can see Luke standing, running his hands through his own messy mop of hair, and blushing a glowing shade of scarlet. He nods as he catches my eye, and hurries to leave.

"Don't go on my account," I say, as he squeezes past me.

"It's fine," he says. "We are – I mean, it's fine. Don't worry, Vi."

I feel terrible for having stopped them. I should have waited. Now I don't want to talk anymore. My stupid childish thoughts seem like a waste of Zoe's time.

I wanted to talk to her about Carl, see what

she thinks about the two of us. I wanted to talk about next year. I've been thinking it through all day, and what I really need is Zoe's reassurance that everything is going to be okay.

It's going to be a tough year of study. I have my research project to complete, I'll be panicking over getting all the competencies in my PAD signed off, and I already know that taking the step to being a senior student is going to be tough for me.

I don't know if I can bear leaving Tangiers Court, leaving Zoe, and trying to get through all of this alone.

"Violet?"

I have been standing in the doorway, blank-faced and silent. After interrupting Zoe and Luke, the least I can do is say something.

"Sorry," I say.

She looks me over, and then reaches out toward me, taking hold of my hands.

"Come in. Sit down. Come on. It's fine."

I must look even more shell-shocked than I feel, because instead of sitting down next to me, Zoe hovers and asks, "Shall I go and get us both a brew?"

"No. Really, I'm okay. I don't know what…I don't know why I'm such an idiot."

"Oh, Violet."

With that, she does sit down next to me. I feel like this is her role in my life. She is the one who says, *"Oh, Violet"*. Whether it's in sympathy when I do something stupid, or amusement on the occasions that I'm being funny rather than plain idiotic. Zoe is my sounding board; that's why I came to talk to her, after all.

I rest my head against her shoulder, and I feel the tears start to stream from my eyes. I don't know if I was even expecting them. It's frustration as much as sadness. I don't know what is wrong with me. It's been a hard year. It's been a hard few years. And I need Zoe.

She does go to get tea, and I don't protest. While we sit on her bed drinking it, I tell her about Carl. She looks shocked, as if she had no idea that there was anything brewing between us. I can't say that I blame her. I don't think I had much of a clue either.

"You've kept that quiet," she says. "So, nothing has happened yet?"

I shake my head. "Nothing. He said that he likes me, and I turned into a tomato and sat there awkwardly for the rest of the evening not knowing what to say."

"Oh, Violet," she smiles. "You like him though."

"I hadn't thought about it," I say.

I can tell from her expression that she doesn't believe me. She raises her eyebrows and gives me that knowing grin.

"Really," I say. "I hadn't."

Her smile snaps off her face, as though something has just popped into her mind that makes it impossible for her to maintain it.

"What? What is it?" I ask.

"I hadn't even noticed. I hadn't seen anything between you. I barely know Carl, and I live with him. Just think how well we knew Luke by this time last year."

"Not as well as you wanted to," I say, trying to lighten the tone.

"That's just it. It's not that I don't want to get to know Carl, I've just been so tied up in Luke. I haven't got to know my housemate; I haven't spent enough time with my best friend."

"Zoe, it's not your fault. You haven't done anything wrong. You have a boyfriend, and you want to be with him. That's completely normal. That's the way it should be." The mood has flipped from her trying to comfort me to quite the reverse.

"We've barely talked about your course, about how you're getting on with…"

She doesn't say the word. I know that she means my anxiety, and the fact that she can't even say it now makes me feel even worse. She was the one I could open up to, but it's true. Carl's the one I talk to now. It was Carl that told me I could beat it on my own. I've been getting on very well thank you without the drugs that Zoe would've had me keep taking.

"I'm fine," I say. "I've been absolutely fine."

She pauses for what feels like a lifetime.

"I think you should have carried on taking the tablets," she says. I'm about to speak, and she silences me. "For the long term. I mean, I think it would be better in the long term if you got some support now. Next year is going to be tough."

"Especially if I have to do that alone too," I say, without thinking.

The hurt look on her face is like a shard of glass thrust into my heart. I shouldn't have said that. One minute I tell her it's not her fault, and the next I try to guilt trip her. What has happened to us?

She clears her throat but doesn't retaliate.

"If you like Carl then tell him," she says instead. "Don't waste time like I did with Luke. He's made the first move. Don't leave him dangling, or you might lose your chance."

"Right. Yes. Thanks."

In the past we would have sat and giggled and discussed all the ins and outs, the merits, and the possibilities. Now all I get is that. *Tell him.* Things have changed so much. Perhaps it's the two of us growing up, getting older, starting to live in the adult world and have adult relationships. Perhaps we are just growing apart.

"Violet." She says my name, and looks at me, saying nothing else.

"Really," I say. "Thanks."

I don't want to be sitting here with her anymore. I don't feel like talking now. None of this is what I expected. I give her a short, polite smile and get up.

"I have a few things to do," I tell her. "Maybe see you later."

"Violet, please," she says. I shake my head and head for the door.

I don't know where I'm going, or what I am doing. All I know is that everything is changing. I don't like it, not one bit.

# Chapter Thirty-One

My homelife might be a mess, but my course and my clinical practice are a welcome, pleasant relief. I've loved my placements this year, even the SPOKE days, surprisingly. They've all had their highlights, but I'm so happy to be back on delivery suite.

As soon as I push open the double doors to enter the ward, and hear the thudding of cardiotocograph monitors from within rooms, echoing out fetal heart rates, and the bustle of activity from the midwives' station in the middle of the corridor, it feels like a homecoming. It's busy, that's for certain. There are doctors, midwives, and midwifery assistants milling about purposefully, and I smile my hellos at each of them as I pass.

The chart on the wall in the midwives' office, where the names of the patients and details pertinent to their care are written, is full. Black marker pen scribbles and notes are scrawled in every box. It's busy, and there's a lot of activity behind that busyness. Some days, a full board and a full ward can still be sedate. Early labourers, women who have come a check-up because they are worried, none of them need a lot of immediate input but they need to be here. Today, it looks as though every woman who is with us needs close monitoring or one to one care.

Handover between morning and afternoon staff is long because of the number of women present, but the midwife in charge runs through it as quickly as possible. I don't pick up a hundred percent of what is said about everyone in every room, but I know that I'll get an individual handover from the midwife that my mentor and I take over from.

My mentor for this placement is Margaret, one of the older staff members, and I don't know her very well. The midwife that I worked with last year is on rotation to postnatal, and I'm gutted that I can't work with her again this time. In midwifery, we always try to provide continuity of care to our patients, and the same goes for the mentorship provided to students. Where possible, we work with the same midwife. It's not always possible.

There's a woman in room two with fulminating pre-eclampsia. That's a disease of pregnancy recognisable by high-blood pressure, protein in the urine and swelling caused by fluid retention. Her blood pressure isn't responding to treatment, and they're preparing to take her into theatre for an emergency caesarean now.

"Room four is Reena Carmichael. She's been here for about half an hour. Straightforward pregnancy. Third baby. Five centimetres dilated, head's at the spines, and she's contracting every three minutes. Her membranes are intact."

"Good one for you," Margaret says, quietly, so as not to disturb handover.

I nod, but don't ask anything else until we are allocated to the woman's care, and the midwife who has been looking after Reena during the morning takes us to the side to handover personally.

"How's she doing with the pain?" I ask.

"She hasn't wanted any analgesia yet. I've shown her how to use the gas and air, and that's all she had last time, so…"

I nod.

"She's happy to have a student midwife, no problem," the midwife says.

Most women are perfectly willing to have a student midwife participate in their care. I don't take it personally if women refuse. It's their pregnancy, their delivery, and as much as possible, all I want is to help them to have the kind of pregnancy and delivery that they want to.

Margaret lets me take the lead as we introduce ourselves to Reena.

"I'm Violet, I'm a student midwife, and, under the supervision of Margaret, I'll be supporting you today, if that is okay with you?" I have to get better at my introductions. I always feel like I'm tripping over my words. It's as though I need time to relax and settle into being with someone.

"Fine, yes, no problem,"

Her husband nods and goes back to the task of rubbing her back. He seems to have discovered exactly the right area to apply pressure to.

I stay in the room with Reena for She's standing at the side of the early part of the shift. I know there's a lot of people rushing around outside of the door to this room, and I would rather be here, supporting Reena, than getting caught up in anything else on the ward. Even though it is busy out there, in here there's a sense of calm and serenity. Until the next contraction starts.

Before long, Reena is fully dilated and ready to give birth. She's standing by the side of the bed, and I'm crouching on the floor by her side. I can see the top of the baby's head. There's a brown, hairy, wet shape that moves closer towards me with every contraction.

I've never delivered a baby whilst the mother has been standing up before, but I'm not letting it faze me. I'm completely focused, and I know that everything is going to be fine. I love this feeling of calm and confidence that I get when I'm with women. I could almost forget that sometimes I'm consumed by anxiety. It's like I am a different person when I'm here in my uniform.

I look up at Margaret and she nods.

"Are you okay?" she mouths, and I nod back.

The delivery table is out of my reach, and Margaret lifts the sterile sheet and instruments onto the bed beside me where I can reach them.

"Do I need to lie down? I don't want to lie down. I can't. I…Another contraction. It's coming. I have to push."

"It's alright. Everything is fine. When you feel that urge to push just go with it. Keep listening to me though. In a short time, I'm going to ask you to stop pushing and try to breathe through the contraction, okay?"

She makes an immense groaning sound, and

the baby's head comes closer towards me again.

"That's it. You're doing so well. Baby is nearly here. Keep going."

I'm trying to position my hands so that I can try to control the baby's head as it starts to emerge, and so I can't drop this child onto the floor. Margaret squats on the other side of Reena and puts her hand over mine.

"That's it," she says, just as I had to Reena. "You've got this."

"Uuuuurrrrrrrrrggggggh."

"Okay Reena, stop pushing now short sharp breaths. Try to pant like a dog. Nice and slow. Don't push."

She makes tiny, restrained panting sounds, and the baby's head moves slowly and steadily forward. I have my fingers on his head, flexing it gently, guiding it out as it crowns.

"Perfect Reena, perfect. Just a little tiny push now."

She does exactly as I ask, and the baby's head pops forward. A gush of fluid comes with it and coats my left leg, but I ignore it and focus all of my attention on the delivery.

Margaret is holding a warm towel below my hands. I don't think that she doubts my ability not to drop the baby, but it's my first day back here, and this isn't the most straightforward of positions for me. It doesn't matter though. What is straightforward for me doesn't come into it. This is Reena's delivery, and I'm going to help her to have her baby in whatever position feels right to her.

With the next push, the rest of the baby spurts from Reena's body into my arms. I catch the slippery wet girl in a grasping grab, messing up my top and my pants, despite wearing a disposable apron. It doesn't matter. It just doesn't matter.

Margaret lifts the towel up, and wraps it over the infant, mopping away the mucus and fluid.

"She's perfect," I say. "You were amazing, Reena."

Reena lets out a grunting noise and flops onto the bed.

It feels so natural; the whole birth feels like I have been guided by Reena and her body, and what she wanted to do. Rather than feeling scared or uncertain, it empowered me. I hope it had the same effect on her.

I'm still buzzing when I sit in the midwives' office with Margaret, writing up the notes.

"How do you feel?"

"Great," I say. "That was amazing."

She looks at me, as if examining my thoughts.

"You handled that so well."

"Thanks. There's nothing to it really, is there? I mean, the delivery is the easy part, sort of."

"In some ways it is. The skill comes in supporting the woman through labour, knowing what to look out for, how to make sure she and the baby are safe, and that she has everything she needs. The birth? Aside from making sure that the baby is born safely, uncomplicated deliveries are pretty straightforward."

"I hope they're all straightforward," I say.

"I wish they were," Margaret replies. "But they are not. You'll learn how to handle those situations though. Don't worry."

I nod. I've not actually been worrying at all. I don't feel at all anxious, and I didn't have any anxiety when I was supporting Reena's birth. I felt calm and in control. Not that I was controlling her, but that I was in control of myself. I knew what I was doing. I knew what to say, how to act and react. Everything was completely natural to me.

Whatever I am going through personally,

being here, being on my placements gives me release and relief. I hope it is always this way, but at the back of my mind I have the fear that I will see things, experience things and have to deal with things that are far more difficult than anything I can yet imagine.

Today though, I'm full of confidence and enthusiasm, and I let those feelings carry me.

# Chapter Thirty-Two

The atmosphere between Zoe and I hasn't improved since our chat. We're being civil with each other, but the change in our relationship is obvious to both of our housemates. I want to be able to talk to Zoe about the amazing birth, and all my experiences on delivery suite. Instead, I keep to myself and stay out of her way.

I've subscribed to a list of potential house shares from the university's accommodation office, but I haven't plucked up the courage to contact any of them yet. It feels so final, picking up the phone and arranging to go and see somewhere new.

Some of the houses are groups of students who've already spent at least a year together and are looking for someone to take up the place of a student who's left the house. I don't want to be that person. It'll be hard enough living with people I don't know, never mind trying to fit in with a gang who are already friends. The irony is not lost on me.

I'm sitting in the garden, flicking through the list of houses when Carl comes out to join me. Nothing has changed between us yet either. It's not that I don't like him. I'm not looking for anyone or anything, and if I'm completely honest, I am not sure that I can be anyone's girlfriend in my anxious, messed up, introverted state of mind. If it's a one-off hook up that he's after that's definitely not my thing.

Because I don't know what I want, or what I'm doing, I've avoided talking to him.

"Busy?" he asks, even though he can see that I'm pretty much doing nothing.

"Looking at some house shares," I say.

I don't put my phone down. I keep scrolling, glancing up only to answer him.

"Right." There's a cool silence before he says, "Have I done something wrong?"

"Wrong? No." My short, snappy answer doesn't sound reassuring.

"You've barely spoken to me. It feels like –"

"Sorry," I interrupt.

I don't want to hear him analysing my behaviour. I know that I've been rude, and I'm sure that if he ever did like me, he must be reconsidering. "I've been busy."

"End of term is coming up," he nods. "Have you got everything handed in? How's your placement?"

I look down at the table, gathering my thoughts, and then click my phone shut.

"It's good, thank you. It's been an easy term really." I pause, and then add, "At uni anyway."

"Not so easy at home," he says. "I know. I'm sorry."

I can't make eye contact. I'm shuffling awkwardly in my chair, feeling all of the familiar flutters of my anxiety. I knew that I would feel like this once we started to talk. That's why I have been avoiding this. I have to talk to him sometime though, so now is as good a time as any.

"Don't be sorry," I say. "I'm a mess. It's all my own fault."

"Don't say that. It's not true. Look at how far you have come in the past few months. You were so stressed and anxious, remember. You got so bad that you wanted to take drugs."

He says *'drugs'* as though he is implying that I wanted something illegal rather than the meds that Doctor Fisher prescribed. The word has its intended impact though. I was at the lowest point that I have been in years. I was. Even though things are not great now, at least I feel better than I did a few months ago. I'm feeling anxious right now, talking to Carl, but I am, in general, doing really well under the circumstances.

He reaches across and puts his hand onto mine.

"I know I shouldn't have said what I did. Last time we talked. It wasn't fair of me. I know that you have a lot going on." He is gently stroking my hand, and I'm not stopping him. I know that he is looking straight at me, but I still can't make eye contact. "I put you under pressure, and I'm sorry."

It was barely anything. He told me that he would like to live here next year if I am staying too. That could mean anything. I've tried to tell myself that I was reading too much into it, but by the way that I have been avoiding this conversation, deep down, I have always known.

I nod slightly, and he moves his hand along my arm. I'm sure he can feel the goose bumps that have sprung up, but he doesn't mention them.

"I don't want you to avoid me. I don't want you to feel like you can't talk to me. If I was wrong, if what I said was, well, if you don't feel the same way that I do, that's fine. I want you to know that. I don't expect anything from you."

He keeps talking, but his words swim around my head. The floaty feeling that is taking over my body is stress, not desire. He pulls his hand back.

"Should I go? Shall I –"

I can't speak, but I shake my head.

"Okay," he says.

I love this garden. I love what we have done to it. When we moved in, it was a dark, dingy yard. Concrete slabs, brick walls, nothing worth looking at. Zoe and I planted flowers in pots, strung fairy lights onto wooden frames on each wall. We spent hours looking through Pinterest boards for the kind of look that we wanted to recreate, and then even longer sourcing the table and chairs, adding the bird table to make the yard exactly how we had pictured it.

That was last year. That was when the two of us would sit out here every night, laughing, chatting, being best friends. It seems like a lifetime ago. Now I'm sitting here with a man that I have known for nine months, feeling anxious, wondering what I'm going to be doing this time next year, not even knowing where I'm going to be living. When did life become so complicated?

Carl doesn't leave, and he doesn't force me to speak. When I have finished wallowing in my thoughts, I finally look at him.

"I'm scared," I say. "Of everything. I'm

scared of change. I'm scared of losing Zoe. I'm scared of not being good enough. I'm scared that if I get involved with you, you'll see what a mess I am."

He lets out a heavy sigh, and I think I have ruined everything. I shouldn't have spoken. I should have kept my thoughts to myself, and just given up on the whole idea of, well, of anything.

"I see you, Violet. I see who you are. And I like you. I like you the way you are." He fixes me with his deep, dark eyes, and I can't stop myself from looking back this time. "You are human. You are only human. We all are. We all have our flaws and imperfections. I have plenty of my own, believe me. But Violet, I like you. I know that you have a lot to deal with, but I would like to be with you. I would like to be more than friends."

"That's a lot of *likes*," I joke, my voice wavering.

"I have a lot of like for you," he smiles back. "And Vi, this isn't about where you live next year. We don't have to find somewhere together; we don't have to live together or rush anything. I want to be with you on your terms, okay?"

I nod slowly. Maybe it would be better for us to live separately, date like two normal people who haven't spent a year living as we have. It doesn't sccm to have done Zoe and Luke too much harm though.

"And if you want to stay here - if you want us to both stay here – that's fine with me too."

He's getting ahead of himself. I haven't even told him that I feel the same way yet. I smile as I have that thought. I do feel the same. I really do. Carl is different from other men that I have met. He knows about my anxiety; he has seen me at my low point as well as seeing the mask that I wear for other people's benefit.

Still, despite all that, he likes me the way I am.

"I like you too," I say. I say it because it is time to say it. I say it because it is true. "I have a lot of like for you too."

I do. I really do.

# Chapter Thirty-Three

There are two weeks left until the end of term, and the end of the year. Two weeks of mate date Monday with Zoe. I have no idea what is going to happen next year. She will spend the summer with Luke, and I'll be at home on my own. It's too early to spend the holidays with Carl. I need to take my time, not rush things. I'll have my mum, but I'm worried that the chasm between Zoe and I will grow. If I move somewhere else next year, will I even see Zoe? I can't bear to think about that. My heart is racing and my head is throbbing as I walk towards the entrance of Blackheath's.

As I draw closer, I stop dead in my tracks. Instead of the bouncy petite redhead that I expect to see, there stands a six-foot-tall male. Luke. I am frozen, wide-eyed and wordless as he approaches.

"Hi," he says.

Even though I'm looking around him to see if she is standing there, I know already that it's useless. She isn't going to pop her head up and surprise me. She's not here. It really is just Luke.

"I know this is your date day with Zoe," he

says, holding his hands up, as though he is trying to calm a frightened animal. "I'm sorry. I need to talk to you."

She must be in on this too. Somehow, he has convinced her to let him come here, or she has talked him into doing this. One way or the other – and I don't like either. I don't know whether I should be more confused or angry. This is my time with Zoe. Being on placement, I have barely seen her all week. I arranged today's shift as I do every Monday, so that I can be here for my time with my best friend. I could have worked a late, had a lie-in, but I rescheduled - for what?

Anger is taking over from confusion. It's that emotional, hurt kind of anger that fills you with heat and comes out as tears. I don't want him to see me like this. I don't want to make myself look even more of an idiot than I already do.

"Please, Violet. Don't. We need to talk. I can't let things go on the way that they have been between you and Zoe. Can we get a drink, sit down, and talk for a while? Please?"

His eyes are compassionate rather than judgmental. I almost feel like he wants to reach out and hug me, make me feel better, but he doesn't. I think for a moment *'Zoe would have'* but then I remember that Zoe must have played at least some part in him being here. He's right not to try. If he comes any closer, I will step away, or, worse still, push him away. I think it would be the last straw before I snapped. He shouldn't be here. I don't want this.

People are starting to look at us. Neither of us are raising our voices, at least not yet, but our body language and expressions are enough to draw the attention of passers-by. I expect we look like a couple having a tiff. His face is beginning to show the exasperation of someone that's running out of options. I'd say that is a fairly standard representation of a lover's fight, but I haven't had enough of them to be certain.

"Say something," he says, his voice quiet, but insistent.

His expression is pleading, but I don't know *what* I should say. I don't share his view that we *need* to talk, that's for certain. I need to talk to Zoe, that's what I need. Before I arrived at the café I was excited about seeing my best friend; all that energy has been channelled into disappointment and annoyance.

"Where's Zoe?" I ask. I sound weak and feeble, and I hate the way that the words come out. They make me feel even smaller and more self-conscious.

"She's at home," he says. "Look. You can have your date night another time this week. I need to talk to you. Okay?"

It's not okay. None of this is okay. The words *'date night'* don't sound right to me. Not right now anyway. We refer to this between ourselves as our coffee date or mate date, but hearing him call it date night makes it feel trite or even risible. Is that what Luke thinks about our meet ups? Are they a joke to him? Maybe he has never liked me. He probably thinks I'm in the way.

I should have seen this coming. He wants to tell me to get out, find my own place and give Zoe the space to live her life.

Happily.

Without me.

These thoughts run through my head, but I don't let any of the words or feelings spill out. Instead, I shrug slightly, not letting my eyes meet his. I know that if I look at him now I won't be able to hold back my tears.

We are too close to the entrance. People are pushing around us, past us, to get inside. I need to decide whether I'm staying to talk with him, or whether I should walk away before he can say things that I don't want to hear. What good will that do though? I will have to have this conversation sometime. We live together, at least for now.

A man steers his daughter, still in school uniform, past us, shaking his head at me as he squeezes by. I understand that people must wonder what we are talking about, and why we need to do it in a place that inconveniences them. A woman is trying to manoeuvre her buggy around Luke and I into the coffee shop, encumbered by the phone in her right hand. Even with both hands gripping the bar, she would still have a hard task to move around us.

I step to the side, into the shop, and it seems my decision is made. Leaving will achieve nothing. I won't have seen Zoe either way. She obviously agreed with Luke that he should come here – no matter who had the initial idea. He would never have forced her to stay at home. He's a good person, and they are good together.

I let out a sigh, and nod towards the counter.

"I could manage a latte," I say.

I can almost hear my stomach reminding me that I promised it at least one slice of cake. Somehow I don't feel like it. Not anymore.

Five minutes later, we are sitting opposite each other at one of the tables near to the window. I'm stirring my latte, watching the coffee leak into the foam in creamy spirals. Luke is sitting still, watching me. I can feel his eyes on me, but I keep all of my focus onto the tall glass mug.

Luke picks his words carefully. "I know you've been used to spending more time with Zoe. I know that this has been strange for you." He pauses between each sentence, as though they are stepping stones that he is trying to negotiate, forming a bridge between he and I. One wrong word and he could stumble off and be swept away. "It's strange for me too," he continues. "I don't want you to take this the wrong way –"

If there's any phrase that is bound to make me even more anxious than I already am, it is that. I look up at him, but I know that I shouldn't have. He must be able to read my apprehension. I must look so stupid.

"Zoe. You. Well, you're both adults. You have been together all of your lives, and from what Zoe has told me you have been through a lot together."

Of course she has told him things about herself. How much has she told him about me?

Does Luke know everything that has ever happened in my life too? Why didn't I think about this sooner? There's nothing terrible, but I feel like my past has been invaded somehow. That anger is boiling back up within me.

"She shouldn't have told you anything," I snap.

"That's what people do, Violet," he says, his voice smooth and soothing. "This is what I mean. This is what I wanted to say. You have to let her go. Not all of her. Not your friendship. I'm not asking you to not be friends, far from it. I want you two to always be friends. I know how much she loves you. You are amazing, the two of you together. But Vi, you need to let her live her life and have this relationship with me, and find a way to balance that with finding your own life."

Now he's saying I'm a no-life loser. Is that what it is? I look away again, trying to make sense of his words.

I have a slice of carrot cake on a plate in front of me, but I haven't eaten any of it. I take my fork, and run it along the buttercream, forming deep furrows that I'm sure match the ones on my brow. What do I want in life? Who am I without Zoe? Luke reaches across to me, and puts his hand on mine, stopping me from destroying the cake.

"That came out wrong, I'm sorry." If he was trying to get across those stepping stones before, now he is wading through the water, still trying to reach me. "I know you have other friends, other interests. You are doing a great course; being a midwife is going to be so wonderful for you. I don't mean that you have no life. I mean, well, I suppose I mean that you have to do things for yourself sometimes. Zoe will always be there for you, but you need to be there for yourself too."

"That makes no sense," I say. "I'm always here for myself. I'm with myself every minute of every day."

He looks at me. "You are. But I feel like I'm taking her away from you, that she should be with you, keeping you occupied, and I shouldn't feel like that."

"So, it's about you and what you want?" I push the plate forwards to the middle of the table; I don't want it anymore.

"No. Not at all. I shouldn't have said anything, I'm sorry. I just want you to be happy. I thought I could say the right thing, but obviously I can't."

"And that's what you came here for? To tell me to get a life, and that I make you feel bad? Thanks Luke. I thought we were friends but obviously I was wrong."

He's shaking his head and I can see that he wants to say something, so I stop.

"No," he says. "That's not why I'm here. No."

"Why then? There's more?"

"I feel terrible for having said all of that now. Especially because of why I did come here. It would mean a lot to Zoe, and to me, if you would reconsider your decision to move out."

The words hang in the air like smoke after the candles on a birthday cake are blown out. I don't want them, and I don't want the cake.

"After all that you said?" I mutter. I can't quite believe him.

I'm sure now that he and Zoe must have been through this, arguing about it, to the point that she somehow got him to come here and make it look like it has all been his idea. He clearly has no reason to keep me around though.

"You can be your own person and still live with your best friend," he says. "That's what I was trying to say before. I know it didn't come out right, but I think it's important for you to have balance. You won't have that by moving out and being on your own, will you? I think you would be sad and resentful and –"

"You think you know me so well?" I spit out the words. I don't mean to. I hate being like this.

He's right though. I most probably would feel that way, in a flat share somewhere with people I don't know, sitting alone in my room every night. At least I would get some studying done.

"I don't, but Zoe does. I care about you though. I want things to be right. I want you to be happy. And Zoe too, of course. She isn't the same without you. Over Easter, when you weren't here, it was like there was a piece of her missing. She was never completely at ease, never totally herself. I mean, she was still wonderful, of course, and I still adore her."

He has to say that, because he must know that whatever he says to me will get back to Zoe.

He continues, "I know that you don't want to be dependent upon her, and I understand that, but the truth is, she needs you. You need each other."

"You're right though," I say. "I should have grown out of this by now. I should be able to start out on my own rather than just being an add-on in her life. We can't live our entire lives unable to be apart for more than a few days. It's just…ridiculous." I shake my head slowly as I speak.

"It isn't. Imagine that I said to you that I didn't want to be dependent on Zoe, that I don't want to feel like I can't live without her," he says.

"It's different. You're her boyfriend. You are meant to want to be with her."

"And you are her best friend. You've been her best friend for as long as either of you can remember. What kind of boyfriend would I be to her if I didn't respect that? I saw what kind of a friendship you two had before she and I got together. I fell in love with the person that she is, and she is that person, in part, because of you." His hand is still on mine, and I'm aware of its warmth and weight.

"You want me to have my own life, but you want me to stay so that Zoe isn't unhappy, and so that you don't feel guilty?"

I can't stop myself. My mind wants to turn everything to a negative.

"We both want you to stay because you are important to us. Okay? But I can see that you are beating yourself up about this dependent-independent thing, and I think you need to do something to make yourself feel better about it. Moving out is not the answer though. Please. Reconsider. Think about it."

I think about it. I think everything through from every angle, and eventually, I come to a decision. It's the only decision I could possibly have made. When my mind is set, I wonder why it took me so long. The answer was obvious. I know what I have to do.

# Chapter Thirty-Four

I've set the table, there are meatballs in ragu simmering in the slow cooker, and I've opened a bottle of mid-priced red wine. I've actually already had a most of a large glass of the wine, so it's a good thing I thought ahead and bought two bottles. In a few days I will be leaving, and I want to make sure that tonight is special. There are things that I need to say, things I should have said before now. I can't leave Tangiers Court without doing this.

I stir the pasta, trying to make sure it doesn't stick to the bottom of the pan. Admittedly, I'm not the world's best cook, but I'm putting everything I have into this.

She doesn't know, of course. I haven't told Zoe that I'm doing this. I did tell Luke though, and he and Carl are going to have a few end of term drinks together while I talk to my best friend. I have been stupid. I have blamed Zoe, not externally, sure, but I have blamed her for the chasm in our friendship. It takes two people to maintain a friendship, and I have not been playing my part either. I have wallowed in my own pit of anxiety and self-doubt, and even when Zoe has reached down to try to pull me out, I have refused to take her hand.

When I hear Zoe's key in the door, a heavy wave of apprehension sweeps through me. Am I doing the right thing? Should I have just asked her to chat with me, rather than making this mighty gesture? I feel foolish, and I panic, wanting to close the kitchen door, shut her out, pretend I'm making this dinner for myself.

"Stop it," I tell myself, out loud, under my breath. "Stop it."

I've set the table, the outside metal table that she and I chose together. The sun is still high in the sky, but I have switched the fairy lights on anyway. I want this to be magical, or at least I want to work some magic between us. I want to cast a spell that will make everything better between us. I think I know how to start.

"Zoe," I call, before she has the chance to run upstairs.

"Hi." I hear her voice, but she doesn't come through to the kitchen.

"Could you, er, can you give me a hand with something?" I stutter.

"Sure," she says.

Her voice is not as chirpy as it once would have been with me. She would have rushed to help me no matter what. I can't think about that now. Tonight is for the future, not moping about the past.

As soon as she walks into the kitchen she lifts her head, sniffing the air.

"Smells good," she smiles. "You and Carl?"

I've hardly talked to her about him, despite this being one of the most amazing things that has happened to me. That's what really made me realise, I think. Not just Luke coming to me, talking to me on her behalf. Not just that. I would always run straight to Zoe with exciting news, and this time, I did not. I don't want a future where I don't race to tell her about everything that happens to me. We have been friends too long, and we have been too close to let go of that. I have to do my part; I have to stop being so stupid and selfish.

"I was hoping you would have dinner with me," I say. I feel so nervous asking her. There's so much at stake. I'm trying to keep the feelings of fear subdued.

She looks into the slow cooker.

"My favourite," she says. "Sneaky." Then she looks up at me and smiles. "Of course."

"Just the two of us tonight," I say. "Carl has taken Luke to the bar."

Zoe raises her eyebrows at that. "He knew

you were setting this up?"

"Well, after you sent him as your envoy to Blackheath's…"

I don't want to say the wrong thing, so I stop talking.

"Thanks, Vi. This will be perfect. Shall I set the table?"

I shake my head slowly, and push open the back door, so that she can see what I have prepared. A wide smile breaks across her face, and I realise it's the first time the two of us have been happy together in way too long.

"I wanted to say sorry. I have handled everything really badly this year," I say.

"No," she replies. "You haven't. I have. It's my fault. I didn't balance things properly. I wasn't there for you. I –"

I have to stop her.

"Let's just agree that we both could have done things differently," I say. "We don't have to blame ourselves, or each other. I'm happy that you're happy. I really am."

"And I hope that you and Carl are happy too. You are…?"

I know what she is asking, without her completing the sentence.

"Together?" I shrug. "It's early days. But I

like him." I have lots of likes for him. "I'm going to try not to mess things up." I grin and she smiles and shakes her head.

"Don't be like that. If you are going to give him a chance, he is very lucky. You're the best, Vi. You really are. I'm sorry I haven't told you that often enough recently."

"I'm sorry too," I say quietly.

I need to strain the pasta and dish dinner out. I could use that as an excuse to put off what I want to say next, but I don't. I take a breath and speak.

"I want to stay here with you and Luke next year. If you will have me."

"Have you? I want that more than anything!" she squeaks. "Are you sure? No, I don't care if you're sure. Just do it. Stay. Stay with me."

Her voice is rapid, racing the words in excitement.

"I'm sure," I smile. "I am completely sure. Whatever happens next year, whatever happens ever, you are my best friend, and I don't want to be without you."

We've left the dishes on the worktop in the kitchen, and we're sitting in the last of the evening sunlight when Luke and Carl come home. It feels strange seeing the two of them walk through the door and into the garden. Luke bends to kiss Zoe, but Carl looks nervous and waits for me to stand and plant a kiss on his face.

"Did you two…you know…sort everything out?" Luke asks.

Zoe and I look at each other and nod. The shared smile reminds me of the closeness that we have always had and reminds me that I never want to lose it.

"We are great," she says. "Everything is going to be perfect."

I don't know about that. I don't know what next year is going to be like. I don't know what will happen with Carl, and I don't know how I am going to cope with my final year of training, but what I do know is that I'm going to be here, in Tangiers Court, with my best friend.

For now, that is all that matters.

# lessons

# learned

## je rowney

## the lessons of a student midwife

### BOOK THREE

# Chapter One

I went back to visit my mum a few times over the summer break, but for the most part I stayed at Tangiers Court with Zoe, Luke and Carl.

Carl.

My boyfriend.

I thought it was too soon to spend the whole summer with him, but the more time I spent at home with Mum, the more I wanted to be with him.

It felt strange, at first, being in Tangiers Court, and then being in the town, after lectures had finished and there were no other students around. I went onto campus, just out of curiosity, and the squares were dotted with seagulls and pigeons fighting over the last scraps that had been left behind. Apart from that, there was an unusual, eerie silence. When you're used to seeing a place filled with life and noise and chaos, visiting when all of that has left is quite an experience.

I can't believe how much has changed since I started university. I'm about to begin my third and final year as a student midwife; I'm a senior student at last, but I'm not sure I'm ready for it. I've spent the past two years living at Tangiers

Court. It's had its ups and downs, but mostly it has been great, living with my best friend, and training for my dream job.

When you suffer from anxiety as I do, there's always some degree of underlying stress, but this year the pressure is really going to be on. I have a practice document (my PAD) that needs to be signed off. To qualify as a midwife, I need to carry out a certain number of deliveries, antenatal and postnatal checks, and other midwifery duties, and have a midwife sign my checklist. I also need to pass the rest of my modules, of course. The academic and the clinical elements are equally as important as each other. This year, I need to complete a research project on my own subject choice. I think I already know what I want to focus on, but lectures are a few days away. I'll wait and see what the module leader tells us.

Then there's Carl.

I actually have a boyfriend.

It's not what I planned, and it's not what I expected, but things happened gradually between us and now it's official. So now there's Zoe and Luke, me and Carl, all living here together. Even though it's not what I'd planned, this is pretty much everything I ever wanted. In

2

a year's time, I will be starting work as a midwife; everything is working out perfectly.

There's a voice from behind me.

"You are coming out with me tonight?"

Carl loops his arms around me unexpectedly, making me jump slightly.

I don't want to say no. I don't want to be the boring one that never goes anywhere or does anything. If it were down to me, we would stay at home with Zoe and Luke, watch television, chat and all have a laugh together. Carl is far more sociable than I am. It's the first night of freshers' week, and even though we're old timers, and not the freshers we were, he wants to go out.

I hide my automatic frown and make myself smile instead, even though he is behind me and can't see it.

"If you want to," I say.

"Don't just do it for me," he replies, kissing me on the top of my head. "Only come out if *you* want to."

I want to be with him. We've spent most of the past three months together, but I'm not uscd to being in a relationship and I still can't get enough of him. It's unfair of me to make it seem that I only want to spend time with him because I've been single until recently. It's not that, at all. I enjoy being with him. I love being with him. Of course I'll go out tonight.

I turn to face him and let him see my smile.

"No. I want to. We'll have a good night." I pause and correct myself. "We'll have a great night."

His face breaks into a grin. "It'll give you a chance to dress up," he says.

I know it's probably only my anxiety making me feel this way, but my mind instantly takes his words as a criticism. I have no other reason to believe he meant them that way, but I look down and my clothes and frown. Plain black and floral dress. Thick tights. Flat pumps. Maybe I should wear a cardigan over this dress, soften my curves a little.

"I didn't mean –" He starts to apologise.

"I know," I say, as if I really believe my own words. "Silly. I know."

"Shall I ask the others?" he says.

I'm sure he knows as well as I do what the answer will be. I'm not alone in my dislike of the packed, sweaty bar. The chance of Zoe and Luke wanting to come with us is slim to zero, but I figure it's still polite to invite them along.

It's Saturday afternoon. Zoe has taken Luke into town for lunch and shopping, or at least she told him it was for lunch, and I know she won't be able to resist the shopping. Luke's pretty good though. He never complains, even when he comes along with the two of us. He's happy to carry our bags and wait patiently while we try on clothes that we rarely buy, or stare in shop windows at jewellery we can't afford on our student loans. I don't know if it is because I'm dating Carl now, or whether we've all settled into the status quo, but *the four of us* feels just right. It's like it was always meant to be this way.

If I text Zoe to ask her to go to the bar, the randomness of my suggestion will probably confuse her. Instead I'll wait for her to return. When Zoe gets home, I wait for Luke to go into the kitchen, and then broach the subject as nonchalantly as I can.

"I'm going to the union with Carl tonight," I tell her. "Do you fancy coming?"

The answer must be *no*. I can't imagine that she would want to. She screws her eyes and looks at me, probably trying to work out if I've lost the plot. She knows how I feel about it, so it's no wonder she's looking at me as if I suggested we spend the evening on the Moon.

"Really?" she asks. "Are you sure? You must really like him, huh?"

I grin. She already knows that I do. It's been three months. All summer, the four of us here, happy together. Happy couples. Happy friends.

"Well I guess it's our last chance to hit fresher's week," she says, like she's trying to find a reason to say yes.

It's true. It's our last year. This is it.

I squeeze her in a tight hug. "It'll be bearable with you there," I squeak into her ear. "Thanks Zo."

She laughs. "You're going to be with Carl, you really don't need me."

"I always need you," I say before letting go. "Don't you forget that."

We get to the bar at just before nine, and it's already heaving. The main room buzzes with chatter and pounds with the heat of packed bodies. Even the open area just inside the doors, where students usually cluster around pool tables and arcade machines, is filled with standing students, drinking, talking and laughing, catching up with old friends and meeting new people.

I could have been part of this. I could have been into the social scene, down here every weekend, or even every night. I know that some of these students have been or will be if they've just started their courses. It's something I've never enjoyed though. I don't want to have to queue for hours for a drink I don't particularly want with people that I'm not really that bothered about talking to. That sounds harsh, I know. I've met some lovely people on my course, and I consider them friends, but apart from that I've spent nearly all my social time as I did before I came to uni: with Zoe.

That changed when things happened with Carl.

"Things Happened" is the best way that I can describe it. I didn't plan on having a boyfriend, but I've heard it said that the best relationships are the ones that *aren't* planned.

Zoe is talking to me, and even though she's only a foot away, I can't hear her. I lean in, squint my eyes, and tilt my ear towards her. Carl keeps walking. He has a purposeful stride, and he's making a beeline for a miraculously empty table. His hand is still in mine, but I lag behind, trying to listen to Zoe as Carl tugs at me.

"Wait," I say as loudly as I can without shouting.

He keeps walking, so I let go of his hand and stop to hear Zo.

"It's nuts in here," she says. "I never realised there were this many students."

I nod and smile, then turn back to see Carl, twenty feet off into the crowd, pushing his way through.

Zoe sees him and laughs. "You can tell he's done this before!"

Luke isn't making any kind of valiant effort to find us seats. He's standing behind Zoe, looking shell-shocked. He's more sociable than Zoe and me, but tonight, the first night of freshers' week, looks like it's too much for him. He only came because Zoe agreed, and she is only here for me. I feel responsible and a little bit guilty. She won't hold it against me though, neither of them will.

Carl's made it to the table before we start moving towards him again. I can see him talking to a couple who reached it a split second before him. He looks over in our direction, points at us, and the two students follow his direction and look over at us. I have no idea what he has told them, but the girl nods, the boy smiles, and they walk away into the crowd. I feel a little bubble of pride. Carl managed to get us seats. I flash a smile at Zoe as the three of us hurry over to join Carl at our table.

He's already sitting when we reach him.

I bend to kiss Carl, and he moves his face, leaving me smacking my lips against air.

"Not here," he says.

I smile, and expect a smile in return, but he turns to Luke and starts talking. I glance at Zoe to see if she noticed, but she's not looking. I let out a small, relieved sigh.

"Do you want to get the first round?" Carl asks, directing the question at Luke.

Luke nods. "Sure." He turns to Zoe. "I'm going to need a hand."

"Ugh, okay," she says. She dislikes the sweaty throng as much as I do, but she wouldn't let Luke struggle.

When we've told them what we want and they start to head to the bar, I give Carl a smile, sit beside him, and hold his hand beneath the table.

"How did you persuade those guys to let us have these seats?" I ask

With a straight face he says, "I told them

you're pregnant." As soon as he has said it, he laughs, but I'm speechless.

"What?" he says.

"I…" I don't know what to say. My red cheeks must be telling him everything he needs to know, but he seems oblivious. I let go of his hand, instinctively bringing my arms in front of my body, resting my hands in my lap, covering my belly, even though it's already concealed beneath the table.

I know I'm not as skinny as some of the girls here, but I've always been curvy. It's not as though I've suddenly put on weight.

I want to ask whether I look fat. I want to know if people could really think I am pregnant.

He's already started talking about something else though, and I have to angle myself in closer to be able to hear him. I'm being silly. I know I must be. Carl likes me just as I am. It's funny really, when you think about it. He lied, and it wasn't the most flattering thing he could have said, but he got us the seats, and I have to be grateful for that. Being in this bar on a Saturday night and having to stand amidst the sweaty bodies the whole time would have been too much. I get to sit with my boyfriend, my best friend, and her man. I really can't complain.

Much as I don't go in for the social scene, it's going to be a rough year. I should enjoy myself while I can, because when my lectures and placements start, I'm going to be working hard and studying harder. Carl might want to carry on partying all year, but I won't have the time or the inclination.

When Zoe and Luke get back with our drinks, I don't mention what Carl said to secure the table, and by the end of the night we are laughing so much that it's all but forgotten.

# Chapter Two

It's been great having time off over the summer, especially because I spent it with Carl and Zoe. And Luke of course. Carl's my boyfriend, Zoe's my best friend, but Luke is still a good mate. It's been super being with all three of them. Still, I'm excited to get back to classes, and by Monday morning I am practically buzzing to get into my lecture room.

This year's modules focus on leadership, and preparing us for making the transition from students to actual, qualified junior midwives. It still feels like an immense step, and that's because it is. The newly qualified midwives that I have met on the wards have all had preceptors to support them through their first few months after qualification, so it's not like I will be thrown in at the deep end on my own. There's always someone on hand that can reach in and pull me up if I start to flounder.

Back in the classroom on the first day of term our chatter alternates between excitement and nervousness. This is it. Our final year. We will walk out of here next August as fully qualified midwives, ready to start our new jobs, and begin our dream careers.

Zita Somerville, one of my favourite lecturers, has judged the feeling in the room perfectly, but then again, I'm sure she's been through this before. Perhaps every group of final year students experience the same set of mixed emotions.

I'm practically prickling with apprehension. I'm surprised my anxiety hasn't kicked in, full force, but since I've been with Carl, I've been so much more relaxed and in control of my feelings. He's given me a kind of confidence I never imagined I could have. It's a good job, because I have a lot to learn this year and, as I keep reminding myself, it's going to be tough.

"In less than a year, you will be handing back your lilac tops and navy pants, leaving your student days behind you," Zita says.

She pauses to look around the room, gauging the effect of her words. As anticipated, we are all turning to our classmates, sharing the realisation that this is the final stretch.

"If you don't feel ready yet, don't worry. You're not alone. Throughout the course you've supported each other, and we have supported you. By the end of summer term, you'll be applying for jobs, and looking forward to the next steps in your careers. And you will be ready."

I gulp in air loudly and a little too sharply and let out a flurry of coughs. Everyone turns to look at me, and I feel my face start to burn as I try to calm myself.

"Same," Sophie whispers next to me. She pats me gently on the back, with a concerned look on her face.

I get in control of my breathing and manage to smile.

On the other side of her Ashley is nodding too. Zita is right: we are all in this together.

"Your Practice Assessment Documents are non-negotiable. All your competencies *must* be signed off in order for you to complete the course and qualify. When you go home today, check through your PADs. Make sure you know what you need to do and start to plan towards getting your sign-offs. You should have received your placement allocations. If you need to make any changes, speak to your link tutor as soon as possible."

I'll have placements on each of the maternity wards this year. I need little bits of everything for my PAD: I need to get more checks signed off on the postnatal and antenatal wards; I still need to assist at the births of eleven more babies. That's going to be the challenging part. Antenatal, postnatal, and infant checks are easy to come by. There are lots of women and babies on the wards, and I'm reasonably confident that getting my sign-offs won't be a problem. The deliveries are a different matter.

There's not always a labouring woman when I am on the delivery suite. When I do look after women in labour, they don't always give birth while I am on shift. Add to that the women who develop complications and need to have instrumental deliveries by forceps or ventouse, and those who have unplanned Caesareans, and my chance for getting those sign-offs reduces even further.

"If you need more time in any of the placement areas, it can be arranged. We haven't supported you this far to let you fail. You *can* do this, and you *will* do it."

Zita is saying exactly what I need to hear right now, and from the relieved murmurs that are passing around the room, I'm definitely not alone.

In the morning coffee break I have my first chance to catch up with Soph, Ashley and Simon since the summer break. Soph and

Ashley have been house-sharing since last year and they're thick as thieves. I know they've probably been sharing their worries and excitement since they came back from the holidays. For Simon and me, this is our first chance to catch up face-to-face. He's the first to start off-loading.

"I'm never going to get there," he says. "I have like twenty deliveries to do."

It's not completely about the numbers. Each woman, each baby, each family, they're all important and I don't want to lose sight of that. Still, when we sit around one of the clunky plastic tables on our hard plastic chairs, the conversation quickly turns to our PADs and what we still need to get signed off to qualify.

"Ugh," Sophie groans. "I'm not even on delivery suite for the first placement."

We shake our heads in shared sympathy.

"Good to be back though," I say, trying to lighten the mood.

"It's great being back," Sophie says in agreement.

I don't see these three as much as maybe I could outside of classes, but I care about them and how they're doing. The whole class feels like it's a community; training to be a midwife is a bonding experience. It's hard to explain how it feels to be on the communal journey with these other students. We have something in common that ties us on a deeper level. We all know what the others are going through. We have similar experiences and stresses, and the same joys.

There's a buzz that comes from being present at a birth and helping a new life into the world that you can't get from anything else. Not just that, when you deliver a baby, you're helping to create a family. You're present at the most intimate, special time and that's always going to feel like a privilege. I'll never reduce that to making up the numbers I need for my portfolio.

Of course, I'm worried about getting everything signed off, but I can't let that take over. I have to keep my anxiety under control and focus on what matters, what really matters.

# Chapter Three

Monday afternoons have been established as my mate date time with Zoe. Even over the summer we carried on the tradition, whether we had spent the day together at home or not. This time feels special and safe; in a way it's sacred. Zoe's classes finish at lunchtime today, and mine run on until four, so I wander down from uni to the town centre on my own.

My head is full of everything I have to do in the next few months. A few months. That's all that lie between me and my future as a qualified midwife. Tick the boxes, write my research project, pass my other assessments, including that final OSCE. It's a cold October day, and I'm already cosying inside my duffle coat, but I get an extra chill thinking about that exam.

OSCE is an acronym for the Objective Structured Clinical Examination, a scenario-based practical that I have had to pass each year to continue. The first year I had a major panic attack and had to resit. Last year, I aced it. I'd love to be able to say that I am feeling calm and confident, but speaking in public isn't my strong suit, even when it's only in front of a couple of lecturers and a stand-in patient. That's not until spring; I'm not going to let myself think about it anymore just yet.

Instead, I kick through the leaves, and let my mind wander ahead of me to the coffee shop. For the first two years it was an independent café called *Blackheath's* but over the summer it's been taken over by a Coffee Express franchise. It's lost some of its unique charm, but the coffee is still good, and Zoe and I have our special corner that we aren't going to let go of in a hurry.

Sure enough, when I arrive at the door, I see her, already drinking her extra-hot-extra-shot mocha. There's another mug on the table: my latte, waiting for me.

"Thanks Zo," I say, leaning across to hug hello.

She nods. "It was my turn," she smiles. "At least I think it was."

We don't really keep count, so it doesn't matter. I settle down into my usual seat, tuck my jacket over the back of the chair, and flop my bag onto the floor.

"Busy day?" she asks.

"Aren't they all?" I say.

She tightens her lips and nods. "Seems that way. I've got so much to finish."

Even though we're studying different courses we both have assignments to write and portfolios to complete. She's going to be a teacher; I'm going to be a midwife. Everything that we have worked towards, not only at university, but before that, school, A-Levels, everything, it's finally getting us to where we always dreamed we would be.

"But we *have* nearly finished," I say.

She raises her eyebrows. "You must have had a good day," she says. "Feeling confident?"

I let out a small laugh. "Confident? I wouldn't go that far."

"You're doing great," she says. "When was the last time you had a wobble?" A wobble. I much prefer her referring to my anxiety attacks like that. It makes them sound much less intimidating. "I can't remember," she continues. "It's been so long."

"I know, me neither." I grin. I never imagined I could get to this point. "Carl makes me feel like I can do anything."

"It's not just him," Zoe smiles. "You can take some of the credit for your own achievements, you know."

I wrinkle my nose dismissively and bat the idea away.

"And stop that," she says. "It's true. You have changed such a lot."

"Changed?" I can't help but feel a stab of concern at the word, even though I'm pretty sure she doesn't mean it in bad way. It's a reflex reaction. However much I have changed, my instinct still flips back to self-doubt.

Zoe settles her coffee cup down onto the shiny white Coffee Express saucer, covering up the bean-shaped logo.

"When you started your course you were so excited, but you were so scared. Now..." She pauses, leans back on her chair, and looks at me. "Now you look like you can do anything."

"Well," I say. "It may *look* that way, but I actually feel a lot like a duck."

She tilts her head and regards me silently, waiting for an explanation.

"You know," I say. "I may look calm and serene on the surface, but underneath my little legs are paddling like mad to keep me afloat."

Zoe bursts out into a raucous laugh that has everyone in the coffee shop turning to look at us. The barista glares over in our direction; Silvie, who worked behind the counter at Blackheath's would no doubt have come over to share the joke. Things change. Things always change.

I join in with the laughter, unable to stop myself.

Eventually, Zoe catches her breath, shakes her head, and pats my arm softly. "A duck. That's perfect."

"I waddle like one too," I say, without thinking.

Zoe rolls her eyes and tuts. "Less of that. In fact, less of that and more cake. What do you want?"

She never lets me put myself down; she's always there for me, fighting for me, and supporting me, even when I'm not supporting myself.

# Chapter Four

I already have a vague idea about what I want to focus on for my research project. It's a subject that's close to home, but also something that I know I have so much more to learn about. Maternal mental health. It was a done deal when I went to the mother and baby unit for one of my SPOKE placements last year. We have a module on maternal mental health, but I am hungry to find out more.

I haven't forgotten my visit to the Linden Unit last spring, and I don't think I ever will. I don't expect I'll see Meg, the mother we visited on the unit, again, but I think of her often. Even though I only spent a morning with her, the experience has stayed with me.

Some of the fascination with the topic must come from my own anxiety issues, of course. Not only because I have been dealing with them for so long, but also because I wonder what it will be like for me if and when I decide to have a child. If I'm still going through the ups and downs of anxiety, will I be able to cope with the stresses of childbearing and childbirth? If I struggle at least I will know that there is help and support available. If I struggle I will know that I'm not the only one. Maternal mental health support is so important, and I want to make sure that I always give the best I can.

I must think about exactly what it is that I want to concentrate on. The paper is six thousand words on the subject of my choosing. That's a lot of work, and there's sixty credits riding on this, so I'd better make the right decision. I want it to be interesting, but I want to write about something manageable. There are entire postgraduate courses on the topic of maternal mental health, so I have to take one fragment and focus.

When I discuss it with Sophie, Simon, and Ashley, I get the response that I had expected.

"Maternal mental health? You mean postnatal depression?" Sophie says.

"I was thinking more of antenatal issues." I watch her face change in recognition.

"Right," she says. "I hadn't thought much about that."

We don't have our mental health module until next term, and perhaps she has been fortunate enough not to encounter any women in practice with antenatal mental health support needs yet. We are only on our antenatal placements for such a narrow window of time that it's impossible to experience everything.

"I guess we'll all learn more about it after Christmas," I smile. "I've been really interested in it since I went to the Linden Unit though."

Ashley nods. "I wish I had gone somewhere like that. Might see if I can get a day booked in."

"I totally recommend it," I say.

"I'm going to write my paper on pain relief in labour," Simon says.

We all mumble affirmations at the same time. In a way I'm glad we didn't talk about my project for too long, because I don't want to end up talking about myself. That's one of the many problems with anxiety, once people know that you suffer, they want to know more, they want to try to help you, and whilst that might sound like a good thing, sometimes, most of the time, I just want to be seen as normal.

When we get back into the lecture room, our lecturer Zita runs around the class, asking each of us to give a summary of what we are planning to write about. I think it's to give some ideas to those who haven't thought of anything yet, and surprisingly there are a handful of students that seem to have no clue. I feel lucky to have something that I am passionate about, and then as that thought strikes me I realise that I feel that way because of my own issues, just as much as my experience on the Linden Unit. It's not exactly a blessing.

The class are considering a wide range of subject areas. It's amazing how many niche areas of interest there are within pregnancy, childbirth and maternity care. There's the physiological side – one of the girls wants to explore the effects of hormones in pregnancy, the social element – another plans to write about domestic abuse, which is unfortunately a huge issue, and the emotional and mental health aspects, like my project. Then there's the practice-based issues, such as pain relief in labour or management of the third stage of labour. There's enough research on how to deliver the placenta to make it suitable as a topic for a six-thousand-word dissertation. The more I think about it, the more I realise how little I know and how much I will still have to learn once I have qualified. Being a midwife is about being a lifelong learner; there's always going to be something new to study and understand.

After class, before I go to meet Zoe, I pop into

the library. The clinical side of my training might be the most interesting and enjoyable, but I need to remind myself to get down to the academic work too. It's no easy ride, training to be a midwife. It's a degree course, and rightly so. The amount of detail and depth that I need to include in the written assignments leaves me with two or three pages of references to write every time. I'm not a naturally clever person, and it has taken me a lot of work to get to where I am today. I'll have to put in a lot of effort to make sure this project is as good as it can possibly be. I don't need to come out at the end of the year with a first class degree, and based on my results so far there's not much chance of that, but I need to pass, and for the sake of my own pride and achievement I would like to do as well as I possibly can.

Zoe coasts through assignments and coursework. Even back at school she was so much smarter than I. Of course, Zoe being Zoe she tried to coach me and give me study skills tips, but at the end of the day I lack that certain something that she has in spades. She still offers to read my essays for me, and does the modern-day equivalent of dotting my 'i's and crossing my 't's.

Most of the books and journals are online now, but being in the library makes me feel somehow more focussed on studying. I want to take some proper ink-on-paper textbooks home with me, and the library is well-stocked with a wide array of texts on maternal mental health. This is where I will start. Get an overview, find my direction, make a plan. It sounds so easy, thinking about it like that, but I have a sneaking suspicion that these six-thousand-words are going to be terribly hard work.

# Chapter Five

Before I know it, it's time to be back in my clinical placement. I get the familiar buzz of excitement as I walk through the hospital car park, past reception, up in the lift and along the corridor to the double doors. It's a route I've taken many times over the past couple of years, and if I get a job here when I qualify it will be my route to work for the foreseeable future. Even though I need to focus on getting my PAD signed off and passing my assessments, I can't help but think of the future, dangling just beyond my fingertips.

When I get onto the ward, my mentor, Jade, is already in the midwives' office, halfway through a mug of tea.

"Violet, hi!" She pulls a file off the chair next to her and pats the seat in invitation.

"Hi!" I chirp back. I know I sound overexcited, but it's because I am. I don't see the point in trying to hide it. Being enthusiastic about being here can't be a bad thing.

"Tea's fresh. Welcome home," she smiles.

Home. It does feel like that. Or at least this feels like a homecoming. I flick my gaze over to the board on the wall where all the patients' names are recorded. It's empty. My excitement sinks like a lead weight into my gut. I pour myself a tea and settle back next to Jade.

I know I have five weeks here, but I had hoped to start getting my paperwork signed off today. I don't want to start thinking in numbers instead of thinking about each woman I support, but I'd I don't get my PAD signed off I don't qualify; it's as simple as that.

"It's been a quiet week," Jade says. "I don't know what people were doing nine months ago, but they weren't making babies."

I almost snort my tea out in a heavy laugh, and manage to just about keep it in. That sets Jade off, and we are both in fits of giggles when the ward sister walks in.

"Did I miss something?" she asks.

Jade shakes her head. "You had to be there."

The ward sister shrugs and smiles. "Looks like it's going to be a quiet one," she tells us. "Good chance to do some stock checks."

Jade nods, but my heart sinks again. I know it's something that needs to be done, but I'm here to learn. I'm here to look after women. I'm also here to get those sign-offs on my PAD.

If there aren't any patients, there's not a lot I can do.

I spend the morning checking expiry dates on the bags of fluid in the stock room and making sure the resuscitation units are fully stocked. It gives me a chance to run through some of the neonatal emergency procedures with Jade though. As we check each of the pieces of equipment and drugs on the trolley, she asks me questions, and I quick-fire the answers confidently.

There's an hour and a half left of my shift when the phone finally rings.

"Delivery suite. Student midwife speaking." I say, as cheerfully as I can.

"Hi Delivery Suite Student Midwife, it's Antenatal Ward Student Midwife."

I recognise Sophie's voice immediately.

"Hi Soph. What's up?"

"I've got a lady for you. She's been here since the early hours. Debbie Baker, primp, term plus one. She was having contractions and wasn't sure if she had ruptured membranes or not."

Ruptured membranes sounds terribly dramatic, but it's only a technical term for the waters breaking.

"She's contracting now, every four minutes,

and she wants some analgesia. I've done a VE and she's five centimetres."

VE is shorthand for vaginal examination. The cervix opens up to ten centimetres at full dilatation. In first-time mums it can feel a little bit like a firm long nose with a tiny dimple to start with. It gets thinner and more stretchy as labour continues, until you can't feel any of it at all. The wonders of the human body will never be lost on me.

Five centimetres might sound like it's halfway through labour, but that's not always the case. It's not steady progress, although a rough guide is that cervices dilate at around a centimetre per hour. Women are unpredictable and cervices even more so.

Even at full dilatation, the baby needs to descend down the birth canal before its mother is able to push it out. I would say that birth takes time and it's a long slow process, but there are also those women who sprint from onset of labour to delivery in minutes rather than hours. I hope that if I ever have a baby I'm one of the quick ones.

"Okay," I say. "Thanks Sophie. Nothing else I need to know?"

"Routine pregnancy. No medical history.

Her partner is coming up with her."

"Great. Are you bringing her? I'll get a room ready."

"Yes, I'll bring her up. See you soon."

It's not likely that Debbie will give birth while I'm still on shift, but I love the whole process. Supporting women and their partners through labour is one of my favourite parts of midwifery.

Sophie, Debbie, and a man that Soph introduces as Marcus, Debbie's partner, arrive on the ward within five minutes.

I run through the usual orientation to the ward, showing Debbie where the toilet and the call button are, and I get handover from Soph while Debbie settles in.

"No one about?" Sophie says, casting her gaze over the empty board on the office wall.

"Really quiet," I say. "We've been checking resuscitaires and doing a stock count."

Soph pulls her face without thinking. "Not going to get any deliveries like that," she says. "I need ten more."

"I need eleven," I tell her, and she pulls her face again.

"I know," I say, trying to smile. "Busy downstairs?"

She wobbles her hand in a so-so movement. "Quiet everywhere, I think."

"Typical. I bet they were rushed off their feet until we started our placements."

The university try to arrange our placements so there aren't too many students on any ward at the same time, but there are weeks when we are all in our lecture blocks, and we all have annual leave at Christmas, Easter and summer break. It would be just my luck if every woman in town had already delivered while I was in university.

Sophie pats my hand. "We'll get there," she smiles.

"We will," I say. I know we have to.

When I go back into her room, Debbie is standing by the side of the bed, sucking on the gas and air like it's her life support system. As her contraction subsides I rest my hand on her arm and encourage her to let go of the tubing that's delivering her pain relief.

"Take some breaths. Get some fresh air in between contractions," I say

"I feel woozy," she says, with an unsteady wobble in her voice that confirms it.

"Hop up. Take a seat on the bed for a

minute." I guide her, supporting her as she moves.

The gas and air can do that to some women. Just enough of it takes the edge off the contractions, too much and it can cause a fuzzy dizziness.

Debbie hauls herself awkwardly onto the bed and sits, eyes closed, head pressed back against the two pillows.

Bedding is sparse in the delivery room. There are two sheets on the bed: one that covers the whole mattress and then another that lies horizontally across it, lined with a plastic underlay. It's positioned directly beneath Debbie's bottom, as intended. There's also a large square incontinence pad, the same kind that the nurses use on the wards, but for our patients it's more frequently used for catching vaginal fluids rather than urine. There's usually some discharge during labour, and a little blood loss can be normal too. The other fluid we look for is the water from the amniotic sac. Soph said they haven't had any confirmation that the waters have broken, and as yet I haven't seen anything either.

I carry out a full set of observations as a baseline, check Debbie's blood pressure,

temperature and pulse, listen to baby's
heartbeat, and make a note of how regular the
contractions are, how strong, and how long they
last. Everything is recorded on something we
call a MEOWS chart, which gives an at-a-
glance view of how things are advancing,
changing, or not changing throughout labour.

MEOWS is another of those acronyms that
makes maternity-speech sound like a different
language. I've picked most things up so far, but
every now and again I hear something new and
have to ask for an explanation. Saying
"MEOWS" is a lot easier than constantly
referring to the Modified Early Obstetric
Warning Score, that's for sure.

Everything seems absolutely fine.

I sit with Debbie and Marcus, chatting,
observing, and recording the regular, routine
checks. Without warning, during one
particularly gripping contraction, Debbie grunts
loudly.

"I need to push," she says. "I really need to
push."

I look over to Jade. This is quicker than we
would expect in a first-time mum, but as I've
said, women's bodies are unpredictable.

"All through your contraction or just when

it's at its peak?" I ask.

"At its peak, I think. When it's really strong."

"Okay," I say. "Let me know when you get your next one. Tell me what it feels like." Then I add, "Have you been to the toilet recently?"

"She went about half an hour ago," Marcus says.

"I tried," she says. "I couldn't do anything."

"Baby's head is right down there between the bowels and the bladder. It might just be that you can feel," I say.

As I'm finishing the sentence, Debbie clenches her hands into fists, grabbing the sheet. Marcus holds the mouthpiece up to Debbie's face, and supports her as she takes big deep breaths of the gas and air.

She breathes steadily at first. In and out. Deep and slow. Then, as the contraction builds, her eyes widen, and she lets out another grunt.

"I need to push now," she growls from behind the mouthpiece.

"See if you can see anything," Jade says from behind me.

"Okay Debbie. If you don't mind, I'm going to take a look down below and see if there's any signs that baby might be coming."

She nods her consent. "That's fine," she breathes.

I raise the sheet and look at Debbie's vulva for any signs of movement, or for any signs of an approaching baby. There's nothing yet. I place my hand onto her uterus, feeling the contraction. It's strong and firm, but it doesn't feel like she's pushing.

There's a difference in the feel of an expulsive contraction that's pushing a baby out and the regular labour contractions. If she's feeling the urge, she's not acting on it yet. If she can hold it back then maybe it's not time yet.

"I can't stop," she says. "I really need to push."

"Keep breathing, Debbie. Use the gas and air." Jade says.

When the contraction settles off, Jade speaks to me. "See if you can get her to the loo, and if she's still feeling the urge you'd better examine her and find out what's going on."

I nod and turn back to Debbie to get her consent.

After a slow hobble to the toilet and back, I start the examination. She's still only five centimetres. No change. She's definitely not ready to push yet.

"Can I push?" she growls as her next contraction starts to peak.

"Not yet," I say. She closes her eyes and breathes deeply, and I turn to Jade and hold up five fingers.

"It's not time yet," Jade says. "You're still five centimetres. It's going to be a little while longer."

"No!" Debbie shouts, opening her eyes wide. "I can't do it. I can't. It's too much."

She looks over at her husband, and he rushes to stand back by her side.

"Easy," he says. "You can do it. You can."

"I want an epidural. I want one now," she says.

"That might be a good idea," Jade says. "If you're getting that urge to push already, we really need you to not push. If you push and you're not ready, you can make your cervix swell up, and it will make things take even longer."

"She *doesn't* want an epidural," her husband says. "She was going to write a birth plan. We never got round to it, but she said that she definitely doesn't want an epidural."

"I. Want. An. Epidural," Debbie repeats. "I don't care what I said before; I want one now."

I nod, and Jade gives Marcus a little shrug.

"Sometimes we don't know what we want until we are in labour. No one can imagine what it is going to be like until they are here." Jade turns to Debbie. "It means that you will need to stay on the bed and be monitored throughout your labour. We will keep a track of baby's heartbeat on the CTG monitor here, and Violet will be checking your blood pressure and pulse."

"It's not long since you were last examined, so I'm not worried about the cervix not having changed much yet," Jade says. "But if it does look like things are moving slowly we can give you something to speed things up a bit. If we do that, you'll be glad of the epidural."

"Okay," she says. "Get it now, please."

Marcus speaks gently to his wife. "Are you sure this is what you want?"

The look she gives him is resolute, but I'm sure I see a tinge of sadness.

"I'm sorry," Debbie says. "I need the epidural. I wanted to manage without, but I can't. I'm sorry."

"Don't be sorry, love. If you need it, you need it. I'm right here."

Jade and I smile at each other before she

heads into the corridor to page the anaesthetist. With an hour left of my shift it's unlikely I'll be present at the delivery, but I know that I am learning with every woman I care for, and with every situation I deal with. I wish I could stay with Debbie, but by the time the anaesthetist has arrived, set up and given her the epidural it's time for me to leave.

Debbie looks calm and comfortable, and I know that I have done everything that I could to support her this afternoon. This is the way that it will be throughout my midwifery career. I will deliver many babies, but I will care for women through pregnancy, labour and beyond without having the honour of being present for the births. If Debbie is still in the postnatal ward tomorrow afternoon I'll go up and visit her, but this is where my journey with her ends, at least for this pregnancy.

"Good luck," I say, as I finish handing over to the afternoon staff.

There's a first-year student, a shy-looking girl called Priti, who will be taking over where I have left off. I hope she gets to be present at the birth.

"And good luck to you," I whisper to her, as I pass by and make my way to the locker room.

# Chapter Six

Despite the quiet, slow start, by the end of my
first week back on placement, I have added
three more deliveries to the signed sheet in my
PAD. I'm constantly aware that we are halfway
through November, and time is ticking away. I
need to start my assignment and finalise my
project plan. I'm starting to feel overwhelmed
by the amount of work I have to do and
pressured by the boxes I have to tick to
complete my PAD. When weekend arrives all I
want to do is spend time with Carl.

Even though we have been dating for four
months now, I still sleep alone, in my own
room. It was my decision, not his. If we had met
some other way there's no way that we would
be living together or spending every night
together this early in a relationship. I'm starting
to understand some of the things that Zoe must
have experienced with Luke last year. He was a
housemate, and then a friend, and then her
lover; I didn't realise how complicated that
could be. Exciting, but complicated.

Nine thirty, Saturday morning, there's a light
tapping on my door. I've been awake for a

while, but I'm still in bed, lazily flicking through the pages of a sweet romantic novel that Zoe passed on to me. It's building up to a crucial scene, but as soon as I hear the knocking, I slide in my bookmark, straighten my hair with my fingers and call out, "Hello?"

"Breakfast, Princess."

Carl nudges the door open with a firm buttock, and edges into my room carrying a wooden tray. On it he has laid out cereal, coffee, toast, and orange juice. He sets the tray on my desk. I give him a big grin and shuffle my legs over to the side so that he can perch on the edge of my bed.

"Hey," I say. "Thank you. You didn't need to…"

Before I can finish my appreciative gushing, he silences me with a kiss.

"You've had a busy week," he says. "Anything for you."

This is way better than the romance in my book. This is real. This is what people do when they love one another. And he does. I do. We're in love. This is perfect.

"It *has* been crazy," I say with a smile. "I'm sorry that we haven't seen each other much."

He shakes his head. "Don't worry about it. I

knew what I was getting into. I've been fine here on my own with the lovebirds, watching the same old shows."

I laugh, and he smiles.

"Didn't you go out last night?" I ask. "I knocked on your door when I came home and…"

He kisses me again, and the peck turns into a long, deep embrace. I melt into him and wish that every day were a day off for me. I wish I could be with Carl all the time, but that's not how things are. Most weekends I'll be lucky to have even one day with him, so I should be thrilled to have both Saturday and Sunday at home this week. Zoe suggested a trip to the shops, but I know she understood when I said I'd like to see Carl. Anyway, it will make my regular Monday mate date with Zoe all the better if we wait another couple of days to catch up.

"Hey. Anyone home?" Carl waves his hand in front of my eyes and I realise that I was floating away with my thoughts of coffee, cake and chatting to my best mate.

"Sorry!"

I smile and lean back into him, hoping to repeat the hug we just enjoyed. Instead, he pats me gently and moves to stand up.

"Get your breakfast in you. We're going out today."

"Oh?" I say. "We are? Where to?"

"That, my sweet Violet, is a surprise."

A judder of excitement passes through me.

"I love surprises!" I say.

"I hope you'll love this one," he says, "but don't get *too* excited."

How can I not?

I practically bolt my breakfast, or at least I eat it as quickly as I can without looking too much of a glutton. I don't want Carl thinking I'm a complete pig. He's got the toast spot-on, exactly as I like it. He must have been paying attention, all the times that I've made breakfast over the past few months. The thought makes a little warm glow bloom in my chest. It's such a good feeling to know that there's someone as lovely as Carl that actually *loves* me.

Carl doesn't have a car. I guess there's no point when all we do is walk to uni or walk into town. I'm sure he had one when he first moved in last year, but I wasn't paying nearly enough attention to him then, and it doesn't seem all that important now. Either way, Carl's lack of a car means that he leads me to the bus stop, and then on to the train station, where we catch the 11:42 in the direction of London.

It's the end of November, but as we snuggle together in the train seats, sharing his set of earphones I feel cosy and warm. I still don't know where we are going, but the choice of train has narrowed it down to somewhere in the New Forest (squee! Pony rides! A spa day? No, because he didn't tell me to bring anything. Lunch in a country pub?) Southampton (yes! Shopping and food!) or London (could be anything, but everything I can think of is exciting). Lots of people might have been pestering their boyfriend to tell them where they are going, but I've settled into the thrill of the surprise.

We chat about everything and nothing as the train takes us through the Forest and on towards the suburbs of Southampton City. When we pull into Southampton station, Carl moves to stand up without saying anything, and I scrabble hurriedly to my feet. I haven't finished my three pounds train tea, and I would usually hate to leave it behind, but today I don't care. Today I hold onto my boyfriend's hand, my cheeks glow with the excitement rather than the cold, and I follow.

Along the high street, in front of the tall department stores and glass-fronted clothes shops, wooden huts bustle with throngs of shoppers. There's a heavy scent of cinnamon and sweetness in the air, and my mouth is practically watering as we push through the crowds. Still with his hand in mine, Carl leads me past cabin after cabin, pausing with me as I stop to point at whatever catches my eye.

"These hats!" I squeal, picking up a knitted headpiece with two long flaps, designed to look like spaniel ears.

Carl smiles, and patiently lets me put the hat onto his head. It suits him. Even something this silly can't make him look anything other than perfect. The fact that he is happy for me to put it on him in the first place makes him even more perfect, in my eyes.

"Am I your little puppy dog?" he laughs, trying to give me a puppy-dog-eyed look.

All I can do is laugh back. It's an icy cold day, but I can barely feel it.

Being with him is so easy.

I'm still full from the breakfast he made me when we reach the bratwurst stand.

"Sausage?" Carl asks.

"I…"

Before I can say no, he's ordering an extra large with onions and cheese.

"Same for you?" he says.

"I don't know if –"

Again, he doesn't wait for a reply. I can probably manage it. His is already on the counter, and it smells amazing. He squirts on the ketchup and mustard and leaves me to collect my hotdog as he pays.

"Do you want to get some drinks?" I ask.

He's got a mouthful of food, so he shakes his head and raises a hand.

After he's gulped it down he says, "Let's wait and get a mulled wine or hot chocolate."

He takes another bite and nods in the direction of the large building in the middle of the square. It's a mock Alpine lodge, complete with bar and kitsch cable cars that customers can sit in while they drink. Much as I'm enjoying my bratwurst now that I have it, I can't wait to get a hot chocolate.

"Okay," I grin.

There was a time that I would avoid coming out into crowded places like this. My anxiety would start to rise as soon as I sensed the people all around me, and I couldn't relax until

I got into some space. Now I feel a serene, strange calmness, and dare I say happiness, sitting here while shoppers hurry past us. It's almost as though I am enclosed in a bubble. It's like being in one of those cable cars, high above the snowy hills, but safe from the ground below and protected from the cold.

I finish my food and wipe a smudge of mustard off my jacket sleeve stealthily, so that Carl doesn't notice what a clumsy oaf I am.

Of course, he sees, and he flashes a grin.

"We can buy some for the house, you know. You don't need to smuggle it home on your clothing."

"Just trying to save us some money." I go along with it. "My student loan is already out of control."

He smiles and pats my arm gently, as if in sympathy rather than jokingly. I guess it wasn't all that funny.

"Listen," he says. "Save these seats and I'll go and get the drinks."

"Sure," I shrug.

It *is* busy, and if we both get up and go to the bar we will probably have nowhere to sit when we come back.

He doesn't ask what I want and sets off

towards the lodge.

I sit and watch the couples walking arm in arm, the parents being pulled along by their children from stall to stall. My eye is drawn to a pregnant woman looking at hand-knitted jumpers. Even when I'm not on my placements I'm curious about expectant mothers. She looks about eight months pregnant, and as I watch her holding the knitwear up to herself I wonder what it would be like to have a Christmas baby.

She must be booked to deliver in Southampton, I'll probably never see her again, but I still start to daydream about how her birth will go. I feel a kinship with pregnant women. We are part of the same team, even when I'm not in my uniform.

Carl nudges my arm. "Hey," he says.

He puts a purple mug down on the table in front of me. Hot chocolate, with a thick swirl of cream and chocolate sprinkles. Just what I would have ordered. Actually, I would probably have skipped the cream and sprinkles, even though I want them. I don't want to stuff myself in front of Carl. I mean logically I know that he doesn't care what I eat. I know he loves me (yay!) just the way I am, but a part of me is still hopelessly self-conscious. I remember my dad scrutinising my food and drink choices when I was budding from a child to an adolescent. I'm used to feeling bad about my decisions.

"Hey," Carl says again.

"Thanks!" I grin, blushing. "That looks perfect!"

"Not as perfect as you." He bends and kisses me before taking his seat next to me.

It doesn't feel sickly sweet, it feels right, and I accept the compliment just as readily as the hot chocolate.

"Thinking about your course?" he asks, following my line of vision to the lady I was watching.

"Always," I say. "I mean, not always. That's not what I meant. I mean…"

He smiles and hugs me into him. "I know what you mean, silly."

Will I ever get used to not worrying about saying the wrong thing? I hope so.


When Carl sits down there's a moment of silence between us, and it feels like there's something heavy in the air. For some reason I can sense he is going to say something important. It's like when a storm is brewing, and you haven't felt the rain or heard thunder, but the air is pregnant with the coming change.

I keep quiet and look at him expectantly.

He shifts a little in his seat and takes a drink from his mulled wine, not looking me in the eye. He looks around casually and then clears his throat before speaking.

"I told my parents I'll be bringing you home for Christmas," Carl says. His face is beaming. "I can't wait for you to meet them."

We spent most of the summer break at Tangiers Court together. I assumed that I'd be going to see my mum at Christmas. I haven't made actual plans, but mentally I was sure that was what would happen. Mum will be on her own if I don't go home. I can't leave her alone over Christmas. I'm too stunned to speak. I don't know what to say.

"I'll take you to meet my friends too. There's loads of places I want to go with you."

He gives me a squeeze that feels too tight. He's warm and close and I need some air. I need to think. I need to breathe.

"Okay," I say, without meaning it as an acceptance. "I mean that's a nice idea. I…I don't know. I don't know if I can. I want to. I do. But…"

He doesn't say anything as I stutter my

words, feeling hotter and hotter.

I should have thought about this. I should have brought it up earlier, let him know how I felt before he started to make plans. I've messed everything up.

"My mum has booked a restaurant for dinner Christmas Day," he says flatly. "We make a big deal of it. It's a family tradition."

I don't want an argument; all I want is time to think.

He's gone from looking full of happiness to having an expression of almost anger. I can understand him being disappointed by my response, but it feels like more than that.

"I'll…" I'm trying to think and speak at the same time, and it's not working very well. "I'll have to talk to Mum." It's the best I can manage.

"Okay," he says in a voice that makes me think that it's very much not okay.

I have to say more. I have to give more than this.

"I want to be with you," I say. "I want to spend Christmas with you so much." I do. It's not in any way a lie.

"That's great," he smiles. "I'll tell Mum we are definitely going."

I want to say, '*wait, no,*' but instead I gulp, pick up my mug and drink. It tasted so perfectly sweet before, but now it's somehow sickly.

I don't know how I'm going to explain this to Mum. She barely saw me all summer, and now I'm not even going to spend the festive holidays with her. I sigh softly as the thoughts swim around my head.

Carl is oblivious; he smiles and gently brushes a loose hair from my cheek.

"It's going to be perfect," he says. "Just like my perfect Violet."

# Chapter Seven

The rest of the day feels overcast, the cloud of our conversation hovering above us. It should be a wonderful day, but I have ruined it by not being confident enough to speak my mind. Instead I have contained the worry inside of me, and I can feel it simmering.

When we get back to Tangiers Court, late afternoon, I want to talk to Zoe about everything straight away. Living with Carl means there's not much opportunity for a private conversation. We enter the house together, sit in the living room together, and there's no chance of me slipping out to talk to Zoe without drawing attention.

Perhaps my worry about talking to her is all in my head. After all I talk to Zoe every day; it's completely normal. Knowing that I want to tell her about my concerns makes me feel like I am going behind Carl's back, like I'm doing something wrong. Still, Zoe knows me, and she knows something is off. Even though when I talk to her I'm gushing about the woollen mittens and sickly-sweet fudge, beaming with the glow of the day with my boyfriend, she can still see the burden underneath my smiles.

When I head to the kitchen to make drinks, she pulls herself up to follow.

"You okay?" She leans against the counter while I fill the kettle.

"Yeah," I reply, not making eye contact.

"You don't seem one hundred per cent," she says. "Not coming down with something, are you?"

"No, really. I'm fine."

"Okay," she says, but she doesn't sound convinced.

Once I've added a spoonful of coffee granules into each mug there's not much else I can do other than to turn and face her.

I know that she can see it in my face, or perhaps it's in the way I hold myself, the tone of my voice, I don't know. It's instinctive, the way we pick up on each other's moods.

"Carl's invited me to his parents' for Christmas." I come out with it, just like that. There's no other way of saying it.

"Oh that's…lovely," she says. The pause between her words says more than the words themselves.

"I know. I can't leave Mum alone, can I? It is lovely. Of course I want to be with him, but…" I let my sentence trail off and I shrug.

"Did you say no? What did you say?"

"I said I'd have to talk to Mum, but somehow, I don't know how, it seems like I've agreed to go with him. And now I can't go back on that; I have to find a way to tell Mum that I'm not going to be there. This should be a good thing, you know, having Christmas with my lovely boyfriend, meeting his family, everything."

I've not felt like this for months, not since before Carl and I were together, but now I can feel my pulse quicken and my breathing become unstable. I know I'm on the edge of an anxiety attack, and Zoe can see it too.

"Okay," she says. "It's okay. It's going to be okay."

She puts her hand onto my arm and gently guides me to one of our dining chairs.

"Sit. Come on."

Her voice is steady and calm, and I try to focus on it as she speaks softly.

"Don't worry about it. Not now. We will make it right. Okay?" She's looking at me for a reply, but my mouth is desert dry and my tongue flaps, wordless.

"I'll make the drinks. Just sit here, get some air."

She kicks the back door open and a blast of cold November air rushes in. I feel it thrill over my face, and the cooling sensation works its way into my hot skin.

My heart is pounding, but I take deep, slow breaths, trying to keep as steady as Zoe's voice.

A panic attack.

In my own home.

My safe place.

Zoe has her hand on my shoulder, grounding me. I don't know how I've got myself into this situation. Really, I should be able to talk to Carl, tell him how I feel and explain that I can't leave Mum alone. I should be able to, but if even thinking about it makes me feel like this, how am I going to be able to have a discussion with him? I thought that being with him had somehow raised my confidence, washed away some of my self-doubt and personal fears, seeing as I haven't felt the slightest trace of anxiety since I've been with him. Now that's all up in the air. I don't know anything anymore.

"What do you want to do?" She says it with the emphasis on the word *you*.

I look over towards the door. I'm sure Carl is happily watching television with Luke, caught up in whatever is happening on *Dating*

*Nightmares*, but still, it's possible that he could hear what we are saying. I don't want that. I don't want a confrontation or an argument. Isn't that what had got me into this situation in the first place? Not wanting an argument means that I haven't opened my mouth and spoken my mind. It feels like there's no easy solution.

"I don't want to upset anyone." I look up to Zoe, and the concern in her eyes makes me feel even worse.

"Zoe I'm sorry."

"Don't be sorry. Don't feel bad about having feelings, or about wanting to make people happy." Her voice is both soft and stern. "You've done nothing wrong."

"It doesn't feel that way."

I'm so on edge that I can tell straight away when the volume on the television lowers a couple of notches.

There's a shout from the living room.

"Did you get lost on the way?" Carl hollers.

I flash a look to Zoe and then call back, my voice as stable as I can manage. "Sorry! Nearly done!"

He knows I'm in here with Zoe. Surely he can work out that we are talking.

"Stop apologising," Zoe says. "Do you want

to sit outside for a few minutes?"

I shake my head briskly. "I should take Carl his drink."

Zoe gives me a wide-eyed stare that almost looks like disappointment.

Whatever I decide to do, I'm not doing any decision making right now. Not like this.

"Give yourself some space, okay?" Zoe says, making it sound like a request when really it's a command. "You've been doing so well. You can keep on top of this."

She's so convinced, I have to nod. My heart is still heavy but it's slowing, settling back to a normal rhythm. Knowing I need to get back in to Carl isn't helping but the chill air and Zoe's chill attitude definitely are.

"Vi?" Carl calls again.

"Don't think about it now. We can have a chat about it on Monday," Zoe says. "Okay?"

I nod and get to my feet. I'm steady. I'm in control. I pick up Carl's mug, take it through to the living room, and settle down next to him. He reaches his arm around me and draws me in close. I breathe in his warmth and nuzzle my nose against his chest to fill my lungs with the scent of him.

Everything will be fine. I'm sure it will.

# Chapter Eight

The thing about being a student midwife is that you always have to be mentally present. No matter what's going on in your personal life you have to have your head firmly on your shoulders and your focus fixed on the here and now. Today that feels like a good thing. I want to be able to think about something other than my internal debate over what I should do. Someone more decisive or self-confident might just have been able to speak their mind, but however much I have learned over the past couple of years, I'm not at that point yet.

I've been hushed down and shut up so many times, and I've stopped myself from making my opinions heard when there's even the slightest chance that they might upset someone else. I'm a people pleaser; that's what I do; that's what growing up displeasing my father taught me to do.

I snap myself back to the room and prepare to take handover. I have to leave everything else at the door, off the ward, and out of my head. Today I am on delivery suite. I am Student Midwife Violet Cobham. I am here to support women, and hopefully deliver babies.

There's a lady due up to the ward for induction and I'm the only student on shift today. That means that unless any labouring women arrive before she comes up, I'll be responsible for looking after her. With my mentor of course. I know that I'm going to be kept occupied for the rest of the shift, but I have time to chat to my mentor before our patient arrives.

"How's the coursework going?" Jade, asks.

I sip my tea and shrug. "I'm on top of it," I say. "I'm more worried about getting my practicals signed off."

"No one has ever not managed it, Vi. Don't worry too much."

It's good to hear those words, even though the empty spaces in my PAD shout out at me every time I open my folder.

"What are you writing for your final year project?"

University sometimes feels like a different world to the placement units. Of course I am putting into practice what I learn in the classroom, and I take back to my lectures the things that I experience on placement. Trying to bundle it all together and make sense of everything, especially where there appears to be a placement-classroom divide, is a challenge.

"Um, something to do with maternal mental health," I say. My voice wavers uncertainly.

"There's lots of research on that. You should find plenty to write about."

"Too much," I agree. "I don't want to just focus on postnatal depression though."

"Interesting," Jade says. "What do you want to focus on?"

I pause for a moment before answering, trying to get my thoughts together.

"I want to write something about mental health in pregnancy," I say. "Anxiety." I leave the word dangling, wondering whether to say more. Looking over at Jade, who has supported me on my placements here since the start of the course, I decide to open up. "I have suffered myself, with anxiety I mean, for, gosh, for nearly ten years now I guess." The thought that it has been so long hits me like a sledgehammer.

"I wouldn't have known," she says. "You always seem very confident and competent."

"I feel it," I say. "At least when I'm here I do."

"And when you're not?"

I look away, drink some more of the hot,

milky tea, and pause again.

"Mostly I'm okay. Mostly."

"There's always someone here to talk to. If you need to."

Before I reply, she adds, "And I'm always here too."

"Thanks," I say.

Even though I passed up the chance to talk to a specialist last year, knowing that Jade is here for me if I do need to talk feels like a cosy relief. She knows me just enough for me to trust her, but not intimately enough for me to feel awkward talking to her. On top of that, being able to talk and listen are two of the most important skills of a midwife. She may not be a trained counsellor, but I know she has the supportive experience.

"Really," she says. "I mean it."

"Thanks, Jade."

A thought flashes through my head that maybe I could tell her what I'm feeling today, talk to her about what's on my mind, but as soon as the thought forms, I push it away. It seems silly to be worrying about something that could easily be solved by talking to my boyfriend. When I think about it that way I want to give myself a shake and have a firm word with myself.

"You've already been very helpful," I smile.

"Well, that's good," she says. "That's what I'm here for."

"That and helping me get this PAD signed off," I grin.

She smiles and shakes her head. "Really, you'll get there!"

I just about have time to drain the rest of my tea before the antenatal ward midwife brings our lady up to delivery suite. She's a first -time mum, and sometimes induction can take longer than the eight hours that I have for my shift, but you never know.

I share a positive grin with Jade and make my way to introduce myself to our patient Dina. Whether I get to deliver a baby today or not, I get to spend time with Dina and support her through one of the most special experiences of her life. After talking to Jade I'm ready to focus completely on her and on providing the best care and support I can. Everything else can wait. Today, I am here. Today I am Student Midwife Violet Cobham, and she is confident and competent.

By the time my shift is over, and I am on the

bus into town to meet Zoe, thoughts of Carl are far from my mind. Being on shift has such a positive effect on me; I hope it is always this way, but there's a niggle at the back of my mind that warns me that there are going to be bad days on the ward. I'm not always going to have the energy and enthusiasm of a fresh student. I hope that whatever happens it never starts to feel like work.

"You seem happier," Zoe notices as I join her at our regular table.

I haven't actually thought any more about what I am going to say to Carl, or how I am going to approach him, but she's right. I do feel happier.

"Good day on the ward," I smile.

"Oh?" she asks. "Something exciting happen?"

Did it? Not really. Nothing out of the ordinary. I spent time with Dina, we talked about television programmes and Christmas shopping and how much we both love this time of the year. I checked her vitals, listened to her baby, and together we waited for her contractions to begin. It was routine and unremarkable, but somehow it was still a good day.

I make a casual dismissive hum sound and shake my head.

"Well, it's nice to see you more relaxed anyway," she says.

Not that I have an agenda for the conversations with Zoe, but I had expected that we would spend the whole of our mate date talking about Carl and what I should say to him. Now that I am here, all I want to do is drink latte, laugh with my friend, and carry on feeling the light contentment that being on the ward has given me. I don't want to spend my precious time with my friend moaning about my boyfriend doing something that he obviously hasn't done to intentionally confuse or confound me.

Sometimes I snap into panic mode so quickly that I don't stop to think about what I could or should do. My instinctive response is always to clam up, shut down and agree with whatever other people want. When I have time to think everything seems clearer. I know already that all I need to do is talk to him and explain how I feel. It's as simple as that.

# Chapter Nine

When we get back to the house, Zoe and Luke head up to her room, leaving Carl and I alone in the living room. I want to talk to him as soon as I can, so that the situation doesn't drag on, and I don't spend any longer than I need to overthinking what I am going to say. Talk to him. Explain how I feel. Simple.

We are both sitting on the sofa, angled in towards each other, relaxed and comfortable.

"Carl," I say. I already feel too formal, as soon as I say his name. I soften my voice and continue, "I would love to spend Christmas with you, and I can't wait to meet your family –
"

He doesn't let me finish the sentence.

"I can tell there is a *but* coming up," he says, moving away from me ever so slightly.

My agenda must be obvious. I feel my cheeks burn and I feel a shimmer of nausea. I want to tuck my head away and hide from this conversation. I slowly make eye contact, expecting to see anger, but instead, he looks calm.

I take a breath and continue, starting with a gentle smile.

"There is. I'm sorry."

"But?" he says.

"But I can't. I really am sorry."

"You've said you're sorry. I believe you." He strokes my cheek, and I know he must be able to feel the heat of my blush.

"I…my mum. I can't. I just can't leave her on her own."

He nods slowly with a look of disappointed understanding.

"I'm so sorry," I say. The apology keeps falling from my lips.

"Violet!" he says. "Stop now. It's fine."

I worried since Saturday for nothing. Instead of being embarrassed about telling him that I couldn't go home with him after all, I'm embarrassed that I was stupid enough to think that Carl would be angry.

"Are you sure? I feel so bad. You made plans and you've told your parents, and everything you described, it all sounded so perfect."

He shrugs. "Your mum is more important than our perfect Christmas," he says.

My eyes flicker slightly, as I try to search his words for meaning. I'm still not confident enough to believe that he really is okay with what I have said.

Either way, the image of he and I in front of the log fire in his parents' house, surrounded by warmth and bustle and love starts to fade from my mind. I have to let it go. I'm making the right decision. I'm doing the right thing.

"Maybe we can have a little celebration, just the two of us, before you go home?" I suggest.

He leans back, even further away from me, and stretches his arms above his head.

"What do you think?" I persist.

"I don't know, Violet. Christmas is a special time. It wouldn't be the same, would it?"

I have to look away again as I try to gulp down the ball that's formed in my throat.

I shake my head almost imperceptibly.

"Would it?" he says again.

"No," I say. My voice is mouselike.

I force myself to lift my eyes.

"There'll be other Christmases," I say. The sound is still tiny and weak.

He's not even looking at me. Instead, he's turned his attention to the television, pressing the switch to turn it on and start scrolling through the channels.

"Carl?" I almost whisper.

"I said it's fine. Leave it." His words come

out like a snarl, and he visibly stops himself before continuing to speak in a softer, more measured tone. "What would you like to watch?"

I open my mouth slightly to almost speak, but I don't think that carrying on with this conversation is going to make for a pleasant evening. Instead I force myself to smile.

"Whatever you fancy," I say. "It's nice just being here with you."

He puts his arm firmly around my shoulder and pulls me back toward him with a smooth tug that makes me slide over the sofa into his embrace. I can feel the pounding of my heart pressed into his side. He is firm and immobile next to me, more like a statue than a human.

He kisses the top of my head, his breath warm through my hair. I want to smile and snuggle against him, but I know that I have disappointed him. I've let him down, and I can't relax knowing that I have made him unhappy.

"Carl, I…"

"Ssh," he says, and presses a finger against my lips. "Don't."

And so I don't. Instead of speaking, I sit silently beside him as he watches television, and I try to think of a way to make this up to

him. I have to do what's right for my mum, but
I should also try to do right by Carl. If I can
make him happy too, I might be able to stop the
nauseating anxiety that is taking me over.

# Chapter Ten

There are only two weeks left of term, two weeks to get as many deliveries signed off as I can on my placement and two weeks to feel rubbish about spending Christmas without Carl. Zoe and Luke are going to be in Portland with *her* parents this year. It's a relief to know that she will only be a short walk away from where I'm staying. Home. Didn't I used to call it home? So much has changed, but I miss my mum. I love my mum. That's never going to change.

Being on placement is a welcome distraction. It's a busy morning and Jade and I have been allocated two women today. It doesn't happen often, the ideal is that each midwife only has one woman to care for, but neither of the ladies is in active labour.

"Cherry Brady, room three. First baby; due tomorrow. Been on the antenatal ward with some protein in her urine and mild raised blood pressure. We're keeping an eye on her at the moment. Doctor Barthes is coming after his antenatal round to review. Paula Carter, room six. Thirty-nine weeks. She's had a couple of rapid deliveries in the past, came in about an hour ago with niggles. Just a multip's os, and her contractions have tailed off a bit since she arrived. I'm reluctant to let her go just yet, and Sister agreed we should keep her a couple of hours and await events. I'd have offered her a bed downstairs but they're full too."

It's a difficult call sometimes, trying to find the balance between taking up a room and providing the reassurance and care that's needed. On paper Paula could possibly go home and come back later but having already experienced two precipitate deliveries I can understand her not wanting to take the risk. I know I wouldn't want to.

There are four midwives and I on the shift and seven patients. The maths says we have to do what we can to share the workload. Not every woman can have constant one-to-one care, no matter how much I would love that to be the case. One of the skills I need to develop for my career as a midwife is knowing how to manage my workload and still give the best care and support possible to the women and families I'm responsible for.

Paula is sitting on the bed chatting to her husband when we enter the room.

"There's not much happening," he says

before we have the chance to introduce ourselves.

My eyes instinctively flick over to Paula to gauge her reaction, but she jabs him playfully in the ribs and lets out a low laugh.

"It's easy for you to say that," she says. "You don't have to squeeze a watermelon out of your…"

"We all know where they come out of," he interrupts. "No need to spell it out." There's a lighthearted humour to his voice, and I can feel the warmth in their banter.

"Next time you're doing it," she glowers.

He doesn't have time to argue about the biological logistics as she lets out a groan. Instantly he's beside her, stroking her hair gently and muttering low soft words that only she can hear.

Jade and I look at each other and smile.

"You're doing great," Jade says.

"See," she grunts. "I'm doing great."

"Of course you are," her husband says. "You always do."

When the contraction dies down, Jade nudges me forwards.

"How do they feel now? Are they getting stronger? More frequent?"

"Stronger, yes, a bit. How often are they, Sam?" she says, looking to her husband for the answer.

Sam shrugs. "I wasn't counting," he says. "I was just watching you."

Midwives and birth partners can serve similar roles, but sometimes I'm reminded of how differently we see things. I'm being trained to watch the clock, check how far apart contractions are, how long they last, how strong they are, and ultimately how long labour is taking. All Sam cares about is how his wife feels and whether everything is okay.

Right now, everything is fine.

Reassured, we head to room three to make our introductions to Cherry. She's on her own, filling in a crossword in what looks to be a gossip magazine. I've never really been interested in them, but they often get left on the ward when women have finished with them, so I end up flicking through them in the midwives' office. I know much more about the lives of Z-list celebrities now than I ever imagined I would.

"How are you feeling?" I ask.

"Bored," Cherry sighs. "I've read this mag twice and I've done all of the clues that I can on the crossword already. I'm not getting anywhere."

"No pains? Nothing happening?"

She shakes her head. "I wish."

Pain is a strange thing to wish for, but I've noted that when women are waiting to go into labour this wish is perfectly normal.

I smile. "Have you had any more loss down below?"

"Nothing," she says. "I just went to the loo, and my pad is dry."

I'm nowhere near as frustrated as Cherry is that her labour isn't starting yet, but I do feel a pang of disappointment. Even though looking after two labouring women isn't ideal, at least it would give me more of a chance of getting those deliveries. Every time I think about my PAD, I feel guilty, almost like I am using these women to make up my numbers. I hate thinking of it like that. I know that I need to prove, somehow, that I have had enough experience during my placements, but ticking off the numbers is never going to sit right with me.

Whatever happens today, I will give my best and think about the women, rather than the numbers. Having a student midwife as part of their caregiving team means that Cherry and

Paula will be able to have more support and attention than they would if I were not here. I know that it's an unfortunate truth that sometimes there aren't enough staff around to be able to give every woman what she deserves. I wonder how I am going to feel about this when I am the qualified midwife, on my own with multiple women to support.

One day, hopefully not too soon after I qualify, I'll be allocated a student of my own. Me. Mentoring another student. The very thought of it gives me chills. I'm only just getting to grips with what I am meant to be doing, without having to mentor someone else.

That's a long way into the future. For now, I have to focus on one day at a time. Those days seem to be passing too quickly, and the empty spaces on my PAD are not being filled.

One day at a time.

# Chapter Eleven

The end of term, and my enforced separation from Carl, comes around much too quickly. It's hard to believe I'm a third of the way through my final year already. I have the sneaking feeling that the next three weeks at home with Mum are going to feel terribly long.

Tomorrow Zoe will be driving Luke and I back to Portland, and Carl will be heading back to Leicester. Tonight though, tonight, I have him all to myself.

Or so I thought.

It's probably my own fault for trying to surprise him rather than making plans. I pictured an evening where the two of us would be here alone, get in a takeaway, choose a film, snuggle up on the sofa. I'm easily pleased, and this simple life, being together, is all I need to make me happy.

When I get home, Carl is up in his room. I don't know if it's because his room is up on the top floor with Luke's, and I don't need to pass by to go anywhere else, but I rarely go up there. My room is on the middle floor, across from Zoe's, so it's *en route* from the top of the house to the kitchen and living room. Today I make the trip up the extra flight of stairs and pop my head around the door.

"Hi," I say, hovering on the threshold.

He looks up, startled. "I didn't hear you come home. Hi, Violet."

There's a pile of books behind the door, and I struggle to squeeze into his room.

He stops what he is doing and kneels still on the floor behind his partially packed case.

"Alright?" he asks awkwardly.

"Er, yes," I answer, equally stiff and uncertain. I feel out of place here. "Do you want me to go so you can finish off?"

"You can watch if you want to, but it's not going to be very exciting for you."

He reaches behind himself for a stack of T-shirts and starts to unfold them, and then refold them into the case.

"Right," I say. This is not the evening I had expected us to have. "Do you fancy getting pizza later?" His face is blank, so I try something different. "Or Chinese or something?"

That feeling that I have done something terrible by not going home with him for the holidays is starting to resurface, and with it comes a wave of anxiety.

"Actually I said that I would go out for some drinks with the lads tonight," he says.

"The lads?" I ask.

When he first came to live at Tangiers Court Carl was fairly socially active, but for the past year he has pretty much spent his evenings here, at home, with me. He doesn't talk about any friends, and I can't picture who he means by *the lads*.

"Some guys from my course," he says, as though it is obvious. "A few pints, then probably hit The Basement."

I don't stop myself in time, and my face shows my disgust at the mention of the grotty nightclub. *The Basement* is in the town centre, not really a student bar, but the prices are cheap and it's open until four.

"You don't have to come," he laughs. "Don't worry."

Obviously, I didn't want to go there with him, I wanted him to be here with me. After letting him down over the whole Christmas thing though, I should suck it up and say nothing.

"Thanks," I say. "I don't think it's really my scene."

"No," he agrees. "The girls in there aren't

exactly like you."

My heart skips, and my brain races to unravel the meaning of the words.

"Oh?" I ask, trying to keep the emotion out of my voice.

He shrugs and turns around to grab another pile of clothes.

"Perhaps I should come with you," I say, pairing my words with a sweet smile.

"Ugh," he says. "Don't start that. I won't be late home. We can have breakfast together in the morning before I go."

"What time are you planning on leaving?" I ask. None of this is happening how I wanted it to.

"Depends when I wake up."

It's not a particularly helpful answer.

"Okay," I say. "Let's go out and have a breakfast date before you set off. You'll be starving on the way if you don't eat…"

"And I want to see you before I go. It's not just about the food, Violet," he says.

"I know. I mean, thanks. Er, you too. I thought I might see you tonight."

"We didn't make plans, so…I thought you wanted to do our own thing."

"It's fine. Really. I wouldn't want you to

miss going out with your mates."

"They aren't my mates," he says. "They're lads from the course, but yeah. Thanks."

He smiles and pats the floor next to him.

"Don't hover over there. Come and sit with me while I finish packing."

He reaches a hand up to guide me past the books, and around a pile of clothes to the space beside him. I try not to step on anything and settle down by his side.

"I've not got much more to do," he says. "It's more fun with you here though."

Watching my boyfriend folding his clothes as he packs to leave me for three weeks is far from fun, but being with him is preferable to being without him.

He puts his arms around me and gives me a long, steady hug.

"I'm going to miss you," he says.

"Oh gosh, you too," I say. "So much."

He draws back, and I think he is going to reach out for the clothes again, but instead he places a hand against my cheek, leans towards me and kisses me.

His skin is soft, and I inhale the scent of his aftershave as his lips move with mine. I want to remember that smell while we are apart. I want to take it with me. Really I want to take *him* with me. I don't know how I'm going to manage to be without him when we have spent every day together for so long. I don't want to think about that now. I don't want to think about the time we will be apart while he is here, still with me. I relax into the moment, wrapping my arms around him, drawing him closer.

After he has left, the house is cold and empty without Carl. I try to settle in front of the television, and I order the takeaway that I had planned for us to share. When the pizza arrives, I pick at it, take a few bites, and push the lid back down. I love pizza, especially tuna and mushroom, but tonight it tastes of cardboard. There's wine in the fridge, and though I rarely drink I pour myself a glass. Half an hour later I pour another, but neither does anything for me.

Zoe and Luke arrive home just after nine, and Zoe almost leaps out of her skin when she pushes open the living room door and sees me curled up beneath my blanket.

"Where's Carl?" she says.

Luke gives me a little wave as he passes by behind her and walks towards the kitchen. I raise my hand slowly to return the wave, and

Zoe repeats her question.

"Where is he?"

"Gone out," I say. "It's nothing."

I gesture to one of the armchairs. I want her to sit here with me. I don't want to spend any more time on my own tonight.

"Nothing?" she says. "It's your last night together."

"It's only three weeks," I say.

I wish I hadn't said, because it sounds much worse now that I have spoken the words aloud.

"Where has he gone?" Zoe's voice is high-pitched and interrogative.

"Really, it's fine. He had arranged to go out with his friends."

"Didn't he tell you before? Or didn't he think that it might be a good idea to spend the night with you?"

"I was going to surprise him. I didn't plan anything, so he wasn't to know." Instead of feeling gloomy and grim I'm starting to get defensive and annoyed. My voice is rising. I don't want the conversation to go down this route. "Zoe, please. It's fine."

I see her eyes move to the wine glass beside me, still half-filled with the fruity red that she bought.

"If you're drinking it can't be *that* fine."

"How often do I drink? It's not like I'm an alcoholic! I probably drink less than every other student in the university. I think I'm allowed one or two glasses when I'm feeling a bit –" I stop myself before I say something that she can use against me. Still, she picks up on my words.

"Feeling what? Annoyed? Lonely? Let down?"

I didn't expect her to react like this. I thought we could chat and laugh and do what we would usually do with Carl not around. My cheeks are flaming with emotion. I want this to stop, right now.

As if sent by my guardian angel, Luke arrives at the door, awkwardly holding three mugs.

"Coffee?"

I reach out appreciatively and say, "Yes. Thanks. Perfect."

I drink the too-hot liquid too quickly. I want an excuse not to say anything else. I need something to shut me up and make sure I don't do or say anything stupid. I'm over emotional, probably overtired, and I don't want to take it out on Zoe.

She sinks back into the chair and lets out a

hefty sigh.

Luke opens his mouth to speak, and she shakes her head, quickly and subtly, but I still see it. Instead of saying whatever he was about to he rests his and Zoe's mugs on the table and sits next to her in the second armchair. He looks over to the TV and flicks his eyes around the room for the remote control.

"I'm not watching," I lie. "Here."

I toss the controller over to him, underarm and cautious.

"Thanks," he says, and starts scrolling the menu.

I take a breath and speak. "Did you have a nice evening?"

Zoe pauses for a moment, looking at me, as if trying to decide whether to press me further or let it go.

"It was…great, yes. More than nice."

I grin, and it's genuine. I don't need to fake my feelings now.

"Tell me about it," I say.

And so she does.

When Zoe and Luke turn in for the night at half past midnight and Carl still isn't home, I decide to make my way to bed too. I want to be fresh

in the morning to spend what time I can with
him before he leaves. I wash my face and clean
my teeth as slowly as I can, just in case he turns
up, but he docsn't, and I go to sleep wondering
where he is and what he is doing.

# Chapter Twelve

Ever since I started working shifts my body has become used to waking up early. When I'm on the morning shifts I have to be at the hospital by twenty past seven, all perky and ready to work. My brain hasn't learnt to make the distinction between work days and off days, so I wake at six, and know it's far too early for anyone else in the house to be awake, let alone Carl after his late night.

It's still dark outside, dark and silent. My phone is plugged in to the socket beside my bed and I reach down to check the time and scroll through social media. No messages from Carl. A few exchanges on the group chat between Ashley, Sophie, and Simon, who were, apparently, still awake around two hours ago. I don't know how they do it. I might be a twenty-year-old, but I have the social stamina of a much older, much more tired woman.

There's not much else happening. I check the news, get diverted onto an article about Kim Kardashian, but it's all nonsense that I've already read about in the gossip magazines at work. I didn't care then, and I don't care now.

My feet are poking out of the bottom of the

duvet, and the chill of the morning is nipping at my toes. I don't want to get up and bimble around the house on my own. It's too early for everyone else; it's too early for me. I pull my knees up, curl the duvet around me and reach over for my Kindle.

I've read a decent chunk of a festive-themed chick lit novel that I'm currently enjoying before I hear noise from Zoe's room. Hushed voices, quiet laughter, and the shuffling of bodies. Then, the thud of feet onto the floor, and steps padding across the room, through the door and onto the landing.

"Zo?" I say in a whispered shout.

She pushes my door open slightly and stands in the doorway, leaning lazily against the frame.

"Hey," she says. "Been awake long?"

I nod sadly and click-close my Kindle.

"I've nearly finished my Christmas reading already."

"At least you'll be in the festive spirit for my playlist on the way home," she grins. "Coffee? Toast?"

"Just coffee thanks." I shuffle up to a sitting position. "I'm going out for breakfast with Carl."

She moves her head slightly in

something that is almost a nod.

"Okay," she says. "Just coffee."

There's a thudding noise from Zoe's room, and she rolls her eyes, smiles, and turns to her own door.

"Sorry!" I hear Luke say, too loudly.

I want Carl to wake up and come downstairs, but I don't want him to be woken too early and be in a bad mood. These are our last few hours. I want us to both enjoy them.

Zoe patters downstairs and I can hear her singing to herself in the kitchen. It's not loud by any means, but if I can hear it from here, Carl can probably hear it upstairs. She's not the greatest singer, not that this bothers her in the slightest, and the Christmas number that she has chosen is certainly not the greatest song.

She's still singing when she pops my coffee mug onto the bedside table and motions for me to move my legs so that she can sit down.

"You okay?" she asks.

"Yeah. I'm okay."

"It's gone nine, you know. I'm sure it's fine for you to go up and wake him."

"Maybe," I say. "After coffee."

She gives me a semi-shrug.

"What time should we set off home?"

She changes the subject before we have any chance to teeter on the edge of an argument about Carl again.

"Anytime this afternoon. Mum is making lasagne for dinner, so I need to be back for that. You're both welcome to come over."

"That sounds great," she says. "It's been a while since I had your mum's famous lasagne. I don't know if Luke will be able to stop at one portion though."

"It is pretty good," I smile.

Already I can feel the tension leaving my body and ebbing away. Home. I can almost taste my mum's cooking and smell the rich, delicious tomato sauce. Maybe I should have that toast now after all.

Zoe looks around my room as she starts to drink her coffee.

"Have you packed?"

I make a sound that could mean yes, no, or maybe, and she raises an eyebrow.

"You're going to be busy once Carl wakes up. Have you got much to take?"

"I'll throw some clothes in a case. Nothing special. I got all the Christmas shopping delivered to Mum's."

Her face perks up at the mention, and I am

sure she is about to start probing me for the details of her present when I hear sounds from Carl's room. There's a cough, deep and heavy, almost as though he's been smoking. Then I hear a scraping noise that I can't place, and finally a weak groan and the sound of his feet landing on the carpet.

I should have got up and got dressed. I could have saved time by getting ready, but I didn't think. I've just been lying here like an idiot, and now Carl is going to get dressed and expect me to be dressed too and…

"Calm down," Zoe says. "Calm."

I take a breath in, let it out, and nod in her direction.

"Thanks Zoe. I'm fine, really. I am."

If I tell her often enough, she might start to believe me.

If I say it often enough, I might believe it too.

# Chapter Thirteen

Christmas goes exactly as I expected it to. Mum was so pleased to spend time with me, and I was happy to be home. After the first few days, anyway, when I started to relax, forced myself to stop thinking about Carl and let myself enjoy being there. It did start to feel like home again, with Mum bringing me hot chocolate at nine pm, settling back into the room that she hasn't touched since I started uni.

We talked, we played games, we ate, we drank, and we laughed. A lot. Still, I felt like something was missing. I've been so used to being with Carl. We've spent so much time together over the past year that his absence was inescapable. Is it possible to escape from something that isn't there?

I saw plenty of Zoe and Luke, and yesterday, the Saturday before the start of spring term, she drove us back here to Tangiers Court. So now it's late Sunday afternoon; Zoe and Luke are in the living room, and I'm upstairs, trying to concentrate on reading a book but distracted by the fact I know that *he* will be back any time now. I've been thinking that since I woke up this morning. I sat too long in the kitchen after breakfast, though I knew it was too early for him to be home. I listened for footsteps outside the front door, for the jangling of keys, but there was nothing. I tried sitting with Zoe and Luke, but I couldn't focus on the television or the conversation. Here I am, buzzing with anticipation and rereading the same page in my book over and over because I'm not taking anything in.

Three o'clock passes, and then four. By five I start to make dinner, and when it's cooked, and he still isn't home I sit at the kitchen table and wait. Finally, just before seven, I hear his key in the door. I leap to my feet and run out into the hallway. As soon as he enters the house I throw my arms around him and plant my lips firmly onto his. He's still holding his case, and he lets it fall with a thud onto the floor.

"Mmmf!" he mumbles through the kiss.

"I missed you!" I say, as I pull back to let him breathe.

"I can tell," he replies.

He pauses to sniff the air. "Smells like dinner."

"Yes," I say, breaking into a grin. "It's nothing really. Luke and Zoe have eaten. I waited for you though."

"That's my girl," he says, giving me a squeeze. "Come on then. I'm starving."

He walks down the hall into the kitchen, and I follow, pausing at the door to the living room to give Zoe a big smile and thumbs up. She probably thinks I'm nuts. She's usually right.

We've messaged and FaceTimed each other over the holidays but none of that is any real substitute for being together. I had that sneaking paranoia that I was messaging him too often or interrupting what he was doing. It's stupid, I know but I don't want to be that kind of girlfriend that always has to keep track on what their partner is doing. I don't want to come across as clingy and dependent, even if a tiny part of me does actually feel that way.

We almost trip over each other in the kitchen as I go to pull out his chair and he reaches out at the same time. I give a little giggle that splutters out of me involuntarily.

"Sorry," I say.

He smiles and sits in front of the place setting I've already laid out for him.

Perhaps this is learned behaviour, trying to woo him with food. My mum always used to cook for Dad when he was in a bad mood. I shouldn't downplay it like that. He was often in much more than a bad mood. Or perhaps it's more accurate to say that he was always in a bad mood and she used cooking for him as a way of mitigating his behaviour. It's not like that with Carl, of course. There's no *'bad behaviour'*; I do what I do because I love him, and I want to make him happy. This is one of the ways that I know of.

"Can I get you a drink?" I smile. "I got some beers, or do you just want a cola or something?"

"You really are spoiling me," he says. "Sure. I'll take a beer."

I nod and pull a chilled bottle of lager from the fridge and flick the cap off. Tonight, I've made curry. This is one of Mum's recipes. She cooked it for me last week, and now I am here, in my other life, cooking it for Carl. She calls it *Enthusiasm Curry,* because she puts everything she has into it. I found that hilarious as a child, and it still makes me smile today.

"What is it?" Carl asks as I place the plate in front of him.

"Curry," I say, stupidly. "Chicken curry. Not too hot."

He nods and stares at his plate. It's not a particularly attractive meal, but I know that it will taste amazing. Perhaps I should have played it safe and cooked up his favourite pasta.

I sit next to him, pulling my seat right into the table so I'm as close to him as possible without being in the way.

"Thanks Violet," he smiles.

"I missed you," I say, without thinking.

"Silly," he says. "It was only a couple of weeks."

I want to tell him that it was three weeks, and it felt like months. I want to tell him that I spent every day while I was away wondering if I should have gone with him to Leicester instead of spending the holidays with Mum. That each night when she went to bed at ten I would sit up trying to fill the time with anything other than my thoughts of him because I missed him so much that it almost physically hurt. That I envied Zoe and Luke being able to be together, even though I knew it was ridiculous to feel that way, and despite my couple-envy I was so happy seeing the two of them together.

Next year I have to spend Christmas with him, whether we stay with his parents, or with mine, I have to.

Then it hits me. Next Christmas I will be a qualified midwife. I will have a job and commitments. Chances are I will have to work at least some of the Christmas period. Babies don't stop being born because people want to spend time with their families. Women still need care and support, no matter what date it is. Perhaps I have missed my only chance, or at least my only chance for some time, of spending the holidays with Carl.

"Are you alright?" he asks. "Something wrong with the curry?" He peers into his meal jokingly.

"I missed you," I say again. Telling him that feels better than discussing next Christmas, a whole eleven months down the line. I've already been bouncing around like an overenthusiastic puppy, I don't want to overwhelm him with future plans.

His mouth is filled with another forkful of the curry, so he gives me an awkward smile instead of replying.

"So, how was your break?" I ask.

In between mouthfuls, he replies, "Okay, thanks. It was Christmas."

"And your folks? Your family? Everyone alright?"

He moves his fork slightly, as though shrugging. "They're fine. Everything was fine."

There's a strange tension in his voice, and I don't know what to say next. He doesn't seem to want to give much away about what he's been doing. Maybe he is still annoyed at me for not going with him.

"Did you get to see much of your friends back home?"

"Christmas is over now, Vi. Let's talk about something else."

"Right," I say, stunned. "I'm sorry. I didn't mean to –"

He puts his fork down onto his plate, still half-filled with the curry, and looks at me.

"No need," he says. "It doesn't matter. I suppose I have had a long journey on a packed train. It's not been the greatest day. I'm tired; it's not your fault."

The tension drops from my body and I let out an audible sigh.

"I thought I had –"

"Hush." He places a finger against my lips, and I smile at the touch. "Really."

I want to apologise again, but I can't say anything. He takes his finger away and kisses me, his mouth warm and delicious.

# Chapter Fourteen

I would have liked a few days of holidays with Carl before we both started our lectures again, rather than the few hours we actually had. On Monday morning I am back in uni, starting the penultimate term of my course. Although I haven't been tying myself in knots in the same way I have in previous years, the thought of the OSCE looming at the end of this term is not far from my thoughts.

I also have to knuckle down and get the bulk of my research project written up. It's a year-long module, but if I leave everything until the final trimester I'm going to make life ridiculously busy for future me. I had some time over the holidays to do some reading; not very festive, I know, but with Mum going to bed early and Carl being hundreds of miles away it seemed like the ideal opportunity.

We have the usual module introductions, and then I bundle along to the coffee shop with Simon, Sophie, and Ashley. I'm always either at home, at uni, on my placements or in a coffee shop somewhere. If anyone ever wanted to stalk me they wouldn't have to try too hard. I like routine, and I love latte.

"We'll be qualified midwives this year!" Sophie grins.

"Don't!" Simon says. "I need another three years yet."

Personally, I'm torn between thinking August can't come quickly enough and feeling exactly the same as Simon.

"We'll be fine," I say, trying to make myself believe it.

Ashley nods. "We have to be."

"Have you thought about where you're going to apply?"

Sophie directs the question towards Simon and me. No doubt she and Ashley have discussed it. There's something about the two of them being housemates that makes me feel somehow like an outsider. They bonded more closely from the start of our course, and they've had each other for support here and at home. Of course I have Zoe, and she's been amazing, but it must be great to have someone who understands the demands of our course and our placements. I'm almost envious of them, but I wouldn't swap Zoe for anyone.

Luckily, Simon is answering the question while I space out thinking about friendships.

"I want to stay where I've trained," he says.

"Don't you?"

"Fliss is looking for a job in London, and I want to go with her," Sophie says.

"Nice," I say. "Things are getting serious then?"

Sophie nods. "Nearly two years together." The sparkle in her eyes when she speaks of her girlfriend is almost a cliché. "I'll go where she goes."

"That's good news for me," I laugh. As Sophie and I are based at the same hospital we won't be competing for a job if she moves away. A part of me would prefer to have her stay at St. Jude's though, so we have each other to turn to while we consolidate our practice.

"You're going to stay at the unit then?" she asks, smiling at my attempted wisecrack.

"I haven't thought too much about it," I say. "It's the nearest hospital to where I come from; my family is nearby, my mum. My friends are all round here. I don't want to leave."

My friends. These days that's Zoe, Luke, and Carl. I couldn't imagine moving away. Not ever.

"I moved as far from home as I could when I came to uni," Simon says. "I feel settled now. I'll probably stay here."

Simon has his placements in a different unit, but if he wants to stay in town he might decide to apply for a job at St. Jude's. On one hand it's more competition for whatever positions they have available; on the other hand, I would love to work alongside him and be able to chat with him over our lunchbreaks. The more I think about qualifying, the more I realise how much ongoing support I might need. On paper, I will be ready, as long as I have had my PAD signed off. In reality, I know that I will still have so much to learn when I start to consolidate my practice.

Ashley is reading a garish flyer that someone from Events has left on the table. There's a lot happening on campus, but I haven't participated in much of it at all. She waves the flimsy paper in front of Sophie.

"Shall we go to this? Looks like fun."

"Fliss would love it; she's so smart."

"You're smart too," Ashley sighs. "Who is that keeps getting the best grades in every module?"

"Only because I force you to stay up late and help me get them finished."

I love watching the two of them banter. They do remind me a lot of Zoe and me.

Now that she is with Luke and I am with Carl we don't get nearly as much time together as we could. Perhaps that's part of getting older, growing up and moving on. She will always be one of the most important parts of my life though, no matter what. I can't imagine ever being without her.

"Hey," Sophie says. "Are you up for it?"

I was miles away, lost in my thoughts, and my brain has to catch up with the conversation.

"The quiz?" I cast my eye over the details. Friday, five o'clock, the union bar. "Won't it be busy on a Friday evening?" I ask. My head fills with visions of the packed room, the noisy students, and the impossibility of having a successful slash fun quiz night.

"At five o'clock?" Simon laughs. "No one is out at five; that's why they're having the quiz then."

"It'll only be a couple of hours. We'll be done before the bar starts to fill up." Sophie does her best to try to convince him, but I can already see that he isn't going to need much persuading.

"I expect that's exactly the point," Simon says. "Get people in early to play the quiz and hope they will stick around for drinks later."

"When we win, of course," I smile. We. I said the word thinking of myself, Zoe, Carl, and Luke. Was Ashley planning for the four of us here to be a team?

"We will smash you," Sophie says, and I breathe a silent, relieved sigh.

I said it as a joke, but I am quietly confident that the Tangiers Court Four could take this quiz down. I might not be the smartest, but the other three are practically geniuses. As soon as I think it I start to wonder if that's the right way to pluralise *genius* and reaffirm my suspicious that I am not the clever one in the house.

"You three and Fliss?" I ask.

Sophie and Ashley nod in unison; Simon shrugs and says, "Sure."

"As long as I can persuade my housemates, we will be there."

The thought of doing something different is a thrill. We rarely go out, and if we do it's never as a foursome anymore. Not that I want to double-date or anything like that, but the four of us getting together for this quiz would be a break from the pressure of studying and a chance to dress up and let my hair down, literally.

Ashley folds the flyer and passes it to me.

"Show this to your team. And make sure you point to that section." She taps the upper side, where there's a bright yellow star with the words FIRST PRIZE £250.

"Too bad we will be taking that," I say, and I tuck the leaflet into my bag.

Two hundred and fifty pounds might not seem a lot of money, but Christmas was expensive, and my student overdraft is always bursting at the seams. Every little helps, even split four ways.

Zoe is in lectures today too, so I have the chance to talk to her about the quiz on the way into town. It's a chilly day, the start of the second week of January, but not so cold that we can't walk it. Even though Zoe has a car there's nowhere to park on campus, and I would like to avoid travelling by bus as much as possible. It's close to freezing but walking and talking makes the journey feel like nothing at all.

"Well, it's different," she says. "Does it say what kind of questions there will be?"

I didn't even think about that. To be honest, I don't know much of the detail at all. I tug the flyer out of my bag and read it as we walk along.

"No. General knowledge."

"General. I wonder why they call it that. If it were that general we would know all the answers," she says.

"I'm hoping that you will know all the answers," I laugh. "I'm useless, but I thought it would be fun."

"It will give the lads a chance to show off, that's for sure."

I know that she is being playful when it comes to Luke, and I hope she has the same attitude towards Carl.

"Show off?" I press her further.

"I'm not sure he's as clever as he thinks he is," she smiles. "Not that he's not clever of course, I mean he must be to have landed you…" She pauses so I can give a sweet bow of appreciation. "…but there's a name for that isn't there? When, let's just say *slightly less intelligent* people think they're smarter than they are."

"That rules me out because I have absolutely no idea what you're talking about." I'm starting to wonder if I should have ever suggested this. I am going to be hopeless.

"Carl would know. Of course," she says.

"But he is studying psychology so he

probably should know." I say it with a smile and Zoe shrugs.

"Do you think he will want to go with us? Carl, I mean." I can't conceal the uncertainty in my voice.

"If he doesn't, we can win without him," she says. She looks over to me to gauge my reaction, and then adds, "I'm sure he will want to come. Tell him there's money involved."

"I don't know," I say.

I thought it was going to be a fun night out, but the more I talk about it, the more I see the potential for disaster.

# Chapter Fifteen

When we get back to Tangiers Court after our coffee and cake session I tell Carl about the quiz, trying to sound as nonchalant as possible. I don't want him to feel like he has to say yes. I'm not even sure I want him to.

"Sure. Sounds fun," he says, without hesitation.

He is smart, I know he is. Much smarter than I am. I'm afraid that I'm going to make an idiot of myself.

He gives me a tight squeeze, bringing me in close to his side, and I smile.

"The four of us will make a great team," Luke says. "Between us, we must know something about everything."

"Some of us more than others," Carl says.

He's grinning as he speaks, so I know it must be a joke, but I can't help but feel a quiver of anxiety shake through me.

"If there are any science-y questions you'll ace it, Vi," Zoe says.

She must have seen my discomfort, or maybe she only sensed it. All the same, she knows. She knows me.

"Maybe not everything science-y," I say.

"And I'm not sure 'science-y' is a word," Carl says, but he is still smiling as he pulls me so close to him that his hip jabs into me.

Zoe rolls her eyes playfully. "We'll be on the same team. We will be fine."

"Is there a prize?" Carl asks.

"£250 for the winners," Zoe says. "Not bad, even if we split it four ways."

"Nice," Luke says. "I guess I should revise."

Zoe laughs. "Revise? It's a fun quiz down the union, not your end of term exam. Oh, wait. Did you actually revise for those exams?"

"I did!" Luke laughs back. "A little bit."

"Little bit," Zoe mocks, affectionately.

"I passed," he says, with feigned indignance. She isn't having any of it though.

"Revise," she says again.

"Well maybe those of us who don't have the best general knowledge could brush up *a little bit* before Friday," Carl says, looking at me.

"We'll be fine," Zoe replies. "You can do some last-minute swotting if you like, but I'm only going for a laugh."

I thought that's what we were all going for, but it seems to have triggered a competitive streak in Carl. I'm starting to wonder what I have let myself in for.

On Friday afternoon, we get to the union bar at half past four; there are plenty of empty tables. It seems that Quiz Night is not quite as popular with everyone else as it is with Zoe and me. We have been bubbling about our team all the way here, and I can't help but feel disappointed that there's not a bigger turnout.

I look at Zoe and she reads my emotions perfectly.

"It's early yet," she says.

I can't see Soph and Ashley yet, so maybe she's right. More people might arrive before the start time.

Carl is board stiff beside me; I can feel the tension as I hold his hand.

"It's early," I repeat, to him.

He nods and sniffs. "Sure."

Luke eases the pressure by asking, "Shall we get some drinks in?"

Whether he was offering to buy a round, I don't know, but Carl says, "Great. Lager," and starts to move me towards a table in the centre of the room. I'd prefer to be tucked away by the wall or window, but I go with him, flashing an apologetic look to Zoe.

"Thanks, Luke. Do you mind? I'll just have

diet cola, thanks."

Zoe and Luke look at each other and there's a trace of amusement rather than annoyance in their glance.

"No problem," Luke says.

Other students start to filter in, gathering in groups around the tables. It's much quieter than I have ever seen it in here, not that I have been a frequent visitor by any means.

Luke waves, and I follow his line of vision to see his course mates, Florin, Rajesh, and Damon. They haven't been round to Tangiers Court much over the past year, and Luke rarely goes out to meet them. I'm sure they must catch up over breaks, but it makes me all the more aware that Luke is part of our little bubble now: he, Zoe, Carl and I, together in Tangiers Court. I like it that way; I'm happy.

Luke has never shown any sign of wanting to do anything else, but sometimes, and more frequently of late, I'm starting to feel that Carl wants more time alone. Not because he doesn't want to be with me, or at least not just because he doesn't want to be with me. I'm not paranoid or possessive or anything like that, but I know that before he and I were together he would go out every weekend, and now he spends most of his time at home. I don't want him to get bored, or feel trapped, or...

"Hi, Vi." Sophie reaches down and gives me a hug.

"Oh hey," I say.

"You were miles away. Running over your general knowledge?"

"That wouldn't take me long," I laugh.

Sophie gives me a well-intentioned smile in return. She's with her girlfriend, Fliss, a mousey-haired northerner. There's no sign of Ashley and Simon.

"Oh, they'll be here," she says, as if reading my mind. "They wouldn't dare leave the two of us to defend the team name."

I let out a small squeaking noise and look at Carl. "We haven't thought of a name."

"What?" he says.

His attention must have been drifting too. He has no idea what we were talking about.

"A team name. Soph, what's yours?"

"The Deliverers," she says, proudly. "You know, like, because..."

"You three are midwives," Carl says. "Very funny. What about Fliss?"

"I'm outnumbered," Fliss smiles. "I couldn't think of anything better though."

I can't think of anything either. I know I shouldn't let this get to me, but thinking of an interesting, funny or cool name seems beyond me. I desperately hope that Carl makes a suggestion, because whatever he says, I am going with.

"Deliverers," Carl repeats. "Too bad you'll be delivering the win to us." He smiles amiably and the girls grin back.

"Good luck, team," Sophie says. "We're going to get some drinks and try to bag a table. Looks like they are starting to fill."

She's right. She and Fliss walk off and I look at Carl to see if he has any answers. Who know that the most important challenge would be choosing a name?

"TC," he says.

"TC?" I repeat. As soon as I realise it's a suggestion, I nod, and say the letters again, trying them out to see whether they work. "TC."

"For Tangiers Court, obviously. It's the only thing we have in common, so that's what we should choose."

"The only thing the four of us have in common," I say with a smile.

"Well, yes," Carl says. "Team Tangiers

Court is too long, and it sounds stupid, so we should be Team TC."

"That's fine," I say. When his expression appears less than pleased I change my wording "That's great. It sounds great."

I could say that we should ask the others and have a democratic naming process, but I don't have any ideas of my own, and I don't want to waste the time that it will take for everyone to brainstorm, disagree, agree and end up choosing Team TC anyway.

"It's perfect," I smile, and I rest my hand on his leg beneath the table.

He looks amazing today. I have got so used to seeing him in the clothes he wears to lounge around the house that I forgot how well he used to dress to go out. I don't think I have seen him putting product into his hair for months, and this sweater must be new; I've never seen it before.

"You okay?" he asks.

I'm both nervous and excited, but I'm also happy. Happy to be out here with Carl, sharing something fun together, spending time and building memories.

"Super," I say.

I give his hand a gentle squeeze and he

returns it. That can be our kiss. For now at least.

The quiz is a lot less difficult than I expected. Either that or I know more than I give myself credit for. Between us, Team TC get most of the answers right, and on those we don't, we are able to agree on an educated guess.

We have a moment of dispute when we say that the longest river in the world is the Nile, and the quizmaster tells us the answer on the card is the Amazon, but we're having too much fun to make a fuss.

When the scores are tallied, we have forty-five out of fifty. I'm almost certain that we will be the winners. We couldn't have done much more.

The quizmaster's system for working out who has won is to ask the room if anyone has scored fifty (no!), then forty-nine (no!) and counting down until someone eventually says yes. When no one has claimed forty-six out of fifty I know what is coming next. Or at least I think I do.

When the quizmaster shouts, "Forty-five," Carl immediately raises his hand and says, firmly, "Here."

Unfortunately, a team of lads that I don't

recognise murmur amongst themselves, and then one of them raises his hand, his answers grasped tightly, and says, "Us too."

"Oh pants," I say, causing Zoe to fall into a fit of giggles rather than being upset that we haven't won.

"Do we have to split the money with them?" Luke says.

"Not likely," Carl says beneath his breath. "We have forty-five," he says, in the direction of the quizmaster.

"Ladies and gentlemen, it looks as though we have ourselves a tie-break situation."

The quizmaster reaches forwards and presses a button on the console, causing a dramatic section of music to boom over the speakers.

It's exciting, but I'm trembling in fear rather than the thrill of how close we are to winning.

"Hey," Carl nudges me. "Get it together. We're nearly there."

I nod, straighten out my skirt over my legs without thinking about it, and sit up straight. It's like being back in school, ready to perform, desperate to impress someone, anyone. Most of all, back then, I wanted to impress my parents. Now, I want to show Carl that I'm not stupid. It seems to matter to me more than it should.

There's a pause in proceedings to let people refill their drinks, and to build the dramatic tension, I presume. For those who scored less than us and are already out of the race, there's the decision to be made as to whether they should leave now and get our before the rush starts to arrive, or whether to be glad they have tables, watch the rest of the quiz and bed in for the evening.

If we hadn't made it this far, perhaps I would be suggesting that we leave. As it is, I have another diet cola, and hope with all of my heart that the tiebreaker goes in our favour.

"It's going to be fine," Carl says. "We got this far. Don't say anything stupid and we will win."

It applies to all of us, but the comment is directed at me.

We blend into the busyness of the room, but I still feel like there are a lot of people staring at us: we are one of the two final teams, of course anyone paying attention is going to be looking at us.

"You okay?" Zoe asks the same question that Carl asked me earlier.

They both ask me it with higher frequency

than they should need to. I am okay though. In general, I am mostly okay.

I give her the thumbs up and she returns the gesture. Carl shakes his head and picks up his fourth pint. Hopefully he hasn't drunk so much that he can't get the right answer to the final stage of the quiz.

Everyone that is staying settles back down into their seats, and the quizmaster plays a dramatic three note scale over the PA system.

"If you're ready, let's go straight ahead to the tie-breaker question. First to raise their hand and give the correct answer will be the winner. There's only one question, and this," he pauses, "is," he stops again, "it."

My mouth feels parched, and I reach out for my drink, and then put it down again. If he asks the question while my mouth is full, I won't be able to answer.

"Calm down," Carl nudges me. "It's okay."

I force a smile and lean towards him.

The quizmaster's voice is slow and steady, which is completely the opposite to how I am feeling. He asks the question, "On which organs are the adrenal glands located?"

I know the answer! Biology. Just my subject. I'm so thrilled that I forget to raise my hand,

and instead, I whisper the answer loudly to the rest of my team.

"Put your hand up!" Carl says, stone-faced and stern.

I snap to attention and thrust my arm into the air.

"Team TC?"

"The kidneys!" I squeak the answer out.

"That's it. Well done, Violet," Zoe says.

"Good girl," Carl says.

"The kidneys," the quizmaster repeats. "Team TC, that's the right answer. Congratulations, you are tonight's winners."

I squeeze my fists excitedly into balls and punch the air.

My first instinct is to look over to Zoe. She is grinning and giving me the double thumbs up. I turn my gaze slowly to Carl, expecting to see him smiling back at me. Instead he is reaching for his drink, his eyes wandering the room.

"I did it," I say, unabashed.

He looks at me when I speak.

"Well done," he says calmly.

He pats my seat, and I sit back down. As soon as I settle, he reaches an arm around me and grips my shoulder, leaning to kiss my cheek.

"Well done," he repeats.

The thrill of the win is strong. Zoe and Luke are hugging, and I see Sophie and her team waving from their table. I wave back, grinning.

"Would the representative of Team TC please come to collect the prize?" the quizmaster says.

My excitement is stopped dead in its tracks. I don't want to have to get up in front of all these people and collect the money. Having everyone staring at me, watching me walk over, fumble the cash, and probably smash into a table or two on the way back is not my idea of a fun way to end a lovely evening.

Zoe leans across to me. "Hey. It's okay. I can go."

"Let me," Carl says, getting to his feet.

Zoe had already started to push her chair back so that she could stand, but when Carl speaks, she smiles politely and pulls herself in to the table.

"No problem," she says. "Make sure you bring it back," she adds, jokingly.

"I'm not going to skip the country with two hundred quid," Carl says, flatly, and he begins to walk over to where the quizmaster stands waiting.

Even though it was a team effort, and I won the tie-breaker question for us, seeing Carl collect the money makes me feel as though I am an onlooker, watching him win rather than being a part of it. I wish I had the confidence to get up in front of everyone, but that's simply not who I am. As he holds the cash, there's a ripple of dull applause from around the room. The clapping is for Luke, Zoe and me just as much as it is for Carl, but I find myself joining in with the crowd.

Zoe and Luke are looking around, enjoying the congratulations, and I feel like a spare part. I'm not good in public situations, I'm sure that's all it is.

As I try my best to relax and enjoy the victory, I feel a hand on my shoulder, and my body snaps to attention. It's only Sophie, with Ash standing beside her.

"You were great!" Sophie grins.

"I'd never have encouraged you to come along if I knew you were going to stop us winning," Ashley says, beaming.

The heat rises to my cheeks. "It was mainly the others," I say. "We were lucky to have that biology question at the end, really."

"I told her it was the kidneys." Sophie gestures towards Ashley.

"You! I knew it. Of course I remembered that."

"*Now* you remember."

The two of them look at each other in mock outrage as they exchange banter, and it serves to make me feel less self-conscious and more comfortable. I'm immensely grateful to them for that, but I don't say so.

"Have you had a good night?" I ask.

"We'll probably stay on," Ash says. "What about you?"

It's already begun to get much busier than I would like in the bar. I guess what Sophie said was true: the organisers expect the quiz teams to stay around for the rest of the evening.

"I —"

I'm about to reply when Carl returns. Sophie and Ashley are blocking his way back to his seat, and they shuffle awkwardly to the side to let him in.

"Well done, Carl," Ashley says. They've only met each other a handful of times, but she is always bouncy-friendly with everyone.

"Thanks," Carl replies. Without a shred of modesty he says, "I knew we would win."

Ashley and Sophie both laugh as though he is making a joke, but he remains straight-faced. They let the laughter fade and look at each other before turning back to me.

"I don't know," I say.

"Know what?" Carl asks.

"They were asking whether we were staying on in the bar."

Carl looks up at the two girls. "You don't know Violet very well, do you? It's Friday night. She will be wanting to get home for her hot chocolate and whatever rom com is on TV."

That does actually sound a lot better than sitting here, surrounded by strangers, pushing my way through crowds every time I need the loo or want to get another drink. Although I probably shouldn't, I shoot a look at Zoe, and it seems to confirm to Carl that he was right.

"The pair of them. What are they like, eh?" Carl smiles at Soph and Ashley. "I think she will be going home."

I turn back towards him. I can read the meaning behind his words.

"You're staying out then?" I ask.

"You don't mind, do you?"

Of course it's a perfectly reasonable thing for him to want. I have no intention of stopping

him, even though I would like to be at home,
curled up on the sofa with him while I enjoy
that hot chocolate and rom com. Even if I did
want to persuade him to come home with me,
it's not like I would start trying to talk him
round in front of my friends.

"Sure. I'll head back with these two," I say,
pointing at Zoe and Luke.

I want to ask whether he will be late, or who
he will hang out with, but I don't want him to
think I'm nagging him, and I don't want the
girls thinking badly of me. For someone who
thinks she's becoming more confident I
certainly care a lot about what other people
think.

Despite being thrilled about winning the
quiz, as I expected Zoe and Luke are ready to
go home too.

I lean to give Carl a kiss goodbye and he
swerves so that I end up brushing my lips
against his cheek.

"Not here." He says it firmly and I have a
strange sense of déjà vu.

"Sorry," I say. "Later then. You owe me."

He smiles, but his eyes don't show any signs
of sparkle.

"See you later," he says.

As we start to walk away, he calls out to me, "Be careful on the way home."

"Okay," I say, uncertainly. It seems like a strange thing to stop me for, but at the same time, it's sweet. He might be awkward in public, in a different way than I am, but he cares about me.

# Chapter Sixteen

Carl didn't come home until after I had gone to bed, but on Saturday morning he is up bright and early, banging around in the kitchen. Because of my habit of waking early it's not a problem for me, but I hope that Zoe is up in Luke's room or they are going to be awoken too.

My eyes are still heavy, so I lie in bed, listening to the noises below, trying to make out what Carl is doing. He's at the oven, that's for certain. I can hear the clanking of pans on the hob. He is definitely making more than toast. That night out has either made him very hungry or very happy. If I am getting a cooked breakfast as a result, I don't mind which it is.

I'm back on placements on Monday; getting some quality time in with Carl this weekend is my only goal.

I don't have to wait long until I hear a gentle tap on my door.

"Violet," he says in a whisper loud enough to wake the next-door neighbours, let alone our housemates.

Pulling the cover off, I leap to the door and open it. I would rather he had just let himself in, but despite having a strong, trusting relationship we still never enter each other's rooms without invitation. Living together this early in our relationship means that we need to have some boundaries, and it's working well so far.

He leans forward immediately and gives me a firm toothpaste-taste kiss.

"Good night?" I ask.

"Late night," he says. "Then I couldn't sleep, so I've made pancakes. You ready to eat?"

"Pancakes?" I say. That's not quite what I expected. "When did you learn to make pancakes?"

"Uh, over Christmas," he says. "They might not be perfect, but they look okay."

"Thank you!" The last thing I want is to sound ungrateful. I'm actually thrilled, just somewhat taken aback.

"Coming down?"

I can't help but be aware of all the noise we are making on the landing between my room and Zoe's, and now that he has mentioned the pancakes, I am suddenly famished.

"Try to stop me," I say, and he does a cute little dodge on the landing, playing along with the literal meaning to my words.

"No really," I smile. "Let's get this

breakfast!"

True enough, there's a pile of fluffy golden pancakes on the table, and coffee for each of us.

"I don't know what I have done to deserve this, but it's amazing. Thank you," I say.

He ruffles my hair softly, then sits down next to me.

"Nothing," he says. "Nothing at all. I felt like doing something nice."

The glow in my heart is as warm as the pancake I fork into my mouth. I thought today was going to be a write-off, with Carl staying out so late last night, but it appears to be quite the opposite. The joy of winning might have helped him into this good mood; whatever it was, I like it.

The rest of the day continues in the relaxed, loving way that it began. We take a walk into town, through the gardens, and he's happy to wait while I stop to feed the squirrels. We sit for a while by the river that runs down the centre of the park. It's cold, but it's crisp. With no wind to chill us, the January day is near-perfect. We walk hand-in-hand, and my mind never wanders to thoughts of PADs, OSCEs or assignments. That can all wait.

Carl and I spend the entire day together, just the two of us. It's a rarity now, and I keep getting distracted thinking about how days like this don't come around often enough. That's part of my anxiety. It won't let me live in the moment and enjoy myself, I always have to be thinking about what could go wrong.

We have dinner at home and, as is our usual Saturday routine, we crash out in the living room with the others It's Zoe and Luke's turn to share the sofa, while Carl and I sit as close as we can on the armchairs. I don't mind too much. I can usually rest my head onto his shoulder and snuggle up to him despite the two thick chair arms between us. Tonight, he's leaning away from me, his knees tucked under himself, tapping away at his phone.

I want him to come closer, but he looks comfortable, and when I move towards him, he shuffles away. We've had a perfect day, and he has been so attentive and caring. I make myself comfortable on my own chair and try to let it slide.

"You okay?" I ask quietly. I don't want to disturb Zoe and Luke's enjoyment of *Cooking Queens*.

He nods, without looking at me, and points

to the screen, as if indicating I should focus my attention there.

"We don't have to watch this," I say. "If you want to do something else, we can."

"I'm fine," he says. "Settle down."

Those two words have the opposite effect than that which I assume he intended. I don't feel at all like settling down.

I look over to Zoe and Luke to see how they respond to Carl's tone, but Zoe just smiles. Perhaps he didn't mean to sound as condescending and snappy as he did, but the Carl that I am sitting next to now is so different from the wonderful boyfriend that I spent the day with.

"What's wrong?" I press.

"Violet," he says, a little louder this time. "Seriously. Give me some space."

This doesn't make any kind of sense. He has flipped his attitude towards me a full one-eighty since we were out earlier. The pancakes, the walk, they were so lovely, and now he doesn't want me near him.

"Okay," I mumble, but the way he spoke to me is needling into me too deeply for me to ignore.

I can't get comfortable. I want to *settle down*

and have a relaxed, cosy night, but this is the opposite of that.

I pick up my mug from the side table, slip my phone into my pocket and take myself off to my room. Perhaps we both need some space, even if I don't know why. He might have used up all of his emotional batteries, being with me all day and being so wonderful. I know he put a lot of effort in, maybe he has earned some time alone. It must be difficult, living here with me, unable to get away.

I must have been upstairs all of five minutes before my phone beeps. Zoe.

**You okay? Coming back down? xx**

I don't want to be in Carl's way, and I definitely don't want to create tension, so I send a quick reply.

**I'm fine. Little headache. xx**

Zoe's response is a sad face emoji, and then a second text.

**Need anything? Paracetamol? Water? xx**

I should have known that her caring side would kick in. Why did I make up such a stupid lie?

**Just overtired, I think. Thanks though xx**

It's probably true. I've had a long, busy day.

Taking to heart what Carl said is understandable. I'm overreacting.

**Let me know if you need anything xx**

I reply with two kisses and lay my phone onto the bed beside me.

I could be overreacting, but there's a niggling doubt inside me. I have the feeling that something is wrong. I've found recently that I am developing a sense for this kind of thing. I think it's something to do with the course. It's a kind of hypersensitivity, picking up on the tiniest signs that something is not quite right. On the wards, this is helpful, but here, at home, with my already anxious mind, it feels quite the opposite. When things are good, I make them bad, when they are bad, I turn them into disasters.

Carl has done nothing wrong, and I have enough to worry about with the things that I was not thinking about earlier, my exam, my assignments, and my placement. I should focus on those, and not try to create problems that don't exist.

And I really shouldn't start lying to Zoe.

# Chapter Seventeen

On Sunday I try to play it cool, give Carl some distance, and even spend some time with my head in the books. Being together is one thing but being together too much is another. As far as I'm concerned, I could spend my every waking hour with him and still want more, but I understand that it could make him claustrophobic. He's always needed more space than I have, but lately his desire for distance is increasing.

Despite wanting to be with him, I'm almost grateful that I start back on my postnatal ward placement this week. I'll be out of the house for three evenings, which should give us the right balance of time alone and time together. It's perfect really. Being on placement doesn't allow my brain the time to mope about not being with him when we have those hours apart.

Frustratingly, I have a day off on Monday, but on Tuesday morning I am back to the ward. Much as I love my postnatal placements I'm not filled with enthusiasm for this block. I have four weeks here, and then three on antenatal before the holidays. It's not long, not long at all considering this is my last placement in the

Margaret Beresford Unit before I qualify. Am I ready? I'm about to find out.

My postnatal ward mentor, Geri, gives me the customary welcome back to the ward and gets straight to the point.

"I'm going to give you these two women and their babies to look after, okay? You can take handover from the night staff, introduce yourself and do everything that needs to be done."

She looks at me as though it's a done deal, not up for discussion, and knowing Geri, that's just about the long and short of it. Everything that Geri has done for me during my placements with her has been for my own benefit, even though I may have questioned that at first. If this is what she wants me to do, she must believe that I can do it.

My stomach is a tangled knot, but I nod. I have Geri as my safety net. I have the whole team. That's the thing with midwifery, even though you might be responsible for an individual woman, child and family, there are always other people on the team that you can call upon.

I repeat this thought to myself as I say, "Sure," and give Geri a smile.

It's been over a year since I was last here, but everything is fresh in my mind as though it were yesterday. The sound of the chatter, the women talking, the occasional cry of a baby, the voices of the staff; it all creates a pleasant hum. The tall windows let the spring morning sunshine fall into the middle of the Nightingale ward in a lemonade coloured wash. Everything feels good. I feel good, and I realise that I haven't felt this way for a while.

I'm thinking about the day ahead, planning the routine in my mind. Take handover, introduce myself to the ladies, work out if there's anything they need straight away before they have their breakfast. Check the babies have fed overnight, don't forget that. Eight o'clock, after breakfast, we do the drugs round. It's usually a one-midwife-job, apart from those meds that need to be signed for by two members of staff, but I, or one of the other students on the ward if there are any, accompany the midwife that's doing the round. I may have passed my medicines management module last year but it's an ongoing learning process. There are always new things to find out about.

After the drugs round I have the rest of the

morning to carry out the daily checks, chat with the ladies, and do whatever else needs to be done. By then it will be lunchtime, almost time to go home. Time passes quickly when you're busy, and on the postnatal ward most days fly by.

Today I've only got two women and their babies to look after. When I am a qualified midwife, I could have half of the patients in the ward to care for. There's a big difference, and I know that Geri is only testing my ability to organise my workload.

Once all the rounds are completed, I stop at the bedside of the first of the women. Jane Judd had a Caesarean section two days ago and she's been tucked away in a side room with her baby. Clinically, she's fine. Her wound is healing well, the baby, a boy called Jasper, is feeding well, and everything seems normal.

"How are you feeling this afternoon?" I ask.

"Bored," she says. "Stuck in here on my own, away from everyone."

"We try to room anyone that's had a Caesarean in a side room, so that you can get enough rest and, well, you have your own bathroom here."

"I'd rather be with other people," she tells me.

Although her vitals are all normal, there's a pale dullness to her face.

"I'll see what we can do," I say.

There are spaces on the Nightingale ward' it would be easy to transfer her.

She doesn't smile.

"Okay, thanks," she says.

I have a niggling feeling, one of those instincts that I've been developing while I've been training here. Something feels off. I don't know what it is, but I haven't been wrong before.

"Is everything else alright?" I ask. "Is there anything you'd like to talk about?"

She picks up a magazine from the side table and starts to flick through it.

"No, no," she says.

Her eyes are moving over the page, but it doesn't look like she is reading. What it looks like is that she is pretending to read.

"Are you getting enough sleep?" I ask. I want her to tell me what's troubling her, because I am fairly sure now that something is. What I don't want to do is to pressure her and force her to shut down.

"When he lets me," she says.

Her voice sounds as though she is trying to make it sound light and happy.

"I have some time spare. We could bath him, if you'd like to?" I suggest.

"I don't want to bath him; I just want to rest. I want a break from him, that's what I want."

The words come out before she even realises she is saying them. As soon as she has spoken, she raises her hand to her mouth, dropping the magazine onto the sheets.

"It's okay," I say. "It's okay."

Before I can say anything else, she is sobbing into her hands, and I'm reaching over to offer a hug. She accepts it, and rests her head against me, letting the tears out.

"How long have you been feeling like this?" I ask, in a soft voice.

Did I miss the signs earlier today? This isn't the first time I have been in the room.

"It, I don't know, it just came over me, all of a sudden. Maybe it's been building up. I feel so useless. I can't do anything for him. I want to, but I'm...I'm useless."

She starts to sob again.

"You're not," I say. "You had major surgery. You've been through a lot."

She nods, but her expression doesn't reflect that she believes me.

"Let's have a chat. I'll get you a brew and we can sit here and talk for a while, okay?"

"Okay," she agrees.

It's a good place to start.

The sun is still shimmering when I exit the double doors at the front of the unit and make my way to the bus stop. It glints off the car windows like sparkling diamonds. I know I have done something worthwhile today. I wanted to be a midwife so that I could make a difference for women, and I feel like I genuinely have. Jane might have a long way to go, but she will get there. She'll have whatever support she needs from the team on the ward and beyond. That really is a good place to start.

# Chapter Eighteen

When I get home, the house is silent. Zoe is on placement this week too. Our practice blocks don't always coincide, but this week we have an overlap. It's strange to imagine her as Zoe, the student teacher, rather than as Zoe, my best friend. I wonder what she is like in the classroom. I know that Student Midwife Violet is a bolder, more confident version of me, but I can't imagine Zoe having to change anything at all to be a great teacher. She always knows what to do and say, it all comes naturally to her. She's cool and calm, and I'm sure she can handle anything. Perhaps I'm like that too, when I'm in the hospital. Maybe that's how people see me.

I flop onto the sofa, flick on the television, and open my phone. I don't think Carl is still in lectures, but they seem to change every week, and I can't keep track of them. It's tough being on a course where we have lectures five days a week, but at least it's easy to work out where I am. Lecture block or skills lab, simple. Wherever he is, he hasn't messaged me. There's no reply to the last text I sent at lunchtime.

The TV is tuned to the last channel we all

watched, but instead of last night's *Medical Dilemmas* it's a crazy game show called *Talk Me Through It*. Couples take turns trying to explain to the other person how to do something. The first person sees only the instructions, and the second sees only the things they need to make whatever it is that the first is trying to describe. I could just imagine Zoe and I on the show. She would be hilarious. I'd be completely useless of course, but that's all part of the fun.

It's unusual but not unpleasant to be on a placement day where I'm not knackered. This is the start of my block of clinical practice and I know it will catch up with me after the first few days. It would be even better if my boyfriend were here for me to spend the evening with though.

My phone is still in my hand, but my attention is all on the TV. There's a buzzing sensation within my grip and I almost drop the phone in surprise. I had planned to text Carl and I almost expect to see his name on the screen.

It's not him though, and it isn't Zoe. It's a message on the group chat that I'm on with Sophie, Ashley and Simon. I could have guessed without looking if I had waited, because the first buzzing is followed by a series of other incoming messages and their accompanying vibrations.

I click my phone and read through, still keeping an eye on the television.

Unsurprisingly I can't concentrate on both things at once, and I try to turn my focus to the TV. It's getting late though, and all I can think about is where Carl could be and why he isn't home yet. He's usually back around the same time every day, like clockwork. He knows when I usually eat, and he knows I usually make dinner for him too.

I message him again.

**Are you on your way home? xx**

It's gone six o'clock, and I thought he would be here by now. He still hasn't replied to the message I sent earlier. I'm starting to think that something could be wrong.

I don't have time to dwell too much, as the front door rattles open and Zoe clatters in.

"Alright?" she says, peering into the living room.

"Yeah," I say. It sounds unconvincing, even to me.

She pauses for a moment, slides her bag into the room, then says, "Hold up. I'll get the coffee."

I give a thumbs up and a smile, and turn the volume down on the television in preparation.

Within five minutes we are cosied up, each with a brew in our hands, deep in conversation.

"So what's happened?" Zoe asks.

"I don't know," I say, honestly. "He seems kind of off. I can't put my finger on what it is, but something doesn't feel right."

Zoe sits silently for a moment, and I'm about to start talking again when she finally leans back and speaks.

"Are you sure this isn't your anxiety talking?" She says it kindly, and in a way that I can't possibly interpret it as a criticism.

The thing is with Zoe I always know she has my best interests at heart. She's on my side, not that there are sides. Not that there's some battle stirring between Carl and me. It's probably nothing. She's probably right.

"You're probably right," I say.

I mustn't look sure of my words because Zoe raises her eyebrows and shakes her head.

"I'm not saying it's definitely that, Vi, but think about it. You went out at weekend. Everything was fine, wasn't it? Has he given you any reason to feel this way?"

It's my turn to pause for thought.

"Not specifically," I say, drawing out the word.

"But? There is a 'but', isn't there?"

I nod. "You know when you have that feeling, and you can't shake it?"

"Like when I went on that date with Billy Bell?"

She shudders for effect. She's been pretty lucky with dating, but that one, that's a story for another time.

I remember only too well.

"Just like that."

Now Zoe nods, taking a mouthful of her brew. A serious look settles on her face.

"Maybe you're right then."

When she says the words I know they are not what I wanted to hear. I wanted her to tell me that everything is going to be okay and that I am imagining things.

Perhaps I should have grasped at that lifeline she threw me and clung to the idea that my stupid anxious mind could possibly maybe be playing tricks on me. I don't want to be right. I don't want there to be something wrong.

"Do you think so?"

My voice has morphed to a husky whisper. I

don't want to say the words, because I don't want to hear the answers. I don't want to believe that there could be something *really* wrong.

She sets her coffee cup onto the coaster and raises her hands.

"Vi, I don't know. It's hard being on the outside looking in. I see the two of you together and you look happy, but I know that doesn't mean that you are."

"It's not that I'm unhappy…" I start to say.

"You were unhappy enough to need to talk about it," she says. "I'd say that meets the definition."

I let out a heavy sigh. "Look at us. We should have better things to talk about, shouldn't we?"

"We should, and we probably do, but right now I want to listen to you talking about what is on your mind. There's nothing wrong with sitting with your best friend, drinking coffee and talking about relationships. It might not be what the glossy magazines think we should be doing, but it's the reality of life, isn't it? Girls…women…want to understand their partners."

"Or at least understand their own lives," I

say.

"Yeah, that too," she agrees. "But you have that sorted, don't you?"

"Do I?" I'm genuinely surprised by the idea.

"Sure! You're almost twenty-one and you already know exactly what you want to do with your life. That's quite something."

"You too," I say, as if trying to mitigate my togetherness.

She shrugs. "We are both impressive then. We have somewhere decent to live, we have great career prospects, and we are both healthy and –" She pauses and looks as though she is thinking about something.

"What?"

"Oh, you know. I forget sometimes, about your anxiety. You've been on top of it for so long…"

"On and off," I correct her.

"The past eighteen months or so, you've been better than you have in years."

"On and off," I say again, and this time she shrugs and nods in acquiescence.

"On and off," she repeats. "But still, things are, in general, pretty good."

"So I shouldn't waste my time worrying about Carl?"

148

Lessons Learned

"I'm not saying that. It's obviously bothering you, so seeing as you are in a good place apart from whatever is going on between the two of you, perhaps you should talk to him. Clear things up."

I can't help but think about this time last year, when Zoe had recently started dating Luke, and she and I seemed to be drifting apart. Then it was Carl that I turned to for advice and support. He was there for me. He listened to me. He told me to talk to Zoe, in much the same way that she is telling me now. I let things stew in my mind. The tiny seeds of doubt and worry start to sprout into tendrils of anxiety that invade my every thought. It's almost as though I need someone to give me the push, every time I am feeling uncertain, to go ahead, to work through my problems rather than letting them overrun my mind.

149

# Chapter Nineteen

I have it in my head that I will talk to him when
he gets home. When he arrives, bends to kiss
me, and I feel the same warm wooziness that I
have been feeling for all these months I can't
bring myself to ruin it by talking about
problems that might not exist. Things appear to
get back on track. We do the same things that
we have always done, and everything seems
normal.

It must have been my imagination, I tell
myself. My imagination protests and puts the
blame squarely onto my anxiety, and I can't
help but agree. This is the most serious
relationship that I have had, and it's a lot
different from the casual teenage dating I have
done before.

It's almost as though I was playing at being
girlfriend-boyfriend in the past, and now I am
deep into the role and I never really had time to
prepare myself. Even though I was single for
quite some time before I met Carl, it's almost as
though I didn't spend enough time growing
from a teenage girl into a young adult woman. I
didn't have time to get to know myself before I
got to know him. Somewhere along the way, a

piece slipped out of place, and I've not been able to function at full capacity since.

My need to make people happy, and to put others before myself is what drew me into midwifery, but when I apply that to a relationship, instead of appearing caring it comes across as clingy.

I have so much to think about that worrying about my relationship is the last thing I want to do. I've noticed though that the more problems I have with Carl, the more time I spend with Zoe. She always makes time to talk to me now, especially after I told her how I felt last year when she had just started dating Luke and I was feeling lonely and vulnerable.

Because I didn't want to sound completely self-centred, I didn't use those words. Making Zoe feel guilty about not spending time with me because she wants to be in a relationship and have time with her boyfriend too would be beyond the pale. I have to handle my own emotions; I have to deal with my own relationship issues, even though I know that Zoe is there now whenever I need her, whatever I need her for. Our friendship is solid, no matter what happens.

So, I carry on. I try to put my doubts to the

back of my mind, focus on my studying, getting
through my placement and not letting my mind
get carried away with itself. It seems to work. In
fact, it's working absolutely fine right up until it
isn't anymore.

The evening before my OSCE, Carl offers to
give me some space so that I can revise. Last
year he offered to run through the scenarios
with me, but there has been no suggestion of
that this time around. I've practised with Zoe,
and got together with the gang from my course
though, and now all there is to do is to make
sure I know absolutely everything about the
potential scenarios that I might get tested on.
Simple, right?

   The exam will focus on emergency situations
like postnatal haemorrhage, what to do if the
baby's shoulders get stuck during delivery, or if
the umbilical cord pops out of the birth canal
before the baby is born. For a simple, natural
life event there's a lot that can go wrong during
childbirth. It's part of my job to know how to
respond, and I need to know that off by heart.

   One of the first steps in nearly all the
emergency drills is to call for help. Pull the
emergency bell. Shout. Get someone else in

there. I will have to know how to handle the situation, but I won't be alone.

I've written all of the steps for all the emergency situations onto postcard-sized cards, and I am drilling myself on them over and over. There are mnemonics for some of them, to help me, and all the other midwives, to remember what to do and what order to do it in.

I'm running through the card that I've headed "Shoulder Dystocia" for what I am sure is the hundredth time when there's a buzzing from beneath the duvet at the bottom of my bed. I instinctively reach down, fumble through the cover, and pick up the phone.

As soon as I feel it in my hand, I know it's Carl's and not mine. It's lighter, and slightly larger, not so much that it's visibly noticeable but I can feel the difference. He must have left it by mistake when he went out earlier; he's never usually without it.

I should put it down somewhere that I won't knock it onto the floor, and leave it alone. It's too late though. I've already looked at the screen.

**Are you coming over tonight? xxx**

The five words alone wouldn't necessarily have grabbed my attention. Carl has friends, even though he rarely goes out with them anymore, I know that he texts his mates and spends time with them sometimes now. Not often, but sometimes. It's normal, it's healthy, and it's probably something that I would be doing too if I didn't live with my own best friend. Zoe and I have our weekly mate date and impromptu trips out when we both have the time and opportunity. What kind of girlfriend would I be if I wanted Carl to stay at home with me every night?

**Are you coming over tonight?**

It's the three kisses at the end of the text that reach into my chest and grip my heart with a cold, icy hand. I almost expect it to stop beating; I can barely breathe. I'm glad I am already sitting, because my head is dizzy, and my legs are trembling.

Of course, the name of the sender is also on the screen, or at least the first letter of the name of the sender. Carl has stored the name in his phone as simply '**B**'.

**B**

Who the heck is '**B**'?

I stare at the screen, reading the five words and taking in the three little **x** marks.

His phone is locked, but I know how to open it. He doesn't have a passcode, and unlike my phone he doesn't need to press his thumb against the pad to open it. There's a pattern, a swipe across and then diagonally down from top to bottom; if I run my finger over the screen I can read the other messages that he and B have sent to each other.

It could be completely innocent. Some people add kisses to every message. Ashley is always throwing them into the group chat. Zoe and I exchange them all the time.

I sit up and my revision cards tumble onto the floor. Normally I would scoop them up straight away, get them back in order and focus my attention on the task in hand: revising for tomorrow. That's the most important thing right now; that's what I should be doing.

**Are you coming over tonight?**

Coming where? Who are you B? Why do you want my boyfriend to 'come over'?

I have a half-drunk spinning sensation in my head that I can't shake. The phone is like a brick in my hand, weighing me down. I want to drop it, but I hold on, looking at the screen, wondering whether I should open it up and see what else is hidden inside.

Zoe is out with Luke. She would know what to do. She will know.

I put Carl's phone gently onto the bed beside me, as if I am afraid that it will run away if I move too suddenly. Instead of opening his phone, I open my own and tap out a message to Zoe.

**I need to talk to you xx**

Typing the kisses hits my stomach like a punch.

I don't stop to think; I click send and wait for Zoe's response.

I expect her to text back, but instead of the chirping of a message, my phone rings.

"Hey, what's up?" she asks as soon as I answer.

She sounds like she is trying not to sound worried. Poorly concealed concern filters through her voice.

"I saw something, and I don't know what to think."

I explain about the message, almost stuttering and stumbling over my words as my emotions take over.

"I thought you were revising," Zoe says, before she even starts to respond to what I have told her.

She's buying time, thinking about what to tell me, I know it.

"I was. I have been. That's kind of gone out of the window now."

"Well, you need to get it back," she says. "Unless you're going to break into his phone and read through his messages there's nothing you can do apart from wait."

I hear her sigh and then she asks, "Do *you* think he could be seeing someone? Is that what this is?"

"No," I say. It's my instinctive response, but if I really believe that why is the message affecting me so badly. Things have not been perfect between us, but that's no reason for me to think that he would be with someone else. "I mean, maybe." I pause, and then say, "Yes."

I can hear Luke in the background at Zoe's end, asking her what's wrong. She must look as shocked as I feel. She moves the phone away from her mouth and talks to him, quickly explaining, and then comes back to me.

In the distance, I hear Luke say, "Do *not* read his messages. It's only going to lead to bad things."

"I think Luke's right, Vi," Zoe says. "You need to talk to Carl. Give him chance to explain what's going on. It could be nothing."

"It could be nothing."

It could be something.

It could be everything.

# Chapter Twenty

When I say goodbye to Zoe, I take Carl's phone, place it into my drawer and shut it away. I don't want to see it or think about it; at least I can do something about one of those things.

It's true that our relationship has felt different recently, but isn't that because of the stress of our final year, just like we said it was? I still want to believe that everything could be okay. I want to believe that everything is in my head, but I have that sick feeling, that nauseating intuition that is insistently telling me that there's something going on.

Carl arrives home sometime after eleven. He stops in the kitchen below and I can hear him walking across the lino floor. He turns the tap, pours water, pauses, walks again. I am focused on every step he takes because all I can think about is wanting him to come up here so that we can discuss the message. That's not all I can think about. Not really. Despite everything, my thoughts are also focussed on how much I really do not want to open this can of worms.

Now I could play dumb and nothing would change between us. He would come into my room, kiss me, and everything would be exactly as it has been. As soon as I start to ask him about the message, things are going to change; I know it. Still, I have to do it. I need to know. Even if it is nothing, my over-anxious mind needs an explanation, or I am going to worry myself into a state.

Finally, I hear his feet on the stairs, and he pushes my door open.

"Hi," he says, walking across to me.

He perches beside me on the bed and reaches over to kiss me hello. I can't stop myself from withdrawing. I should have played it cooler, tried to act in a more natural way, but my anxiety has burst through to the surface and there's nothing I can do to conceal it.

"What's up?" he asks. When he pulls back I can see the hurt in his face, and I think for a moment about making something up instead of going through with the conversation I know we need to have. "I left my phone somewhere," he says. "I'm sorry that I didn't message you if that's what's wrong."

That's enough to tip me over the edge. If he hadn't mentioned the phone maybe the conversation would be calmer, but I feel so worked up that I lash out.

"Yes, you left your phone. You left it on my bed. You had a message while you were out from your friend **B**. Is there something you'd like to tell me?"

As openers go, I know immediately that it is a bad one.

Carl looks stunned, and then the anger breaks through.

"You read through my messages? What the hell do you think you're doing? What gives you the right to check up on me? Is that what you were doing? You don't trust me, so you decide to snoop around in my phone. One time I happen to leave it here, just one time, and you do this? What is wrong with you? Why would you do that?"

His voice gets louder and faster as the tirade of questions roll off his tongue. He's up on his feet now, standing by the side of my bed, looking down on me. I feel like a cowering mouse.

"No, I…"

He doesn't give me the chance to explain what actually happened.

"There I was thinking that you had an important exam tomorrow and you needed me out of the way so that you could revise. No.

161

That wasn't it. You wanted me out of the way so that you could nose through my phone. And my room as well? Have you been up in my room going through my drawers? Checking through my pockets?"

Even though he is standing, he leans closely to my face and spits his words at me.

"Carl, stop," I say.

He stands deadly still, glaring at me. I shouldn't have said anything. I shouldn't have picked up his phone. I shouldn't have looked. It was innocent though, all of it was. I never intended for any of this to happen. Now I have ruined everything.

"What do you want me to say?" he asks. "Whatever I tell you, you seem to have already made up your mind. You think I've done something wrong; I can tell by that look on your face. When I come home you're usually all over me, and today you can't even kiss me. You don't have to say anything, that says it all."

He's right, of course. I saw the message and instead of giving him the benefit of the doubt I called Zoe, I didn't even consider that there could be an innocent explanation. Carl is my boyfriend, and I should have trusted him.

"I'm sorry," I say, quietly.

"What?" He sounds incensed, his voice booms in my face.

"I said I'm sorry," I repeat, as calmly as I can manage.

"You crossed the line, reading my messages. I can't believe you would do that."

"I didn't. I mean, I picked up your phone by mistake and I saw what was on the screen. I would never –"

"You accidentally picked up my phone and then you accidentally read my messages?" He laughs acidly. "Sure, Violet. Sure, that's what happened."

"You must have left it."

I try to explain, but when I speak, he cuts me off, stopping me from getting the words out.

"I never expected this of you," he says, shaking his head. "Accusing me like this. Show me your phone. How about I read through your messages?"

"There's nothing in there. Nothing you'd be interested in. And I didn't read through your messages. It was only that one, on the screen. I never opened your phone."

"But you know how to, don't you? You've made sure of that. I've seen you watching me."

He looks at me for a response and I can only

nod. My phone is on the bedside table, and he snatches it. Stupidly I reach out to try to take it off him.

"What? You don't want me to look? I thought there was nothing to see. If you've nothing to hide then I can look, can't I?"

I wish I had never started this, but I did, and now I am stuck in a bad situation that I don't want to make any worse. Even though I know there is nothing on my phone that Carl shouldn't see, my anxiety is building up to a point that I know I must look guilty regardless. I can hardly breathe let alone find the energy to argue.

"Yes," I say resignedly, and I flop back against the wall to watch.

"Open it."

He holds the phone in his hand so that I can press my thumb against the pad without being able to snatch it off him. I wasn't going to. I don't care. I can't fight him; I don't want to.

I put my thumb on the pad and as soon as my phone opens, he whips it away and starts to scroll through. Instead of moving so that I can't see what he is doing, he reads in a way so that I know exactly what he is looking at. He's trying to get some sort of reaction from me, but all I have is submission.

He flicks open my social media and runs through the private messages. There's a couple of exchanges I have had with other student midwives that I've chatted with online, and some threads about book swaps. His expression starts to change from anger to a bizarre amusement.

"Is this it?" he asks. "Is this your life?"

"What?" I stutter.

"Is this all you do? I mean I don't want to find that you've been talking to other guys, but I expected something interesting at least."

Something inside me snaps, and I sit up sharply.

"Give me my phone back." My face is poker straight and I am deadly serious.

He speaks back to me with the same sharp directness. "I haven't finished yet."

I reach across again, flailing for my phone, and he holds it away, out of my grasp, and gets to his feet.

He's moved on to my phone call log. I know, even though I can't see anymore. I know because the next thing he says is, "You called Zoe. As soon as you saw that message, you called Zoe."

He holds the phone out towards me, accusingly.

"Everything that happens, everything I say, everything I do, it all gets back to her, doesn't it? Do you have any thoughts of your own that you don't run by her first?"

"That's not fair, I –"

"Is it fair on me? Is any of this fair on me? What did she tell you to do? Did the two of you have a lovely little chat about how terrible I am and how I definitely certainly positively must be cheating on you?"

He throws the phone at me, and luckily it thuds into my abdomen rather than striking my face. Still, he has crossed the line, and I can't accept this.

I take a deep breath and try to make my words sound as calm as possible. "I have my exam tomorrow. I can't deal with this now."

"What's more important to you? Sorting things out between us or your stupid exam."

The words land like a slap and I recoil just as though it was a physical blow.

My instinct is to blurt out, *'You, you of course,'* but I pause and that's all it takes to tip him over the edge, if he wasn't there already.

"I knew it." He practically screams the

words at me.

"Carl!" He turns to walk to the door. "Please. You are important. You are."

"I am important. I know I am. Just not important to you." He spits the words out. "You were the one that started this. You wanted this argument and now you've got it you can't handle it. You can't start accusing me of things and then expect to schedule an appointment to talk about it."

There's a tap at the door, and I hear Zoe's voice. I didn't hear her come home, and I wonder how long she has been able to hear what's going on.

"Everything okay?" She sounds hesitant, a slight tremble in her voice.

"Fine," Carl says. "We're finished."

Finished talking or *finished* finished? The question jolts through me, but I can't speak. My mouth has turned to useless jelly.

He pulls the door open and pushes past Zoe, his feet stomping on the stairs up to his own room. The second he is gone I bury my face into my hands and let the tears out.

Zoe runs in and sits next to me, her arms around me before her rear hits the duvet.

"Hey. It's okay. It's okay. What happened?"

I hear the door move and flick my eyes up to see Luke pushing it closed from the landing. He must have been behind Zoe, backing her up, being there for her.

I shake my head and snort back snotty tears.

"Come on," she says softly. "Hey."

Her hand smooths my hair in gentle strokes, and I rest my head on her shoulder.

"I've made such a mess of things," I say.

"So, he hadn't done anything wrong? He hasn't? What did he say? What was it all about then?" She pulls back to look at me and bites her lip. "I'm talking too much," she says. "Tell me what happened."

I give her the short version of events and she sits expressionless and listens. When I have finished she finally speaks.

"So he didn't deny it," she says.

I had missed that less-than-minor detail amidst my anxiety.

"Well, no," I say. "But he was so angry that I had been looking at his phone. I couldn't really keep asking."

She sighs and shakes her head. "And what was the shouting about? Does he know your exam is tomorrow? He must do. Are you ready?

No, don't answer that now. Tell me why he was yelling at you. I just wanted to burst in here and…well, I don't know what, but Luke stopped me. He said, *'Be cool. Don't make things worse.'* Worse? I ask you. What's worse than someone yelling at my best friend. Well, I know…" She stops herself again and reaches out to wipe my tears.

"I don't care about my exam. I've messed everything up. I'm so stupid."

"Violet Cobham you are not stupid. You are not. And the fact he is making you feel this way gives me even more reason to doubt him."

"She's probably just a friend, Zoe. He's allowed to have friends. It's not even a case of being allowed. I don't have the right to allow or not allow anything," I say through my bubbling tears.

"You have a right to expect him to be faithful and honest and not treat you like an idiot."

"I am an idiot," I mumble.

"You should go up there and sort this out. Ask him, straight up. Ask him what's going on. Find out who this **B** is."

It's the last thing I want to do, but I do need to finish my revision and there's no way I can even think about my exam with this hanging over me.

I tighten my lips and look at Zoe.

She gives me a reassuring smile.

"Whatever happens, you are going to be okay, Vi. I promise."

Even though my heart is beating out of my chest, I steel myself to get up and say the words that need to be said. As I push my hands into the bed to stand I hear Carl's feet on the stairs.

"Wait!" I call after him.

I get to the landing in time to see him opening the front door.

"Carl, please. Wait." I shout the words, and they sound so alien, so desperate.

He pushes the door and leaves the house without so much as turning around to acknowledge me.

I've really made a mess of this. I've ruined everything.

# Chapter Twenty-One

When morning comes, Carl doesn't show for breakfast. Either he got up early to avoid me or he's hiding away in his room. Although part of me wants to talk to him, and to get some kind of reassurance that everything is going to be alright between us, there is also a part of me that is relieved that we don't have to go through another argument this morning. I have to get my mind focussed on the exam ahead of me.

I know it's going to be tough, and with Zoe on placements I'll be walking into uni alone. I force myself to think about drills and mnemonics, repeating them over in my head like particularly dull mantras, blocking everything else from my mind. It feels impossible. Carl keeps creeping into my thoughts. No, not creeping; the thought of him crashes in, like an uninvited party guest. Each time my attention drifts to him, I start running through another list, repeating it over and over until all I can think about is the exam.

I get to the skills lab five minutes early, just as I planned, and after the all-too-familiar wait in the corridor, my legs are like jelly when I walk into the room. This is it. My third and final OSCE. I have to pass. I have to focus.

I can't believe how easily I breezed through this last year. I was so confident then, so sure of myself and my knowledge. Now I feel completely unprepared. I did what I could last night, but the feeling runs deeper than that. I don't only feel unprepared for the exam, but also for the end of my course, for qualification, for practice as a midwife. There's a chance that my insecurity and self-doubt have been kicked up a notch after what happened last night, but there's also a chance that I really am not ready for this.

I try to smile at Zita to conceal my fear.

"Hi Violet," she smiles back, and it feels warm and reassuring. "You know Sarah and Amanda." She gestures to the second lecturer and the woman who will be standing in as a patient.

I nod. Thoughts of Carl and our stupid argument are cycling through my brain, pushing out all the things I need to remember for the exam. I can't think about him now. I can't let my brain wander to working out who B is and what she is to Carl. I have to stop this, right now.

It's so much easier thought than done.

"Hi," I say weakly.

Hearing my own voice makes me snap to attention. I reach up and straighten my collar, wipe a stray hair from my forehead and take a deep breath.

"Hello," I say again, and this time my voice rings out strong and steady.

My lecturer grins. "That's better."

She wants me to succeed. Sarah wants me to succeed. Even Amanda, the stand-in patient, who barely knows me, wants me to succeed. I have to want it too. I have to want it enough to focus, to put all of my mental energy into the here and now and ace this exam.

Once we have begun, everything starts to fall into place. I have drilled the mnemonics into my memory bank efficiently enough that I can pull out the information I need when I need it.

The first scenario is shoulder dystocia. It's not something that occurs often, and I haven't experienced it in practice, but if it does happen I'm going to need to know what to do. In a routine birth once the baby's head is born, the shoulders are delivered with the next push. The upmost (or anterior as we call it) shoulder slides beneath the mum's pubic arch and the rest of the baby follows in one, sometimes slippery, motion. In a small number of deliveries the shoulder gets stuck against the bone: that's shoulder dystocia. It's risky for the baby; being stuck in the birth canal can lead to nerve damage, brain damage, and even death.

This OSCE is not a paper exercise. The lecturers aren't testing our memory recall skills. They need to know that if, or when, we experience these situations in practice we know exactly what to do. Acting quickly and correctly can mean all the difference.

My mind flicks into gear as I respond to the scenario. My instincts kick in, and if Carl were to walk into the room now I wouldn't even give him a glance. This is how it should be. When I am in my uniform, with woman, all that matters is giving safe, supportive care.

When I leave the skills lab, I'm buzzing with the thrill of knowing that I've aced the OSCE. I knew everything I needed to know, and I did everything I needed to do. Despite last night, the lack of sleep and the distraction of my row with Carl, I kept my head.

As soon as I think about last night, my mood drops an octave, and my smile turns into a frown. I've passed the toughest assessment on my course. I should be happy, but instead I'm walking home worrying about whether I even still have a relationship. That's without even thinking about everything that led to our argument in the first place. All that rowing and for what? It didn't achieve anything. I can feel the anxiety gripping me like a tight hand around my wrist, drawing me back from the happiness that I should be feeling. What's going to happen to us? What's waiting for me when I get home?

My phone buzzes, still switched to silent from the exam room, and I jump as I feel it vibrate against my side. I half-expect it to be him. I want it to be. I want some reassurance. Just a few words. '*We'll talk when you get home.*' Even something as formal as '*Hope your exam was okay.*' I'd take it. I'd take anything right now.

It's not him though. It's Zoe.

**How did it go? xx**

Of course it's Zoe. She's always there for me. No matter what. That doesn't stop me from feeling a little pang of disappointment as I read her name on the screen instead of Carl's.

I stop at the traffic lights, waiting to cross the road and tap out a reply.

**Fab xx**

I add a smiley face emoji, even though I don't feel much like smiling.

I send the message and turn my attention to the road. It's not quite rush hour, but the traffic is picking up and there's no way I'm getting across unless I wait for the green man to flash up.

I sigh and type a follow up.

**Are you home? Have you seen Carl? xx**

I stare at the words on the screen until I hear the rapid beeping of the pedestrian crossing. Shaking my head, I pop my phone back into my pocket without sending. What can she say that is going to make me feel any better? Nothing. Not by text message anyway. I raise my head, focus on the way forward and try to let myself enjoy the cocktail of relief and satisfaction from making it through the exam – without the side order of self-doubt and anxiety.

There's no sign of Carl when I get back to Tangiers Court, but Zoe runs to meet me.

"Tell me all about it," she grins as she ushers me down the corridor towards the kitchen.

There are already two mugs on the table, filled with fresh tea, and she's laid a plate of biscuits out as though we are having a party. I know she is trying to be sweet, but the strangeness or seeing them there is somehow jarring and I swallow my smile.

"Sit, come on," she says, relentless.

I can't help but return her smile, and I tuck my jacket onto the back of the chair and settle in front of my mug.

I'm aware of myself listening for signs of Carl's presence. I can recognise the sound of his footfall, somehow different from Luke's. Not heavier, but more defined. Firmer, maybe. It's something I've become tuned in to. Now, there is only silence. No Luke. No Carl. Zoe and I are alone here, the two of us sitting beside each other in our home.

I'm about to speak when Zoe edges in. "Tell me about your exam."

I'm sure she knows that I want to talk about last night, that I want to thrash out the details of my argument with Carl and look for some suggestions on what to do next. Instead of pushing it, I take a biscuit and start to tell her about the OSCE.

The mugs are emptied and filled again. I stop myself from eating more biscuits because it's nearly half five and time to be thinking about dinner rather than snacking. Still, it's just the two of us. We go from talking about my exam to discussing her day and the portfolio she's putting together for her course. Although we are studying for different career paths there are many similarities between what we are doing. We've always been that way, the same in so many aspects, but different enough to be our own individual selves.

Her face glows.

"So, I went to my supervisor and she said she would have done the same thing," she laughs.

An aura of confidence emanates from her as she tells me about how she handled a particularly tough situation in a class this week.

"You have to go with your gut," I nod, understanding the principle, even if I don't understand the exact situation. "As long as your supervisor agrees you must be on the right track."

I haven't taken the time I should have to reflect on how much Zoe has changed, developed and grown since we have been at uni. Looking at her now, I can see it. She's a little older, of course, but she is so much wiser, so confident and comfortable in who she is and what she is doing.

The thought catches in my throat, and without saying anything I lean over and throw my arms around her, squeezing my best friend in a tight embrace.

"Hey! What's that for?" She laughs and encircles me with her arms too.

"I just wanted to. I had to," I say, pressing my face into her hair. I know she can hear the smile in my voice anyway. "You're…I don't know. It sounds silly. I'm proud of you. It does sound silly, doesn't it? But, I am. Look at you, so…together." I pull back and look her in the eye. "You're going to be an amazing teacher."

"Oh Vi." I swear that's a tear in her eye. "You silly, silly…" She shakes her head but doesn't stop grinning. "I look at you and I think exactly the same thing. Everything has come easily to me. I haven't had to cope with any of the things that you have, not now, and not before we got here. My life has been an easy ride. Think about how you were back when you did your first OSCE. You've fought back and here you are breezing through your exam today."

I get an instinctive blush of shy humility and

have to look away.

"Own it. Own your success."

She's like my personal cheerleader. This started with me complimenting her, and she turns it around every time to make me feel good about myself.

I nod. "I own it," I say, "but you're going to have to take some of the credit."

She shakes her head resolutely. "I'll take the credit for my success, and I absolutely acknowledge that you have made a huge difference. Do the same."

I don't say another word. I pick up my mug and hold it out towards her.

"To us and our well-deserved successes," I say.

"To us and being awesome," she grins.

We click our cups together and drain the last dregs of the tea. It's not champagne, but it's a celebration, and we deserve it. I believe that I deserve it, I really do now.

The sound of a key in the front door snaps me back to the reality of life. I know it's Carl before he pushes into the house and stomps upstairs without so much as looking whether I am home. Zoe and I are still in the kitchen, tucked away at the back of the house, but he didn't call out, he didn't pop his head in. He doesn't care.

Zoe matches the change in my expression with one of her own. Her smile melts into a look of tender sympathy.

"I should…" I start to say.

She shrugs slightly. "You don't have to go running," she says. "Maybe it's better if you don't."

Maybe it is, but I can't stand the atmosphere of words left unsaid. I need to clear things up with Carl.

"Last night…" I say, and then I can't find any more words.

"Last night must have been horrible," she says. "Last night was last night. You don't want to go through that again, do you?"

"No."

Where has that confidence gone? I sound deflated, like the hope and happiness have been squeezed out of me. I settle back into my seat, trying to relax, but feeling the tension stiffening my body.

She lowers her voice. "I didn't want to get you talking about it. I thought we could just…you know…have some happy time."

"I know," I say. "Thank you."

My voice is as hushed as hers. I know how sound carries in this house, even with two floors between us and Carl.

"But it is what it is," she says. "Tell me what's going on. What did he say? What did he do?"

My sigh is long and draining.

"You know what you saw. If you want answers, you demand answers. You deserve the truth," she says.

"Do you think he would really do that? What do you think?" I ask.

She breaks eye contact for a moment and appears to consider the answer.

"I don't know what to say, Vi. I only see things from the outside."

"That doesn't help much," I say. My voice is coarse, and I don't mean to sound so ungrateful. "Sorry," I add. "I…"

Before I finish the sentence, I hear the thudding of footsteps coming back downstairs. I instinctively put my finger to my lips and make a shushing sound. Zoe sits silently beside me as we listen to Carl's descent.

He walks into the kitchen, and without looking at Zoe, he addresses me.

"When you girls have quite finished talking

about me, do you think you could have the decency to talk to me instead, Violet?"

I choke up, wordless, and nod timidly.

*You girls.* That's the exact term that Dad used to say when he would flip out at Mum and me. It's not completely out of context here.

"Actually..." Zoe begins to speak.

"Actually nothing. I wasn't talking to you."

He throws the words at her, and for a split second I read surprise on her face. She soon recovers her composition though, and replies.

"Actually, we were talking about Violet. Not that it's any of your business what we talk about."

She may have told me that she didn't want to pass judgment, but Carl's tone isn't helping to show him in a positive light. I don't want the two of them to start an argument though I couldn't bear to be in the middle of that.

*You girls.* It's too close to the bone.

# Chapter Twenty-Two

By the end of the week, Carl and I have barely spoken to each other. If there was a chance to save what we had, I missed it. From the moment I brought up the messages it has seemed like there's no going back. Carl is distant and defensive, and there's no talking to him.

I've tried.

I've really tried.

I want to believe him, and I want to trust him, but all that has happened is that he has become increasingly detached.

I don't know what I can do. All I know is that I have to do something.

He's been up in his room since he came back from uni today, and when he comes down, although I don't want him to think I'm ambushing him in any way, I walk nonchalantly behind him into the kitchen.

"Can we talk?" I say it as calmly as I can. I don't want him to think I'm about to make a scene.

"There's not much to talk about," he says.

"So, is this it? Is it over between us?"

I don't know what response I expected, but I

thought perhaps, just maybe, a part of him might want to work through this.

"Over?" he says. "Yes, it's over."

He turns his back, reaching up into the cupboard for his mug. His hand brushes past the mug that I usually use, but he only picks out his own.

"Can we, I mean is there..." I should have thought about what I was going to say, because now I am standing in the kitchen, close to tears, mumbling towards his back, and it doesn't feel great.

He spins dramatically and faces me.

"What? What are you trying to say? Come on, get it out."

"Why are you being like this? What changed? Why are...just, why?" I don't want to cry. Not now. Not in front of him. I never thought he could be like this. Last year he was such a good friend, so solid and supportive. Then he was a great boyfriend. Now? Now I barely recognise him.

"Nothing changed. Maybe that's the problem," he says.

I don't understand what he is saying, and it must show on my face.

"I can't handle this," he says. "I'm going to

move out."

"What? Where would you go? You don't have to…"

"I can hardly stay here with you and your friend who clearly hates me."

"She doesn't…I mean she sticks up for me, that's all."

"That's all? The pair of you are impossible. There's no room in your life for a relationship with your course and your friend, and your ridiculous paranoia. I thought you were done with that stupid anxiety."

I thought I was too.

"It's not stupid. I can't help it. Don't you think I've tried to…"

"You've tried nothing. You said you were going to get some help, and what happened there? You never bothered. You just hide behind it, use it as an excuse for everything in your stupid life. That's what hasn't changed. You haven't changed."

"My life isn't stupid either," I say, but my words don't sound certain.

"I felt sorry for you, okay? Last year when Luke and Zoe were all loved up and you were rattling around the house on your own, obsessing about these panic attacks or whatever they are. I felt sorry for you. I stopped seeing my mates so I could spend time with you, and now that I want to actually do something other than be stuck here with you all the time, it's a crime. You're unbelievable."

There are so many things I want to pick apart from that diatribe, but all I say is, "Doing something and doing someone are two different things."

I regret it the moment the words tumble from my mouth. Maybe I am stupid after all.

He glares at me and shakes his head slowly.

"What's the point?" he says. "I'm moving out. This is over. Whatever this is. It's over."

I know it's not what I should say, but my instinct is taking over my brain. "Did you ever actually like me?" I ask.

He looks at me, his face expressionless.

"Did you?" I ask again.

I want to shut up, I really do, but my heart is thudding so hard in my chest. I can't think clearly. I'm not saying or doing anything right. Perhaps I never do.

Without replying, he walks to the door, moving within inches of me but not touching.

"Carl!"

He doesn't turn around.

He doesn't stop.

He doesn't answer the question.

Instead, he leaves me standing alone in the kitchen, and I finally let the tears flow.

Although I can barely concentrate on anything, I spend the rest of the evening working on my research project. The final assignment is a six-thousand-word literature review and discussion on my chosen topic. Maternal mental health in the antenatal period; I thought that was a great idea. When I started work on the project, I thought that I would focus on anxiety, but I found so much information on so many other mental health issues that I had to read more.

Learning about how best to support women has also given me some strategies for supporting myself. At the back of my mind, or perhaps not quite as far as the back, I must have known that this would happen. I didn't get the support from my GP or the counselling service that I very nearly accessed last year, but now, at the end of my three years, I feel more confident and in control than I ever have before. At least I did. I thought I did.

I have grown, not only grown older, although now I am in my early twenties rather than being the teenager that I was when I started my course. I have grown in confidence. I have grown in terms of my knowledge and skills, but isn't that the whole point of coming to university? No. Not the whole point. What I have learnt in the classroom and on the wards has been so much more than the contents of a book, or the slides from my lectures. I've learnt from the experience of the midwives that I have worked alongside, and the lecturers that have coached and mentored me through the theory. I've learnt from Zoe

I've learnt from my relationship with Carl, or at least I hope that I have. I don't want to think about him right now. I don't want what happened, what is still happening, between he and I, the way he has behaved, the way he's making me feel, any of it, I don't want that to cast a shadow over my experience. I don't want it to cloud my happiness. Passing my course, learning the life lessons along the way, that is my achievement, and I am going to celebrate it.

I know he is in the house, in Tangiers Court, the place that Zoe and I found and made our home. He's just upstairs. I could go and try to talk to him, to say something, anything to try to put things right, but I know that it's too late. It's too late because he has let me down. This isn't my doing. I haven't failed, I have been failed.

Did he actually ever like me? He didn't reply, and I can't let myself become obsessed with what the answer, the true answer, would be. What I do need to do is to like myself. At the moment I feel fragile and my heart is heavy with loss, but a part of me, the stronger part, knows that I can learn from this and move on as a stronger person.

Eventually.

# Chapter Twenty-Three

The week before Easter break, as I'm coming towards the end of my antenatal placement, Carl moves out. I'm surprised that he has stayed as long as this; the past five weeks have been unimaginably uncomfortable. We have tried to avoid each other in the house, but the atmosphere has been a thick fog of awkwardness.

When Zoe, Luke, and I have been downstairs, watching television, Carl has kept himself hidden away up in his room. It's almost felt like the beginning of last year when we barely saw him or spoke to him. When I barely knew him.

It's wrong to think of it like this, but if Zoe and Luke weren't together perhaps Carl and I would never had become a couple either. We drifted into the relationship at a time that I was vulnerable and weak; I'm not saying that he took advantage of that, not at all but perhaps if I had been spending more time with Zoe I wouldn't have felt the need to fill my time with something (someone) else.

Up until Carl, Zoe had been my only confidante, my only true friend. I thought I had been lucky enough to find a boyfriend who would fill that role too, but I was wrong.

While I'm on my antenatal placement, I realise that Zoe isn't the only person I have to talk to. I've drawn the Sunday afternoon shift with my mentor, Becky, this week, and there are only three women staying with us right now.

The busiest time for antenatal ward tends to be weekdays. Women are referred in by their GPs or community midwives, and there are fewer opportunities for referrals at the weekend. Most of our intake on Saturday and Sunday tends to come from delivery suite. Women who attend for blood pressure checks that aren't in need of constant one-on-one care, or those whose waters have broken but they aren't in labour yet; there are many reasons why women might stay on the antenatal ward, but today there's a lull, and I'm appreciative.

I should want it to be busy. Being busy means there is more opportunity to learn. The more I see, the more I experience, the more I can reflect on. Right now, I am finding it difficult to focus, and it must show.

We've done the drugs round, which took us all of ten minutes, and we're settling back in the office with tea and a box of chocolates that one of last week's patients left for us. There's a copy of *What's New?* magazine, a trashy gossip mag that I would never dream of buying, but that seems to be the staple read of people who are stuck in a hospital ward with not a lot to do. I'm about to reach over for it, when Becky speaks.

"You seem a bit distant today," she says.

It takes me aback. My first thought leaps towards whether I have been acting unprofessionally, or not engaging with the patients fully. Whatever is going on in my life, I must put their needs first. When I am here, I am Violet Cobham, Student Midwife. Violet the Heartbroken Idiot has to stay at home.

"Sorry," I say.

Becky picks up on my surprise and shakes her head. "You haven't done anything wrong. You're not your usual self though. I've hardly seen you smile all day."

I have a choice. I can throw back a joke, try to deflect from what is bothering me, or I can open up and chat to Becky about how I am feeling.

I don't know her particularly well. I've had three placements on this ward, and she has been my mentor for each. Not that we have worked every shift together, there have been times when she hasn't been around when I have been on duty, and of course I usually try to avoid late shifts on Mondays. Still, we have talked.

It was Becky that encouraged me to visit the mother and baby mental health centre at the Linden Unit last year. Without her prompting me, I would have missed out on so much. Although we have never talked about it again, she told me then, when she was suggesting that I visit the unit as one of my SPOKE optional placement days, that she had suffered with mental health issues. She might actually understand how I feel.

"I'm…" I start the sentence before I have even decided what I want to say. How much do I want to tell her? I take a breath, try to calm my heart rate, and speak again. "I'm not sleeping well. The anxiety is, well, it's pretty bad at the moment. I split up with my boyfriend, or at least he split up with me, which is the same thing, of course, but you know what I mean, and, well, I feel rubbish."

It's not the most concise of explanations, and I stumble over the phrasing, but I get the words out.

"Oh Vi. I'm sorry to hear that. Do you want to talk about it?"

Do I? I haven't even told Zoe about the way that my anxiety has been bubbling away since Carl dumped me. My sleep pattern is all over the place, I can't concentrate on anything anymore. I don't want to worry her. We both have to study; we both need to focus. I don't want to monopolise her attention, not now.

"I feel so stupid," I say. "Inadequate. Like I wasn't good enough for him. I feel like if I was more interesting, or at least less boring, he wouldn't have left me. There's something wrong with me."

I can't make eye contact. Even though I never made it to see a counsellor, I imagine that this is what it might be like. Becky has been a midwife for a while, and I'm sure she must have counselled plenty of patients. Probably not quite as many daft students though.

"You can't think like that," she says calmly. "If he left you, for whatever reason, it doesn't mean that it was your fault."

"I think there was someone else. I found a message. He never said there was, he never admitted to it, but everything fell apart after I confronted him."

"You read his messages?" she asks.

Her voice doesn't contain any traces of judgment, it sounds more like she is trying to clarify what happened.

"No," I say. "Well, yes. One message. It was on his phone screen. I didn't mean to, and I couldn't unsee it."

"It is pretty difficult to unsee things," Becky smiles. "Was everything alright until then?"

I nod, and then I reconsider. "Maybe not, no. I felt like something was off, but I didn't know what it was."

"Sounds like you've had a tough time of it. I can see why you're feeling down. I know from my own experience how easy it is to take things to heart and blame yourself for everything that goes wrong."

I can feel a lump growing in my throat. I'm worried that I'm going to burst into tears, right here in the office. My back is to the door, at least no one would see me if they walked past, but this isn't right. I shouldn't be doing this, not here.

"I shouldn't have said anything," I sigh.

"My role as your mentor is to support you," Becky says, leaning forward and placing her hand on my knee. "We have time to talk, and if that makes you feel any better at all, let's do it. Okay?"

"I was fine before I met him. Not fine. I mean I had the anxiety, but I didn't need a boyfriend. I didn't need this. I didn't want to fall in love and be let down and feel like –"

"Like rubbish," Becky nods. "No one should be able to make you feel that way. What would you say if it was one of your friends that this had happened to, and they were telling you about it?"

Zoe. What would I tell Zoe if she were moping around, losing sleep over some guy that clearly doesn't deserve her?

It's not that simple. Anxiety doesn't stop grabbing hold of you and shaking you just because you tell it that you want it to leave you alone. Once it gets hold it sinks its claws in and hangs on for dear life. I want to say that I would tell her she'd better off without him, and that she should forget him and move on, but I know that isn't going to make me feel better. There's no instant miracle cure.

"I'd tell her to be good to herself," I say.

Becky drinks her tea and appears to toss my words over.

"That's a good start," she says. "Be good to

yourself."

As she finishes repeating my advice back to me a buzzer rings down the ward. I instinctively start to stand up and respond. Instead, Becky taps my leg again.

"I'll get it," she says. "Take a minute, okay?"

I nod silently and let her go.

Being good to myself has never been easy. Anxiety causes me to be unnecessarily hard on myself, but I never know at the time quite how unnecessary it is. Just like Carl, it makes me believe that I am useless, of no value. Being good to myself means fighting against that, giving myself a break, and a chance to move forward.

It's what I need to do, I know. There are more important things in my life than worrying about a man who was *not* good to me.

# Chapter Twenty-Four

Little by little I try to make a change. When I lie awake in bed at night, worrying about why he left me, wondering what is so wrong with me, I try to distract myself and push the thoughts away.

The break-up still stings, but I am trying to look for the positives. That's the only way that I can deal with this.

I've tried not to obsess over the details. I have to accept that there are some questions that are going to remain unanswered. Did I do something wrong? How long had it been going on? Who was she? Why? That, most of all: why? It's unknowable.

Instead of letting my over-anxious, self-doubting brain take over and punish me for whatever it is that I did or didn't do, I am trying to focus on my research project. I'm meant to hand it in after the final block in uni, before our last placements. They like us to be able to focus on wrapping up the PADs and concentrating on our clinical allocations, but that means I only have just over a month to finish my assignment. That may sound easy, but I've gathered so much information that trying to work out what to include and what to leave out is a major task on its own.

The house is quiet, with Luke asleep on the sofa downstairs and Zoe across the landing in her room, working on her own dissertation. Sure, we could take our laptops and sit next to each other at the kitchen table, but we would soon turn away from the walls of text on the screens and start to chat about much more interesting things. Being supportive sometimes means being apart. Knowing that she is knuckling down to her work makes me more determined to get stuck into mine.

I'm getting there, slowly. The bulk of my paper is about anxiety in pregnancy, and I have written up most of what I have researched. I click onto a tab to open a search engine, and momentarily I'm distracted by one of my social media accounts. It's not because I see something that I have to read; I've not received any notifications, and it's not a funny cat video that pops up and takes my attention away from my assignment. I wish that it were. I would have much preferred that. Instead, I have a thought that stops me in my tracks. I forget what I was about to search for, and I stare blankly at the screen.

Carl.

I'm thinking about Carl.

Specifically I'm thinking back to the day that turned out to be the beginning of the end: when I confronted him about the message.

The first thing he looked at when he opened my phone was my social media. That was where he expected to find some kind of sign that I had been up to no good. To be fair, I don't think he really expected to find anything. Anybody that knows me would be able to confirm that I am at my happiest at home with close friends and family. Having one relationship is hard enough for me, never mind two-timing anyone. I barely use social media, compared to a lot of girls my age, and even if someone tried to send me untoward messages I probably wouldn't see them.

But Carl went straight to my inbox.

I should be closing this browser page and getting on with my database search, I know, but now that I have the thought in my head, I can't get away from it. Morbid curiosity is driving me to dig deeper. I bring up his profile and read his *'About Me'* details. His name, date of birth, hometown, are all listed. His relationship status is set to single. He either changed that back quickly or he never updated it at all. I don't care, it doesn't matter, but it does make me pause for a moment.

I can see his friends list, so I scroll through, looking for a girl whose name begins with **B**. He has over a thousand friends. I, on the other hand, have eighty. I have friends from high school, family members, uni students, and some of the midwives. Everyone on my list is someone that I actually know and want to keep in touch with. I don't think he has actually met Lauren Jade from Alabama, but I could be wrong. Most of the people on his list are indeed girls and young women. There are a couple of lads from his course, whose names I vaguely recognise him saying, and some based in Leicester, so I assume they are friends from home, but the majority of pictures show perfectly posed pretty selfies.

"What were you ever doing with me?" I ask myself the question out loud, and it hangs heavily in the air.

This isn't evidence of anything. Without trying to hack into his account, which I have no intention of doing, and I wouldn't even if I had the first idea how to, all I can say is that Carl knows lots of attractive girls. There's no rules against that.

I can't scroll through the full list of friends, and I have no idea how to search for B amongst the many names. This is hopeless. All I am doing is making myself feel bad, and it's stopping me from doing my work.

We had something, and now it's over.

Unfortunately, although I have failed to gain any new information about Carl, I have also failed to gain any new information for my assignment. My head is spinning, and I know I should never have let myself think about him, let alone creep through his social media. I click back onto his profile page and look at his most recent photo. He's a looker, that's for sure. How did I ever imagine that he would really be interested in me?

Forget it. I can't possibly concentrate on my essay now. I close my laptop and walk as quietly as I can across to my door. I am going to hate myself for doing this, but sometimes my emotions take over, and I can't reason with them. I step onto the landing and listen against Zoe's door. Her fingers are tapping away at the keyboard, so she is either on a roll with her essay, or she is playing around on the internet too. Either way, the sound of my footsteps hasn't disturbed her. I walk to the stairs, but instead of going down to the kitchen, which is probably, almost certainly, what I should do, I start to climb up.

I know he is gone. There is no trace of him here anymore. He took everything, threw away his rubbish, washed his bedding and wiped away any signs that he ever lived in this room. It's empty and cold, and seeing it like this hits home. I was barely even up here, but this room was his. I suck in a deep breath, trying to catch the scent of him, but there's nothing. Even that has been erased.

Before I can stop myself, tears are spilling from my eyes. So many questions. So much that no amount of research would ever be able to answer. I can find out how to help other people, but who is going to help me?

That question, it seems, does have an answer.

"Hey," a voice comes from behind me.

Startled, I don't know whether to wipe my eyes or speak, and I whirl around without doing either.

"Oh no," Luke says. "Oh, Vi. Come here. It's okay."

And so I do. I step across the landing, into his outstretched arms. His hug feels safe and warm, and it's exactly what I need.

"You shouldn't do this to yourself." He says the words into my hair. "He didn't deserve you. I know that is probably one of the biggest clichés in the book, but that doesn't stop it being true."

I reach up awkwardly and try to wipe my eyes so that my mascara doesn't end up on his T-shirt.

"I feel so stupid," I say.

"It wasn't your fault. Whatever happened wasn't your fault."

More clichés, and this time I definitely can't agree.

"I feel stupid for feeling like this now. I feel stupid for missing him when he treated me like an idiot."

"You are a lot of things, Violet, but you are not an idiot. My wonderful girlfriend would not have an idiot for a best friend, that's for certain."

I make a tiny sad laughing noise that makes me sound like a piglet. With Luke though, I don't care.

Zoe's footsteps sound their way up the stairs,

and she joins us on the cramped upper landing.

"No one invited me to the party," she smiles, and wraps her arms around both of us, creating a group hug.

"Violet was making herself feel sad," Luke says.

"Anything to get out of studying," Violet says, and I can hear the smile in her voice.

"A girl has to work hard to get a hug around here." I sniff back my tears and relax into the hug.

The door to Carl's room is behind me. All I can see is Luke's T-shirt. All I can feel is their arms embracing me. With them on my side, I can get through this.

I have to get through it.

However bad I feel about what has happened with Carl, and however confused I am about why, I can't let it take over my thoughts. Although I have made it through my OSCE, which is by far the most daunting of my assessments this year, I still have assignments to hand in, my research project to complete and, of course, always hanging over me, the rest of my PAD to get signed off.

I'm tumbling towards my final term, and that in itself is enough to make me feel the pressure.

# Chapter Twenty-Five

Compared to the emotional turmoil of going home for Christmas without Carl, being able to spend Easter with my mum with no fear of divided loyalties is actually a relief.

Once Easter break is over, I have a final four weeks in uni before I am due out onto placements. I want to be on the ward, getting the last of my paperwork signed off.

Being in uni feels like a waste of time now. There's only my research paper to hand in. The lectures are focussed on the transition from student to qualified midwife, what to expect from our preceptorship periods and, perhaps most immediately important, advice on how to approach our job interviews.

We are lucky. There are going to be a handful of jobs available at all the local units. That doesn't necessarily mean that we will all get taken on at our first choice of hospital. It doesn't necessarily mean that we will be offered a job at all. There is still a procedure to be followed, and we have to impress the Head of Midwifery and whoever else interviews us.

Interviews fill me with dread; all the attention focussed upon me, with so much opportunity to make a mess of things is almost unbearable. My whole future will be riding on how I perform, what I say, and what they think of me. I can only hope that the second interviewer is someone that knows me. Not only because they might forgive me more easily if I slip up, but also because knowing someone will make me feel more relaxed. A little bit more, anyway.

I've already filled in my application for St. Jude's before I start back on my placement. It finally strikes me that my delivery suite mentor bears almost the same name as the hospital that we work in. Jade. Jude. It's close. I can't help but take it as a positive omen. Not that I necessarily believe in that kind of thing, but anything that helps me to feel more positive and less terrified has to be a bonus. Either that or I am stretching it, trying to clutch at anything to give me some hope.

I am stretching it. I'm stretching it really thinly, I know.

At the beginning of my placement I have six deliveries left to have signed off. Every time I open up my PAD those empty spaces still mock me. This has hung over me all year. I don't want to wish away the end of my course, but I want to have everything done and dusted, signed and sealed, and yes, very much delivered.

By the last week of my placement I have one more delivery to tick off on my PAD checklist. I've conducted all of the postnatal, antenatal and neonatal checks that I needed to; those sheets are filled with signatures and ready to be submitted. I've written statements and reflections. This is it. This is my last week, and all I need to do is support one more woman to deliver her baby. I have to see one more life into the world. That's not hard work, it's a privilege, but the pressure of needing this one thing so that I can complete my PAD and submit it feels intense.

If I don't manage to deliver a baby this week I'll need to stay on for more shifts after I'm meant to have finished. That's the worst-case scenario. I have all week to do this. I have longer if I need it. I can do it. I will do it. It's fine.

I repeat that over in my head as I walk into the hospital and up to delivery suite. Still I feel the tension of anxiety fluttering through every inch of my body.

"It's fine, it's fine," I repeat to myself, this time out loud, softly, beneath my breath. "It's fine."

As I get to the double doors of the unit I pause, take a deep inhalation, and try to compose myself.

The ward is eerily, disappointingly quiet. There's a distinct atmosphere when it's busy, even without the noise from the rooms, the air feels somehow charged. Today, it is calm and peaceful. By the time I get to the midwives' office I have already resigned myself to an uneventful day.

Jade nods at the board, as blank as I expected it to be, and says, "Sorry."

"Oh gosh, it's hardly your fault," I smile, despite my disappointment. "I have all week, really it's okay."

"And if it doesn't happen this week, you can stay on," she winks.

I know she is being playful, but I really don't even want to think about that. I have all week; I'm sure something will happen.

"You should have been here yesterday," one of the other midwives says. "Board full of women. There was a second-year student here, got three deliveries. Shell, it was. Do you know her?"

Shell, the name sounds familiar. Well, good for her. Perhaps she won't have the last-minute panic that I am having.

"If you'd called me I would have come in," I say.

I'm joking, but it strikes me that if someone had called, I would have been here, regardless of it not being my planned placement day. Maybe that's what it will come to; I'll put myself on call. I can't miss then.

I'm tossing the thought over in my head when Sister speaks. "Someone did phone up earlier. First-time mum, having niggles. Didn't sound like much was happening, but you never know."

"You never know," I agree.

"Have you got anything else that needs to be signed off?" Jade asks.

I pull my PAD out from my bag, and flick through, showing her the relevant pages.

"Just my end of course meeting with you and the placement mentor, Deb, and this."

The list of names, all in my trying-to-be-neat handwriting, of the women whose babies I have delivered during my course. Even with the gaping hole at the bottom where the final sign-off will go, it feels like a huge achievement. I remember every single one of those women, their babies, and my experience of supporting them. I hope it will always be this way; I never want to forget anyone. I hope it will never become just a job.

"I know," Jade says, reading my expression. "All those women," she smiles.

She has been beside me, or behind me, for nearly every delivery. We have worked together through most of my time on the ward.

"Thank you," I say. It comes from nowhere, and it feels so insufficient. "Really, thank you. You've been great."

She shrugs and smiles again. "When you have qualified, you'll have the privilege of mentoring students too. Don't forget how you feel right now, at this present moment. The excitement, the trepidation. Hold onto it."

I nod. I won't forget. I'm sure I won't.

# Chapter Twenty-Six

We chat for what seems like an hour until we're interrupted by the ringing of the ward phone. It's an outside call, I've learned how to tell the difference.

Sister picks up and talks to the person on the other end of the line. By the time the call ends, I know that we are getting a visitor. I look at the ward sister expectantly for the details.

"Yes, it's a lady for you," she says. "Not the one who phoned up before, someone different. Second baby, thirty-nine weeks, sounds like she's in labour. Here." She holds out a scrap of paper with the woman's hospital number so that I can pull the notes from the file.

"Anything else we need to know?" I ask. I want to make sure I get everything ready and get everything right.

"Nope," says Sister. "Routine pregnancy. Waters haven't broken yet. Last time everything was normal." She shrugs. "Get the notes and have a read while she's on the way."

Nodding, I glance quickly at Jade and then set off for the clinic where the records are kept. All the way there, all the time I am browsing for the notes, and all the way back the only thing I can think about is how this could be it. My final delivery.

My patient today is Hester Healey, and as Sister rightly said, there is nothing remarkable in her notes. The main hospital file has all of her medical history, as well as her obstetric records. She's been to clinic for a routine visit, but most of her care has been out in the community. The only other notes in her file are from an appendectomy some years ago, which won't have any bearing on her delivery. Routine. Normal.

When I return to delivery suite, I manage to fill a jug with water for Hester and take it to her room before she arrives. She's a petite brunette, and accompanying her is her rather tall husband, Jeff.

I introduce myself, take a history, and pop back into the office to talk to Jade.

"Everything okay?" she asks.

"Seems fine," I say. "The contractions are getting stronger and lasting longer. She doesn't want any pain relief yet."

Jade nods. "I think you can take the lead on this one. You know I have to be there for the delivery, but everything else, unless you need me, you should go it alone."

I instinctively look over to the ward sister, and she also nods in confirmation.

"You'll be fine," she says.

I did feel fine before I knew I was going to do this alone. Now, I feel more nervous than I ever have previously on my placements.

"You will," Jade says. "You basically do everything anyway, right?"

She has given me a lot of opportunity to lead and learn how to support women in my own way, that's true. But she has always been physically by my side too.

"Okay." I look her in the eyes. "Thanks. This will be good practice."

"Anything at all, ask."

With that, I go back into Hester's room.


Not having Jade with me makes me feel as though I am missing a limb. Of course, I have explained to Hester and Jeff that I am a final year student, about to qualify, and that Jade is only a few steps away.

"Must be lovely being a midwife," she says. "I couldn't do it myself, with all that blood and..." She screws her face up rather than finishing the sentence.

"There's not all that much," I smile.

"Have you always wanted to be a midwife?" she asks.

"Since as far back as I can remember," I say.

"I'm a project manager," she says. "That's not one of the jobs people dream of, but I love it."

"That's what matters," I smile.

Our chatter is broken by the onset of a contraction. Hester focuses on the tightening of her abdomen and the rising pain, breathing deeply throughout.

"That's it," Jeff coaches her. "Keep breathing like that."

Everything seems as straightforward as her first delivery, and as routine as the rest of her pregnancy has been. We carry on chatting between contractions, and it feels like we are building a bond. I love this part of midwifery. Even if I don't end up delivering the baby I know I will have had a great experience today.

I pop out to the office for my lunch, and Jade steps in to support Hester and Jeff, and to carry on with the check-ups. We carry on monitoring pulse, fetal heart rate, and contractions frequently, as well as keeping an eye on blood pressure and urine output. Her waters still haven't broken, and she hasn't had any bleeding, but we keep a check on any vaginal loss too.

I've been on my feet for hours, but it doesn't feel like it, and as soon as I sit to eat my sandwich, I wish I were back in the room. I don't want to miss anything.

Typically, I'm about three bites in when Jade comes back into the office.

"She's getting the urge to push now, Vi. I don't think she'll be long."

I look at the bread in my hand, and then back at Jade.

"You'll probably be okay to finish that. Don't give yourself indigestion. I'll set up a trolley."

"Thanks, Jade."

I try to take my time over the rest of my lunch, but all I can think about is getting back into the room and getting my head back into the situation. I gulp down the rest of the food, swill it down with my tea, wash my hands and get back to work.

Jade has just finished setting up the trolley, and she's standing up by Hester's top half, stroking her hair and speaking softly.

"Everything's set. I don't think you need to

do an examination; I can see some movement down there during contractions now."

"Okay," I agree. "Let's see what happens then. Alright, Hester?"

Hester gives a quiet grunt of acceptance.

"Is that urge to push getting stronger?" I ask. She nods.

"Try to have a quick drink before your next contraction," I suggest.

Jeff leans over, from the opposite side to Jade, and hands her the little cup of water.

"That's it."

I've learned all of the things I should say and do. There's so much to remember. I have to make sure that I am thinking of Hester's comfort as well as monitoring what is happening with the labour. This is as much about making her experience as positive as possible as it is delivering her baby.

She thrusts the cup back at her husband as the next contraction starts to build.

"Well done," I say. "I'm going to have a look down below, see if I can see anything, okay?"

Hester is trying to focus on the breathing, just as she did before, but as the contraction gets stronger, her body gives a forceful push.

Jade was right. I can see the top of baby's head move towards me as Hester pushes. It's a little dark circle, up in the distance, but I recognise it for what it is. With each push I see a little more of the circle.

"Brilliant," I say. "Baby is moving."

I reach up and press the heart rate monitor onto Hester's abdomen, making sure there's still a strong, steady heartbeat, and that it isn't slowing with the contraction. It sounds perfect. I take the opportunity to look at Jade, and she nods supportively.

The contractions come every couple of minutes. Sometimes, with some women, contractions can space out at this point, but Hester's remain strong and regular. Each time she pushes I see her baby move closer towards me down the birth canal. Pushing is sometimes a two-steps-forward-one-step-back process until the baby passes around the natural curve of the pelvis. When it gets to the point that baby's head doesn't slide back anymore between contractions, I know she is nearly there.

"Shouldn't be long now," I tell her. "You're doing so well."

Hester tries to smile. Her face is sweat-lined and she's resting her head against her husband between contractions. Jade has hold of a damp cloth that she has been wiping Hester's face with to cool her down.

"Nearly there," Jade says.

"Okay, love. Nearly there," Jeff repeats.

It takes two more contractions for the head to crown. Hester pants when I ask her to pant, and baby's head is born. Looping my finger around, below baby's head, looking for any sign of the cord being wrapped around there is an instinctive move to me now. I notice though as I'm doing this that the baby has remarkably chubby cheeks and the head is bigger than I have seen before. A strange sick feeling hits my gut, and I look over to Jade, trying to appear as calm as possible.

"It's a big baby," I say.

When I palpated Hester's abdomen, the baby didn't feel particularly large. I don't think I missed anything. There's nothing in the notes to say that any of the other midwives who have assessed her suspected that this could be a big baby. Even Jade, who has been in here and cared for Hester on my break, didn't think anything untoward. But this is a big baby, and a big baby plus a not-so-tall woman can lead to shoulder dystocia. I may have passed my OSCE and be trained to deal with an emergency situation, but I don't want it to actually happen. My usual calm and controlled exterior is starting to crack. I can't let it show.

"How much did your first baby weigh?" I ask.

"Seven and a half pounds," Jeff answers. "Is this lad going to be bigger?"

"We're about to find out," I say.

Jade is beside the emergency buzzer; she knows the drill too.

As the next contraction rises, I say, "Push now, Hester. As hard as you can."

I guide the head, tying to move the anterior shoulder under the pubic arch. My heart is thudding out of my chest. It's too hot in this room. Everything suddenly feels too close, too much for me to deal with.

It moves. The shoulder moves. It seems like minutes rather than the seconds it actually takes. The baby slides out of the birth canal; a healthy, chubby boy, just as Jeff said.

"He's fine." I take a deep breath of relief.

"Well done," Jade says, and I know she is talking to me, just as much as to Hester.

My mind was running through the mnemonic, thinking about what I would need to do if the shoulder hadn't delivered, and also second guessing whether I should have picked up on something sooner.

When we get back into the office, Jade speaks to me.

"Well spotted," she says. "Nine pounds, spot on. Quite a bit bigger than her last."

"I missed it though."

"Me too," she says. "And everyone else that's been looking after her. But when you saw it, you knew. That's the first step."

As we drink tea and fill in the notes we talk about what we would have done and what we could have done. Reflecting on practice, on individual cases as well as on our general experiences is an important part of training and will carry on being important when I am working as a qualified midwife. It's a constant learning process, and I will never know everything there is to know. What I do know is that there is always someone to talk to, always someone to share my thoughts with, and always someone to support me.

I finish typing the records into the computer database and sink back into my chair. It's been an unexpectedly draining day. The clock shows ten minutes left until the end of shift, and I want to take Hester and her baby up to the ward myself and handover before I leave.

"Thanks for today," I say to Jade.

"No problem. You did great."

I smile and get up to go back to Hester's room.

"Are you forgetting something?" Jade asks.

I stand and think, and nothing comes.

Jade points at my PAD folder, sticking out of the top of my bag.

I can get my final delivery signed off. I did almost forget, even though that seems unimaginable. I was caught up in the experience and focussing on the task at hand. My sign-off sheet became the furthest thing from my mind. As I always hoped, it has been about the experience, and about supporting women, rather than about ticking off the numbers. That said, I can relax and enjoy the remaining days of my placement now, without having to worry about how many babies I do or don't deliver.

I hand my file to Jade, and she signs her name at the bottom of the list, below all her other signatures.

All I can do is smile proudly and thank her again. For everything.

# Chapter Twenty-Seven

The rest of the week feels a lot more relaxed, now that I'm not chasing deliveries to till in my PAD. I actually make it to supporting forty-four women in delivering their babies by the end of my final shift on Saturday morning. Then that's it. My last day on placement. My final day as a student midwife. It's surreal.

My last day on placement is also the last time that I will see a lot of my course mates. We've arranged a get-together in the union bar to celebrate the end of the three years. Even with my dislike of the bar, I am too emotional to worry about that today. My brain doesn't know whether to be happy or sad, excited about what I have achieved or afraid of what might happen in the future. I'm all over the place, but I have made it.

By eight o'clock, I'm in the union bar drinking diet cola, and I don't even feel like I'm missing out. Sure, I've tried to have a few drinks when I've been out here before, but it never ends well for me. I don't enjoy the way alcohol affects my anxiety, so I have finally made the sensible decision not to drink. It actually feels like quite a weight has been lifted. Even though I am still not particularly comfortable in such a large crowd, at least I am doing it on my own terms now, and making my own choices.

That feels good.

Tonight is a chance to say goodbye to Ashley, Sophie, and the other girls from my course. I'll be seeing Simon on the wards if we both get the jobs that we have applied for, so it's a '*see you soon*' rather than '*goodbye*' to him. I'll keep in touch with Ash and Soph though. I can't wait to hear what their new hospitals are like, and what experiences they have in their careers. We are on our own, but we are together. We are a community.

Zoe and Luke have come out with me, and somehow Luke has persuaded Zoe to join him and his course mates, Rajesh, Flo, and Damon, around the pool table. I've never seen her play before, and I've chosen to stay at the table and save our seats rather than join in. It's a reasonable excuse. I really couldn't bear to make a complete idiot of myself trying to take part in a game I have absolutely no clue how to play.

I'm going to sit here for ten minutes, soak in the atmosphere without having to stumble through the crowd, and drink my non-alcoholic drink. This is the last time I will be here. I'm going to try to enjoy it.

And then I see him.

Not only do I see him, but he's seen me first, and he's walking in my direction.

Carl. Of course, Carl.

He looks different, somehow, but in many ways still the same. The same man I fell in love with. The same man who dumped me.

I should be over it by now. Seeing him walk towards me shouldn't make me feel physically sick, but it does.

"Violet," he says.

His voice slurs enough to let me know that he's had more than a couple of drinks. Would he have come to talk to me otherwise? He's got a glass with him, sloshing around a measure of something that looks like it's probably whiskey. I never knew he drank that; I never really knew him at all.

"Carl," I reply.

My eyes dart around the room, looking for Zoe and Luke, hoping that they are heading back to the table. Of course, they aren't. I can't see the foyer or the pool table from here, but I know they haven't been gone long enough to be due back just yet. How long does pool take? I don't know how much time I can bear spending with Carl.

He slouches into the empty chair beside me and leans in towards me. The alcohol that has no doubt made him feel the need to come and talk to me hangs heavy on his breath.

"So good to see you," he says, in a mock-posh accent. It doesn't suit him.

I want to give him a snarky response. My instinct is to lash out and say that is it most definitely not good to see him, but that's not the kind of person I am.

"How's things?" I ask, instead.

"Everything is peachy," he says. "Just peachy. Looking forward to getting out of this place and going home."

For a moment I think he means the bar, but it strikes me that he's probably referring to the end of uni and moving home to Leicester. This thought comes with a strange feeling of relief. If he goes back there I won't ever run into him again.

"That's…good," I say.

I'm trying to pick my words carefully. I don't want a conversation, let alone an argument.

"You're looking…" He pauses, letting his eyes appraise me in a way that makes me feel even more uncomfortable. "…the same."

"Well, thanks," I say, not rising to the bait.

I'm not going to start an argument with him. Not here, not now, not ever.

"I wanted to say so-"

"Don't," I say, cutting him off. "I don't want to hear that you're sorry."

He laughs. He actually laughs. It's an ugly, twisted laugh, and I wish, wish, wish that he would disappear.

"I wanted to say something," he says, his voice trying to steady itself. "I thought I should come over and…" He waves his hand in front of his face like he's batting away smoke, and says, "…clear the air."

"Well, yes. It's very clear now, thank you," I say.

I haven't a clue what I am supposed to say. I thought I would never see him again. There was a time that I wanted to see him, that I thought that seeing him might be a good thing. This is not a good thing. Not at all.

He laughs again, and I don't feel any of the trademark sensations of anxiety. I feel anger. I look him dead in the eye and I ask the question that I have wanted to ask ever since we split up.

"For my own peace of mind, tell me. Were you seeing someone else?"

My voice remains calm and steady. I don't let my emotion spill out, even though it's trying to.

"That's how you get your peace of mind is it? Have you been torturing yourself all this time? Let it go. Move on. We're young, Violet. We should be having fun. You should be having fun."

He raises his glass to me.

"Get a drink. Get a few. Live a little."

I keep a hold of my emotions. I have to stay calm. I have to stay in control of myself.

"Thanks," I say. "You know I don't really drink."

"You don't really do anything. That's the problem."

I don't rise to it. I look him dead in the eye and say, "It's not a problem for me. I love what I do. I love who I am. I'm sorry you felt differently."

That seems to slow him in his tracks. I think he's going to give up, turn away and walk off, but as he starts to move he stops again.

I'm not prepared for what comes next.

"Do you know why I was with you?"

"What?" The question seems to come from nowhere.

"Do you know why I was with you?" he uses exactly the same words and the same tone.

What kind of a question is that? We got on well. We were friends. He was lovely, back then, back when we spent our time chatting and laughing. I don't know how to answer, so I stand, silent, wishing he would go away or that I had the sense to walk off rather than listen to this.

"I'll tell you why." His face is right up close to mine now. His breath is heavy with lager and whiskey and something else that I can't even recognise. "You were vulnerable. That's why. I started giving you some attention. I knew that you would lap it up. You were...well, you were so focussed on poor little Violet. Poor me, my friend has got a boyfriend and I'm all on my own now. Poor me, I can't do my exams because I'm too scared. Poor me –"

"You can stop right there." It's Zoe. She's standing beside him, and although I know she would never physically accost anyone, I can see the rage bristling through her.

I raise my hand to stop her. "Zoe, it's fine," I

say.

I turn my attention to Carl. "You dated me because I was vulnerable, and because it was easy for you. I think that says a lot more about you than it does about me. Are you happy? Are you really happy now? You don't look it. But I tell you what, Carl. I am. I'm happy. I have everything that I could possibly want. I passed those exams. I finished my course. And yes, I have my best friend, and I love her. I don't care what you say, or what anyone says."

Instead of biting back he looks at me, long and hard, and then looks at Zoe. He starts to clap, slowly.

"Well done, Violet," he says. "Well done. I thought you were going to be a little mouse all your life, but maybe there is more to you. Good. Good for you."

Perhaps a part of him means those words, but they sound hollow.

Zoe flashes her eyes at me, as if asking a question. I can feel it. I know she wants to know if I'm okay, and if she should say something. I give her a tiny shake of the head. I want to handle this myself.

"It was great to catch up with you," I say, and I try to make the words light and pleasant, even though they mean goodbye.

Taking the hint, Zoe settles into the seat to the other side of me. We turn to each other and start to chat. The two of us form a bubble that he is not a part of, and he sits on the outside, looking like he has no idea what to do. Although I am trying to look nonchalant, the adrenaline that is pumping through me is making me dizzy, and I can barely focus on the conversation.

"Well, I have to get back to Bella," he says, putting all of the emphasis on the first letter of her name. "She'll probably be thinking I've run away with someone." I can't help but look at him when he says it. "Right, Vi?"

Without another word, he stumbles to his feet, turns his back, and disappears into the crowd.

# Chapter Twenty-Eight

My course has ended, my placements are over, and I've done everything I need to do to qualify. Handing in my dissertation and my PAD feels surreal, but it also feels like a huge weight has been lifted.

I can almost relax and enjoy a few weeks off before I start work. Almost. First, I must get through an interview and be offered a job.

During my course I've given presentations, stumbled through the three OSCEs and talked about myself and my progress at regular meetings with my placement supervisor and my mentors. I'm trying to see my interview as just another meeting, but I know it's not. I know that it means everything. If I mess up now, all the work that I have put in over the past three years will have been for nothing.

And yes, it's interview singular. I want to stay at St. Jude's hospital, so it's the only position that I have applied for. I tossed it over in my head for a long time, but I think I am making the right decision. I know that if I want the job, I must do my best. It's a way of focusing my mind. If it all goes horribly wrong, I could look around and see where else there are vacancies, but I want to stay here. I want to be near to Mum. I want to stay close to Zoe and Luke. This is my life, the life that I have been building, and I want it to be my future.

The night before my interview, Zoe, Luke, and I are sitting in the back yard at Tangiers Court. We've been out here so many times over the past three years. The fairy lights flicker along the trellis, Luke has fired up the chimenea that we picked up cheap on one of our Saturday shopping trips, and we've got our terribly boring diet colas on the white metal table that Zoe and I bought right at the start of our tenancy.

Three years. Has it really been that long?

"How are you feeling about tomorrow?" Luke asks.

He's got his chair pulled right up to Zoe's so that he can drape his arm around her shoulder. She's leaning into him, resting her head on his chest. They look perfect together; they are perfect together.

"As prepared as I'll ever be," I say.

My smile is genuine, but I'm smiling at the two of them, rather than because I am particularly confident about the interview.

"Do you want to go through any more questions?" Zoe asks.

"You've spent long enough helping me," I say. "What I don't know now, I never will."

Two hours we spent, her asking the mock questions and me mumbling through the answers until I could reply without mumbling at all.

"You'll be fine," Luke says. "The interview is just a formality anyway, right? They know you. They know that you can do it."

My mouth feels dry, and I take a gulp of the ice-cold cola. It doesn't help.

"Hey," Zoe says, reading my expression. "Really, you're going to be fine."

"I can't believe I've come this far, to be honest. I don't want to mess it up now."

"I believe it," she says. "And you have come this far despite everything. Despite your anxiety. Despite…"

"That guy," Luke says, interrupting her.

I allow myself a tiny laugh.

"That guy," I repeat. "Yeah, let's just keep it at that."

"He got off lightly. If Zoe ever cheated on me, I don't know what I would do, but we definitely would not be together anymore, and *I* certainly wouldn't be moping around wondering what I had done wrong. She'd be gone. Gone." Luke is resolute, but I doubt he has anything to worry about there.

"Alright, alright. Never going to happen! I shouldn't have even mentioned him," Zoe says. "But you've had a lot to contend with, and still, you have done it. You've completed your course. You got your PAD signed off; you finished all your assignments. You're ready."

I nod. "I hope so."

"Me too," she says. "I'll need you to coach me for my interview next week."

Luke runs his hand along her arm in a supportive rub.

"Zoe Colebrook, soon to be Miss Colebrook, teacher extraordinaire," I smile.

"Unless we get married before she starts work of course," Luke says, without a hint of irony.

Zoe snaps her head around to look at him.

"Just saying," he shrugs.

I would love to say something useful, but instead I make a high-pitched squeaking noise as my excitement slips out.

Zoe looks completely gobsmacked, staring at Luke in a stunned silence.

"Is that a *no* then?" he asks.

"Was that…I mean were you…are you actually serious?" she stammers.

As romantic proposals go, I don't think this would win any awards, but the look on his face tells both of us that he is completely serious.

"Zoe, the past two years with you have been perfect. You are perfect. I never want to be apart from you. Will you be my wife?"

My head is whirring. We're only twenty-one; I can barely hold down a relationship, never mind even think about being with someone forever. Forever is a terribly long time. Still, these two, they are right. They are both perfect, and they are perfect together.

"Luke," she says. "I would love to be Mrs Zoe Buxton. I…yes…yes, I want to be your wife. Yes."

He squeezes her so tightly that I'm afraid she's going to burst. I give them a good thirty seconds to hug each other before I throw my arms around the two of them, crouching awkwardly behind their chairs.

"I'd better get to be bridesmaid," I laugh.

"That, Violet, is a given," Zoe grins through the happy tears that are streaming down her face.

# Chapter Twenty-Nine

I'm too excited about Zoe and Luke to be nervous about the interview. For the first time since I started my placements at St. Jude's I make my way to the Head of Midwives' office on the Margaret Beresford unit. I pop my head into the midwives' staff room, but Geri isn't about today. If everything goes well, if I get through this interview, I'll be back here working alongside her in only a few weeks' time.

It feels unreal. It *is* unreal until I make it happen.


After the interview I walk back to Tangiers Court. I want some time on my own to think about how it went, and how the past three years have gone.

I channelled everything that I've learned over the past three years into that interview. Not only the theoretical knowledge that I gained in lectures or the clinical experience that I have begun to build on my placements, but more than that. I have grown as a person and developed in ways that I could never have imagined. Part of that is growing older. I have gone from a fresh eighteen-year-old school leaver to a twenty-one-year old future midwife.

I've doubted myself, I've doubted my ability as a girlfriend, but worst of all I have doubted my friendship with Zoe. Now, if I didn't make a complete mess of today, I am going to be starting my dream job, and I know that Zoe will be there by my side, on my side, always.

As for that guy, I'm trying not to think about him. I don't want to give him the headspace. He doesn't deserve it. I was vulnerable and convenient. What does that make him? Whatever it is, I am far better off without him in my life. I wasn't bothered about looking for a boyfriend before I met him, and I am not particularly bothered now. I don't want to be with anyone who doesn't make me feel the way Zoe feels with Luke. Their relationship, with all of its banter, and unconditional love and support is an absolute gold standard. I love them both so much.

It's easy to be positive on such a glorious day. It's the beginning of August, and there's not a cloud in the sky. My black dress was perfect for the interview, but now it's absorbing the heat. I want to be at home in the garden with an ice-cold drink and some cooler clothes. I can kick back, read a book, and wait for the phone to ring.

I don't have to wait too long. I've just about had time to change and settle down in the yard with Zoe when my phone starts to buzz. I know it must be from the hospital.

I don't answer straight away, instead I look at Zoe. She nods.

"Go on. This is it. You've got this."

I take a deep breath and click the button to take the call.

"Hello?" My nervous squeak of a voice creeps out of me. I clear my throat. "Violet Cobham."

I listen to the woman on the other end of the phone line. Zoe stares at me, searching for signs of emotion on my face, but I try to keep a deadpan stoniness.

At the end of the call I put my phone down and look at her.

"Don't do this to me!" she says. "You got it, didn't you? Tell me that you got it."

I can't hold back any longer. My straight face cracks into a wide grin.

"I got it. Zoe, they want me. I'm going to work at St. Jude's. I'm going to be a midwife!"

She grabs me, almost too enthusiastically, and we tumble back on the sofa, squealing and laughing like over-excited children.

"I never doubted it," she finally says, as we calm ourselves enough to sit.

"I doubted myself," I say.

"I never doubted you." The laughter is gone now, and all I feel is the support and love that flows out of her.

"So, this is it," I say. "The end of three years. The end of Tangiers Court."

"This is the beginning," she smiles. "Violet Cobham, midwife."

"Zoe *Buxton*, teacher," I say, placing the emphasis on what will be her new surname.

"Zoe Buxton, wife." She says the words with a smile, but then her face becomes stony serious.

We look at each other in silence, taking everything in.

"You're right," I say. "This is the beginning."

Dear Reader,

Thank you for reading the **"Lessons of a Student Midwife"** series.

If you have enjoyed this book, please consider leaving a review on Amazon and/or Goodreads. Reviews help readers to discover books, and help authors to find new readers. It would mean a lot to me if you would take a few minutes to leave a review.

If you want to read more about Violet and Zoe, check out my standalone novel **Ghosted**.

If you would like to find out more about new releases and special offers, including information about the rest of this series, please sign up to my mailing list. I'm currently giving away a free full-length novel to everyone who signs up. Visit **jerowney.com** for details.

You can also find me on social media as @jerowneywriter.

See you there!
J.E. Rowney